CARLA

MASK OFF
A Sergeant Knight Novel
Volume One

Blue Café Books

Published in the United States by Blue Café Books, Atlanta, GA.

IBSN 978-0-9790638-3-1

Editor: Constance Poitier
Cover Design: Richard Anthony Evans

The words on these pages are dedicated to those who are trying to find love after loving...and losing.

When you are happy,
You enjoy the music,
When you are sad,
You understand the lyrics.
- Anonymous

Tamara Butler	Andrea Cobb
Travis Cure	Carl DuPont, Sr.
Dr. Carl DuPont, Jr.	Alanna Foxx
Frank Leggett	Derrick Mathis, III
Ja'Qonna Mathis	Sgt. Jared Ojeda
Jasmine S. Parker	Constance Poitier
James Poitier	Shawna Smith
Nacirema Stewart	Robert C. Thomas
P. Ware	Daemon Woods

This project would not have come together without each of you. I wholeheartedly appreciate you working with me to bring this story to life. Thank you for answering my endless questions, talking me off the ledge, wiping my tears, and giving me support.

xo,
Carla

@writewithcarla

#WhoIsSgtKnight

Show me where you are taking Mask Off! Tag me in pictures of you enjoying this great read!

MASK OFF

A Sergeant Knight Novel

Volume One

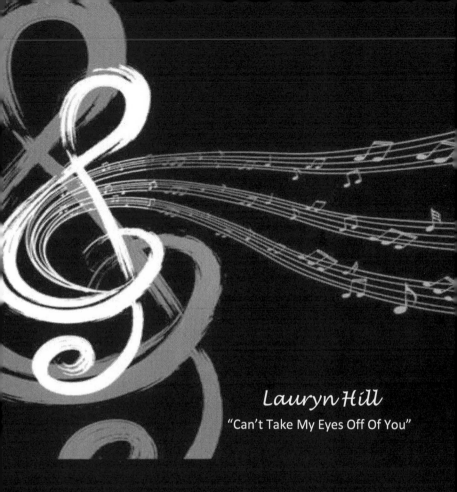

Lauryn Hill
"Can't Take My Eyes Off Of You"

You're just too good to be true,
  Can't take my eyes off of you...

Chapter 1

Londyn's eyes opened before the alarm clock on her phone had the chance to awaken her. She awoke with a strange intuition that something just wasn't right. She tapped the home button on her iPhone to check the time, then rolled her eyes. With time ticking down, she only had 13 minutes before the alarm sounded. Thirteen! That was just enough time to be irritated, but not enough to get more sleep. She laid there relishing being enveloped by the sheets.

Per her usual routine, she prayed, thanking her Heavenly Father for waking her up, keeping her and her family safe through the night, and keeping them in perfect health, mentally and physically. She hopped out of bed and turned the light on to go wake up her boys, when something out of the norm caught her eye. There was a used condom in the middle of the floor.

"What the..." she spoke out loud to herself. She just stared at the half-unrolled condom lying in the middle of her bedroom floor. Londyn was completely in awe. It was only inches from the jeans that lay sprawled across the floor leading out of her husband's closet. The same jeans she saw him wear out of the house the night before.

Londyn's stomach became instantly queasy. It was clearly evident that their marriage was headed for divorce, the one path she made clear that she didn't want to go down. Yet, there she was, wondering how reckless could he really be. Did he care so little that he somehow managed to let his used rubber find its way into their home? Into their bedroom? What if the boys found it before she did? How would she have explained it to them? It was in the middle of the floor! She quickly snapped a picture on her phone of the condom, jeans, and shoes all in the same frame to make sure it was undeniable given the climate of their conversations. Then she took another picture, a close-up of a white residue stain on the crotch of his jeans. *Ugh!*

"Maaaaaa," a groggy 11-year-old Kingsley moaned. Londyn stepped on the condom to cover it with her feet. She thought, *Thank God I have on socks!*

"What's up Ace?"

"I don't wanna go to school!" He plopped face-down on her bed.

"Maaaaaa," a groggy 11-year-old Kingston groaned. "Me either," and he plopped face-down on the bed next to his brother.

Londyn couldn't help but laugh. They tickled her. They were so much alike without even trying to be. Really they couldn't help it being identical twins.

"Why not, Deuce?" Londyn nicknamed them according to their birth other. Kingsley was 17 minutes older than his twin. When she found out that she was pregnant with twins at 23, she could not have been happier. Finding out they were boys was music to her husband's ears. They were such a happy family. Kaden did not miss one obstetrician visit, not one class, and was there for their birth. It meant so much to him to be a good father to his kids. He always wanted them to feel his presence and know that he was there for them in every aspect of their lives.

Life was good for Kaden, Londyn, and the boys until the phone call came that no one ever wants to receive. As soon as the phone rang, she felt a funny pain in her stomach. Londyn's mother, Deshawn, answered and gave a string of yeses and unh huhs. She asked, "Are you sure?" then turned to face Londyn. With her back to her mother, she somberly asked, "Kaden is dead, isn't he?"

Kaden was tragically killed in a car accident. The twins started walking just days before he passed. It was by far the saddest day of Londyn's life. She was in such disbelief. Like, why did her husband have to die so young? There were so many mean and cruel people in the world who others would argue that the world would have been a better place without. Why was the candle blown out on his life?

That was the day her heart broke; she thought her life had ended right along with her husband's. She'd never quite been the same since. Her smiles weren't as wide, her eyes weren't as bright. She would never feel completely whole again. She trusted the Lord knew best. Eventually, she was able to find solace in that. It took her a long, long while.

Micah, her current husband, was there to help her over the hump. Micah was Kaden's best-friend. He'd always had a sweet spot for Londyn. He idolized what a perfect family life looked like and thought his best-friend had created that. Kaden and Londyn seemed to flow through life so effortlessly. So when Kaden passed, he felt it was his duty to step up to be a man for her and a father for the boys. Not everyone shared his sentiment. Kaden's family was not happy about it. They felt like the transition happened a bit too quickly; like perhaps the new couple had been fooling around all along even though there was nothing anyone could point to that showed Londyn had eyes for anyone else except Kaden. His family still couldn't wrap their minds around Kaden's best-friend stepping into his shoes.

To Londyn, Micah was the one guy who she felt she and the boys could trust. At least they weren't starting completely over with a stranger. Feeling helpless put her in a very vulnerable state of mind that she couldn't get past. So, Londyn and Micah tied the knot and he adopted the gregarious Kingsley and Kingston who were laying across her bed.

"Because, I already know everything!" Deuce exclaimed.

"Is that right?" she egged him on and darted to the bathroom to grab a paper towel.

"I'm the smartest one in my class, Ma!"

"Ditto!" Ace lifted his head off the bed for the split second it took to say the word.

"What is the molecular formula for nitric acid?" she asked, swooping up the nastiness still calling her bedroom floor its home and balling it up.

"What is a molecular formula?"

"Exactly! Get up! Get up!" she tickled them. She knew that's what they really wanted. "Let's get rid of that stinky morning breath and those crusty little eyes!" They laughed and laughed, then ran out of the room to get ready for the day. They would probably make enough noise getting ready to wake their dad up. She didn't care. He shouldn't have been sleeping on that side of the house in the spare bedroom. He'd moved over there a few months before.

For now, the dirt was documented. Her focus was on getting the boys moving to get them to the bus stop on time, then on to her satellite office, the coffee shop. She'd started going back to the coffee shop around the time her husband found it repulsive to sleep next to her.

The coffee shop was like a real-world *Cheers*. Everybody knew everyone's name. There was a group of consistent morning regulars of about 40 people or so, who were in and out between 7 and 10 a.m. Then there was another set of regulars who considered the coffee shop to be their office. They all mingled and chatted with each other. Being the newest member of the crew, she was amazed that they were genuinely interested in the happenings of each other's lives. It didn't take long for her to fall into the groove. Going to the coffee shop helped her to be in the company of others. No matter that the majority of the conversation was meaningless, having a living, breathing person who she could touch was good enough for her.

Being a stay-at-home mom, working from home was sometimes a bit of challenge. Especially as of late. She was totally unmotivated. She'd watched her family life fall apart, not once, but twice. Both times, she felt helpless to do anything about it. As a talent manager, she was even more unmotivated. There was a small amount of royalties rolling in, just enough to help her connect the dots her half of the bills made. Her only client, Libra, was a singer/songwriter/actress who never made it above C-list, but was planning to really make a comeback effort after enjoying her newest role as a mother. As long as *some* money was filtering in, Londyn didn't feel the need to overwhelm herself any more than she already was.

"Lunnnn-dennnn!" her best friend, Kenzie, sang into the phone. Londyn jumped back as the voice from the ear buds boomed in her ears.

"It's Friday. Don't you have heads to fry, dye and lay to the side?"

"Gosh! You are so country!"

"My blue-headed Grandma Mable used to say that. God rest her soul," Londyn's voice dropped thinking about her beloved. Her grandmother, with only a 6th grade education, was an entrepreneur at a time when blacks in the south were under Jim Crow law; but, she didn't let that stop her. She owned the first and only beauty shop in the black neighborhood while her sister owned the only restaurant. The Britt girls made their own way in life. Londyn's friends used to tease her saying, "Everybody ain't a-a-a-ble like ol' blue-haired Ma-a-a-ble." Now she was pursuing entrepreneurship above and beyond anyone believing she could make it happen. Like her grandmother, she believed in herself and pressed beyond the disbelief of her friends, family and/or husband towards her goal of trailblazing.

She realized that the drive of entrepreneurship pulsed through her veins more like ol' blue-haired Mable. There were no other women in the family trying to do the same. Londyn wished her grand-mother could give her the scoop on how they went from nothing to something over the obstacles they faced.

"Yes, I do have heads...one in the chair and two under the dryer. But that's not why I called."

"Yes, we can go. Yes, Micah will watch the boys. No, I didn't ask; but if he has plans, I'll get a sitter. Yes, I'm dranking so we can have a good ol' time!"

"Well, alriiiiiiight! See you at 8:30!"

"See you then." Londyn ended the call on her phone and plugged her ear buds back into her computer to slide back into a Pandora groove. She was putting together a proposal for Libra to get a potential sponsorship for her re-entrance back into the spotlight. It was going to take a concerted effort to get a C-list star back on the radar in a B-list way, especially with her being a new mother, people were more hesitant to bring her on. She texted Micah to ask if he would keep the boys and he agreed. Then she let him know about his indiscretions. She began with the picture of the condom near the jeans.

Londyn: Can you please be more careful?

Micah: So, having sex with dudes in our bed is what's hot in the streets?

It was just like him to turn everything around on her.

Londyn: Location. It's next to your jeans.

Micah: That's not mine

Londyn: Ummm...

Micah: It must've gotten stuck in the cuff of my jeans

Londyn: Yeah, when you took it off

Micah: I went to the strip club last night. That's not mine. And frankly, I'm

upset that you would even insinuate that it
is.

Londyn knew that the rubber was still in her trash at home. He wouldn't think enough to throw it out into the big trash or remove it from the trash bin under the sink. The fleeting thought to have it tested crossed her mind.

That had happened to a co-worker years before. She was called by a man who said he thought her husband was sleeping with his wife and wanted to test the condom he found. She gave the man some kind of hair from her husband's hair brush or bristles from his toothbrush or something like that. The results were conclusive, her husband was having an affair.

Londyn also knew that there was no point in going to that length. Proving that the used condom was Micah's was a complete waste of time and energy. Months before, Micah was sitting on the porch smoking a cigar. Londyn sat next to him. His words came out of nowhere.

"I'm not happy." He spoke without tearing his gaze away from the movie on his iPad.

"What do you mean?" She asked, her stomach immediately feeling ill. That's how her body responded to stressful situations, she always felt like she had to run to the bathroom.

"I'm just not happy."

"Ok, what do you want to change?"

"I don't want to be married."

"Ok…so…do you want to go back to counseling?"

"No."

"Do you want to take some time apart?"

"No."

"What do you want *me* to change?"

"Nothing."

"I'm so confused."

"I'm leaving," Micah finally said.

"To go where?"

"Away from you."

"Where is all of this coming from?"

"I haven't been happy for years. I know you aren't happy either."

"I mean...I'm good. I thought you were good too. We have our normal issues, but what couple doesn't? We still love each other, so we can try."

"No. I'm not in love with you. I'm tired of trying. I'm tired of faking. Londyn, I don't want to be married to you anymore."

"Faking?"

Londyn sat there looking at him in disbelief. This wasn't the first time they'd been at this juncture. Or even the second. Any time he threw the big "D" word at her, she ducked it and begged. Londyn was no angel. She'd done her job to muddy the waters, but she'd also tried to make up for her mistakes. Micah felt like it was his job to hurt her back. So it was tit for tat. Then, they started counseling and Londyn felt that things were moving in the right direction.

There was so much emotional work that was done. Boxes of emotional baggage stored away in each of their minds and hearts. They loved each other, but had hurt each other in more ways than one. Fingers were being pointed, blame was being passed; they were more concerned with the opinions and comparisons to their friends, than they seemed to be with each other. They welcomed their own views 'from the outside looking in' impressions of their friends' relationships and marriages into each session. They had begun to judge each other's actions by the way their friends reacted in their relationships.

As their counselor pointed out, treading through a relationship this way only brought more pain and hurt. It was so unnecessary because, "No one is here in this room with Micah and Londyn *but* Micah and Londyn," the counselor said. "Leave Kenzie, Nika, D.J., Fred, and whoever else where they are. The only people in this marriage are you two. The only people who can save this marriage are the two of you. The only people whose voices matter, are the two of you."

His words were so profound. For Londyn, it's as if she had not even considered that her marriage didn't include half of the civilized world. For Micah, he looked at his partners' relationships and marriages like they were the gold standard. "Comparison is the thief of joy," according to Teddy Roosevelt. That's exactly what was happening to them.

Londyn began to view their marriage through a different set of eyes after that divine revelation. In the age of oversharing on social media, comparing your life to friends, followers, and anybody else with an open profile seemed inevitable. Rather than look to others, Londyn was determined to only compare her marriage to Micah to the happier, more hopeful version of their marriage from the past.

They fought and struggled to knock down walls of mistrust, open up wider lanes of communication, and open pathways of making love. Not in the physical sense, although their bedroom skills were rejuvenated, but in the sense of speaking each other's love language. Their counselor spoke of the importance of making love to each other in the receiver's love language, not in the giver's love language. Basically, giving someone what they would value and appreciate, versus giving them what you want them to have. They hadn't seen the counselor in over a year, but Londyn was happy with the turnaround. Clearly, she was the only one.

The sweet stench of his cigar curled into her nose. It was a smell she'd learned to appreciate. When he smoked with his boys and came home to her, she'd bury her nose in his dreads and inhale deeply. The enormity of the words her husband just spoke weighed on her, although not as heavily as they could have. He'd said, "Maybe I should leave your ass," enough times for her to think the words coming out of his mouth were more cigar smoke curling into the air.

"When are you moving out?" She called his bluff.

"In a few months. I'll wait until school gets out." *Damn!* He was actually thinking this thing through. She stood up and walked back in the house. Stunned, she sat on the couch and let the TV watch her. She didn't know what to think. That was then, this was now. In the slow progression, Micah was spending more and more time out of town, and wasted fewer words speaking to her. When he preferred to sleep on a blow-up mattress on the other side of the house rather than sleep in the king size bed next to her, she knew it was over.

So, the condom didn't surprise her as much as it bothered her. She really was losing. None of that would matter when she and Kenzie got to The Spot. The Spot was a neighborhood watering hole, kinda hood, but not too crazy. The food was good and Kenzie was in tight with the bartender so half of the time, they didn't even pay for drinks.

After being carded at the door, Londyn strutted in. She was comfortable in tight jeans, and an olive green shirt that was a size too big, but that was the way it was supposed to fit. She showed a little cleavage and pulled her naturally long, thick hair into a disheveled, high bun. She didn't need much make-up and a dive like this didn't require much beyond tinted lip gloss and eyeliner. Standing at 5'4", the high heel sandals gave her an extra four inches. Her cocoa brown skin glistened under the red light as she walked to the bar to find Kenzie.

"I should've known there weren't going to be any seats," Londyn huffed. It didn't bother her, but she would have preferred to sit, especially since being a stay-at-home mom, wearing heels on her feet would not be comfortable long.

"Hey boo!" Kenzie said turning around. She was so pretty. They both were. Turning heads was not new to them. Kenzie favored Beyoncé, not in the ugly girl whose mama told them they were cute kinda way; but in a legit, they could be related kinda way. She was the same complexion, too. She wore her hair in a cornrowed design and big, bamboo style earrings made out of wood. Kenzie liked to be Afrocentric, #blackpower. "Londyn, you remember Nicole," Kenzie pointed to the friend standing next to her.

"Hey Nicole!" Londyn and Nicole exchanged hugs.

"Hey girl! We haven't been here long. Seats will open up soon. Gotta keep our eyes open," she said with a sweet smile. Londyn had only met Nicole a handful of times, but each time, she seemed so pleasant to be around. Londyn didn't mind Nicole hanging out with them.

Nicole and Kenzie were engaged in a conversation, but Londyn didn't feel like leaning all the way over to them. She took inventory of her surroundings. Directly in front of her was a guy, slouched down in his bar stool glancing back and forth between the oversized TVs and his phone. Next to him was a heavy dude with gold-rimmed, clear glasses from the Asian hair store and three-week-old braids who was licking the wing sauce off of his fingers. On the other side of him was a couple boo'ed up. They were so close, they could feel the wind from each other's eyelashes when they blinked.

Londyn's gaze fell on the game overhead. Not really being a basketball fan, she could care less about the teams playing or what was at stake. "Is that Tim Duncan?" she asked nobody in particular. The guy slouched on his phone, shook his head yes. It was so loud with people yelling over the DJ spinning that Londyn was surprised he could even hear her. "Oh my gosh!

His old ass! He's been playing since I was in college!" she roared with laughter. The guy laughed and turned his head to the side to acknowledge her without looking at her fully. "How can he still be playing?" she leaned into his ear asking. This time, he looked at her, then jumped back, sat up in the chair and smiled. She had his attention, she could see that he thought she was attractive.

He leaned back over, explaining the ins and outs of players' rosters, something she would not remember within a week's time, but it pacified her curiosity. There was talk of pay scales, salary caps, positions, and player longevity that if they had been talking football, she would have been able to offer a little more input. But between the cute stranger and fact checking his knowledge on her on phone, she hadn't noticed Kenzie and Nicole snagged seats a few bar stools down.

Londyn politely thanked him and made her way down to her friends. Standing...the odd man out. Kenzie had already ordered her a drink and handed it to her.

"He's cute," Nicole wasted no time.

"Mmm hmm," Londyn responded unbothered.

"He's looking at you."

"Chile please. What am I gonna do with that little boy. He's 12," Londyn said laughing. "Plus, why would I entertain anyone?"

"Because your husband is!" Kenzie interjected.

"UGH!" Londyn rolled her eyes.

"Do I need to remind you about breakfast the other day? You think he's worried about you? Because he's not. That man told you he was leaving and you still in here talking 'bout why would I entertain anyone?" Kenzie mocked her. All of the ladies laughed.

Londyn needed no reminder. Micah had gone to pick up breakfast for him and the boys, knowing she was awake. She was taking advantage of sleeping in because it was a Saturday morning. When she asked where was her food, rummaging in the empty fast food takeout bags, Micah snorted, "You were laying in bed pretending to be sleep, so I didn't get you anything."

"But I texted you, so you knew I was awake." Micah shrugged and kept eating. Londyn hopped in the car and drove to Kenzie's house. She needed to get away immediately!

"Seriously, he just needs space. He'll come back. They all do." Londyn spoke confidently bobbing her head to the music.

"In the meantime..." Kenzie amped.

"No, man! Leave me alone!"

"Listen," Nicole said, her eyes had not left the cute stranger's face. "If you don't go down there, honey, I will. He is *too* fine."

"Ladies! Ladies! Ladieeeeees! He has a nice looking face, but we can't really see what that body looks like. And! He looks too young."

"How young is too young? He looks like he's in his early 30's." Nicole was not hiding the fact that she was sizing him up. "He's still looking this way. Uh oh, Londyn, he wants you."

Londyn looked down past the five or six bar stools to where he was. He tipped his head and mouthed 'Come here.' Shaking her head and laughing, she walked back down to where he was. It was a total trap.

"What can I do for you, sir?" her southern upbringing evident in her manners.

"What are y'all talking about? She keeps laughing," he said. Londyn looked over her shoulder and saw both Kenzie and Nicole laughing.

"We're trying to guess how old you are."

"How old do you think I am?" he smiled.

"They think you're in your early 30's. I don't think you're a day over 25," Londyn spoke nonchalantly.

He sat up in his chair proudly, "I'm 25 and a half." Londyn rolled her eyes and busted out laughing.

"The fact that you added that half shows how young you are!" She ran back to her girls. He could see them all fall out laughing when Londyn leaned in to tell them what he said. He called Londyn back. He thought they were laughing with him, they were laughing *at* him.

"How old are you?" he asked.

"34."

"Ain't nothin' wrong with that." This time when he spoke, his face was serious. "I like 'em older."

For the next 15 minutes or so, Londyn was back and forth between the cute stranger and her girls. A rowdy, obviously young, man walked over to their cute stranger and patted him on the back. They dapped each other up and the newcomer pointed in the direction of two tables with a group of guys waving. He called Londyn down again.

"Do you want my chair? I'm gonna go sit over there."

"Thanks," she responded genuinely smitten, "but I want to sit with my girls and there's no room to squeeze a chair in down there."

"Do you want to sit down?"

"Yes, but..."

"Yes or no. Don't worry about the rest." *Oh!* Londyn looked at him quizzically and decided to see where this was going.

"Yes."

"Let me pay my tab and I'll get you a seat." She walked back over to her friends. When she turned around, the cute stranger was standing up. Londyn, Nicole, and Kenzie's mouths all dropped. Sitting down, they couldn't tell he was holding like that. He gave a quick chuckle when he saw their expressions, but he was used to it. Women looked at him like that all the time. Londyn tore her gaze away, trying to save face. She turned the complete other way and said into the air, "Damn that boy is fine!"

"*Ooh* yes he is!" Kenzie agreed.

At that moment, the bar got quiet. Forget what cheesy 'can't understand a single syllable' rap song was blasting through the speakers. When he looked at her under that red light, she felt a gust of wind that took her breath away. All Londyn heard was Donna Summer crooning, 'Ahhhh, love to love you babaaaaaaay!' Everybody else in the place disappeared. They stared at each other for what felt like an eternity to them both. He loved how girl-next-door pretty she was. She wasn't trying too hard, unlike some of the other women in there looking like they were down for whatever. He leaned his head to the side and Londyn was lost in his eyes, looking like he could swallow her whole and leave no trace. Kenzie and Nicole saw what was happening and were feverishly tapping each other.

He stood 6'2" about 225 from what Londyn could tell. Very nicely packaged. His beard was pristine and so was his fresh cut. He was about two shades darker than Londyn's brown skin tone, with beady little eyes. His buddy tapped him again which jolted them both out of their wishful thinking back to reality. At the bar. Surrounded. By other people.

The cute stranger spoke into the ear of the guy sitting next to him, the lady he was with and so on down the line. Londyn watched as all of the people got up and moved down leaving an empty stool next to Kenzie. She looked at him in amazement. This man had literally disrupted all of the people between his chair and Kenzie's chair asking them to move themselves, their drinks, plates, and whatever else down so she could have a seat. She was in awe. He was such a gentleman, and she didn't even know his name.

He looked at her, winked, then pulled the chair out. He hugged Kenzie and Nicole. The smile wiped off of Londyn's face. She even felt a tinge of jealousy. Then he hugged her. Saved the best for last. His embrace was so warm and heartfelt; the hug he gave her wasn't as quick as the hugs he gave her girls. He pulled back and looked in her eyes.

"C'mon Baby! It's time to celebrate!" his friend said. He held both of her hands in his.

"What's your name?" he asked.

"Londyn. What's yours?" She couldn't help but cheese as he bent down to talk to her, looking her straight in her eyes. He easily stood six inches taller than her even in heels.

"Knight."

"Knight?" Londyn started laughing again. His over eager friend, also standing a robust 6'2" or 6'3" and a slightly bulkier 240 pounds, wouldn't leave. His hand was on Knight's shoulder nudging him to bust a move.

"What?" He asked wanting to be offended, but her easy laugh broke him down.

"Do you always introduce yourself by your last name?" She asked with a straight face. *You can be my knight any day,* she thought.

"Baby Knight is his name lady! You're pretty and all if I do say so myself! If he don't want cha, I'll take ya!" The friend pushed him along. He still had Londyn's hands in his as they were ripped apart.

"Girl! If you don't go get that man! He was all over you, Londyn!" Nicole said, "I got wet just watching y'all!" They all roared with laughter.

"I don't know friend. He looks like he has a *skrong bike*!" Kenzie said and Nicole high fived her. Every so often, Londyn would turn her head and he would be staring right at her. Getting at Knight should have been a no-brainer. But her situation was complicated and about to get even more so. She didn't want to drag him into whatever was about to happen. Not that she believed Micah's repetitive threats.

Once Knight left the bar area, Londyn didn't even want to be there anymore. Nicole teased her about finding out if Knight had a strong back to please her sexually and he could be a real life Knight in shining armor. Londyn laughed and left the jokes as they were...jokes. It felt like a piece of her had left. In her mind, she would've gone to the car and let him have his way with her. Despite her marriage being in the crapper, Londyn still couldn't touch that man.

Knight gazed over wondering what the reservation was. He noticed her nice size wedding ring, but she was giving him too much for that to be a problem. The smiling, the eye contact, the hand holding. He figured it was his age. They were almost ten years apart. To him, it was fine, but he could see that it bothered her. Well that and when she said something about him seeming to have common sense, he told her he didn't. But they'd laughed about that.

The celebration for him was going full on. He was sure that they would end up at a strip club. How could they not? Atlanta was notorious for its strip clubs. He didn't even need the celebration, he would have rather had more time to finesse Ms. Londyn. He planned to catch her walking out to exchange numbers. There was no way she could deny him.

Musiq Soulchild
"Love"

Love...
So many people use your name in vain
Love...
Those who have faith in you sometimes go astray

Chapter 2

Sitting at dinner, Londyn was excited to talk to this prospective client. She was another up and coming artist, however, different from when Libra got started, this young lady already had a following. When Libra hit the market, things still had to be done on a grass roots level, pretty much from day one. Fast forward about six years, Instagram and YouTube were making any and everybody famous. She was a fan of one of Libra's songs and had become a super fan. Finding Londyn, Libra's manager, was the icing on the cake.

K Beezy desperately wanted Londyn to represent her. She felt that she was hotter than Libra, not in a disrespectful way, and a fresh face to Londyn's roster could actually help bring Libra up with her. With the rap name, K Beezy, Londyn's first impression was a bit taken aback, but her lyrics and delivery were the truth.

K Beezy showed up with her sister and BFF; she never went anywhere alone. Even though she initiated the meeting, her sister had to be there. She was a very good judge of character and was always on the lookout to make sure people weren't taking advantage of her younger sister.

The ladies ordered drinks and appetizers and were shooting the breeze. The heavy work stuff came when the dinner orders were placed. K Beezy dove right into asking questions about Londyn's management style and asked her frankly about Libra's stagnant career. Londyn made it clear that she was there to support and push her client, but not overwhelm her. Libra had begun working on a new album, but when she found out she was with child, made motherhood her first priority. They were planning a strategic comeback campaign for her to begin in the next 12 months; however, now, she was dedicated to spending the time with her baby that she could never get back.

As they were talking, Londyn received a text from Micah.

Micah: Call me when you get a chance.

The text seemed odd. He hardly had two words to say to her in the last month or so, would barely even sit in the living room to watch TV with her and the boys. Since she left the house early that morning, she immediately thought something was wrong with the boys.

"Excuse me ladies. My husband just texted me. Let me make sure everything is alright." She quickly went to the 'Favorites' list on her phone and found the name 'Hubs' with a wedding ring emoji on each side. The phone seemed to take forever to connect, but it didn't ring a full ring before Micah answered.

"Hello," he answered.

"Hey. I got your text. What's wrong?"

"Nothing, where are you?"

"I'm in a meeting."

"I just wanted to give you a head's up so you aren't alarmed. I moved out today."

BOOM!

"You what?"

"I moved out today," he spoke so matter-of-factly. Her world began spinning. The restaurant was so loud and so quiet all at the same time. She instantly looked up at K Beezy, but couldn't see her clearly through the tears that were already forming.

"You moved out?" She couldn't process what he was saying, but in true mommy fashion, felt she had to hide her emotions. Immediately.

"Look, I just didn't want you to come home and see an empty house." *An empty house. What did you take?* she thought.

"You weren't supposed to move for another few months. You are starting this shit off all wrong! We said we would talk to the boys before you moved a thing! And you moved without saying anything to me this morning? I came in the room and said goodbye to you before I left. You didn't say a word! And our boys? They *saw* you pack and move? NO! This is not going down like this!"

"Look...do you want me to bring them to you or are you going to get them from the sitter?" He asked not finding any fault in the way he handled things. Londyn was fuming. The ladies at the booth were quiet listening to her end of the conversation. They were becoming just as invested as she was.

"*You* bring the boys home! Don't spend the night anywhere else until we talk to them together like we agreed! You can start your new life wherever you want...tomorrow!" And she ended the call, then threw her phone in her oversized purse. Doing things this way, Micah had full control of the narrative. He could have told the boys anything. Whatever it was, the two of them had not agreed to it. It was yet another way he wanted to show that he was in control.

Londyn looked up at the ladies in the booth, took a deep breath, tried to talk and exploded in tears. She was talking to them, but they couldn't understand a word she was saying. She was absolutely mortified. Every time she tried to get herself together, she exploded again.

She opened her eyes and an older white man was rubbing her back and offering her his handkerchief. When the first Pearl Harbor sized wave of emotion was out and she opened her eyes, she noticed all of the tables with a view of her booth were staring at her. She started crying again. Sheer embarrassment.

"Londyn, we'll take care of your tab. Just go, get yourself together. We can handle this another time," K Beezy said holding Londyn's hand from across the table. Londyn apologized profusely.

"Frankly," K Beezy's sister said, "your husband is a jerk for doing that. Especially if y'all had already talked about it, he could have told you then he was getting ready to move out. Such a coward. Men, I tell ya!" she shook her head.

Londyn apologized again, snatched her bag and darted through the door. She had to beeline through the standing room only vestibule with patrons tortured by the delicious aroma of P.F. Chang's while they waited to be seated. She walked double time, with her head down, through the people frolicking around the mall's stores and restaurants, then around the valet parking line, dodged on-coming traffic, and finally made it to her car.

She sat there. Looking at nothing. Feeling nothing. Hearing nothing. Just sat there. The only way she knew she was even alive was the sound of her heart beating. And it was beating so loud it sounded like it was coming from the speakers in her car. She looked down and saw the loose, hot pink camisole top vibrating.

This is so crazy. My husband left me for real. She looked down at the three and a half carat diamond wedding set she had, the one that just minutes ago K Beezy and her girls had complimented her on. The sunlight danced around in the diamonds sending radiating sparkles of red, blue, yellow, and white all around the interior roof of the car. The ring meant nothing. Marriage was in the heart. Her marriage to Micah had been over for a while. She felt it once he told her he was unhappy. Even with the many divorce threats through the years, he'd never said it quite like that. But never in a million years did she think that he would leave. Now that he had, she was left holding the bag. Again. How could he not want to work on it? She thought as long as he was in the house, he would change his mind. Surely, he'd come around to realize that he loved her and the boys enough to work it out. How could he not want to take time apart and come back once he figured out where his unhappiness stemmed from? How could he turn his back on them? Well, in reality, he was turning his back on her, hopefully not the boys.

The boys were his heartbeat, just like they had been Kaden's. After their father died, Micah's calls to check on her and the boys turned into frequent visits. They'd play with the boys together. Sometimes, Micah would watch them for her so she could get out of the house or get some rest. Eventually, the visits turned into outings with the four of them.

Chinese delivery, movie marathons, and play-time at the park were the things their weekends were made of. And they were happy. Kaden used to always get on Micah about flirting with Londyn. Micah was now free to make his move. It just felt like the natural thing to do. She felt no objection to opening up her heart to him. They fell in love and became an item. She felt good having a man who didn't shy away from her being a widow; someone who could take her broken pieces and love them back together.

Through the years, things became somewhat challenging. They went from being best friends, laughing and talking during the night to barely talking at all. Londyn got a job, then was laid-off when the economy tanked. Having twins was hard to juggle keeping them in daycare. It seemed like one of them was always sick and she was wasting a mortgage paying to hold their spots.

Managing Libra fell into her lap, and thankfully money was coming in. Londyn and Micah would host parties at their house on the weekend, even a few couples' game nights. Their house was the fun house for a while. All in all, they were making it. They were just a young couple trying to tap into the American

Dream like everybody else. She became a serial entrepreneur and with each business venture, Micah grew colder.

Through it all, Londyn had done her share of dirt and he made her pay dearly for it. When Micah started ignoring her, poking fun at her lightly fluffy weight of 150 pounds at 5'4", coming home without speaking and closing himself up in the office, hanging out and not coming home until a highly disrespectful hour for a married man, she reconnected with an old friend from college. Their friendship turned into a dependence because that's the only place she was getting attention. She talked to him every single day. Even though he was in a whole different state, it felt like he was right there with her.

Of course, when Micah found out, he was furious! And rightfully so. There was some back and forth, but ultimately, Londyn let her old friend go. The opportunity for things to go further and turn sexual had presented itself, but nothing happened. She couldn't go through with it. Micah didn't believe her, nor did he believe the guy when he called and asked, "Do I need to pack her shit and send her to you?"

Micah was devastated. He had every right to be. The wife who, in his mind, he was working hard to provide for, whom he had taken in as his best friend's widow with two kids had turned her back on him. She tried to get him to see the relationship that developed was not intentional. She was lonely. Asked him to spend more time with her. Londyn didn't feel like she could talk to her friends about her marital problems because they all thought The Charles Household was perfect, like they had that Will and Jada kinda love, that Method Man and Mary J. 'You're all that I need, I'll be there for you' kinda love. The kind that would last forever. Plus, none of them were married, so they wouldn't understand. Or she just plain didn't want to deal with their judgement. She certainly couldn't talk to her parents about it and her friend happened to resurface at that precise time she needed attention.

Micah made her pay for it dearly. He caused a rift between her and two of her best friends that they almost did not recover from. He did the absolute unthinkable. Still, they stayed together. Micah and Londyn had lived through another such incident that could have ripped their family apart and didn't. She strayed emotionally...again. He tried to pay her back by hurting her...again.

They started marriage counseling. Londyn had gotten to the point where she felt everything between them was good! If they had survived all of that crap, there was no way they were going to get a divorce. They were in it for the life sentence. On the porch when he told her he was leaving, Micah said he had been fronting. He had never gotten past how she violated his trust the first time, looking outside of their marriage for emotional comfort. The funny thing was, he only looked at her indiscretion, and only seeing his as a reaction to hurt her the way she hurt him.

Having her entire marriage flash before her eyes as she sat in the mall parking lot, it all seemed so surreal. *How did we get here?* In truth, she wasn't sure he knew the answer. One thing was for sure, he was done with her ass.

There was no way she could go home. Londyn recalled a non-profit fundraiser event going on not far from where she was. She reapplied her make-up and put on some peppy music, then found the location. She tried to pretend that she was enjoying herself, laughing and joking until putting a fake smile on her face became too much.

Later, pulling into her driveway, she knew what loomed in her immediate future. *Here we go.* She pressed the garage door opener and gasped. When Micah told her he moved out, she was thinking clothes and shoes. He took everything.

Everything that he brought into the house. She hadn't realized just how much stuff was *his* until that very moment.

"Oh...my...God...what has happened? Lord? What has happened?"

She was in complete shock. She called a friend who she loved dearly, but they only spoke every few months. The kinda friend who understands that life happens and you may not talk every day, but you two can pick up where you left off.

"Londyn! Hey girl!" Her friend answered chipper and upbeat.

"It's gone," Londyn whispered, "it's all gone."

"Londyn! Londyn! What are you talking about?"

"Micah...he's gone. He called to say he moved out today. I just got home. I don't think this is what I was expecting." Londyn was completely in shock, her voice barely above a whisper.

"What do you mean *he* left *you*? After you stayed with him after that hotel bullcrap? He's lucky you didn't kill him then!"

"I can't go in the house."

"You said it was all gone."

"In the garage. All of his stuff from the garage. It's all gone."

"You haven't even been in the house yet? You need somebody there with you. You don't sound good, babe." It was then that Londyn realized, she was still sitting in the driveway, truck running with her foot on the break. She put her Yukon in park, got out and sat on the cement. She hung up the phone and cried. It's like the lights from her truck were shining spotlights on where Micah's stuff was supposed to be.

Eventually, she made it in the house and saw that even more stuff was gone. He didn't take any of the big items, but anyone who had been in their house would immediately notice certain things were missing. She didn't know how she was going to make it.

She walked straight to her room and put her wedding ring in the jewelry tray. Just seven years ago, their families had watched them say their vows. Standing in front of an intimate crowd of just under 75, they looked in each other's eyes, proclaiming their love for each other 'til death did them part. Neither of them had died, but their marriage did. So did another piece of Londyn's heart and belief in love.

She began to wonder if Micah really, truly loved her or if he'd married her out of feeling a sense of obligation to his dead friend, Kaden. Maybe he was trying to get her over the hump of becoming a new mom and a widow within the span of 12 months. Maybe he'd fallen out of love years ago when they started having issues, but felt it was his duty to stay.

The marriage counseling that Londyn thought was a fix, was only a band-aid for Micah.

She took a long shower to wash the day away and as she put on her pajamas, she heard the pitter patter of big twin feet rumbling through the kitchen. She hugged them and told them to take showers, Mommy had a migraine and was going to bed. Really, she couldn't bear the thought of looking at Micah. He'd be able to tell that she'd been crying and seeing his eyes would send her back into a tailspin of sadness. As if it could get any deeper than it was at that moment. His single act that day had deepened and widened the emotional tornado spiral that began when her husband died leaving her to raise two boys. The uncertainty, the questions.

If Londyn saw Micah, her mouth would rattle off the questions that had been rummaging through her mind over the last few hours. Questions she knew the answers to, but could not understand. If she saw him, her normally calm demeanor would increasingly ramp up to yells and screams and fighting and crying, fortifying her heartbreak and bringing the boys into a world too wild for their 11-year-old hearts to be exposed to.

Londyn was a vessel of empty sadness. A place where love had left an achy reverb of the sounds of her tears. She wanted nothing more than to go to sleep and wake up spooning her husband like the day – or last eight months – had never happened.

The next morning, they talked to the boys who both cried. They got it, but they didn't. Yes...Daddy is moving. No...he's not coming back. Yes...he's going to live somewhere else. Yes...they would be able to see him. No...he's not mad at them, he and Mommy just don't get along right now.

There wasn't a dry eye in the room when he left. Later that night, Ace called to ask Micah if he would be back so they could see him before bed time. See, they got it, but they didn't.

The next few weeks were full of confusing Q&A periods from Ace and Deuce. They had soccer practice, which they were late getting to if they even made it. They had school, for which they missed the bus almost every day and Londyn had to drive them through the parent drop-off line in her jammies....and a hair wrap. They had soccer games, where the start whistle was blowing as they ran on the field. They had boy scouts for which they pretty much went AWOL. And forget home cooked meals. Fast food every day.

Londyn could barely bring herself to get out of bed, brushing her teeth and leaving the house was asking a whole lot. While they were at school, her days were filled with crying herself to sleep again...waking up and crying herself to sleep again until the bus came. Her streaming tears intermingled with the falling water from the shower. Everywhere she went, to get gas, food or any necessary departures from her car, to pick up the children, drop them off for practice, her towel-of-tears was always nearby. Whenever the boys came home, she'd say she had a migraine and close herself up in her room. It just all hurt so bad. The marriage she thought they'd strengthened still crumbled at the foundation. Her husband had given up on her.

"Mom, can we *please* not eat fast food again today? Can you cook for us, *please*?" Deuce asked one morning as they got ready for school. Londyn rolled her eyes at the thought of mommying.

"I'll see what I can do." She had gotten to the point of sadness where she told her mother, "If you want to see your grandchildren alive, come get them." Not that Londyn thought she would do anything to hurt them, but she was being less and less of a mother to them. They arranged for her mother to come get her beloved grandboys as soon as the school year ended.

Londyn didn't want the workers at her neighborhood Publix to see her looking a mess. She was a regular there, had real conversations with the employees and other stay-at-home moms who frequented Publix like it was a real hot spot. She washed her face, threw on some athleisure wear, as if she could even remember what the inside of a gym looked like and headed to the store.

Usually, she would have a list of ingredients for the recipes she found on Pinterest. Ever since she and Micah had gone to counseling, she'd been trying to do better. She was the new school type of woman with barely-there cooking skills. She had mad bedroom skills, though. Micah told her spaghetti wasn't real cooking, so she'd turned to Pinterest to help her be more adventurous in the kitchen.

Today...spaghetti it was. No-brainer, fun food that she could do to give her boys something homemade and not put herself out too much. And her husband wasn't there to complain.

"Mmm hmm," she heard behind her, but didn't pay attention. She was on a mission. Entertaining aimless conversation or turning guys down was not even on the list of things she had the energy to do.

"Mmm hmm," she heard again, this time closer. Still, she turned the opposite way and walked down the aisle. *Oh gosh, not today*, she thought knowing whoever it was had her in their sights. "It's not often I'm interested in a girl and she gets away. Especially when I give her my bar stool to sit in." Londyn paused...whizzed around and was standing face-to-face, well, face-to-chest with Knight.

"Ohhh, it's the basketball guru," she said trying not to blush. He looked ridiculously handsome even under regular lights.

"Knight."

"Mmm hmm, whatever."

"Ms. Londyn, how can I reach you so we can talk about things more interesting to you than point guards or diced tomatoes?" He asked picking up a can and putting it back down.

"Well...usually, when you want to talk to someone, you ask for their phone number."

"May I have your number?"

"No."

"I saw you wearing a wedding ring the other night." He glanced at her hand and saw it was missing.

"Yeah...relationship status #complicated. Are you on social?"

"Instagram."

"Open it up." Knight opened his Instagram and Londyn snatched the phone out of his hand. She found her profile and followed herself from his phone. "I'll holla." And with that, she turned around and walked out of the aisle. Knight could see she was gonna make him work.

Sly & The Family Stone
"Family Affair"

It's a family affair,
It's a family affair,
It's a family affair,
It's a family affair.

Chapter 3

Apollo Knight IV, the baby of four boys from his father, but the only child between his parents. His father, Apollo III, had three sons with his wife. He named them all after Greek gods and warriors: Castor, Titus, and Ares. He left his wife for Apollo's mom, who was his side chick.

Back then, it was nothing for a man to have outside kids and keep his family together, he was jonesin' so hard for Apollo's mom, that he actually left home. It was the talk of the town. Apollo's mom was a pretty, firecracker of a woman. Lil' Fran could drink grown men under the table and run circles around anybody in gin rummy. She was out to have a good time. And she did. Stealing Apollo III wasn't what she set out to do, but he was such a strapping young man, she couldn't keep her paws off him. Well, they say, if you can take a man, he didn't belong to whoever he was with. The old adage was true.

It wasn't long before the black community on the south side of Atlanta was brewing with rumors that Apollo III and Lil' Fran were an item. His wife, Regina, ignored them at first, but soon enough, she found them to be true. It wasn't long before she received a call, "You need to go get your man. He's over there right now." That's just what Regina did. She drove over there, knocked on the door and yelled for Pops to come out. When he did, she gave him the lashing of his life with a thick, black leather belt.

She whipped him all the way to his truck, then followed him home. He walked in to his three young sons, at varying stages of awkward little boy growth and snaggletooth mouths laughing, "Ooooh, Mama gotchu!" He tried to reach out for them, but they were too quick with him being sore and welted from his own beating.

A few weeks later, it was more of the same. It got to a point, where she just called Lil' Fran's house and told him to come home. It was clear that he wasn't letting go of Lil' Fran. Francesca had her hooks in that man so deep, Regina had the mothers of the church trying to pray off the voo doo. No amount of holy oil, prayer, communion, or late night moanings in the prayer closet could send the voo doo away. Because there was no voo doo, just love. Real true love. Apollo was head over heels for Lil' Fran.

Regina had finally had enough. She had already lived through two affairs with her husband, but now going through a third one after a decade of marriage and three growing boys, she couldn't do it. Not to mention, he was at the point where he didn't even try to conceal it anymore. She refused to be embarrassed in her community and in her home. She knew that the example her husband gave the boys was how they were going to be as men. Sista girl wasn't raising no jive turkey, sorry ass, excuses for men. She wanted stand-up men, productive members of society who knew what it meant to be a family and to be *present* for their families.

Regina packed up 9-year-old Titus, 8-year-old Ares, and 4-year-old Castor and took a trip to her hometown.

"Where are you going?" Pops asked her.

"Home."

"You can't take my boys!"

"Who's going to look after them if you're running behind Lil' Fran?"

"Regina..."

"God don't like no lukewarm Christian and I don't like a lukewarm man. You need to make a choice, me or her. When I come back, I want my husband back. Home! For good!" She marched out, her jheri curls bounced with every step. She hopped into her blue, hatchback Toyota Corolla and screeched down the street.

When Regina got back, Pops was gone. Her plan worked the way it was supposed to. If he loved her and wanted to keep their family together, he would have. If he wanted to go to Lil' Fran, he would have. But what he wasn't going to do was keep laying up in the bed with both of them. Regina was not going to have that.

Pops didn't divorce Regina for a while. He kept her and the boys on his benefits and all. He and Lil' Fran had Apollo IV. Just as a dig, Lil' Fran let him do what Regina never would, name a son after him. Regina didn't care about Lil' Fran and her actions. She was petty and immature. It wasn't a contest, Regina let him go and she was able to hold her head high because of it.

Halfway to Knight's double-digit birthday, Lil' Fran up and left. Pops raised his son alone until Regina stepped in to help. Apollo IV, who everybody called Baby, became a legacy firefighter just like his brothers, father, uncles, and grandfather. The whole family tree was all male! The only females were married in. One of the older brothers, Ares, had played a short stint in the NBA. After two years, he became a firefighter as well.

Seeing Londyn in the store was so funny to him. He was hard pressed to remember a time when he wanted a female and she dissed him. And he never had to be patient. He got what he wanted, and what he didn't even have time to want. Women threw themselves at him. All of the Knight boys were lookers. Baby Knight was no different, although he was the runt of the group. They were tall, boasting naturally athletic frames, with strong, handsome facial features looking like the Greek gods and warriors they were named after. They could have made a Knight Family Firefighter Calendar that would have been a bestseller! Even Pops could pose shirtless!

He had seen Londyn twice. Once with her ring on and once with her ring off. He made mention of it to her and all she'd offered was that her relationship was complicated. He was young, but with older brothers, he'd certainly been privy to his share of complicated relationship squabbles. Especially with that Castor, the knee-baby. He was always getting into something. He'd finally recently settled down with his baby mama. The only thing settled was the ink on their marriage certificate. Titus was married with a handful of boys; Ares had a son, but his fiancée passed away giving birth to him. Ares was never the same after that. Castor, probably the best looking of them all, was a skirt chaser. If it had legs, he wanted to see if he could get between them.

At least now, there was a connection between he and Londyn and he hoped that she took advantage of it. He didn't want to be pushy, but he would definitely let her know he was interested if she took too long. Her age didn't scare him one bit. He had too much going for himself to be fooling with young girls anyway. College educated, well into his career, recently been promoted, good credit, and had money in the bank. On top of all that, he was a gentleman. After his mother left, his dad went back into his philandering ways. But when it came to Regina, Pops treated her with the utmost respect and dared any of the boys to do any different. Aside from cooking, she never lifted a finger. Regina was their queen.

Knight had a full package to offer Londyn. As he sat in his yard daydreaming about the fact that she was still pretty in regular daylight, without make-up, and without him having alcohol in his system, Castor exploded in his ear.

"Baby Knight!"

"Castor Knight," he spoke in his too cool vibe. Castor had a larger than life personality. Growing up in a house with three boys, he had to make himself stand out to get attention. Knight was the opposite, very cool and reserved.

"What it do Baby?"

"Why do you have a duffle bag?" Knight laughed.

"Jasmine again!"

"What do you mean, Jasmine again? You the one who keep messin' up. That's a damn shame! How you think your boys feel every time she puts you out?"

"Like their mama is crazy!" Castor roared with laughter. He and his wife had been together for years and this was nothing new.

"For real, for real. Castor. You gotta tighten up. That girl ain't been nothing but good to you. I don't know what you married her for if you weren't gonna be good to her. I don't even want to know what happened. I know it was your fault."

"It was."

"I already know. Don't be like Pops, man. Tighten up! Take your ass home and make it right."

"That's easy for you to say. Look at your situation."

"Look at it. I'm not married. I live at home and I don't have any kids. If you love her, and you want to be with her, then do right by her. It's that simple."

"It's *not* that simple though. I mean, sometimes it is, but not always."

"You coming at her with new girls, different girls. You got these chicks out here thinking you're gonna leave ya wife and you know ya ass ain't going nowhere. Whatever you want, you need to get it at home."

"But there are things my wife won't do."

"You better convince her to do 'em."

"Man, whatever. I don't even know why I'm talking to your ass about this. You have no idea what it's like."

"Nah, I don't. But you ain't bringing that bag in my house. Go home. And quit playing both sides of the fence!"

"This my daddy's house fool!"

"Mine too! I pay bills here," Knight stood up and Castor saw he was serious. Castor only had 15 pounds on him. They were practically the same size. If they started fighting, it would've been a dead heat...until one of them tired the other out.

"Bruh, I'm not doing this with you today."

"I don't want to either. Go home, Castor." Knight didn't budge.

"Imma call Daddy!"

"Call him! I'll tell his ass the same thing. Bye Castor!" Knight gathered his ice-cold beer and cell phone, and walked inside.

Yo Gotti
"Down In The DM"

It goes down in the DM,
It go down,
It go down in the DM,
It go down,
It go... down

Chapter 4

Londyn almost, had the boys ready to go for the summer. It was normal for them to be away, but this summer would be different. She needed a break like none other. She was barely holding it together. With them gone, she could have the real breakdown that was looming over her head. She could feel herself unraveling more and more each day. She loved her kids but if there was any chance of her preserving what was left of her and reinventing the new person she needed to become, the time away was very necessary.

When she bent the corner to her house, the garage door was up. Before the thought that she had left it up had even crossed her mind, she saw Micah's car. *What the hell is he doing here?* She quickly checked her text thread from him. *Nope, nothing saying he would be here. Dang, we haven't talked in days.*

When she opened the door to the mud room, he was sitting right there at the boys' computer. She opened the door and looked at him.

"Hey," he said not even looking at her.

"Why are you here?"

"Kingsley said there was something wrong with the computer. I came to fix it. Don't worry, I'll be gone soon."

Londyn walked into the living room and turned on the TV. About five minutes later, Micah came in behind her.

"Alright, I'm leaving now."

"Bye," she said as dryly as possible. Not out of spite, but really, what did they have to talk about?

"You wanna do it?"

"Do what?" She looked at him confused. As far as she knew, he took 95% of his stuff when he left and she was in no mood to clean out the hall closet. The one with all of the memories of happier days, the earlier days filled with such promise.

"It. We got about 10 minutes before the boys get off the bus. Gimme some," Micah gyrated his hips looking like he was doing the Pee Wee Herman. Londyn burst out laughing. Loudly. "Damn! You sleeping with somebody else already? Cool."

"I'm sure the boys will be happy to see you."

"Forget that, they'll be alright. I'm out." And he left. Her mouth flew wide open.

A few days later, when they were exchanging the boys, Londyn asked for the garage door remote. She'd thought long and hard about the fact that he really had complete access to her whenever he wanted. She wasn't trying to be mean, but it was a show of force. There was no reason why he should have the garage door opener and the key lock code to her house and she didn't have access to where he was staying. If he wanted to come and go as he pleased, then he should have stayed in the house.

"Why do you want the opener back? So you can give it to the guy you're having sex with?" Micah yelled.

"Kingsley and Kingston," Londyn said back through clenched teeth. The boys were right there. Sitting in Micah's car with the windows down.

"Why do you want it back now? It's been a month since I moved out!"

"You don't live there anymore. If you want to come over, you need to call first."

"That's my house too."

"Not any more. Give me the opener," she stood with her arm outstretched.

"You want the damn opener? Fine! Here it is!" Micah threw the garage door opener at Londyn's car and it cracked into two pieces on the hood. She picked it up and put it back together. He kept yelling, she got in her car and drove off. Then he called.

"You don't want this to get ugly! Do you hear me? I will make your life hell!" Londyn hung up the phone and kept driving. He sent the same thing in a text. She didn't respond.

Once the boys began their summer vacation, they were hardly out of the driveway before the tears began to fall. It was such a relief to just be like, 'eff it'. Without having the boys depending on her, she could wallow in whatever this dark, sunken place was that she was in. She could take her time and go through the motions. Londyn, had experienced heartbreak in the form of death, but not a break-up. Kaden was her first committed relationship; Micah was her second. So she thought it was going to be like on the movies. You know those romantic comedies where the women cry, listen to sappy love songs, binge eat and scarf down ice cream. Then at some point not long after, the man comes back on bended knee. Her situation was not like that at all.

She could barely hold down any food. In fact, her mom said that she had noticeably lost weight. She'd tried to eat, but usually, all she could handle was a smoothie or some fruit. Anything else was asking too much of her. Lucky for her twins, they got to choose whatever they wanted for dinner every night. Except that by the time they left for summer, even they were tired of fast food.

She developed a strange addiction to love songs. Raheem Devaughn in particular. It felt like the only place she could find love was between his verses and choruses. She'd listen and sing along until she was crying so hard, the words were barely audible over her cries. Her phone would ring and she wouldn't answer it. When she stopped posting to social media, that's when the calls and texts really started to come.

Normally, Londyn posted two, three, or four times a day. When her profile was quiet for almost a week straight, her cyber buddies were sending out APB's. Text messages came, she ignored them; except for a select few people who knew that her husband had moved out and barely left a trace that he'd ever lived there. On the days that she did shower, in the dark with incense burning, she stood under the water until the water ran cold.

During this time, she reflected on every second of their marriage. She thought about everything she could remember that she had done and how he'd responded to it. She thought about everything that she could remember he had done and how she responded to it. She replayed conversations, fights, happy times. Londyn was searching for the trigger, the pivotal moment when it all went south, or perhaps the writing on the wall that she'd turned a blind eye to. She was more than willing to take her part of the blame, but she had also been more than willing to try to work on things. A marriage took two…two people to make it work.

There was a certain point when Micah treated her so…blah…Ace asked, "Why are you living with Daddy if he treats you so mean?" That made her sad. She was determined to make her marriage work. Londyn wasn't going to leave her husband. Whatever issues they had, she felt like they could get through them. She loved him, she knew he loved her too, even if he had his own retarded way of showing her.

Of course, she got angry again that Kaden died on her, leaving her to be in this situation in the first place. Knowing it was a natural reaction in the process of grief didn't minimize her anger in any way. She was sure he wouldn't have done this to their family. He wouldn't have given up on them, he wouldn't have walked away.

All of the things Micah wanted were shallow surface fixes. He wanted her to wear make-up, when she did, he said it was too much. He wanted her to get her hair done, but didn't offer to pay for it. He wanted her to lose weight. He wanted her to dress better. He wanted her to make his doctor and dentist appointments. He wanted... He wanted... He wanted... None of it really mattered anymore. He made the decision for both of them. Now, she had to live with it.

Londyn was a total mess. She needed a distraction. She was just so sad. She knew hiding from people wasn't good, but she didn't want to answer questions and pretending to be happy hurt more than laying on the couch crying. Her mom always said she was transparent when something was bothering her.

"Trouble getting your little ones down during nighttime?" A drab lady in non-formfitting khaki pants and a horrible generic button down asked on a commercial. *Knight, I should call him.* She was bored and sad. She really didn't feel like talking about her home life to people who didn't know, nor did she feel like explaining her feelings to those who did. She wanted to talk to someone who wouldn't make her failed marriage a topic of discussion.

Londyn opened her Instagram and scrolled through her followers until she saw the avi with his pic and sent him a direct message. The message just had her phone number.

Knight got a notification that he'd received a message from her. A sexy smile crossed his face that was as wide as the Nile is long. He saw the number and called instantly. They chatted for a few minutes and set up a date at a coffee shop. He was eager to see her. He joked that she owed him a cup of coffee for waiting so long to reach out.

The next day, Knight arrived at the coffee shop and glanced around quickly, she wasn't there yet. Just like he arrived at his own celebration early, punctuality was important to him.

Londyn arrived just a few minutes later. He ordered and paid for their drinks; tea for him and a Frappuccino for her.

"Ok Knight. So, do you really introduce yourself by your last name?"

"Yes."

"Why?" She asked laughing. Looking at him across the table, she realized that this was the first smile to don her face in ages. It certainly helped that he was *very* easy on the eyes. She quickly let her eyes dart around the room.

"Because, I like it. And my first name is probably funnier than my last."

"Try me."

"Nah boss!"

"C'mon Baby Knight!"

"*Ohhhh!* Look who was paying attention! I'm the youngest of four boys, that's where they get Baby from." She was attentive to him. She instantly won points for that. His brother had said it in passing the night they met and she didn't bring it up in the store, but she remembered.

"Buuuut, that's not your government. You know mine, so fess up."

"Ugh!" He sighed in faux aggravation! "Apollo."

"Like the Greek god?"

"Yes! Most people jump to the man from the housewives show. Pops named us all Greek names. Go figure."

"Ok, Apollo Knight," she chuckled. "That's a hell of a name. What were y'all celebrating back when we met?"

"I got promoted to sergeant at the firehouse," he replied and noticed that Londyn jumped when the door flung open.

"*Oooh.* Sergeant Knight?" She asked eyeing the door. "That's sexy as hell! Sergeant Knight," she tasted his name on her tongue. "Sergeant Knight, the firefighter. That's actually pretty dope."

"I got something that's even more dope than that."

"Oh yeah? What's that Sergeant Knight?"

"I can show you better than I can tell you." Her eyes opened wide. He caught her all the way off guard with that. Londyn put her hand over her face and he removed it. "I've been waiting for months to see you. You don't get to hide that beautiful face." He was pouring it on thick.

"Full disclosure," Londyn gave him a quick blurb that explained her recent separation from her husband and that not many people knew they were separated. Once Knight heard that, he could see that being out in public was really making her nervous. He commented as such.

To tell him he was wrong would have been lying. She asked him the necessary questions. He admitted that he was fresh out of a break-up too and didn't have any kids. Londyn didn't ask for specifics, but as fine as this man was, his ex had to be dumb as hell. They agreed that they were not looking for anything serious, just somebody to talk to.

"You know, it's cool if you call me Baby."

"Sergeant Knight, if I call you Baby," Londyn warned, "it's gonna mean something totally different than you being the youngest of four boys."

"How about Big Daddy?"

"Oooh boy! You definitely gotta earn that!"

"Mmm hmm, I think we can work that out."

They sat and talked for nearly an hour. As time flew by, Knight could see that she was becoming increasingly jumpy, so he called it. He walked her to her truck, opened the door and hugged her tightly. With her still in his arms, he leaned in for a kiss. Londyn hit him with the swivel neck, but he caught her. Once their lips met, he felt her instantly relax in his grasp. She snatched herself out of his arms and they looked at each other for a good second. Londyn hopped in the truck and sped off.

Knight was left standing there confused. He could tell she wasn't one of the trifling, cheating types and what she'd said about her husband was true. She was far too jumpy and nervous.

From that point on, they spoke every day. He called her in the morning, during the day, at night. They even started falling asleep on the phone, junior high school style. It was so refreshing to have someone to talk to, who wasn't in her immediate circle asking empathetic 'How are you?' type questions. Knight was a great distraction. Of course, there was the usual sadness over Micah and her family breaking apart, but Knight gave her a reason to smile.

There was talk about future goals, life for each of them growing up, the usual getting to know you type stuff. He told her the importance of family to him and one day having a family of his own, which is why he couldn't understand how Micah could walk away from them. Being raised by his father, made him long for a relationship with his mother. He was grateful for Ms. Regina, but it wasn't the same as having his own mom around. He missed her not being there in his life. He was sure deep down a part of her missed being there with him as well. There was no way Knight was going to willingly not be in the same house as his children. He made that perfectly clear.

```
Knight: Thinking about you
Londyn: What are you thinking?
Knight: All good things
Londyn: Better be.
Londyn: How did you sleep last night?
Knight: Ok
```

They became fast friends. There was so much to learn about each other. Despite the age difference, they were both born and raised in the south with the same values and morals, so they easily clicked. Londyn hadn't been in this phase of a relationship since forever. She could barely remember a time when she was getting to know someone like this. She'd known Kaden in college and with he and Micah being best friends, she inadvertently learned Micah's behaviors, likes and dislikes so once they began a relationship, it wasn't starting fresh.

Knight was so funny, he kept her laughing. At first, it was hard to act upbeat, but after a time, it wasn't an act. He made her laugh just being himself. Whatever it was between them, she appreciated every second of it. She just needed an outlet, a distraction. And he was harmless. So when he told her he was going on a trip out of the country, she was bummed. They'd been talking for two weeks! The thought of his voice not being the first one she heard every day, interestingly enough, seemed like a foreign concept to her already.

"I have to pack," Knight said as they were talking in his ear buds while chillin' at the firehouse in between calls and cleaning up.

"Where are you going?"

"Bahamas."

"Bahamas?" Londyn asked surprised. "How long will you be gone?"

"Just five days."

"So, what am I supposed to do for five days if I can't talk to you?"

"You'll be alright."

"No I won't!" she joked. "I need to hear your voice," she whined in a baby voice.

"Need?"

"Yes, I'm at that point already."

"Well, I'll make sure I call."

"Never mind. I want you to enjoy your trip. Who are you going with?"

"A group of friends."

"You're going to the Bahamas with a group of friends?" Londyn asked not hiding her disbelief.

"Yeah from school," Knight confirmed. "I'll make sure to call you."

"Have fun. Enjoy your friends. I'll miss you."

"I'll make sure you won't even have a chance to miss me."

Sure enough, Londyn spoke to Knight every day of his vacation. He didn't call as early in the morning, nor did they talk all day, but the fact that he made it a point to call Londyn was good enough for her. To her surprise, it was the first time he FaceTimed her.

He got a kick out of her shrieking, then giggling like a little school girl when she answered the phone. Even when he was away from her, he felt like something as small as that would make her feel special. And it did. He could feel her melting in his hands. He was patient enough to take his time with her. Knight knew her situation was a delicate one. She was fragile, so was her heart. Not to mention he appreciated that she wasn't throwing herself at him the way he was used to. She was making him work for it.

Knight: I bet you are missing me right now

Londyn: Wishful thinking…

Knight: Or is it true?

Londyn: LOL!

Knight: I wanna see you when I get back

Londyn: Maybe that can be arranged. Are you having fun?

Knight: I'd be having more fun if you were here

Londyn: Bye!

Mary J. Blige
"Not Gon' Cry"

While all the time that I was loving you,
You were busy loving yourself,
I would stop breathing if you told me to,
Now you're busy loving someone else.

Chapter 5

The boys had been gone for a couple weeks. Londyn didn't have much time to really miss them between sulking and crying over her marriage, then cleaning up those tears and changing morbid thoughts into cheerful ones when Knight called. Just going through the extremes was exhausting. Sad about Micah, happy for Knight to entertain her. It was true, going through a divorce was like mourning a death. The crazy part was, they had only separated. As quiet as Micah had been since the boys began their summer vacation, she wondered if he truly was enjoying himself out there in those streets.

She knew that Micah would be visiting the boys and taking them away from her parents for Father's Day weekend. Londyn made a conscious effort not to bad mouth him around the boys when he moved out. She was sure he would still be a good father, even if he was tired of wearing the title of husband.

When Kingston called Londyn, she was excited to see what they were up to. She spoke to or FaceTimed them at least once a day.

"Hey Ma!" Kingston's bright, smiling face appeared on the screen.

"Hey Deuce! How's it going?"

"It's going good. You wanna talk to big head?"

"Yes," she smiled, laughs were hard to come by.

"What's up, Ma?" his matching face brother appeared on the phone.

"Kingsley! Wassup witcha?"

"Coolin'...ya know!" he replied.

"So what are y'all getting into?"

"We're about to go to the pool."

"Yeah, but we're waiting on Jennifer, Daddy's friend!"

Carla DuPont

Kingston interrupted, hopping back in the frame.

"Jennifer?" Londyn asked more as a reflex than a question.

"Yes, she's coming too." *BOOM!* Londyn just froze. Kingsley kept talking, but nothing was registering.

"Ok, ok...Mama will talk to y'all later," she said quickly and she hung up. No good-byes or I love you's.

Londyn instantly started shaking. She placed her hands over her face so that when she exhaled, it made a loud sound. *Who the hell is Jennifer? I don't know any Jennifer. And he has her around my kids? On Father's Day?* She texted him.

```
Londyn: Who is Jennifer
Londyn: ???
Micah: A friend
```

Tears exploded from her eyes. With her hands still over her face, her legs began to bounce rapidly. It seemed to her almost like she blacked out for a minute. She did the only thing she could do on auto-pilot, call Kenzie.

"Hey Londyn!" Kenzie answered. All she could hear was Londyn wailing in the phone. It took a minute for her to get the cries out enough to speak. Even then, it was a whisper.

"This mutha...this mutha...I can't...believe..." the words came between sporadic, forced breaths.

"Calm down, Londyn. Calm down. It's ok," Kenzie coaxed, "breathe, hun."

"I...can't...oh my God...why...is...oh my God!"

"Come to me. Where are you?" Kenzie asked and the call dropped. The drive from Londyn's house to Kenzie's house was a good 40 minutes, doing 10 miles over the limit, with no traffic. Truth be told, going anywhere in metro-Atlanta, it's expected that the trip will be at least a 20 minute ride.

There were so many thoughts going through Londyn's head as she drove the distance to her friend's house. She didn't know who this Jennifer was. As long as they had been together, Micah hadn't mentioned any friends named Jennifer. How good of a friend could she be for Londyn to have known Micah for at least 12 or 13 years and never heard of her? To make matters worse, the way Kingston said her name, it was so matter-of-factly. It was as though the boys knew her. This couldn't have been her first time around them. And there was no way Micah had met her in the time since he moved out and already introduced the boys to her. Her mind was a swirling cesspool of thought after tragic thought. Before she was even finished thinking one thought, it was being phased out by another.

The tears never stopped, from the moment they started. Her shirt was wet from the tears dripping down. The wall of tears was almost impossible to see through. Londyn blindly made turns and stopped at red lights and made more turns. She arrived at her destination in just 20 minutes.

Kenzie saw her pull up and met her at the door. "Damn girl! You grew wings." Londyn collapsed in her friend's arms and cried like a baby being stripped away from its mother. Kenzie walked her into the bedroom where she was doing laundry; Londyn grabbed a pillow off of the bed and fell into the fetal position on the floor. Once she was finally able to stop crying, she spoke softly.

"He already introduced the boys to somebody else," her voice was barely above a whisper. Kenzie muted the TV so she could hear better.

"What did you say?" Kenzie asked popping her head like an angry black woman.

"Micah already has a new woman around my kids," this time her voice sounder stronger. "The boys called to talk and..." her voice trailed off again. Kenzie's husband, Joshua, peeked his head in the bedroom door startled by Londyn curled up on the floor. He looked at his wife, who by this time was also in tears. Kenzie shook her head and Joshua left as quickly as he'd come.

Kenzie sat on the floor next to her friend. She couldn't begin to imagine what Londyn was feeling. Her own marriage wasn't perfect, but damn near. She and Joshua were great communicators and they'd learned how to give each other space when it was needed. As a couple with no kids, they both saw being childless as a benefit. With children involved, parents have much more added stress on themselves and each other. Each child brings its own personality, and a whole 'nother set of likes and dislikes and attitudes and temperaments and behaviors.

Kenzie and Joshua agreed neither of them wanted children and practically decided to get married on the first date. It had been a challenge for both of them to find anyone who felt the same way. Most people who didn't already have kids, were either chomping at the bit to have them or wanted them down the line. Kenzie and Joshua were a match made in heaven.

That didn't mean Kenzie couldn't find empathy for Londyn. Seeing Londyn this way hurt her. Of course, she had been offering words of encouragement all along when texting and calling Londyn. Some of it helped, some of it didn't. It just depended on whether Londyn was in the mindset to receive it or not. In a moment like this, there wasn't much to be said. There weren't any words that would comfort her. Kenzie just rubbed Londyn's head as she wiped her own silent tears.

Joshua walked back in the room. Standing a nice 5'10", stout from eating cornbread and hog maws his whole life, he headed right for Londyn. Her face was actually frowning. He reached down, grabbing both of her hands and pulled her into a standing position.

"Come on, Honey," he said looking at his wife. He put his arm around Londyn and escorted her through the house onto the balcony. The grill was smoking and a bottle of merlot was sitting in a hammered, stainless steel ice bucket. He opened the wine and poured servings in glasses in front of the seat where he placed Londyn, as well as the seat where his wife sat.

The only thing that could have made the view more perfect is if it were a beach. However, Londyn didn't feel like she was settling looking at the tall trees that provided the perfect amount of shade to make sitting on their extended porch enjoyable under Georgia's summer sun. They swayed in the gentle breeze, the leaves noisily playing with each other. The smell of the grill was enticing, although Londyn couldn't imagine she'd want anything to eat.

As the sounds of 90's R&B played from the speaker, Londyn wondered what was happening to her life. This was such a far cry from a year ago, hell even six months ago. In a strange, yet comforting way, she wanted to talk to Knight. She picked up the phone, then decided against it. He had become her happy place, she didn't want to burden him with the issues between her and her husband.

Joshua busied himself going back and forth between the grill and the kitchen until the hamburgers and corn were finished. Kenzie knew exactly how Londyn wanted her burger, so she prepared it. Londyn was more interested in seeing the bottom of the wine bottle than eating. She only mustered taking two bites. After they were finished eating, Joshua brought out more goods. He fired up a joint and put it in rotation. Londyn wasn't really a smoker, but figured she'd take anything short of crack cocaine to take away her pain. As she inhaled, looking up at the colors painted by the setting sun, she wished the pain, hurt, and confusion would all just go away.

Marvin Gaye
"Sexual Healing"

And when I get that feelin',
I want sexual healin',
Sexual healin', oh baby,
Makes me feel so fine,
Helps to relieve my mind,
Sexual healin' baby, is good for me,
Sexual healin' is something that's good for me.

Chapter 6

Knight had waited long enough. Although he spent his days pretty much talking to Londyn, they had yet to meet up in person again. Londyn was content having a pen pal on the phone to talk to who could take her mind away from the lonely confines of her house. Now that he was back from vacation, he suggested they go to the movies. It was dark, so nobody could see them and he was sure Londyn would feel comfortable.

When he suggested it, he held his breath thinking she'd turn him down. She agreed and he was so excited. Although there was still a big piece of him that thought she was going to stand him up.

"Good morning beautiful," he said when she answered the phone that morning.

"I think you have the wrong number," she joked.

"I'm looking for Londyn Charles."

"Oh, well you have her," Londyn tried to swallow hard so she could clear the grogginess from her voice to leave a soft, sexy morning tone.

"Good morning, beautiful."

"Good morning, Sgt. Knight. How did you sleep?"

"I slept ok. Look, you aren't going to stand me up today are you?"

"I wouldn't dream of it!"

"My feelings will be hurt if you do."

"Well now, we can't have somebody pissing off Sgt. Knight, can we?" They both laughed.

In all honesty, she'd had second, third, and fourth thoughts up until she saw him walk to the ticket machine. *Sweet Jesus, this man is fine.* It was more of a glide. His walk was so cocky, like he just knew he had it going on. And if that's the way he thought, he was right. But he wasn't cocky at all, at least he didn't come across that way.

Knight stood admiring Londyn's hip switching from side to side. He didn't mind being plainly obvious that he was staring at her, which made her stomach jump with butterflies. She shook her head and laughed so nervously she couldn't even look at him. He leaned his head to the side, just like the night they'd met.

"Ooooh weee, girl! You got what I *want!*"

"Hey Sgt. Knight," she replied and he snatched her up in his arms. He planted one kiss on her cheek. They'd spent so much time on the phone they felt like they really knew each other.

Knight had every intention of making his new lady friend feel comfortable on their date. He led her right up to the very top row of the theater. There was one other person halfway down the row. Since they were at a matinee, the place was virtually a desert with only a handful of people in the whole theater. Londyn, still nervous to be around him in person, unconsciously sat with her arms folded. She was much more comfortable looking at him on her iPhone.

By the time the credits rolled, Knight had put his arm around her. It was his goal to make the most of having her there in the flesh. The truth was, he went to sleep thinking about her and woke up thinking about her. Her proof was on her phone by the good night texts and when he called her the first thing in the morning. He loved hearing her voice in his ear on his way to work, in between calls, after work on his way home. She'd become a fixture in his life. As much as Londyn felt like Knight was saving her, he felt the same way. There was something so warm about her, so genuine. He could really appreciate that. If all she wanted was to jump his bones, he would've smashed already. So clearly, sex wasn't all on her mind. He could barely get her to see him in person.

Knight lifted the armrest between them so he could pull her in closer. He heard her giggle, then kinda fall across his lap as she adjusted to get comfortable.

"Sgt. Knight."

"Yes."

"Why are you hard?" She asked honestly. They had literally done...nothing.

"You're beautiful. I'm attracted to you." She looked at him almost surprised at his response. The movie screen illuminated their faces as they looked at each other. Just like in the bar the night they met, nothing else mattered; they were all alone. He pulled her face up to his and kissed her so passionately, she couldn't stop if she wanted to.

It was the kiss he'd dreamt about and it was more perfect in actuality than he thought it would be. Her lips were so soft, he easily got lost in them. With his other hand wrapped around her, he brought Londyn in as tightly as he could. She didn't resist at all. He put his other arm around her and practically put her in his lap. Londyn moaned when she felt what was pressing against his sweats. Height and good looks wasn't all he had going for him. He rubbed his hand down her back and into her pants. *Skurrrrr!* That's where she stopped him.

"Unh uh," she said. "No, Knight. I didn't shave," she laughed. He already knew women used that as a tactic to keep themselves from going too far.

"I'm a grown ass man. I don't care about no hair."

Londyn's eyes clamped shut. This was going way further than she anticipated. She thought they were just going to watch a movie and maybe grab a bite to eat. Now, she was in the movies with his finger toying with her wetness.

"Mmmm," she moaned softly while he fingered her, and he pulled her mouth to his. He hoped her whole body felt the electric shock his had. He gently took his hand out of her pants. She grabbed it and used her tongue to suck his finger clean.

"That was for me," he said. He looked at her with a passion in his eyes that was beyond words. He hungrily kissed her trying to taste the remnants of her. He knew then he was in trouble.

"We can't do this," Londyn said. She gathered herself, pulling the armrest down.

The next morning, Knight called and he didn't have the normal chipper tone she'd grown used to.

"Londyn," he started.

"Well, good morning to you, too." She was nervous that he was going to leave her alone after the stunt she pulled the day before.

"Come see me."

"Ok."

Knight sent her his address. He was surprised at how easily she obliged him. She didn't joke, didn't whine, didn't reject him. He was glad. He'd thought about her the whole day after leaving the movie, which was normal, but he simply couldn't get her out of his mind. Their connection was far too strong. He could tell that she was feeling him, too, by how wet she was when he touched her. They had only been around each other maybe ten minutes.

Londyn took a shower and hopped in the truck on her way to see Sgt. Knight. When she arrived, she was hella nervous. Much more nervous than meeting him for the movie. She turned the engine off and sat in the truck for a second to collect herself. She was so nervous to see him. Nervous to be around him in person. Nervous that something could happen and she'd be powerless to stop it. She'd barely made it out of the movie unscathed. Seeing him on his turf was going to be a battle.

She was somewhat distracted by the beautifully manicured yard and vibrant flowers. As she pep talked herself into not driving off, he emerged from the house. She closed her eyes, then she smiled. He opened the door for her and hugged her after pulling her out of the car.

"How was the drive?"

"Long."

"It wasn't bad," he laughed escorting her to his bedroom. They sat on the bed watching Law & Order for two seconds, before he pulled her closer to him and went in for another kiss.

"It's too early for all that," Londyn pushed him off.

"It's never too early," he said pulling her back over. Slowly, his hand crept up her shirt and Londyn felt the air on her stomach.

"Noooo! NO!" She jumped.

"What's wrong?" he asked. Watching his reaction to her, she realized that her exclamation was just that, loud.

"I'm sorry. I can't do this."

"What's wrong Londyn?" he asked gently. She hated that he was such a gentleman.

"I just...I. *Ugh!*" she said frustrated. "I haven't been with anybody new in a looooong time."

"Ok..."

"I'm nervous. Nobody new has seen my body since I was *your* age." He laughed. Londyn's fears were legit. Dating and body image goals had changed a lot over the past decade. Girl-next-door-cute had been killed by filters, titty jobs, butt implants, and smart lipo. She didn't have one of those bodies. She was nicely shaped, but she didn't have a big butt, big boobs or a flat stomach. Stretch marks and gently sagging boobs were the war wounds of childbirth.

"You're fine," he laughed and went in for another kiss. This time, to his surprise, Londyn sat up and put her feet on the floor. There was an awkward silence between them. "What would you need to be comfortable with me?" He asked honestly.

"A dungeon. I need complete darkness," she laughed a sinister laugh. The house he shared with Pops was quite impressive, but with two stories above ground, she knew there wasn't a room in the house that was completely dark.

Knight stood up, walked around to the side of the bed she sat on, leaning his head to the side as he stared at her. She looked up at him. Fine. Well-defined body with tattoos on his chest, stomach, and arms. Tattoos that weren't visible when he wore clothes. He extended both arms holding his hands open. He hoped she would place hers inside of his; she did. As they neared the hallway, he noticed that she was shaking.

"Are you really that nervous?"

"Yes."

"Why?" He put both hands on either side of her face, looked her in the eyes and said, "Londyn, you're beautiful!"

"Of course you're going to say that when you got me here in your house and you want some ass." She looked at him with a blank face.

"Wow. Your husband must have really done a number on you."

The truth of the matter was, Londyn got complimented all the time. It just came from strangers, random people on the street, not from her husband where she needed it to come from the most. Even his friends took time to notice dope nail polish, or new hair style and made it a point to tell her. Who cares if the world thinks you look good. If *your* world, the person you're doing it for, doesn't notice, it hardly matters what everyone else thinks.

Knight opened a door with a stairway going down into a basement. From where she parked, Londyn didn't see a basement level. He took her to a room that was completely dark.

"Is this dark enough?"

Londyn smiled in awe. This was the type of thing that Kaden would have done. She responded by taking off her shirt. Of course, he couldn't see this, but when he reached for her in the dark, his hands caressed bare flesh. She heard him smile.

They kissed like they had been waiting their whole lives for this moment. He backed her up to the bed. Londyn climbed back far enough for his tall stature to be fully supported by the bed and began running her hands up and down the length of his back. Not missing a beat, he kissed her on the neck and put on protection at the same time. A squirt of lube and he was ready to go.

My goodness! What am I even doing in here with this lil' boy? Londyn was more nervous than excited. She had not been with anybody other than Micah in almost ten years. Not to mention, she still loved him and believed in her heart of hearts that their marriage was going to be restored. At some point. She also found it strange that someone as attractive as Knight would be as interested and turned on by her as Knight seemed to be. Surely, he was just aiming to add another notch in his belt. The young ones just wanted to conquer.

As he mounted her, he felt her wince in pain.

"You want me to stop?"

She wrapped her legs around his waist and he took the hint. She was still shaking, but he wanted to make it a good experience for her. Knight wasn't about to have somebody walking around calling his sex game whack. As they found a rhythm, the chemistry between them was undeniable. They both panted, enjoying each other's skills. Being in total darkness heightened their senses, making each touch, each kiss and each stroke more intense because of the element of surprise. They didn't know each other in that way to know what the other liked or was going to do. They couldn't see what the other person was doing, they could only hear and feel. That made switching positions more fun.

When Knight climaxed, she pulled him down on top of her and clawed at his ripped back. He collapsed his full weight on her and she held him tightly. Knight smiled and kissed her on the neck. He couldn't believe she'd actually gone through with it.

"That was good," he volunteered.

"You think so?" she asked. In her mind, she hadn't really done anything. There was so much more she had to offer, even though they'd just had a lengthy session, he'd done all the work. She was too nervous to really get into it, although she enjoyed herself. It definitely wasn't a wasted trip.

"Yeah!" He spoke confidently, followed by a more timid, "You don't?"

"It was cool," she said rubbing his head. He turned the light on and grabbed his phone as he walked into the bathroom.

Their second encounter was much like the first. It was full of excited energy. Only this time, when Londyn grabbed the knob to walk into the basement, Knight stopped her.

"Nah, baby. I want to see it all this time!" She was mortified! Her eyes bugged out as he walked her backwards to his room. He led the way so she entered the room with her back first. The sun was shining brightly in the room. She was so nervous that, again, she was shaking like a leaf. He thought it was kinda cute that she was so nervous. Londyn thought for sure the youngin' would take one look at her naked body and be turned off. She had become accustomed to having sex in the bed, at night, under the covers. In the event that Londyn and Micah frolicked around in the daytime, she usually had her shirt on. Through the course of their marriage, her confidence had gone from boiling over to the back burner to not even cooking on the stove.

Meanwhile, she looked at his body...which seemed perfect...to her. Tattoos danced across his pecks and stomach. Muscles well defined. Using his hands to hover over her in a push-up position, she admired the muscles that flexed out of his arms as she coursed her hands around them. His legs and thighs were solid and well-shaped from years of playing basketball. Nice teeth and waves in his hair, ya boy had it going on! *Gorgeous and handsome as shit! I don't know why he even wants me. He could have anybody.*

Knight took his precious time with her. The first time, he was so excited, there wasn't much foreplay. This time, especially in the daylight, he wanted to make sure she knew she was appreciated.

"What are you trying to hide?" he asked looking down at her lying naked on the bed. Londyn instantly became more self-conscious.

"My stretch marks and mom boobs," she said wrapping her arms tightly around her body. He stared at her face, she stared at the wall. She couldn't even bare to look at him. He grabbed one of her arms and she resisted letting him move it, so he playfully tugged to open her up. Then he unfolded the other arm.

"Your body is beautiful, Londyn." Her motherhood war wounds were not looked down upon, but instead were celebrated. He sucked her breasts, and swirled his fingertips down and across her stomach before planting kisses over her stretch marks. Londyn felt slightly more comfortable. Slightly. It was still daylight. Her shirt was completely off. They were still new to each other.

He moved slowly at first to get her used to his size, then skillfully maneuvered her to an orgasm before he got one. She squeezed the back of his neck, pulling him deeper into her as her body tingled from head to toe.

After he was satisfied, Knight grabbed his phone and shorts from the floor.

"There's a rag on the counter," he said pointing to the bathroom. She freshened up and walked over to him. She leaned down and kissed his cheek as he lay watching TV. He kind of brushed her off.

"Alrighty then. Guess I'll head out."

"Bye," he said not moving from his relaxed position.

"So, what are you going to tell your friends?" he asked as she hit the hallway.

"That the youngin' has a strong back," she yelled. Knight got what he wanted. Londyn knew she would never see him again.

TLC
"What About Your Friends"

What about your friends?
Will they stand their ground?
Will they let you down again?
What about your friends?
Are they gonna be low down?
Will they ever be around?

Chapter 7

Londyn aimlessly flipped through channels until she found one of her old favorites, Sweet Home Alabama. No matter how many times it came on, that was one of the movies that she couldn't get enough of. It was a story of a couple who grows completely apart and live totally separate lives, yet manage to find their way back to love. She honestly wondered if that's what would happen between her and Micah. Yes, he had somebody else, but Jennifer had nothing on the years Londyn and Micah shared; nor the family they were raising. Londyn missed her husband, but more than that, she missed the friendship they'd built over the last decade and somehow lost over the last 12 months.

On the break, an air freshener commercial aired. Londyn shook her head as she remembered an incident surrounding air freshener that happened between herself and Micah.

One day, that same commercial aired, or one just like it. They all seemed to be the same even with a team of genius marketing execs. On the commercial, people were walking into their respective houses inhaling deeply and smiling because their houses smelled so good. It made her recall an incident between them.

"I want my house to smell good," Micah commented. Londyn made a mental note. The next day, while he was at work, she went to the store to pick up those same plug-in fresheners. She put one in the kitchen and another on the other side of the house in the boys' bathroom, which also served as the guest bathroom.

"Why did you get this?" Micah asked when he came home that day.

"Because you said you wanted your house to smell good," she said smiling. He smiled at her. By the third day, he came home and took them out of the walls.

"Can we just let these go now?" He was stating more than he was asking. Londyn was crushed.

Reflecting on that incident made her think about how confused Micah was. If he didn't know what he wanted, he surely couldn't know that he wanted her or their life together. She completely understood. She understood that he needed time away. She understood he wasn't happy. But she didn't understand him leaving for good.

In her mind, nobody was happy in their mid-30's. Growing up, you have this idea of what your life is going to be like, how successful you are going to be and how much money you'd like to have. Everybody thinks they'll be living on Easy Street at the ripe old age of 35...that is, until you hit 30. By that time, you realize that life isn't all you thought it would be. You are introduced to glass ceilings, corporate ass kissing, being skipped over for promotions and job positions you are perfectly suited for. Some people get physically ill or have accidents that impair them. You fall into periods of sadness and depression. Friends and loved ones pass away. In general, life happens. Not to mention you and your spouse are growing and maturing, and that's if you are blessed enough to find a spouse. The things you wanted for yourself change. Like Micah had even said to Londyn once, "You've changed."

"You damn right I have! How can I be the same person I was eight years ago. You shouldn't want me to be the same person I was eight years ago. People evolve. It's called growth!" Londyn responded.

In a house of four different people and their individual sets of personalities, desires and temperaments, change was inevitable. In fact, change was the only permanent thing to be expected.

Londyn was slowly coming to grips with the fact that in Micah evolving without her, she was no longer a part of what he wanted for his life. As painful as it was for her, she understood that his wants and needs had changed to the point where she could no longer make him happy. She didn't want to be angry or bitter about it and prayed every day that God would take the anger and bitterness out of her heart. She prayed that she could act in love...speak in love...think in love.

The process was not going to be an easy one. She'd not futurized herself as a single parent. He wanted the kids more than life itself. That was the one thing she thought would help keep them together. His actions of already having someone around the boys showed her that there was somebody else on his mind and in his heart. She had to live with that. And the cliché she'd entrusted in her heart that if you love something, set it free. If it comes back, it's yours. If it doesn't, it never was.

Stephen: Hi Londyn, how are you?

Stephen was a longtime friend of Micah and Kaden's. Londyn was a little skeptical to even respond. How much did he know? Had Micah told him about moving out? She went back and forth in her mind about whether or not to answer. He must've sensed it because after a few minutes, he sent a follow-up text.

Stephen: I'm just checking on you and the boys.

So he knew.

Londyn: We're good! How are you?

Stephen: Don't give me that PC BS, how are you really?

That meant he *really* knew.

Londyn: You know…it's been hard. But it is what it is. You can't make somebody love you.

Stephen: Do you need anything?

Londyn: Peace of mind.

Stephen: It'll come eventually. Just know I'm here for you. If you need anything, don't hesitate to HMU. I mean it. I know this mess between y'all is tough, but I'm not taking sides. I'm here for you Londyn.

Londyn: Thanks Stephen. I appreciate that.

"*Hmmm*, that came out of nowhere," she said to herself. But she appreciated it. Still, he was Micah's friend who loved her and the boys only as extensions of Micah, she felt. Then again, he was one of the only people who consistently reached out after Kaden passed. She didn't know how honest she could really be about her feelings with Stephen. Nevertheless, it was comforting that he took the stance to be neutral.

Interestingly enough in marrying her dead first husband's BFF, she remained in the same social circle. She gained another family, but the friends remained the same. She didn't have to endure the scrutiny of impressing and winning over a whole new set of guys. Nor did she have to learn a whole different set of personalities.

She knew they were sympathetic to her loss, especially having the twins who were barely one-year-old at the time. Going through this separation with Micah, she was sure that they would be choosing sides. Most of them anyway. How could they not? When you're together, everybody knows it; when you break-up, seemingly even more people find out. Most of the females she hung out with were the significant others of Micah's friends. Because he'd started telling his crew he was leaving her before he even told her, they were already looking at her with sad, puppy dog eyes.

"How are you doing Londyn?" they'd ask when they saw her and give her a hug.

"I'm good," she'd say, thinking all was right in her world.

"Are you sure?" or "How are you *really* doing?" She'd nod and smile that things were fine. Unbeknownst to her, Micah had already let them in on the secret. Even after they had the real 'D' talk about getting a divorce, Londyn was still reluctant to say anything to anyone. She felt dumb telling her friends that her husband was planning to leave her and he was still sleeping under the same roof as her. She didn't want this to become one of those situations where friends and family were involved only to hold the grudge of this indiscretion longer than she would. Then, later on they would bring it up, throwing it in her face down the road after everything was all good.

She knew she'd lose friends. She was just unsure of who they would be. It didn't take long for her to feel iced out and forgotten.

A few days later, a large manila envelope came in the mail. The return address was a stamp that read 'The Law Office Of" on the first line. Londyn's heart sank. She walked back in the house and sat it on the dining room table, collapsing in one of the wooden chairs. She stared at the envelope. Stared. And stared. Her mind was completely blank, at first. But as her wheels started grinding, the tears began forming.

Why is the envelope so heavy? What do we have to fight about? He's filing for divorce already? How is this happening to us? Is Jennifer pushing him to do this? He can't be ready to make it permanent already? Why?

She folded her arms in front of her and fell over on the thick envelope. She screamed and cried. It was just too much to handle. She should have listened when a friend told her to kick him out when he said he didn't want to be married anymore. Maybe, that would have forced him to see that he did love her, that he did need her. Instead, the ball had been in his court all along. He decided their marriage was over. He decided to leave. He decided not to forgive her for anything she'd done. He decided...to file for divorce.

Micah was serious. He wanted no parts of a life with her. Londyn was then firmly convinced that if he hadn't been such good friends with Kaden and had been around since day one with the boys, that he would probably have been gone from their lives as well. Thank God he still wanted to be a father. There is no way she could strip him away from them. There were going to be obstacles that they faced as black men in America that she could only empathize with. She would never know first-hand what being a black man in America felt like. There were also going to be things that she, as a woman, could not teach them. They needed a man to do that. Micah was going to be that man.

Again, she cried out through tears, "Lord, please... *please*...hold my hand. Let my words be of love, not hurt, not anger, not bitterness, not woe. Lord, comfort me in this season. You are the potter and I am the clay. Put my heart back together again. Piece my spirit back together. Help my mind function so that I am able to take care of my children. Lord let me not be overwhelmed with life. Take away my suicidal thoughts. Lord comfort me."

She stood up and ceremoniously removed an oversized oil painting of the two of them from the wall that was a proud wedding gift from her parents. She dragged herself to the bed she once joyfully shared with her soon-to-be ex-husband and cried herself to sleep.

Mary J. Blige
"Share My World"

Share my world,
Don't you leave,
Promise I'll be here,
Whenever you need me near,
Share my world,
Don't you leave,
Promise I'll be here,
So baby don't you have no fear.

Chapter 8

Knight was getting used to his new position at work. Coming from a pedigree of smoke eaters, firefighters from back in the day who worked in a time before they wore protective gear when fighting fires, he knew Pops was proud of him. Hopefully, he had a long career ahead of him. His dad had been a chief for what seemed like forever. Pops loved being in the field, as his father had and he shared that passion with all four of his boys. Pops was probably the only man in the history of the modern world to have all four of his sons in the same profession.

The house he shared with Pops was a roomy, four bedroom with a completed basement. The three stories was more than enough room for two men who were hardly ever home, especially with scanty love lives. Pops had his rotation of women, but they all knew their places. They knew better than to just pop up on him. Knight rarely brought women home. That was just his way. He knew, honestly speaking without being boastful, that he had the recipe to make them go crazy over him. Not crazy in a good way, bat shit crazy. Didn't want the crazies popping up, slashing tires and doing drive-bys. To him though, Londyn was special. She got to come to his house.

Pops spent a lot of time in the yard. He had a green thumb and planted lots of trees and flowers around. Being a southern boy, Pops even had a little vegetable garden. It made him poke his chest out to make spaghetti from tomatoes he grew with his own two hands. Knight wasn't that good at it, but he still tried to fool around out there. It was the perfect garden oasis to relax in to get away from a stressful job.

There was a wide, round patio table that sat six and an umbrella big enough to offer everyone who sat under it a little shade. Next to that was a collection of wicker chairs and ottomans with soft blue and lime green hues. Further beyond that, still on the wooden deck, was a water feature set between two long lawn chairs. All of this cozy backyard décor was courtesy of one of Pops' ladies. She picked out and arranged it all. The Knight men could easily host a small gathering for 10 guys who could spread out back there without being cramped. A couple of fans on either side of the deck, coupled with the tall trees produced a beautifully, cool and relaxing atmosphere, even in summer.

"So, I heard what happened with you and Castor," Pops said. He was on his knees tightening up his box of annuals. The honey yellow petunias were a perfect complement to the pink and white begonias.

"Mmm hmm," Knight responded waiting for the rest of the speech.

"Now you know with all these rooms we got in this here house, you should've just let ya brother go on in there."

"No Pops. He's using us as a crutch. You're enabling him to keep messing up."

"Ain't no sense in him being there. That girl doesn't want him there."

"Well, she needs to kick him out for good. Not, put him on the couch, take him back, put him out, take him back. Half of the time, he's acting up so she will put him out and he can go do his dirt."

"Look son, you don't know a thing about the woes of married life," Pops stopped moving and looked at him dead on.

"He's a grown man! Let him lay in the bed he made! You want him to mess up his marriage like you messed up yours, huh?"

"If I didn't, you wouldn't be here."

"I would've still been here, even if you hadn't left Ms. Regina. My mom prolly wouldn't have run off though."

"How you figure?"

"She couldn't handle being a mom and a full on woman to you. She was happy being on the side."

"I don't..."

"That's enough about her," Knight was instantly irritated at the thought of his mother. He couldn't wrap his mind around an absentee parent, much less an absentee mother. Women were natural nurturers. How could she just leave him like that? Leave Pops? Sure! But not her own flesh and blood. It just wasn't right. Pops knew exactly how Knight felt about Francesca. There was such a love/hate emotion there. "This is about Castor and Jasmine. Quit giving that boy a crutch. He ain't right and you know it."

Knight took a swig of his beer and that was the end of the conversation. True to his word, Castor ran to their father thinking Pops could get his baby brother to change his mind. It hadn't worked.

The next morning, Knight called Londyn on his way in. She was definitely becoming his peace, his happy place as well. She let him know she was going out of town on business for a few days. She was trying to tighten up a deal for Libra's return at the end of the year and felt like it would be better negotiated in person.

"Don't send me out of town like this."

"Like what?"

"I need to see you."

"Here, I'll FaceTime you."

"No, boy!" she snickered. "I want you to give me some," she said shyly anticipating the rejection.

"When are you leaving?"

"Tomorrow morning."

"I can't, you know I'm headed to work now."

"Mmmmmm," she moaned sounding like a spoiled brat. He could picture her on the other end pouting out her bottom lip.

"Sorry sweetheart."

"Fine, bye!" she hung up. He looked at the phone blinking. She was serious. A few hours later, he called her back.

"Where are you?"

"Where do you need me to be?"

"Meet me at my house in an hour."

"I thought you had to work! What happened?"

"Do you want it, or not?"

"I'll be there in 58 minutes," she laughed. Londyn was beaming from ear to ear. She was sure that after Knight had gotten his fill of her, she would not hear from him again and if she did, it would be sparingly...on his terms. Not only had they continued to talk every day, but here it was, she'd asked him to come through for her and he had actually gotten off work to do it! She couldn't believe it!

When she arrived, he greeted her in the driveway in boxers with a hard-on. He was biting his bottom lip, with his head leaned to the side. She had seen that head lean enough to know what it meant. She excitedly ran over to him. He calmly grabbed her hand and led her into the house, straight to his room.

She slid out of her sandals and before she could do anything else, he lifted her arms straight in the air. He ran his hands from her waist all the way up to her wrists, then back down again. *What the hell is he doing?* she thought. As he came down, he gently tugged at her shorts and pulled them down to the floor, then tossed them across the room. He gently gathered her shirt from the bottom and pulled it over her head, then maneuvered her in silence and with complete ease. His touch was so incredibly gentle. Using his feet, he tapped her ankles to widen her legs while bending her torso toward the bed. He leaned himself over her, kissing her from the nape of her neck down to her waist, put on protection, then slowly entered her from behind. He hadn't even said, "Hi."

"Is this what you wanted?"

"Yes," she spoke softly.

"Say my name."

"Sgt. Knight."

"Am I your big daddy?"

"Go harder."

He turned her over so he could look in her eyes while he plowed through her. His stroke was not as gentle as his hands had been. They both got what they wanted. She wanted it rough; he wanted to watch the faces she made while he gave it to her that way.

When they were both satisfied, he grabbed his phone and shorts on the way to the bathroom. He took a quick shower.

"I'll see you later, Sgt. Knight," Londyn said. She'd wiped off and was now fully clothed, purse in hand, headed for the door.

"Wait."

"For what?"

"Please, just wait. I'll walk you out."

"You don't need to do that," she laughed. The first time she went to his house, he walked her out just to make sure she left; the second time, he didn't even get out of bed.

"Londyn," he said looking at her.

"O...k..." she made an 'oh shoot, I'm in trouble face' and sat back on the bed. Once he was ready, he grabbed her hand and led her back outside. She loosened her grip to make a beeline for her car. He lightly tugged her back and she recoiled, coming face to chest with him. He grabbed her face in one hand, still holding on to the other and kissed her. He hugged her like he meant it, then gave her a forehead kiss.

Londyn immediately noticed the change in the way he sent her off. She thought, *This must be it, the final sendoff. Now, for sure, I'll never see him again.*

"You know, it's gonna be hard to stop seeing me when you go back to your husband," Knight acknowledged.

"You mean, it's going to be hard for you to dump me when you realize that I'm not going back to him and you might be stuck with me."

"After all that time, one of you is going to go back. Since he left, he's going to come back to you." Londyn pulled away from his grasp.

"Nope! I got divorce papers in the mail." Knight's face immediately showed total surprise. "Oh...and he already introduced the boys to his new girlfriend!"

"He what?"

"You heard me." Knight ran behind Londyn. His driveway was big and wide. Being big men, he and Pops both drove trucks, and Pops had a sportscar as a toy. They needed room for all of that. He grabbed her arm and she ripped it away. Knight could see she was instantly annoyed by this topic of conversation. Usually, when he could get her to open up about her failed marriage, her tone was somber. Now, he saw her pissed.

"He introduced the boys to a new girl? What's wrong with him?"

Londyn shook her head with the straight face not even attempting to act like she was trying to find an answer to that rhetorical question.

"She's his friend," Londyn said using her fingers to put air quotations around the word friend.

"It's way too soon for that."

"Oh, but they've already been around her a few times."

"How? He's only been gone like three months?"

Londyn turned on her heels and got in truck and drove off. He stood there looking at her.

Inhale...exhale...trying to release the tension of hurt and tears before they built up enough to release. His scent still lingered on her. She inhaled deeply. This was probably one of her favorite parts of it all. The length of time their bodies were in contact was about 45 minutes. He could last! But, catching waves of his scent on her as she moved through the day were pleasant reminders of how good he made her feel. The sound of her phone ringing jolted her from feeling like the soccer moms in those detergent commercials whose lives seemed to revolve around doing laundry. The ones who just inhaled deeply through the whole commercial.

"Are you ok?" Knight asked in his cool voice.

"Yes," Londyn looked at herself in the pulled down visor mirror. Somebody needed to see her puzzled face, even if it was only her.

"Was it good to you?" He asked nervously on the other end. There was no reason for him to be nervous. He'd seen and heard her reaction, he already knew the answer to that question.

"Yes, Sgt. Knight." Londyn laughed, "Are you ok?"

"I am. I just wanted to make sure you got what you came for."

"Twice!" she burst out.

"I know. That's what big daddy does." They both laughed.

"Is it weird that...when I leave you, I don't immediately shower? I mean...I can still smell you on me."

"No sweetheart, that's not weird at all."

Sweetheart? As they both drove to their respective destinations, they continued to chit chat about random things.

"I'm so hungry," Londyn said. "I want some hibachi."

"Go get you some."

"I don't feel like driving all the way to Buckhead for Benihana's and my other little spot doesn't open until evening."

"You know what Londyn? I want to date you."

"Huh?"

"I see now from today, you only want to have sex. I feel used," he joked.

"I thought that's all you wanted."

"With all these minutes we clock on the phone? I mean...at first, maybe. But not now. And as long as you made me wait? You know I want more than just sex."

"Well...you know my situation. And even though I'm sure my marriage is over, you also said you were just getting out of a relationship and didn't want anything serious."

"You're not the kinda girl to just sleep with and keep it moving. I really like you."

Londyn sat silently on the other end of the phone. *Eyeroll emoji*, she thought. People always said being just friends was impossible. At some point, somebody catches feelings. In her early days before Kaden, Londyn was good at smashing and moving on. She never caught feelings. With this, she thought it was a perfect little arrangement. He had sense, was a gentleman and was a hard worker. He seemed a little emotionally void deep down, but she couldn't put her finger on where that was coming from quite yet. Until today, he'd just let her leave him when they were finished rolling around in the bed.

Now, he was saying he wanted to date her. Then again, dating didn't mean he wanted a relationship. It just meant a step beyond Netflix and chill.

"Hello?" he asked.

"Yeah, yeah. Ummm, that's cool." Knight could hear that she didn't sound immediately enthused.

"Are you on birth control?"

"Where did that come from? You're weirding me out today."

"Since it looks like we're gonna be involved, just thought I'd ask." *Involved?*

A few days later, Knight called her to invite her to lunch. He wouldn't tell her the name or the type of place it was, beyond that it was lunch and he was on a tight schedule. He had a meeting at corporate so he could slide in lunch before returning to the station.

He texted her the address which put her in a plaza. It was so early, that the restaurant parking lot was basically deserted. At 11, restaurants and food places were just opening, but their typical lunch crowds didn't flood until after noon. By that time, Knight and Londyn would be long gone. Since she couldn't look for the restaurant because he refused to give her the name, she looked for his fire department SUV. She parked a few spaces away from it. It was then that she saw the restaurant was a hibachi spot. *And he listens? This just keeps getting better and better!*

Knight was sitting in a booth facing the door so he could catch her walking in. The maître d was all over the place because they had literally just opened their doors. When Knight saw Londyn walk into the restaurant, he smiled widely to match hers. She was smitten by his thoughtfulness and he was taken by her beauty. The last few times he'd seen her, she was coming for one thing and one thing only. There was no need to dress up or put on make-up just to rub her face on his sheets.

He stood up to greet her. He hugged her tightly. "Hug me like you mean it," he said. She squeezed him, as ordered.

"So, how is work?"

"Ya know, it's work," he chuckled.

"How are you getting adjusted to the new position?"

"It's ok."

"C'mon Sgt. Knight! Give me more than that! Is it hard? Are the guys giving you a rough time?"

"Nah," he smiled, touched she seemed to genuinely care about what was going on with him. "They don't give me a hard time. It's more paperwork and more responsibility."

"You can handle that, though," she winked and smiled.

"Yeah, there is one. His name is Otto," Knight told her all about his conundrum with his co-worker turned subordinate. They talked all through lunch. Conversation came easily for them. It was like they'd known each other much longer than they actually had. Knight paid the tab, Londyn thanked him and they walked out to their cars.

"You look nice," Knight complimented her on the black sundress she wore. It was short and flirty. She accessorized it with a chunky, gold necklace that wrapped around her neck three or four times and gold bracelets.

"Thank you Sgt. Knight," she replied. He chuckled because he couldn't believe she would rather call him that than Baby or Apollo, or even just Knight. She insisted on saying Sergeant Knight. "I wore this for you," she did a southern girl twirl in the parking lot.

"Well, it's working," he said appreciating how her butt jiggled under the soft, cotton fabric.

"Let's do it."

"I don't live anywhere near here."

"No! In your truck! Or mine!"

"Londyn."

"C'mon. I wore this dress for easy access. You know you want it."

Knight closed his eyes and breathed deeply. Then he looked at her, put her made-up face in his hands. "Londyn. I like you. For real. I don't want to just have sex with you. I meant what I said when I told you I wanted to date you. Take you out. Spend time. Don't get me wrong, that cat is everything!" Londyn hit his arm and they shared a laugh, "But I'm really feeling you."

"So, are we doing it in the truck or not?" They both laughed again. He hugged her and pecked her on both cheeks, then on the lips. He opened her door and kissed her again on the forehead before thanking her for joining him for lunch. He loved that she acknowledged him taking her out for hibachi after she'd mentioned it a few days before.

Londyn looked in the mirror to reverse out of her park and thought, *What is happening here?*

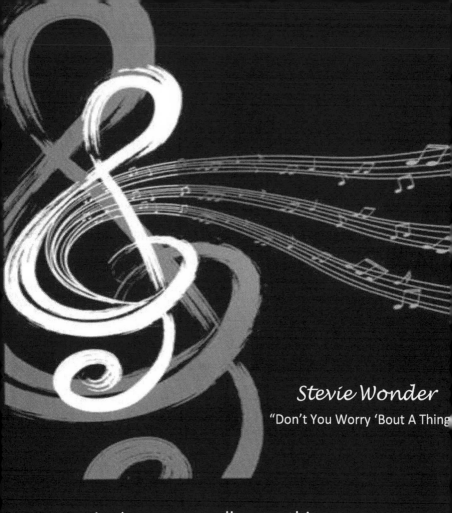

Stevie Wonder
"Don't You Worry 'Bout A Thing"

But don't you worry 'bout a thing,
Don't you worry 'bout a thing,
Don't you worry, baby,
'Cause I'll be standing on the side when you
check it out.

Chapter 9

Londyn's days were filled with positive affirmations, Netflix, not eating, half-ass working out at the gym she'd just joined and conveniently avoiding social media. Just like most millennials, she had easily gotten sucked into the time warp of using her thumbs to scroll her way into other people's lives. Getting on to alleviate her own boredom, or to see what was going on in the world quickly turned into a lost hour of other people's opinions, jokes, and food posts.

The beauty of social media is that it's not real. But that part is also most easily forgotten. Everything has to be snapped 'for the Gram'. The millennial generation spends more time adding filters on pictures than living in and enjoying those moments. For the most part, people only post pictures that make them look successful and accomplished; happy and smiling; celebratory and festive; sexy and desirable. Only the brave, emotional post-ers, upload long soliloquies about being sad, their horrible baby mama/baby daddy drama, being wrongly mistreated at work, hateful co-workers, and bitter type posts.

Londyn knew that people only posted what they wanted her and their other few hundred or couple thousand friends and followers to see. They hid behind the truth of their pain, dissatisfaction in their relationships, unhappiness with their stations in life and mediocre jobs. Not wanting to be out done by the branches of the family tree they couldn't stand or classmates who voted them Most Likely To Succeed, people lie about how successful they are, who they know, and where they are traveling to.

Londyn opened up her Facebook...

I hate when people almost run you off the road!!! They need to pay attention to the rest of us out here!!!

They probably just got fired or got a call that their mother is dying and were racing to the hospital.

Ladies...before you go through your man's phone and hit me up, you should probably ask him who I am! Don't ask me who I am to him!

Hmmm...interesting.

Today I attended a funeral for a five year old boy...

Nope...can't bear to read the rest of this...

Hey family and friends sorry I haven't posted anything in the last 2 days.

I'm sure nobody cares. Really.

Happy anniversary to theeee greatest husband everrrrrrr!!!♥ ⚪ 🏫 I love you sooooo much! You are the best husband a women could ever ask for! You are such a good provider to our kids!!! Their great kids because of you! Thank you for being my best friend!!! I can't wait to spend our hole lives together!!!

Ugh! Chile please, you just posted last week about him cheating on you with one of your friends and you kicked

him out. Now he's the best husband everrrrrrr? And I see
incorrect grammar. Ugh.

Social media was such a cesspool of b.s. Londyn's weak
emotional state was putting her in a poor mind frame.

```
Summertime vacay. James talked me into zip-
lining! What a rush!
```

Awww!

As Londyn stared at the last post, a picture of her friend
James and his wife, Kesha, tears filled her eyes. She had known
James for years and knew what they had was real. Not to say
that they didn't have their share of problems like every other
couple, but they genuinely loved each other. Londyn wasn't in a
place to look at other people's happiness. She wasn't happy. She
was quite confused.

She hadn't heard a peep out of Micah since their day-
long marathon of texts where she asked him not to introduce
the boys to random girls and to keep them out of his personal
affairs. It was none of their business who he was screwing and
with it being this soon since he left, she knew 'his friend' had
been around before he packed his bags. He insisted she was just
a friend, then proceeded to blame Londyn for 'making' him leave
because it was her fault the marriage failed. Everything was
always her fault. They texted back and forth until his response
was so long, that it wouldn't fit on the screen. The text literally
had three lines of words, followed by ... When Londyn tapped
the text, it opened up into a Word document on her phone. She
didn't even bother reading it, just responded, 'ok.'

Seeing James and Kesha looking refreshed and happy in
some exotic locale standing with a lush, green rainforest behind

them instantly made her sad. Her heart pined for the familiar; it ached for her husband. Micah was silent to her, wherever he was. The only peeps she heard from him were daily posts where he talked about dropping dead weight to be happy and finally being free.

Wow! She was the dead weight that was holding him back. *Hmmm.* She, alone, was keeping him from living a great life. She was keeping him from being his best self. She was the thorn in his side. *Damn.*

James and Kesha gave her hope that she could, one-day-eventually-but-not-in-the-immediate-future be happy again. It made her feel like love still existed even if the love she felt for someone who didn't want to even look at her was burning a hole in the bottom of her heart.

She clicked on the box to change her relationship status. The options were bleak, but none of them said brokenhearted and confused, although 'It's Complicated' came close. Labeling her profile with any of the options would have notified the 238 friends she and Micah had in common that Londyn had just changed her relationship status. That would have sent a cascading firestorm of texts and calls, adding unnecessary nosiness that she was not prepared to deal with. So she chose the three dashes that signified *no* relationship status. Just clicking that option made her shake her head.

Facebook, in its infinite wisdom asked Londyn, 'Do you want to see less of Micah Charles?' There was a rambling about how making the choice would affect her feed. She chose, 'Yes.'

As she began thinking herself into a deep, dark abyss of aching sadness, Knight called. He asked how she was doing as if he genuinely cared. She opened up about her fears of being a single mom. Not that she didn't think Micah would still be there for the boys, but the day-to-day nuances were going to be all on her. He wouldn't be there to back her up when the boys got flip at the mouth, or needed a quick smacking across the head. It would be totally up to her to figure out dinner, get them ready for bed, do homework, and all the other stuff that went into running a household that she'd never really had to do alone.

The thought of school shopping for uniforms and shoes alone was something that pained her. Micah usually bought their shoes; she'd always taken care of the rest. She mentioned as much to Knight.

"I guess I'm going to have to break down and ask him to get shoes for the boys. I just don't want to ask him for anything."

"You don't have to."

"When they come back, I want to have everything ready. I don't want to have to take them to the mall. Do you have any idea what that's going to be like?"

"I suuuuure do! Them boys'll have you buying all kinda stuff."

"Exactly!" They shared a laugh.

"I'll take you."

"No, I wasn't saying it for that."

"You didn't ask...I'm telling you. I'll take you shopping for the boys. You don't have to ask him for shit."

"Mmm hmm, we'll see." Londyn didn't bring up the conversation of the boys' school shopping again. She did not want Knight thinking that she was putting him up to taking her shoe shopping for Kingston and Kingsley. Her sons were not his responsibility. If he took her shopping, it would be on his own. In all of their conversations over the next few days, he never brought it back up again. Then...

"What are you doing?"

"Chillin'! What's up?"

"Get dressed, we're going shoe shopping!"

Knight knew Londyn thought he forgot about volunteering to take her to the mall. He was excited. They'd been doing a lot of eating out, but this was going to be different. And talking in person was much different than talking on the phone. He would be able to drink in her mannerisms, gestures and look into her eyes as they spoke.

The truth was, he was excited to be taking her shopping. He enjoyed spending time with his nephew, Hermes. Hermes' father was Ares, the second born son to Regina and Pops. Ares was raising Hermes alone, so all of the brothers chipped in to help. It wasn't the most stable of situations, with them all having rotating schedules, but it was all Hermes knew. Hermes was nine years old, so close to the age of Londyn's boys. Knight knew they would get along well. He toyed with the idea of getting them together, taking all the boys to Six Flags or some place, but he knew Londyn wasn't ready for that yet. Especially after seeing how she reacted to Micah introducing them to somebody else.

Knight was eager to have his own family. He told Londyn that he wanted a wife and kids more than anything. Two or three little clones running around would fill his heart with joy. Naturally, when he brought up the conversation about having more kids, she told him that she did not want any more. She admitted that if she was in a serious, long-term relationship with a man who didn't have any kids, she may be open to giving him one. However, after being widowed and having a failed marriage, she was hesitant to walk down the aisle again. At 35, having been through two marriages was enough.

Taking her shopping was something that he truly wished he would be able to do one day for his own boys. Yes boys. He was convinced that looking at four generations of only boys in his family, he would certainly be having all boys.

He arrived to pick her up at her house. She was on the phone when she opened the door and held up the one church finger asking him to be patient for a few minutes. He sat on the edge of the couch and beckoned for her to come back to where he was. She walked over to him and he positioned her in between his legs. He lifted her shirt up and started kissing her stomach, then unbuttoned her cutoff shorts. He shimmied them down just a tad, and kissed all along her panty line. Londyn pushed his head away from her and went to put on her shoes.

She was so self-conscious walking into the mall with him. Of course, black don't crack, but she did look a tad older than him. Londyn didn't want people thinking she was his suga mama. Then again, her friends thought he was about five years older than he was, so technically, they would look around the same age. What did it matter anyway? The people at the mall were complete strangers. Hell, they could be siblings for all anybody cared. She drove herself crazy with random thoughts walking behind his sexy, swagged out stride trying to keep up with him. At first. Until he noticed she was lagging behind.

"Move them little baby legs!" he joked looking behind him.

"Sgt. Knight! Your legs are like two times as long as mine!"

"Let me slow down for the baby," he said pausing a half of a second for her, then reaching out his hand for hers. Instead, she grabbed his bicep and they swagged on inside the mall. Somehow, by the time they walked into the first store, he was a few paces ahead of her again. There was a pretty, young girl in her early 20's standing at the threshold welcoming customers in.

"Mmm...hello," she said with one of those damn-boy-you-fine faces. "What can I help you find today?"

"Nothing yet, thanks," Knight said walking past her. She was looking at him so hard, that she didn't even notice Londyn. Her head followed Knight into the store. He picked up a shoe and turned around to show Londyn. The sales associate was standing right there...between them.

"What size do you need?" She asked happily.

Knight craned around her to look at Londyn. "What size?"

"Six," Londyn said smiling. The sales associate still didn't acknowledge Londyn.

"She's rude as hell," Knight started as soon as she walked away.

"Yeah, she's got her eyes on you boy!" Londyn winked. He brushed her off and kept looking at other shoes.

The sales associate came back, "Here you go, size 6 in black."

"Oh, we need two pair."

"We only have one size 6 in black."

"Sweetheart," Knight looked at Londyn, "what do you think about that?" Then he looked at the sales associate, "We have twins." She rolled her eyes. Londyn shook her head no. "Mama says that won't work," he grabbed Londyn's hand then walked out of the store.

"Ooooh weeee!"

"She didn't like that, huh sweetheart?" Knight laughed still holding her hand. He noticed that she hadn't even balked when he called her sweetheart.

"Not at all!"

"Got me out here feeling like I got step-kids before I even have my own!" *Step-kids? I thought we were just having fun, she thought.* Londyn looked at him kinda crazy, then shrugged it off. They had meaningless banter back and forth about the girl until they got to the next store.

"What do you need me to get for you today, love?" An associate at the next shoe store asked. Cheesing so hard you could see all 32 of her teeth.

"Ask Mama what she wants," he pointed to Londyn, "we're shopping for our boys."

After a little back and forth with a sales associate who wasn't nearly as rude, they found a pair of shoes. During the wait, Knight found a seat on a bench, while Londyn perused the rest of the store. She made it all the way to the front of the store where a full-body mirror had the perfect catty corner view of where Knight was sitting. Londyn noticed the girl who greeted them at the front had made her way to the rear of the store. She stood next to Knight talking to him. He was glued to his phone.

Londyn kept looking at other shoes and random shirts with cool, athletic sayings and artistic sketches of supposedly famous athletes she had no clue who they were. All the while, she maintained a slick view of the back of the store through the mirror. The girl talking to Knight, positioned herself in front of him, still talking. He turned his whole body around to the opposite side of the bench. She walked to that side of the bench and stood in front of him. He looked at her, stood up and walked toward Londyn. Londyn quickly averted her gaze to keep him from noticing the mirror. He gave her a kiss and smacked her on the butt.

Once the shoes were paid for, Londyn thanked him and took the bag off of the counter. He reached his hand out and she placed her hand in his. He shook his head 'no.' What he really wanted was the bag. Knight was a gentleman; his father had raised him that way. He was not about to let her walk through the mall carrying a bag as long as he was around. It was just one more thing to make Londyn gush over him. He reminded her of Kaden in that way. Kaden was such a gentleman.

"Why are you looking at me like that?" Knight asked Londyn. He already knew what look that was.

"It's hard for me to be around you and not jump your bones right here," she spoke candidly.

"Maybe I'll let you jump my bones when I drop you off. You still have the condoms I left at your house, right?"

"Ummm," Londyn looked up toward the ceiling in thought, "we can stop by the drug store on the way to my house." Knight stopped his pace, the smile erased from his face.

"I bought a three pack and we only used one. What happened to the other two?"

"Knight, I'll pay for more condoms. It's not a big deal."

"You should still have two more," he said looking at her with the straight face.

"We can buy more."

"Nah, nah," he shook his head.

"You're counting condoms?"

"Yeah, when I buy them. I left them at your house for *us* to use, not for you to use them with somebody else."

"Boy, I have them. Dang!" she burst out laughing.

"You better!" He just laughed at her, then kissed her forehead.

"It's not like you care anyway," she tested the waters just a tad.

"Try me."

"I am hungry. Let's go to the food court." Londyn changed the subject.

"Nah, we'll go to Chipotle down the street when we leave. There are a few more stores to go to."

"I don't like Chipotle," she pouted.

"Too bad. It's healthier than this other crap."

"I really don't like Chipotle! They don't have as many toppings as Moe's!"

"Too bad. I'm driving, I say Chipotle," Knight said giving a good ol' Kanye West shrug. She smacked her lips and rolled her eyes. They shopped for another hour or so, then on to Chipotle. Londyn grudgingly placed her order, shooting a nasty stare at Knight the entire time. Already spoiled from the mall, she didn't even bother to grab the bag. Once back at Londyn's, she busied herself putting the TV trays in the living room and getting cups. Knight was busy getting undressed. Knight saw that she was eager to eat, but he was just as eager for something else. He caught her by surprise, turning her around to his naked body. She hadn't even seen him undressing.

"Oh...ok," she got with the program. How could she not? This fine man was standing there, not chiseled looking rock hard, but still perfect. And he was fully erect just thinking about the good good he was about to get. After a hot, sweaty sex session, Londyn hopped in the shower.

Londyn took her precious time showering, then lotioning her body down. When she walked into the living room, she noticed Knight stretched out on the couch watching TV in his boxers.

"Why aren't you eating?"

"I was waiting on you."

"But now, your food is cold."

"That's alright."

"Sgt. Knight, what am I going to do with you?" she smiled. He was so sweet, so self-less. He didn't make a grand announcement that he was waiting or rush her out of the shower so they could eat together. He just waited patiently.

Knight openly admired her body. Didn't try to hide it in the least. He hungrily stared at her breasts in the semi-opaque tank top she wore. Her dark nipples pressed against the tan color. He didn't take his eyes off of them as she brought his food over to him. She felt like Loretta Devine's character, Gloria, in the film version of Terry McMillan's *Waiting to Exhale* when Gloria is walking away from Gregory Hines and knows he's watching her switch across the street.

He ran his index finger along the side of her leg. Leopard print leggings looked painted on accentuating her shape. Londyn didn't say or do anything, just made a mental note. *Either he genuinely likes what he sees or he's pouring it on thick.*

Micah wouldn't have waited on her to eat. He liked his food piping hot. Even beyond that, the days of wooing had long since vanished. Having spontaneous sex was even more of a challenge, especially with the boys. There were the occasional stolen moments of quickies and spontaneity, however, those too, like the happy times, had faded.

Londyn and Knight had just had rough, mind-blowing sex. He worked any frustrations he could have possibly had out on her and still was equally, even if not more so, attracted to her. Knight gave her the look she was used to getting before sex, not after. It felt so good to be desired. It seemed like so much time had passed since she felt that desire from Micah. Their bed had grown increasingly cold, although after trying their hand at counseling, Londyn thought they were in a much better place, it still didn't compare to the heat they once shared. She blamed herself. She beat herself up for ever confiding in her old friend emotionally.

She pushed the hurtful reflections out of her head and focused on the man beside her. They ate, then stretched back out of the couch to boo up, watch TV, and talk.

Khalid
"Saved"

But I'll keep your number saved,
Cause I hope one day you'll get the sense to call me,
I'm hoping that you'll say,
You're missing me the way I'm missing you,
So I'll keep your number saved,
Cause I hope one day I'll get the pride to call you,
To tell you that no one else,
Is gonna hold you down the way that I do.

Chapter 10

Knight: We gotta stop this. I don't wanna fall in love with you.

That was the text Londyn woke up to. She rubbed her eyes and read it again. *Well, he finally got around to it*, she thought. She was expecting one of them to cut it in the beginning. After they had sex a time or two. She would've cut it off if his sex was trash and she expected him to cut it for any plethora of BS reasons. Either way, the fact that he had been around as long as he had was already surprising. She'd take that as a win and keep moving.

His reasoning was what took her for a loop. *Why would he even say fall in love? Who was talking about that? We both said we didn't want anything serious. We were both getting out of relationships. Falling in love though? Well, we have clocked a million hours talking on the phone all day...every day. We've been going out and spending time together.* As Londyn reflected on that, she realized the whole setup was definitely more than she'd anticipated. Cut buddy to bang her back out at most, but definitely not spending quality time hanging out and phone conversations as long as they were back in junior high when that's all you could do because parents wouldn't let you see each other.

So maybe it was more than Knight banked on as well. *Maybe going shopping with me was a shock to his system*, she thought. *Maybe shopping for the boys put a sense of responsibility on him that made him re-evaluate our situationship. He sure didn't act like it. Maybe all of the butt smacking, holding hands, and kissing sunk in after he left because he shole was acting like he was having the time of his life. All smiling and happy when we got back to the house. He was acting like he couldn't get enough.*

Oooh and when he put her legs on his shoulders! Mmmmm, it felt so good!

Whatever his reasoning, she wasn't about to chase him. She was already in a situation with a man who left her because he didn't want to be with her, now she was in two. Londyn had no intention of going after either of them. If she'd asked Micah over and over not to leave given the years, friendship, and raising two boys together and he still left, she was sure pleading to Knight would result in the same thing. There was nothing but laughter and great sex between them.

No doubt she would miss his conversation and company. She would certainly miss the sex. It was amazing. But, she had big girl problems to deal with.

Knight sat at his desk staring at his phone. He placed it in the center of his desk after he sent the text. Londyn always texted right back. Always. If it took more than five minutes, he was surprised and she always answered when he called. He sat there with his hands clasped, index fingers touching like he was making a gun with his hand. He rested his chin in the hook between his index fingers and thumbs.

Otto tapped on the door and walked in without having the go-ahead. Knight looked up at him instantly annoyed. He'd just sent Londyn a text cutting things off with her and was anxiously awaiting her response. In his experience so far, she'd been pretty level headed, even with the way she handled things with her husband. But that didn't mean anything. He'd seen girls go zero to 100 real quick. She knew where he lived and could easily find his job. Not to mention she was already going through an emotional heartbreak from her ex. He didn't want to push her over the edge.

Otto had been working at the station for twelve years. He was there when Knight was transferred in. Otto had been trying to become a sergeant for a while. He didn't have the chops. Everybody could see that except him, of course. When Knight got promoted, Otto had a fit. He felt like he had been passed over for Knight. He also thought Knight was getting preferential treatment. Otto toyed with transferring to another station house, but decided to stay and make Knight's life miserable instead. He acted like it was Knight's fault that he hadn't gotten promoted.

"I didn't answer," Knight said.

"But you would have and you would have told me to come on in. So here I am." Knight just rolled his eyes.

"What is it this time?" Knight asked clearly annoyed.

Then a call came through with instructions resounding over the firehouse intercom. He snatched his phone off of the desk and they both ran out of the room jetting to the truck. The call was for a car accident on 75 heading north, so both the ladder engine truck and ambulance were needed.

As Williams gunned it, lights and sirens to the scene, the other men got dressed in their full bunker gear. The men were filled with an excited adrenaline. Calls like this didn't come every shift. One of the attractions to being a firefighter was the unknown. Each day, walking into work, there was no telling what was going to happen. It was fun...problem solving at its finest; putting out fires literally and figuratively while saving lives. Still, with whatever hoopla was going on around them, they had to remain calm. Calculated in their actions, calm in their words.

Once they arrived, Williams positioned the ladder truck to establish scene safety. They needed to close off as many lanes as possible to keep cars from speeding too close to the scene of the accident. Otto, already wearing a reflective vest, hopped off to guide him and direct traffic, while Sterling put up cones. They left one lane of traffic inching in the far left lane.

Knight radioed to dispatch, "Dispatch, Sgt. Knight, ladder, Firehouse 9, we're cutting off lanes 1, 2, and 3 on 75 north at Forest Park," while Josten ensured that the vehicle had been turned off. Knight did a quick, visual scene assessment as he walked over to see Josten applying immediate first-aid to the patient pinned inside his car. He noticed one person standing with a bleeding head wound, but who was talking.

"I need you over here!" A middle-aged woman demanded a few feet away from Knight. "My son needs help!" Otto rushed over to help her. After a few seconds, Otto ran back over to Knight to let him know the teenager would need stiches, but he was otherwise doing fine.

There was another patient reclined in the passenger side seat of the third vehicle. Sterling yelled, "Need a medic!" Williams ran over to assist. They put a neck brace on her.

"Hey! You! My son's head is bleeding!" The woman shouted at Knight again.

"Ma'am, I understand that," Knight maintained his cool, "could you please step aside."

"We have a three car MVC," Knight radioed, "where the patient is conscious, pinned. We need another ambulance."

He saw that the victim who was pinned inside of his car didn't have compression syndrome, a condition where being pinned adversely affects circulation to the point where a limb would need to be cut off or he could possible lose his life; but he was in bad shape. Still, there was no need to call Life-Flight to airlift him. Their biggest concern was figuring a way to get him out of the car and to a hospital. Otto brought spreaders. He and Josten worked to position them so they could rescue the man. His leg was stuck and bleeding; he was screaming in pain. As they were working, the second ambulance arrived, Knight pointed them in the teenager's direction.

The men worked to get the car open to a point where they could get the patient's leg unpinned and get him out of the vehicle. When they finally freed him, they put him on a gurney and Sterling applied a tourniquet to stop the bleeding. All was well, everybody would be ok.

Once they were back at the station, Knight checked to see if Londyn had responded. She hadn't. Almost two hours had passed and he could not believe that she had not breathed a word to him. No calls, no texts, no DM's. Nothing. He went back into their text thread to see if the message had even delivered. Underneath the blue bubble at the bottom of their thread was the word 'delivered.'

The silent treatment he could not handle. He went into his recent calls and tapped her name which was at the top.

"Hello," Londyn answered sounding unamused. It was a far cry from her normally excited tone.

"Londyn."

"Sgt. Knight."

"Did you get my text?"

"Yes."

"And you just not gon' respond?"

"What do you want me to say?"

"Something. Say something."

"Something," she obliged him.

"Londyn."

"Sgt. Knight."

"C'mon, stop playing," his tone was urgent.

"I'm not playing. I honestly don't know what kind of response you're expecting."

"What did you think about my text?"

"Ummm...I thought, ok. Something is clearly wrong with me if both of my men no longer want me," Londyn looked down at her nails. She needed a manicure, the melon-colored gel polish was growing away from her nailbed. "I mean, I'm not going to beg you to stay with me. You said you were just getting out of a relationship and didn't want anything serious, and clearly you meant it. You got what you wanted. You busted a few nuts, now it's time for you to bounce."

"Is that really what you think?"

"What else is there for me to think, Apollo?" He could tell she was feeling some kind of way. She'd never called him Apollo. "We talk every day, we hang out, we just went shopping for my sons and the word step-kids came out of your mouth. I didn't ask you to take me. I never asked you to *date* me. That was all on you. I was perfectly fine keeping this in the bedroom. Now, all of a sudden, you want to stop dealing with me? I can't make you want to be around. So if that is where you are, I have to accept that."

Knight exhaled deeply. There was something he needed to tell her. It was weighing on him. He exhaled loudly, again. Londyn deserved better than this. She was right in everything she'd just said to him. He just couldn't bring himself to tell her, so he thought cutting things off would be easier. In the two hours since he'd sent the message, he was tormented. He didn't really want to lose her, he didn't know any other way to handle it.

"Londyn. I don't want to lose you."

"Apparently you do. You just broke up with me."

"I don't. You know how I feel about you."

"I thought I did. I thought we were good, but apparently not."

"I love you, Londyn. But you know...your situation is a lil' complicated."

"How so?" She skipped right over those three magical words most women die to hear. "I haven't brought you any of the drama that Micah brings me. I keep all that away from you."

"You are still married."

"Not in the heart. That's where it matters. He's already sent divorce papers. I think you and I both know where this marriage is heading."

"You are still married, Londyn. You can decide to take him back at any point. Not to mention Kingsley and Kingston. That man is going to have a fit when he finds out about me!"

"That's my problem, not yours. I'm not going to put you in any type of danger, Knight. I mean it. But I totally understand if this is too much for you to handle. Good-bye."

She hung up on him. He looked at the phone. She had really just hung up on him. He closed his eyes and hung his head over the desk. So that was it. They were done. It ended just as easily as it began. For that he was thankful, but he was sure he would regret breaking it off.

On Londyn's end, she kept hearing Knight say, "You are still married." It played over and over in her head. He was right, she was still married, but it sure didn't feel that way. No part of her life felt like she was married. Hadn't felt that way in a long time. Micah had moved out months ago and before that, he'd spent months in the guest bedroom and before that all but quit talking to her. They were not waking up together, they were not sleeping together, they barely even spoke. They'd only had sex twice that year before he moved out. Not that that came as a complete surprise. How could they possibly make love when there seemed to be little love between them?

There really *was* more Knight needed to say, he just couldn't let the words escape his mouth. Things with Londyn were over and she would never know the truth.

It was eating him up that she would think he was just a young guy trying to hit it. The thought of not hearing her groggy a.m. voice, that she thought sounded sexy, upset him. He half-heartedly smiled just thinking about it. In the beginning, she tried to sound alert, like she had been up for hours. As they became more comfortable, she didn't try so hard. Still, she tried not to sound like a Barry White voice double.

He stared at his phone. Half expecting her to call back, half knowing she absolutely wouldn't.

Travis Greene
"Intentional"

All things are working for my good,
Yeah,
Cause He's intentional,
Never failing

Chapter 11

For the next seven days, Londyn's phone was dry. Her Ace and Deuce were living life on vacation; her parents sending pics of them at the beach, cooking, hanging out. Knight was gone, Micah didn't care if she was breathing or not. It was not a good place to be. She relived scenarios from both relationships. She tried to accept the fault of both failures. She tried to find where she had been the cause of the downturn of things. At 0-2, clearly *she* was the problem.

She could easily see how incidents earlier in their marriage could have incited Micah's behavior, but not Knight's. Maybe her being still married really did spook him out. She couldn't help that. She still couldn't bring herself to open the large manila envelope that sat all by its lonesome on her dining room table. It was starting to collect dust. She had yet to muster the courage to look inside. It was so thick. She wondered what she and Micah had to argue about that constituted so much paper. It looked like almost half of a ream. She passed by it no less than 20 times a day. And 20 times a day, she ignored it. The envelope had practically become a part of the landscape. It's mere presence alone reminded her of the failure that she was.

Londyn met with a colleague for lunch. Amberlee was a business coach who was an emerging force in the industry. Being that she helped entrepreneurs think outside of the box, Londyn thought they could put their heads together to figure out a unique spin on Libra's image and comeback.

She was mixed, black and Hispanic, although she looked white. She had long, straight hair that drove her crazy because it would barely hold a curl. She was tall and slim, having none of the traits from her black heritage aside from juicy lips. Amberlee greeted Londyn standing up from the table to give her a hug and kiss.

"Hey manager to the stars!" Amberlee spoke in a sultry alto. Always calm, always sexy.

"Whatever, business coach, 100,000 followers strong! I'm trying to be like you when I grow up."

"Actually, that's 102,000 followers strong, organic, not bought," they laughed. "Londyn, when they talk about me, make sure they don't forget to say, but she didn't buy her followers though!" They both cracked up.

"What's going on Amberlee?"

"You know, just trying to make it out here. Trying to move on up like The Jeffersons."

"I see you out here moving and shaking. It's hard to get a hold of you."

"Except it's not. You have a direct line, not many people have that," Amberlee said earnestly. Londyn looked in her eyes. Her friend meant what she said. They had only known each other for about two years, but their relationship came easily. It was a mystical connection that they were both moving in the same direction and needed each other to fuel the trip. They were both genuine people, which is hard to find in Atlanta. Most people only care about who you know and whether or not you can get them a wrist band for a VIP section for free drinks.

"I'll drink to that," Londyn put a straw in her freshly poured glass of ice water. The waiter placed them on the table when Amberlee arrived.

"So, you wanted to talk about Libra, right?"

"Yes, so..." Londyn began when Amberlee's phone rang.

"Hold on. Hello...yes...I'm here...Sure!...ok." Amberlee turned her attention back to Londyn. "My girl Melody is in town. I told her to meet me here after you and I met, but she's early and wanted to know if she could crash our lunch."

"If she's your girl, I'm sure she's cool. Melody who?"

"Melody Waters, she's a..."

"Thee Melody Waters?" Londyn's eyes got wide. Her eyeliner was perfect on those almond shaped eyes she got from her mama. Now she was very glad she decided to polish her look off before leaving the house. In her feelings of rejection and despair, she started to feel like it wasn't even worth the effort. Who was checking for her anyway?

"Yes," Amberlee was tickled.

"She's my mentor...my auntie...my BFF...in my head." Amberlee roared. "I have been following her moves for years! Now you're telling me she's going to be sitting right here at this table?"

As Melody approached the table, walking as gracefully as a gazelle, Londyn tried hard not to spazz out. The last thing she wanted to do was come across like one of those super fans from social media who followed someone's every move; but that's what she was for Melody. Thank God for social media, otherwise, it would be harder to model herself after such a bomb ass queen.

Amberlee, who was taller than them both, stood to hug Melody. Melody was closer to Londyn's height, maybe an inch or two taller. And she was thick! Gorgeous feminine curves that even the straightest woman could appreciate. Her hair was naturally curly in a cute short cut.

"Melody, this is my friend, Londyn. She's a talent manager." Melody walked to Londyn's chair.

"I'm a hugger," she said and met Londyn with a warm embrace.

"I see you finally made the big chop!" Amberlee noticed.

"Yeah," Melody fingered her cut. "It was time. It's all juices and berries for me from here on out. No more creamy crack!"

"Oh, I need creamy crack. That's the only way to tame this mane," Londyn said. Her hair was thick and long, but she usually opted for a ponytail or bun of some sort. The ladies chatted about how hungry they were and what they'd planned on ordering. After they placed their food and drink orders, Melody dove right in.

"Girl, let me tell you about Jason." Melody stopped. Her eyes darted to Londyn. Londyn had made her feel so comfortable, that she forgot they didn't know each other.

"She's cool. She's a vault," Amberlee vouched for Londyn meaning, anything Melody wanted to say, she could and know that word would not get around.

"Ok," Melody seemed a bit relieved. "We are at such a stalemate. It's like we aren't on the same page at all. We used to be so connected, I don't know what's happening."

"Do you think there is somebody else?"Amberlee asked honestly.

"I don't think so, but I'd be a fool not to consider it. We argue so easily and it seems like we argue over nothing. Like absolutely nothing. I don't get it. I'm so frustrated!"

"My husband and I got to a point like that. He could literally look at me and tell what I was thinking. We could watch a car commercial and he'd say, 'Did you see his shoe was untied?' and that would be exactly what I was looking at. Then we got to where you and your husband are."

"What did you do?"

"You try to get back to each other. Get back to the basics of the relationship. You're probably not spending as much together as you used to, are you?" Londyn asked.

"No, we aren't."

"So that means you're both growing, but growing apart because you're not around each other as much, so you aren't talking as much either. It's easy to get caught up in your business, which I have been mesmerized by your successes by the way."

"Why, thank you," Melody jumped in moving her eyebrows up and down quickly.

"Being an entrepreneur is hard, trust me I know. But juggling a relationship, a business where you do just about everything *and* taking care of kids? That's a lot. Something usually suffers. Unfortunately, more often than we'd like to admit, it's our relationship. Plan some down time for the two of you. If you can't get away for a weekend, then do something like lunch far out of the city or a leisurely walk around a park. The goal is to have more than just an hour-long meal to reconnect. An hour flies by, especially if the kids are there. Plan it for just the two of you. A few hours. Then follow that up with calls and texts throughout the days afterward. You'll be amazed how that works. Oh...and put that thang on him, girl!" They all laughed.

"But you didn't answer the question. What did you do?"

"I tried to plan little movie nights at home. Money was tight for us. Finally, he agreed, but he didn't want to watch the movie I wanted, so I let him pick it out. He sat on one couch, I sat on the other. He didn't want me to touch him. Then his friends hit him up to go out and he did. I was so sad. Later, I told him to make the next date. I'm still waiting, but I don't think he's planning it now." Londyn admitted, Amberlee put her head in her hands.

"What?" Melody asked.

"His lawyer sent me divorce papers in the mail a few weeks ago." Londyn made a painfully obvious forced smile.

"I'm sorry to hear that."

"Me too. I tried to do token things. Give him compliments, take him out to eat, go to the movies, buy him just because gifts. This was all before he wanted out. It just didn't work for us. Your situation will be different. You have to believe it."

"How has it been...you know, going through this transition?"

"Impossible."

"How so?"

"I don't know what to do, which way to go. Some days, I don't even get out of bed. Divorce is like mourning a death I keep hearing. And it is. It's the death of a relationship, a walking death. Instead of mourning a picture of a loved one who has died, the person is living but dead to you and treats you as if you are dead to them. Thank God my parents took my twins for the summer. I'm trying to get my mind right for when they come back. In general, I'm just sad. Really sad." Amberlee reached out and patted her on the back.

"You know what? Tonight, I'm going to a revival. You should come with me. It will be so good. This thing between you and your husband sounds kinda fresh. You should come as my guest."

Londyn was no holy roller and she was no saint, but she did have a relationship with God. She attended church regularly, prayed, and did devotions every day. She'd been praying for encouragement and direction. She didn't think it was a coincidence that one of her favorite virtual mentors was looking her in the face. If Melody met with Amberlee when they originally planned, Londyn would have never met her. Now, here she was inviting Londyn to a revival.

Londyn considered maybe this was exactly what she needed to help pull her out of her slump. A spiritual reviving. By the end of their girls' pow wow, Londyn was convinced. She had nobody to go home to, so why not hear a word from the Lord.

As one of the special guests, Melody was escorted up to the second row with Amberlee and Londyn in tow. The church was completely packed and service had not even begun yet! It was standing room only. They must have been saving Melody a seat, because otherwise, the ladies would have been in the vestibule area watching the streamed version on TV rather than the in-person standing-so-close-the-pastor-is-sweating-on-you version.

At first, Londyn was a little apprehensive because the energy was so high; but the minister gave her a sense of calm. A lady led the church in a few songs and the energy was crazy high. A full band turnt for God had the church rockin' in no time. Londyn bobbed her head, but she wasn't standing up clapping and stomping like those around her who were used to that type of worship. Interestingly enough, her focus fell on a man who sat on the side of the stage where there were about three rows of four chairs each. All of the seats were filled. The others were up rejoicing along with the crowd. The man who Londyn noticed, noticed her as well. They stared at each other for a few seconds, still bobbing their heads to the praise and worship.

Later, she would come to find that he was delivering the message that night. She instantly felt bad for staring at a man of the cloth like that. He captivated her. Their spirits saw something in each other.

His sermon was about asking God for a manifestation of revelation; asking to be shown direction. Again, Londyn felt like this was not a coincidence. His sermon was exactly what she'd been praying about. He spent a bit of time exploring the possibility of sadness being in God's will.

"Most argue that God doesn't want that for His children," he stated. Then in a mocking voice, "My God wants me to be happy and prosperous and healthy and living my best life." The congregation waited intently, hungry for more. "But if you are surrendering to His will, then you may not get your way. Think about a child who wants to eat candy, eat candy, eat candy. As a parent, you know what will happen if they keep eating candy. They are going to get sick, right?" The congregation shook their heads in agreement. A few laughed out loud, presumably because they had experience with their kids getting candy-wasted.

"Well, if you take that candy away from your child, especially once they've had a few pieces, they are going to cry and scream bloody murder! But *you* know what is best for them. And in taking away the candy, you are taking away the possibility of them getting sick which would hurt them more in the long run. That's what your Heavenly Father is doing!"

The congregation began leaping to their feet, clapping and giving him encouragement. "Alright pastor! Preach preacher! Say it ain't so!"

"If you are sad because you submitted to His will and He took something away, know that He is going to replace it with something much better for you in the long run. Yes, your sadness may be in His will for you. Let Him take that candy away from you! He's just keeping you from further pain and hurt." The crowd erupted.

Londyn had never thought about it that way before. So it *was* possible to be sad, frustrated, and hurt and still be in God's will. She decided then and there, to stop praying that God would bring Micah back, but that she remained in His will.

Meanwhile, Knight was antsy and frustrated. He could not understand why Londyn had not attempted to contact him. Being ignored was not something that sat well with him. Who walked away from Baby Knight? Even though he was the one who cut things off, he felt like he'd been rejected. Again, not a feeling he was used to feeling. Normally, it was the other way around. Girls began to show their true colors after he'd sexed them down a few times. Their actions of calling non-stop and texting back-to-back led him to discard them. He wasn't above blocking them either.

This was so different. During the course of their relationship, he pursued her. He called her most of the time. He initiated the visits and the dates. Since he'd told her they needed to cut things off, Londyn made no effort. In his heart of hearts, he expected her to miss him and reach out. Even the toughest chick could only last two or three days without reaching out in some way. Not Londyn. She was a damn mountain not to be moved. She didn't even tag him in posts on Instagram anymore. She'd lasted twice as long as he anticipated. Could he really blame her though?

Any time his phone alerted him to a new text or started ringing, his heart jumped a little. He'd look at his phone with slight hopefulness only to be let down. Again and again, at least 20 times a day. How had it been so easy for her to let him go like that? Didn't she care at all? He'd told her he loved her. She didn't even acknowledge him. Maybe there was somebody else. He didn't think she had time to entertain anybody else. She never led him to believe there was anybody else. Any time he wanted to see her he could. Had she replaced him already? That easily? In Atlanta? The city where the odds were 20 to one? And he was such a prime catch?

Knight: I miss you.

He knew she couldn't resist that. She *had* to say something back. They say absence makes the heart grow fonder. He was missing her ass like crazy. If she cared anything at all for him, she was missing him, too. No response.

Knight: Londyn, I miss you.

Why was she playing hard to get? He already *got* her. Although, now it seemed like she *got* him. Almost every time he called her, she was home. Her lifestyle seemed to be pretty relaxed beyond her openly admitting to being sad about Micah and withdrawing from everybody. Now with the boys gone, she was straight chillin'. Knight just knew Londyn was sitting on her plush grey couch, wrapped in a throw blanket staring at his notifications on her lock screen.

`Missed Call: Knight`

"Damn!" He said. A week ago, she was responding to his texts within minutes. Thirty minutes, two texts and a call? *This girl is not giving in. I said I miss her*, he thought. No way she was ignoring him like this. No way she was looking at her phone, not acknowledging he was trying to get in contact with her. Did she forget he knew where she lived?

`Missed Call: Knight`
`Missed Call: Knight`

She was playing for real now. Surely, she hadn't forgotten about him in a week. Knight was beginning to feel like he'd really made a mistake. Londyn was the wrong girl to cut off. She was not having any part of his attempt to hear her voice. She was not massaging his ego by making him feel wanted or needed.

Londyn felt the ever so slight vibration of her phone. She didn't want to look at the screen. It didn't matter who it was, she was trying to connect with God. She knew herself well enough to know that if she saw who it was, she was going to feel obligated to respond. If it was a text, then she'd start texting back and miss the message. If it was a call, then she'd hold up her church finger and walk out to the atrium to return it. Again, missing the message.

The phone vibrated again. Her phone had been such a wasteland, she was curious as to who was trying urgently to get in touch with her. Before the thought that something could be wrong with the boys completely formed, she snatched her phone out of her purse. If something had happened to her overactive 11-going-on-21-year-olds, rambunctious but loveable sons, she needed to know.

"Knight?" she said out loud. Of course with the congregation on its feet, clapping and egging the pastor on, nobody but God Himself heard her. Amberlee glanced over to look at the screen being nosey. "Calls and texts. I wonder what he wants," she felt comfortable talking to herself knowing her voice was overshadowed by the swelling praise of the crowd. Londyn didn't even bother opening her phone. Whatever he wanted, it could wait. As she started to put her phone back up, his name flashed across her screen again.

She really hoped that he was ok. Seriously, what were the odds that something was wrong and he was calling her? He had a slew of brothers, brothers in arms at the fire house and a dad to fly to his rescue before he had to waste a get-out-of-jail-free card on her. Londyn dropped the phone in her purse and stood to her feet to tap back into the high feeling of the spirit in the building.

```
Knight: WYD
```

Knight was getting hot. Literally. He could feel the heat rising off of his body. Why was she making this difficult. What was so hard about hitting him back? Maybe something was wrong with her. Had she taken Micah back? She could have just told him so he would leave her alone if that was the case. No, if she took Micah back, he knew she would have told him. He quickly checked her Instagram. Only one post in the last week and it was a picture of food. It was a beautiful plate of shrimp and grits from a restaurant he took her to the week before. So clearly, she hadn't taken her husband back.

```
Knight: LONDYN!
Missed Call: Knight
Knight: Where are you????
```

He was flat out annoyed.

```
Missed Call: Knight
```

```
Knight: So I guess you're sleeping with
somebody else now
```

She could have at least been woman enough to tell him that she didn't want to deal with him anymore. Wait. He'd already done that. *Damn!* This was all his fault. The longer she didn't respond, the more intense his thoughts got. He stared at his phone in his hand. He didn't even have the heart to lock the screen. He just looked blankly at the one-sided text thread wondering if she would grace it with a bubble filled with letters...that formed words...that let him know what she was thinking.

The benediction came. Londyn, Amberlee, and Melody walked each other out to their cars, hugged and shared a few encouraging words. Melody thanked Londyn for the advice and wished her the best in her situation.

Londyn inhaled and exhaled deeply, then pulled her phone out of her purse again. Usually, she didn't hang out in parking lots once she got in her car. She'd heard years ago that women were victims of rape, car-jacking and being robbed because they get in their cars and don't immediately lock the doors or pull out. So she made it a habit of getting in her car and getting in motion right away.

Since she was in a busy church parking lot, she knew she was safe. It was well lit and there were so many people walking to their cars trying to leave, she would be creeping through the parking lot anyway.

"Wow Sgt. Knight," she said. Clearly there was something on his mind. As she held the phone, reading his texts, the screen flashed his name. "Hello."

"Where have you been?" The familiar sound of his voice sent a shiver in the pit of her soul. She closed her eyes envisioning his face as she slumped in the driver's seat. "I called and texted and called! What the hell are you doing?"

"I was in a revival," her voice wasn't excited or upbeat. It was after midnight. He couldn't tell if she was tired of irritated. He'd never irritated her to know what she'd be like if that were the case.

"A revival?"

"Yes, a revival. Special services held at churches."

"I know what a revival is. You didn't see me calling and texting?"

"I was paying attention to the message."

"What was the message?" He asked unbelieving.

"That you can be sad and still be in God's will. He will take you from a situation you want to keep you from getting into a worse situation."

"Are you sad?"

"Yes," in truth she was. She hadn't heard from Micah and Knight had cut her off. Knight had swindled her into becoming her happy place, then just like that, he was out.

"Why, babe?"

Babe? Fool, I haven't talked to you in a whole week! "What's up, Sgt. Knight?"

"I miss you. I want to see you."

"L...O...L..."

"I do, for real, Londyn. Let me take you out tomorrow."

"Yeah, sure. Text me tomorrow. I need my GPS to get home. Later."

She wasn't interested in just holding an aimless conversation with him. She owed him no favors and had already done too much by answering the phone that late. As far as she was concerned, they were over. He wouldn't be getting too many more responses during booty call hours.

The Staple Singers
"Let's Do It Again"

Let's do it in the mornin',
Sweet breeze in the summer time,
Feeling your sweet face,
All laid up next to mine,

Chapter 12

Kenzie and Londyn couldn't get to The Spot fast enough. The only people Londyn had been around that week were the regulars at the coffee shop. They were good people, but the interaction was associative at best. Knight had reclaimed his spot in her call log, but she was treading a little lighter this go around.

Kenzie had a very eventful week at the salon. She had a stylist who up and quit without warning, leaving her a week's roster worth of clients to fend for themselves. Of course being the proprietor of the establishment, Kenzie was not about to have two dozen clients negatively rambling about her shop, so she and the other stylists did their best to squeeze them all in.

"Londyn sweetie!" Kenzie shouted over the music. She waved Londyn down.

"Why are you waving like you're stranded on the side of the road?"

"I wanted to make sure you saw me."

"Kenzie...who can miss you? You're as bright as a highlighter with a big afro puff on the back of your lil' peanut head!" Kenzie laughed reaching out to hug her friend. She wore her light-brown hair cornrowed to the middle of her head, releasing into a beautiful afro with hints of natural gold highlights adorned with shells on the braids.

"When are you gonna let me do something to this tired ponytail in your head?" Kenzie asked scrunching up her face. "You need to come see me soon."

"I do too!" Nicole snuck up behind them. They greeted her warmly.

"There's nothing wrong with my hair. I don't go anywhere really. It would be nice to have somebody else wash it though. Scratch this scalp," Londyn laughed.

Carla DuPont

Londyn's phone lit up with a picture of Knight in his uniform on the screen with his name across the top.

"Oooh, so Sgt. Knight got a picture added to his contact. Go Sgt. Knight!" Kenzie said, subconsciously bouncing to the trap music.

"Is that the youngin'?" Nicole asked surprised. Londyn smiled and nodded.

"Sgt. Knight," Londyn picked up. She closed the other ear with her finger and bent her head down as if that would help her be able to hear. "Text me. I can't hear in here!"

"You still talk to him?" Nicole asked rhetorically. "Wow, that's impressive! These days, dudes wanna tap it a few times and be out."

"I know you heard me!" Kenzie yelled nudging Londyn with her shoulder. Londyn rolled her eyes and smiled. "A pic on his contact?"

"I mean, he's a hot fireman. Why not?"

"You know what that means, right?"

"I can see who's calling?"

"No! It means he's special."

"He might be. Just a little bit," Londyn held her hand up pinching her thumb and index finger together.

"I thought he cut you off," Kenzie inquired.

"He came back."

"They always do," said Nicole. "Be careful, Londyn."

"For what? Neither of us wants anything! Just a little companionship to pass the time. We are both just getting out of relationships. Nobody is trying to jump into anything."

"Right." Kenzie looked at her with the straight face. "If you keep seeing him, you know what's going to happen. Look, you already put a pic on his contact! Next it'll be emojis!"

"Somebody's catching feelings!" Nicole added.

"Emojis don't mean anything."

"Yes it does," Kenzie and Nicole yelled in unison.

"OMG!" Londyn shook her head.

"Jinx!" Kenzie said.

"Your old ass talkin' 'bout some jinx!" Nicole blasted pushing up her glasses.

"I'm just saying, in situations like these, somebody catches feelings. I'd hate to think that he's playing with you," Kenzie said.

"Kenzie Love, I appreciate your concern, but I'm good. My mind is so messed up, I couldn't take him serious if he wanted me to anyway. I'm reeling from this separation with Micah who acts like he doesn't give two thoughts about me. I have to consider my own feelings, and the feelings of my boys. That's going to be a lot. When they get back from summer vacay next week, the reality of not having Micah home is going to hit hard."

"You're right."

"Knight is a good distraction. Right now, he's helping to keep me off the ledge. He doesn't even know it, but he's my happy place. He's the one place I can go where talking about Micah...divorce and depression...and love are not really on the menu. Maybe as a sampler from the appetizer menu, but that's it. The few other people I talk to always bring it up. I'm tired of talking about it! I don't want to talk about it. I talk about it enough to myself!"

"That's a problem," Kenzie laughed.

"My life has been completely turned upside down. Honestly, I think about it non-stop! With Knight, we don't talk about it. He might skim the surface, but if I can redirect he keeps it moving."

"Ok, hun. If you think you have it under control, so be it. Just be careful."

Knight invited Londyn out to eat. It was their favorite pastime. He was in great shape. Mostly genetics, sprinkled with a little working out. She was a little fluffy, but still small by most standards. She had a post-baby pudge that she never got rid of, but it didn't stop her from getting attention.

"Be there at 3. Don't be late."

"I won't," she said.

"I'm serious. You know how you are. I don't feel like waiting on you."

"If this is how you're starting it off, then I'll just see you later. I'm not in the mood for attitude."

"No, I want to see you. I just want you to be there when we agree to be there."

"Bruh…"

Knight could hear the irritation in her voice. He was always prompt. It annoyed her. Knight got that from Pops. Pops was early everywhere he went. If you told him to be somewhere at 5, he was there at 4:30 feeling like he was late.

Knight arrived and circled the parking lot. He didn't see Londyn, so he shot the breeze scrolling through social media on his phone. He looked at the time, 2:50 and she wasn't there. 3:00 and she wasn't there. 3:05 and she wasn't there. He was hungry and his stomach was grumbling for sushi. 3:10 and she still wasn't there.

Knight: Where are you?
Londyn: At a table waiting on you.

Two minutes later, she saw him stroll in. He still gave her butterflies. She easily brought a smile to his face. She wore her hair down, which was unusual for her. The soft curls swept away from her face and cascaded down her shoulders. He found her just as she said, sitting at a table waiting on him to get there. He was surprised, she'd never beat him anywhere.

"It's about time!" Knight said.

"What are you talking about? You're the one who's late."

"I was sitting right out front waiting on you to get here."

"I didn't see your car," Londyn said.

"Well, I didn't see you walk in."

"Man! I left the house early just so I wouldn't have to hear your mouth. Then ran into a traffic jam," she said shaking her head.

"You know how Atlanta traffic is."

"Don't I know it! I tried my best," Londyn said beaming. She was so proud of herself.

"You got here early, so you claim. And...I still had to wait on you, so whatever." As soon as the words escaped his mouth, he could see the smile erase from her lips. She slammed her eyes shut and bent her lips in. "Don't hold it in. Say it."

Londyn just looked at him quickly annoyed. First by him, then by traffic, then by him again. She had nothing to say. Knight knew he was out of line for his comment. He was already treading on thin ice after ghosting on her. He was only just working his way back in. They'd only been back in the saddle for a few days. Now here she sat, made-up face, which was a rarity for them, with the most beautiful eyes staring angrily at him. Even mad, he thought she was sexy.

The waiter came over asking for their drink orders. Londyn let him know they were ready to place their food orders. If she wasn't starving, she would have gotten up and went right back home.

Knight ordered sushi and Londyn ordered hibachi from the grill. She could never finish it. No matter where they went, he ended up eating off of her plate anyway. They fought over the fried rice though. He thought she was cute, eating as much as she could before she had to give in and let him have it.

The drinks came first, then the food shortly after. The space between them was filled with light talk. Londyn enjoyed hearing his stories from work. Being in the face of the public, he encountered all kinds of people and the stories kept her thoroughly entertained. Ninety percent of firefighter work calls have nothing to do with fighting fires. They were mostly medical calls and accidents with the occasional running to burning building scenarios. As much as he liked talking to her about it, he appreciated her reaction to him. She was genuinely interested in what he had to say. She always asked how his days were, and how was work. She made him feel like she cared. But right then, he knew he was getting to her.

"Sgt. Knight, you don't have sex with me enough to rush me. You need to be glad I came up here to eat with your ass at all," she snapped. He knew she was right. There were few places he'd rather be than with her. She was beautiful. Her eyes. There was something in her eyes that drew him to her. Even though he could see the pain in them, she didn't bring any of that emotion to him. She didn't burden him with her drama, although he would have gladly taken it off of her mind if she felt like opening up to him. Knight looked at Londyn as a breath of fresh air.

"What are you going to do about your husband?"

"What do you mean?"

"Are you going to take him back?"

"What is there to take? He's not acting like he wants to be back. I'm totally open to it. I'm pissed about that damn girl meeting my boys, but if he was open to it, we could make it work. Or at least put the subject on the table."

Londyn knew that was probably not what he wanted to hear. She had no reason to lie. She'd kept it honest with him from day one. There was no need to start skating around the subject now.

"So if he asked you to move back home, you'd let him?"

"Not right away. There's a lot that needs to happen, but the door isn't closed." Knight nodded his head. He totally understood. "I never thought it would get to this point. I didn't think he would leave. Then again, he did file for divorce already. I think he's done."

"I'm sure he'll come back. I would if I were him. You're beautiful. You're a good mom and you have a lot going for yourself. And oooh, that body. Girl, you know what to do!" He said, she rolled her eyes. "I don't know why he left to begin with."

"Welp, that's on him."

"He can stay away a little longer. I'm trying to get some more of that."

"Some more of what?" Londyn smiled, slyly, for the first time since he doused her excitement about being on time. She aimlessly pushed the rice around on her plate with her fork.

Knight leaned his head to the side and bit his bottom lip.

"Check please," Londyn raised her hand to get the waiter's attention. Knight paid the tab and they were out of there. He led the way to the highway and they quickly hit 75 in a 55.

"You need to stop that speeding!" He teased calling Londyn on the phone. He watched her in his rearview.

"I'm keeping up with the flow of traffic."

"You're right behind me!"

"You're the flow I'm trying to keep up with," she responded sounding sexy. He opened his legs to give his swelling a little room to breathe in his jeans. They swerved in and out of lanes like playing musical cars. At times they were behind each other, other times they were on totally opposite sides of the four lanes.

Londyn thought it was funny how they could be together, leave each other and talk on the phone immediately after. It didn't matter if they were going to the same place or not, they spoke on the phone until they got wherever they were trying to get. Merging from 285 to 75, Londyn saw the traffic backing up.

"Let's get off right here," she suggested.

"Nah, let's get off on the next exit." She slowed up and followed his lead. "Damn, you were right. We should've gotten off on the other exit," he agreed a minute later.

"Oh gosh!" she smacked her lips.

"We're right by your house. You don't know how to get home?"

"I don't know where we are," she cracked up.

"That's a shame. I think I know." Londyn hung up as they pulled up to a light. They were right next to each other. With the A/C on full blast, she was jamming to her music just a little bit. She didn't want to really go in because she could feel his eyes staring at her. Her phone rang.

"Sgt. Knight."

"Hey girl. You're so beautiful." Londyn smiled and shook her head in a what-am-I-going-to-do-with-this-fool kinda way. "Look at me." She tried to give him that 'whatever' look. When their eyes met, he winked and blew her a kiss.

"Bye Knight," she cheesed. They missed the whole light change. Her phone rang.

"You said your name is Londyn, right?"

"I did," she looked back at him sitting next to her in his truck and she in hers. His pick-up gave him a feeling of size and power, not that he was compensating for anything. Hers was the boys' paddy wagon, an SUV, making carpooling and trips to the movies with the twins' friends and soccer practices and games easier.

"Your name is almost as pretty as you are."

"Bye Knight!" She hung up, her phone rang again.

"Where your mane at gul?" he asked sounding like a DSBG...down south Georgia boy. His normal southern drawl was sexy to her. That's part of why she liked to hear him talk so much.

"He left me."

"I won't lee you gul! Won't choo let me be ya mane?"

"OMG! Knight you are retarded!" They missed another light change. The lights were easy to miss being that they were in a highly desolated area. They were only a few seconds from red to green to red again. They were both cracking up.

"Londyn."

"What's up, homie?"

"Homie?" He asked raising his eyebrows for clarification.

"Yes...homie..."

"You ready for me?"

"Are you ready to *give it* to me?"

"Make this next light and I'll show you," he said looking over at her. *Lord Jesus, I don't know about this*, she thought. She hung up the phone and let him speed ahead. As they navigated the two-lane street bending and curving through residential areas, she couldn't wipe the smile off of her face. She caught her cheesy grin in the visor mirror. *Dang, I guess I am a lil' cute today.*

Keeping a safe distance from him, she opened her phone's camera and took one selfie. It was perfect. She didn't suffer through the normal selfie struggle taking 30 snaps of virtually the same pose trying to find one that had just the right amount of light at just the right angle. Her eyes looked happy. The picture radiated happiness. It was a glimpse of herself that she hadn't seen in a while. Her phone rang again.

"Do you know where you are now?" Knight asked.

"No. Oh, wait. I think I do, yes."

"Good, we'll be there in a sec."

When they arrived to Londyn's house, he let her pull into the driveway first, then he pulled in beside her. He hugged her from behind and walked from the door to the bed kissing her neck. She turned around. They kissed and undressed each other and themselves all at the same time. He dove on the bed and pulled her on top of him. He pulled her all the way up to sit on his face. Londyn tried to squirm back down his torso, so their faces would be next to each other. Knight picked her up and sat her back on his face.

"I don't feel comfortable like this," she said nervously. He could feel her shaking. He put his arms around her waist and clamped down. She couldn't move. And after a few seconds, she didn't want to. She moaned, and as he felt her body relax, he relaxed his grasp. Her face fell forward into the soft, leather headboard.

Always in control, he picked her up and put her on her back. After putting on protection, he grabbed the inside of her thighs and easily found where he wanted to be. He was positioned on his knees looking down at her. His hips moved expertly to the exact up-tempo rhythm they both wanted. She loved being dominated. She rarely initiated sex with Micah in the end. How could she when she didn't feel like he hungered for her? He didn't seem to appreciate her body or relish in her feminine curves? She did, however, usually end up on top. While Londyn didn't mind working the middle, she much preferred to have somebody else working it for her. She liked throwing it back, versus just throwing it.

"Does it feel good to you?" he asked. Londyn was panting so fast that she couldn't catch her breath long enough to answer. He slowed down and rubbed her face. "Londyn...open your eyes. Look at me." She did as she was told. Knight stared into her soul, moving slowly, yet steadily. "You know I'm falling for you."

"No you aren't," she whispered.

"Yes I am, baby," he said never interrupting his stroke. His strokes got deeper and harder...He put both legs over his shoulders...deeper and harder... He bent down to kiss her... deeper and harder...deeper. He crumbled on top of her at the same time that she lost control. Their bodies moved in harmony as currents of pleasure pulsed through them. That was the first time they climaxed together, but certainly wouldn't be the last. She rubbed her hands up and down his sweat-moistened back while she kissed the side of his face. He rolled over on his back, bringing her on top of him in one swift movement.

They laid there. Neither of them wanted to move and neither of them said anything. They were each lost in their thoughts. His embrace felt incredible.

Knight knew there was more he wanted to tell her. More he needed to say. He told her he was falling for her. He was being transparent. Honest. She was a safe place for him. He loved that about her. She made him feel good, not just physically – although their sexual chemistry was undeniable. She made him feel good as a person.

Londyn was shocked that he hadn't jumped up putting on his boxers and grabbing his phone. That was the first time he'd just laid there like that and held her. Then he'd told her he was falling for her. What did that mean? The boundaries were set from day one. She'd just told him an hour earlier that if Micah wanted to try to work things out, she would. Now he was falling for her? That experience between them was so different than the normal hit and run. He felt it. She felt it. The universe was setting her up, but for what she was unsure.

She listened to the lullaby of blood flowing in, then out, of his heart. The scent of his sweat had become an aphrodisiac to her. He kissed her head...rubbed her hair...drew invisible signs on her back with his fingertips.

For the time being, they both relished in the moment. The warmth between them. That was the first time they climaxed together. It was amazing.

Beyoncé
"Video Phone"

Them hustlas keep on talking,
They like the way I'm walking,
You saying that you want me,
So press record I'll let you film me.

Chapter 13

Life at the fire house was running along as usual. Knight was getting adjusted to his new role. There was a difference in the amount of paperwork that he had to do. In working his way up from Candidate to Fireman I to Fireman II, he had gotten accustomed to gaining different responsibilities. He wasn't abusive with his new power, so he'd earned the respect of his men. All in all, the men wanted what was best for the house, they were a brotherhood, a family, so they respected the rank. In this instance, they respected both the man and the rank.

All except Otto. Knight was younger and he was legacy; both were problems for Otto. He always started with Knight, but Knight didn't let it bother him.

"Knight!" Josten said as Knight walked into the common area, "marry, date, or dump."

Knight chuckled, "Let's go!"

"Halle Berry, Beyonce and Rihanna."

"Hmmm, this is an easy one. Marry Halle Berry."

"Marry Halle Berry?" Williams asked.

"Yeah, 'cause she old! You know Knight got a thang for them old ones!" Josten teased, he was the liveliest of the bunch.

"But she's crazy man!" Williams said.

"Aren't they all?" Knight asked.

"My wife ain't crazy," Sterling said. Williams and Sterling were the older men on the squad, then came Otto, then Josten and Knight were only a year apart.

"That's 'cause you ain't giving her that good D!" Knight said, Josten laughed and gave him some dap. "You can make any of 'em go crazy when you laying that pipe!"

"Man! My wife been with me for 19 years! She ain't crazy!"

"Aye bruh, you ain't doing something right, like Knight said," Josten chipped in. Otto walked past the table where the men were congregated. Knight and Josten didn't pay him any attention, but Williams and Sterling tensed up.

"Nineteen years and she's still putting up with you, huh?" Otto said trying to be funny. The white man trying to joke with black men who all knew he had a problem with Knight.

"At least I found someone to put up with me." Josten and Knight put their hands over their mouths pretending to try to conceal their laughter. It was a horrible attempt.

"PUHAHAHA!"

"You boys are horrible," Otto said.

"Boys?" Josten cut his laughter short. "You better watch all that boy talk. I ain't gon' be too many of your boys, now," Josten warned.

"Chill...chill," Knight interjected.

"So Knight, we knew you'd want to marry the old one. What about the other two?"

Knight's phone rang, "Hey babe," she spoke into the phone. He looked at the boys at the table and got up.

"I liked the sound of you calling me babe."

"Anything exciting happen on your shift today?"

"Nah," he made it to his office and closed the door. "I wish I could wake up to your lil' sexy ass." He spoke honestly. Londyn blushed on the other end. It didn't matter that no one was there to see her, her cheeks flushed red instantly.

"Oooh! First I get babe...then you want to wake up to my sexy ass...what's going on with you, man?"

"I just miss you."

"Sgt. Knight, you just saw me two days ago."

"And I want to see you again. I miss you."

"When you say stuff like that..." Londyn struggled to actually tell him, "you know, calling me sexy, you make me feel some kinda way." She was nervous and giddy even saying it. It had been ages since her husband called her sexy or made her feel that way.

"You *are* sexy. Why would you think you aren't?"

Londyn laughed. "That reminds me of a time when I dressed up for Micah. He was already in a mood and I knew it, but I was trying to cheer him up. I had gone to the bank earlier that day to get some ones. I picked up some rose petals from the florist and bought a slew of candles. I put a chair in the middle of the floor and sprinkled the rose petals down, then lit the candles. I put on this sexy, cute, little something and handed him some ones. Before I could even put the music on, he asked me, 'What the hell are you doing?' I told him I was trying to spice it up. He threw the ones at the wall and said, 'You ain't no damn stripper.' "

"Sheeeeeit! I dare you to try that with me."

"What would you do, Knight?" Londyn yelled in the phone not bothering to try to conceal her laughter.

"Try it and see," he laughed in his calm sounding, low voice. "Why don't you send me something."

"Something like what?"

"Send me a pic of those ta-tas."

"Nooooooo!" Londyn roared. "What do I look like?"

"My baby, sending me a piece of paradise and calm while I brave the streets of Atlanta putting out fires, running into burning buildings, pulling people out of mangled cars, and keeping up with this rowdy bunch of heathens."

"*Ugh!*" she moaned.

"PLEASE!"

"I really don't know about this. This is so weird." Londyn was shaking her head and wondering if this was life dealing with a younger man or if smartphones had drastically changed the landscape of dating. Only once could she remember doing something like that. She'd taken boobie pics for Micah, but it was so long ago. She couldn't remember if she had ever actually sent them. But since leaving #teamblackberry for #teamiphone, she knew she hadn't taken nudes and that was over five years ago. It had been a long time since Micah made her feel confident and sexy enough to even consider sending him a naked picture of herself.

"Londyn, send a pic," he said more as a demand than a question.

"Have a good day, Sgt. Knight," and with that she hung up the phone. She chuckled to herself and fixed a glass of Riesling. She thought back to the way he looked at her after they'd had sex on the day he took her shopping. He didn't seem to mind that her stomach wasn't flat, or that she didn't have the perky breasts of a 21-year-old, much like the ones Londyn was sure her beau was used to. He kept telling her he liked older women, but she was sure he was only saying that so she wouldn't feel so self-conscious.

Maybe he did really want to see her body. In fact, the frequency of their visits had increased which meant they were having more sex. He was always ready, it never took much to get him to rise to the occasion. Another glass of Riesling. She decided to give him what he wanted.

She laid down on the bed, opened her screen and flipped it around. *Click*. She tapped the small picture screen on the bottom left of her screen and the picture was horrible. She rolled her eyes, repositioned herself and took another. *Click*. This one was even worse than the first. The hair wrap took away the sex appeal.

"Oh my gosh! My face!" She screamed. When taking the first set of pics, she didn't think to take them from the neck down. "Ohhhhh NO SIR! I do not need evidence pointing back at me! Not gonna have somebody hacking into my damn icloud and posting pics everywhere!" There had been far too many examples of jilted lovers and hacked iclouds for her to risk putting her whole face in the frame.

Londyn snapped a series of pictures. After about 27 clicks, she found one that she thought he could appreciate. It was a classy, sexy pic of her body's profile from the side. The sheets covered all of the goodies, but her butt cheeks hung out as a teaser. She nervously hit send after creating a new message with it. She dropped the phone, her hands flung to her mouth. She was in total awe of herself. She had gone from barely wanting to meet up with him in public to sending him nudes in a matter of months. Wow! This was so far from what she thought it was going to become when they met. He just made her feel so comfortable.

Knight: Ooooh yes! Send another one.

Londyn screamed! She was so tickled that he liked it. Her heart was racing a million beats a minute. She didn't know if it was from being nervous or because he wanted another one and she had to dish it out. She used one arm to cover her breasts, then playfully put a finger in her mouth. *Click, click, click*, she chose the best one. *Send.*

Knight: Mmm hmm! Keep going!

She stepped it up a little bit. This time, she got both of her boobs in a shot, careful to squeeze her arms just a bit to make them look more round and plump. Teasing with a little nipple. *Click, click, click*, she chose the best one. *Send.*

Knight: C'mon baby.

She was so tickled, but starting to have fun. This time, she turned over on her stomach, tooted her butt in the air, and held her phone over her shoulder to get the best view. "He loves this arch," she laughed to herself. *Click, click, click*, she chose the best one. *Send.*

Knight: Don't stop!

"OH MY GAWWWWWWD!" she fell out laughing on the bed. She stared at the popcorn designs on her ceiling, cheeks hurting from smiling. She was so new to this whole thing. The moments of happiness seemed to be more spurts between the darkness of her depression. But it sure felt good to be able to have fun again. She'd forgotten what it was like to have fun in a relationship. Now this fool had her taking pic after pic. She couldn't let him down, plus she was starting to have too much fun.

Londyn decided to give him a money shot. She spread her legs open and seductively put her hand in front of herself so he could see, but not really. It was definitely more of an illusion.

Click, click, click, she chose the best one. *Send.*

Knight: 😵 😵

After that, she posted the selfie she took when they were playing in traffic to her Instagram and Facebook. One of her homeboys, instantly texted her.

Ant: You're glowing L

Londyn: Really?

Ant: Yeah, you look really happy.

Londyn: 😊

Ant: How are things going? You and Micah finally getting your act together?

Londyn: Chile please! He barely looked at me when we exchanged the boys. They'll be back soon, so we'll see how it goes.

Ant: Well who got you looking all happy and shit?

Londyn: LOL!! I have a friend.

Ant: A friend?

Londyn: Yap!

Ant: Deets

Londyn: Nope, LOL

Ant: L

Londyn: He's my Knight. He's a fire-fighter. I met him at a bar a little while ago. He's cool. Makes me feel confident, FR. Like, he makes me feel so sexy. I haven't felt this good in a while.

Ant: You call him Knight?

Londyn: That's his gov't. I know, I was ROFL when he told me too.

Ant: 😂😂😂 Is he your Knight in shining armor???

Londyn: Shut up cornball! 😂

Ant: Aight, tell him to keep it up. You look beautiful.

Londyn: 😍

Another Bad Creation
"Iesha"

At the playground, ya know,
That's where I saw this cutie,
This girl was swingin' and she looked so fly,
On the monkey bars,
We climbed up to the top and,
She touched my hand that's when I fell in love.

Chapter 14

As the summer began winding down, Londyn knew she would have to get into full mommy mode. Not that she hadn't been a mother for the past 11 years, but this would be different. She was trying to convince herself that it wouldn't be so bad. That she could handle her rowdy tween boys with their totally different attitudes and temperaments. That she could deal with chores and football practices and homework and dinners and making all three of them feel safe in the home without the presence of the man, her husband, when her neighbors had begun to notice that he was no longer coming home.

She wondered if she would be in this situation if she and Micah had had a child together. In the beginning, he wanted them to have a child together. He thought she needed time to heal from Kaden's death and didn't want to rush things. Then as he got comfortable with her, he began to make slick comments about her weight and how much she ate. He told her that before she even considered having another baby, she needed to lose about 15 pounds.

Of course, it made her feel self-conscious, but it was only 15 pounds and she didn't feel motivated to lose it. Micah talking about it only made her feel less motivated and more self-conscious. Instead, she wanted to cover herself up more, started keeping her shirt on during sex and not wanting to change clothes in front of him. His reverse psychology didn't work on her.

She wondered if it was so easy for him to walk away because the only children who called him Dad in the world didn't share his blood. She was instantly upset that she'd never given him his own seed. Then again, she certainly didn't want somebody who she felt had to be guilted into staying with her.

With the boys coming back in a few days, she needed to get her life as best she could. The only problem was, she still didn't know if she was going or coming. She was hurt, mourning the death of her marriage while experiencing feelings and doing things she'd never done with a new man who she was still treading on very thin ice with. Something about Knight just scared her. It just seemed that there was something about him that she couldn't put her finger on. Londyn was usually good about that sort of thing, figuring people out. Knight had her though. Maybe it was just her mind being skeptical. After all, she was on the market for the first time since college. They didn't have any friends in common for her to do her research on him and when she Googled his name, nothing came up. For now, she'd just enjoy his company and try not to let it get any more serious than it was.

She made it clear that he could not meet the boys. It didn't matter that Micah had gone on and started over with somebody else. She was not going to be the mom to introduce her kids to every person who had her attention.

Knight knew that the boys were coming back soon, too. Them coming back would affect him in that he wouldn't be able to go to her house whenever he wanted, nor would he be able to see her as often. He hadn't been around before the boys left for summer, but scrolling through her social media, he could see that she was very hands-on as a mother. The kind of mother he wished he'd had. The kind of mother he wanted for his own kids. He didn't expect his future wife to be selfless, but he expected her to be very active in her family's lives.

He needed someone strong enough to support him and his crazy work schedule, but keep up with the house and kids as well. He would certainly do his part, too. He did not plan on leaving all of the rearing to her. Pops was 100% with Knight because he had to be. Even with Regina helping him, Pops felt like Knight was solely his responsibility. After all, he was the child born to the woman Pops left Regina for. Regina never blamed Knight for her failed marriage or treated him differently than her boys. If anything, she babied him more, because he was the baby of the Knight boys and because his mom ditched him.

Either way, Knight could see that Londyn was going to be consumed with Kingsley and Kingston. He couldn't fight with that. It also meant that she and her husband were going to have to interact. The boys were still far too young to drive or take public transportation, so it was up to Londyn and Micah to get them to and fro. That made Knight nervous because with them seeing each other, he knew feelings would rekindle between them. He and Londyn had a good thing going. He had no intention of losing the grip he had on her.

He loved her. He meant it. She had skimmed right past when he told her, but she heard him. He knew she did. Just how big of an impact the boys coming back had on their interaction was yet to be seen, but it scared him. He had his own life to live, but she had become such an integral part of it.

During one of their normal 15,000 conversations throughout the day, Knight asked Londyn if she had plans for the next day. She told him she was meeting with a few friends from college for a birthday dinner, but nothing fancy.

After his 24-hour shift ended at 7 a.m., he drove to her house. She cooked breakfast while he showered so he could eat before crashing. When he awoke, he joined her Netflix 'Scandal' binge on the couch. They had a round of hot, sensual sex, after which, they both took showers. Since he was a guest in her home, she let him have her shower and she used the boys' bathroom. Even though she felt comfortable around him, she still wasn't comfortable enough to hop in the shower with him. That was a whole 'nother level of intimacy.

When he got out, he found her applying makeup in her mirror with a t-shirt on. She was humming and softly singing some 90's R&B. Not full on singing, but hitting the choruses and key words, the ones everybody sings when they sing particular songs. He stood next to her at the Jack and Jill sinks with a towel wrapped around his waist and began dancing. She couldn't help but laugh. He had absolutely no rhythm...yet, he was so skillful in bed. She couldn't believe it. He was so cute though.

"I have some ones in my purse," she teased. He was clearly performing for her. He was really breaking it down, moving slowly...legs spread wide...water still running down his chest...with his half-chub threatening to pop out of the towel. He stared at her in the mirror winding...winding... winding. Londyn was actually getting turned on. Again.

Knight scooted behind her, held her hands in his and put her arms up in the air while he rubbed his hands up and down her body. He admired her pretty brown tone. "Sing baby," he commanded. Londyn kept singing as her beau admired her body from behind. If there was ever any doubt that he appreciated her...body...he had been slowly erasing those doubts from day one. Londyn could hear Kenzie in the back of her mind, "Have fun, but be careful." With him acting like this, Londyn could hear her guard crashing down like a cliff into the sea.

"C'mon Knight! I gotta beat my face. You know I'm not good at this make-up stuff," she admitted.

"You don't need a lot of make-up," he said, still trying to find the beat grinding behind her.

"I'm going to get lessons," she said proudly.

"For what? You don't need all that. I don't want you looking all caked up and plastic," he said leaning down to rest his chin on her shoulder. "You're beautiful." They stared at each other for a few seconds. She put her hand on the side of his face and leaned into his embrace.

He knew she was self-conscious and he felt as though she didn't have a reason to be. To him, Londyn was beautiful. And he wasn't the only one. He'd seen how other men reacted to her when they were out. He always beat her wherever they were going, so he'd see guys watching her and approaching her before they saw she was with him. It was hard for Knight to understand how she could be so hard on herself. He told her if she wanted to lose the weight, lose it. If not, she was perfect to him.

Londyn was busy thinking about how many times Micah complained about her singing. If they were in the car listening to the radio, he'd threaten to turn it off if she didn't stop. "Let them sing the song. They're getting paid, you aren't," he'd say. Now instead, Knight was clowning right along with her.

"You know you're my baby, right?" he asked.

Londyn looked down and away. She tried to pull away from him, but he wouldn't let her go. He moved her long hair to the other side of her neck and kissed her neck, then down the center of her back. He got on his knees and kissed down the crack of her butt and back up it again. With one hand, he steadied her torso, pushing it over the sink.

Using his tongue, he coursed up and down, around and around her butt cheeks until he was hungry for more. Londyn gasped when he parted her cheeks and she felt the moistness of his mouth. Her head dropped and she naturally arched her back even more. Wanting to feel him, she lifted her leg up and put it on the counter between the sinks. Knight stood up and slid inside her. Even though they had just had sex, it felt like the first time in days.

He coiled her hair in his hand and gently yanked her head back until her gaze met his in the mirror. They stared at each other, saying nothing until she couldn't take it anymore, slamming her eyes shut.

"Unh uh...open up. I want you to watch what I do to you," he ordered. She came just at the words. He never stopped moving. As she tried to gain her composure, he tugged on her hair again, beckoning her to look at him. "I told you...I want you to watch." She came again. She gained her composure and this time, she was ready. She boldly opened her eyes and bit her bottom lip.

Knight looked at her like she was defying him. He put his hand around her neck and squeezed. She came again. "Mmm hmm," he laughed. He knew exactly what to do to her. She turned around, sitting on the very edge of the counter, wrapping her legs around him.

"Oh, so you think that's funny, huh?"

"Yep," he said grinning from ear to ear. Londyn grabbed his nipple with her teeth and tugged, slowly, but with force as she grinded on him. He couldn't escape the hold her legs had; that was a wrap for him. She laughed.

"Guess I had the last laugh," she said, they both busted out laughing. He kissed her feet and went back into the bathroom to clean up.

Londyn was surprised when Knight put on real clothes and not the usual basketball shorts.

"Where are you going?"

"I'm going to hang out, too."

"With who? You don't have any friends," between work, the gym, and Hermes, Londyn could set her watch by his schedule. Very routine. Very predictable.

"Yes, I do," he laughed. He tapped her on the butt and they got ready to leave the house.

She gathered the box of condoms and lube and put them with Knight's things in his bag. When she walked back past the nightstand, she noticed that he'd removed the condoms and lube placing them on the nightstand. Thinking she forgot to move them, she put them back in his bag. Somehow, they ended up back on the nightstand. She knew she wasn't crazy.

"Sgt. Knight. Why do you keep taking this out? This is yours."

"Leave it here."

"No, take it with you so you can be protected. I don't want you bringing me nastiness from any other girls you're sleeping with."

"I only use them with you."

"Hmmph," she sighed and they left in their respective trucks.

Londyn was heading to meet up with friends from her alma mater, FAMU. She sweat and bled orange and green, from the highest of seven hills in Tallahassee, Florida, Rattler Country.

Since FAMU and FSU's campuses were so close and literally half of the state of Florida went to either, there was a lot of co-mingling between students. Some of the girls had attended FAMU, and the others, FSU. It was a small group of ladies getting together.

In college, they had been as thick as thieves. They all converged on Atlanta within two years of each other, but stressful, real world responsibilities like jobs, children, serious relationships, and break-ups had taken their toll over the years. The ladies weren't able to all see each other often, so this was the first time in a while.

"Hola chicas!" Londyn beamed.

"We thought you weren't coming," Nika started. She was the mother hen of the group. "You are late."

"Girl! It's summertime! Chill! You ain't got nothin' else to do!" April chimed in.

"Thanks, April!" Londyn said giving hugs around the table.

"I'm glad you came," Johna admitted. Her hug was the warmest. She didn't want to let Londyn go and Londyn felt that. Londyn hadn't really been forthcoming with the crew. They knew something was amiss, but not exactly what.

"Me too."

"Where have you been? You've been M.I.A. No posting, no commenting. You're quiet in the group chat. What's going on with you?" Johna asked.

"Well, I guess now is as good a time as any," Londyn started. "Me and Micah have split." Hustle and bustle of the restaurant aside, nobody at the table moved.

"Oh no!" Johna's eyes instantly brimmed with tears. "I had a feeling it was something like that. You haven't pulled back this much since Kaden..."

"Damn," Nika added, "I'm so sorry hun. And here I am giving you a hard time."

"Don't you always?" Londyn laughed.

"He's been posting so weird lately. I knew you two were going through something. All his posts are about him being happy and free. He keeps using the word free. Oh gosh, Londyn," Johna let the tears fall.

"Please don't cry," Londyn couldn't fight back her tears anymore either. It was more a trickle than a stream. "I've been praying about it. Just had to take a step back to try to wrap my mind around it all."

"You look like you've lost some weight," Nika said honestly. Londyn was noticeably a size or two smaller. She realized it herself when she'd gone to buy some shorts for the scorching summer and had to get a size 6 when she was used to buying 10.

"Yeah, that depression diet will do that to ya!"

"I can't imagine," Nika said shaking her head. She was married with three kids herself. She was the first one to get married. Her husband kissed the ground she walked on. After Londyn skimmed the details of how everything transpired over the last eight or nine months, Ashley, the quiet one, finally chirped up.

"I found out my husband was cheating on me a little while ago." Ashley had not even hit her first anniversary yet. "My situation is different because we don't have the amount of time invested or any kids. I told his ass to get to steppin'. I wasn't about to be dealing with that shit."

"But Ashley, you never talk. So how did you say it?" Nika joked. They all sort of laughed.

"I printed out divorce papers and left them on the printer. I wanted him to think I was considering it."

"Were you?"

"Honestly, I was. Our first anniversary is next month! How is he already bored with me? He's not. She is obviously someone who he brought into our marriage from the beginning. So, if he didn't straighten up, I was out. Still may be if I get a glimpse that anything else is going on."

"Oh shoot! Look at Ashley tryna boss up!" Nika said.

Johna had two baby daddies. She was all head-over-heels in love in college with the first one and thought they would be together forever. Of course it didn't last. Nobody could quite figure out how her second baby daddy came into the picture, nor how he left. He left as fast as he came, but made sure to drop his seed in her for a reminder of their quickly fizzled love affair. "I don't see what's the point of getting married when you aren't ready. Or if you aren't happy. He should have cut it with ol' girl or never proposed to you."

"You have the biggest heart, Johna," Londyn said. "You've just had some bad breaks with love. I really hope you find the love you deserve."

"Serious though. Like what's the point of telling someone you want to commit to them and you're only committed to yourself," Johna added.

"I went to one of my homeboy's weddings and asked him if he'd cut his side bitch off just minutes before the wedding started. He said he tried," Nika said.

"Whaaaaaat???" Londyn rhetorically asked. She was more in disbelief than anything. "TRIED?!"

"See, that's what I'm talking about!" Johna exclaimed. "That's that BS right there!"

"Yep, this fool said he told his side they needed to cut it off, but he spent the night with her after his bachelor party."

"Nah!" They all collectively yelled.

"Clearly she ain't going nowhere," Nika added.

"Well," Ashley piped up to defend her fresh marriage, "I don't *know* that he was seeing her before. It was my assumption."

"It doesn't matter! The ink isn't even dry on your marriage license yet and he's out here dipping his wand in other hats."

"I forgave him. We are moving forward." Ashley made her peace to let them know that she no longer wanted to discuss it.

Londyn toyed with the idea of telling them about Knight and decided against it. She would keep that juicy morsel to herself. Plus, how would they feel hearing that she was dating someone that much younger than her. To Londyn, it was still a bit taboo. Like what the hell was she even doing with him?

Meanwhile, Knight and his friends were enjoying the scenes at a sports bar across town. Jo Jo and Derek were friends of his from high school. They weren't bosom buddies, but they hung out from time to time.

Even though they both made substantially more than Knight, there was a shadow of envy because it seemed like he was working more of a fantasy job than a real job. He had the cool career. Jo Jo was a banker and Derek a financial advisor. At some point during toddler-to-little boy life, boys play with firetrucks, hats and want to be firemen when they grew up, not dressed up in suits planning financial futures. Knight was doing just that; although it didn't feel like a hobby when he was battling a blaze to rescue the toddler inside who dreamt of wearing the cool firefighter hat one day.

"Say man," Jo Jo said, "doesn't that waiter look like Sheka?"

"Sheka who?" Knight asked in a condescending tone.

"You know Sheka! Sheka, Sheka! Your Sheka!"

"Shole does!" Derek yelled and slapped Jo Jo five.

"Naw, man," Knight wasn't trying to hear it. The girl they were talking about looked nothing like his junior high school love. Plus, there was no way she ended up working in a dump like that.

"Bruh...look...at...her! That's Sheka!"

"Sheka?" Knight tried to casually look in that direction, hoping his friends had already had too many drinks to be seeing clearly. If it was Sheka, he was going to be heartbroken to see her as a waitress at a restaurant.

"Man! Jo! Remember that time we caught him fingering her after school in the custodian's closet?" They all roared with laughter.

"This clown walked out letting us all smell his finger!" Jo Jo added, and they roared again. The girl got closer, but her back was to him. She did look to be about their age, but it seemed like she was keeping her back to them on purpose. Maybe it was her. Maybe she was just as embarrassed to be working there as he was to see her.

"You couldn't tell Baby he wasn't the man!"

"Yep, he was the first one to get some poon too!" they chuckled a little softer, taking sips of their drinks.

"You had 'em all, bruh," Derek said tipping his beer to his old pal.

"Had," Knight corrected him. "That was then, this is now," Knight said coming down off of his reminiscing cloud. Looking back into the past always seemed like a glory parade. Real life, current life, was happening now. That 12-year-old Knight couldn't do a thing to help him now.

"So what are you going to do about ya girl, man?" Jo Jo asked. Knight exhaled deeply looking down at the table. Just then, the waitress turned around. It was Sheka. Their eyes locked and she turned away quickly. Jo Jo and Derek saw the exchange.

"Shit," Knight said. He looked down at the table trying to remember the last time he'd seen her. It was after high school. He was almost certain that they were connected on Facebook, but since he was never on it and really only lurked on Instagram, he hadn't really, *really* kept up with her.

"I knew that was her," Jo Jo said in a more somber tone. He saw the disappointment in Knight's eyes. "We're friends on Facebook. Haven't seen her post in a minute though. I know she has a handful of kids," he continued pulling out his cellphone. He opened his Facebook app, found her profile, then shoved it at Knight. Reluctantly, he grabbed it and began going through her pictures. He saw she'd had three more kids since the scare they'd had with her first. Once she fessed up after the baby was born and told Knight that her newborn wasn't his during their senior year, he was done with the back and forth with her. He never knew who the baby's father was. Nobody seemed to. But after dealing with her for so many years between junior high and high school, she still held a special place in his heart.

"Four kids...and she's a waitress? How is she supporting four kids working here?" Knight asked completely confused. Jo Jo and Derek shook their heads. They continued shooting the breeze, going down memory lane for another hour or so. When it was time to leave, Derek picked up the check.

"I can't let you do that," Knight said.

"Lemme put something on it," Jo Jo chimed.

"What Uncle Sam takes from me in taxes is more than what y'all make," Derek laughed.

Knight kept cash on him, so on the way out, he asked their waitress to hand a note to Sheka. He wrote 'Baby-N-Sheka 4-eva' on a napkin and wrapped $200 in it. He tried to hurry to the car, but she caught him.

"I don't need your damn pity, Baby! Do you hear me?" Knight unlocked his car and opened the door. She ran over to him and stopped him. "Take this shit back!"

"How old is he?"

"Who?"

"The baby who was supposed to be mine?" Sheka's face unballed. It quickly morphed from being pissed to hurt. Knight never got the full story and wouldn't have believed it anyway. All he knew was, she was pregnant, and she was his girl. After Pops and Ms. Regina read him the riot act about not using condoms and made him get a job, Sheka told him the baby wasn't his. He wanted a paternity test, she insisted that he was not the father. "You had all that mouth coming out here, but now you ain't got nothin' to say?" he asked in his sexy voice.

Sheka looked in his eyes. The same eyes she saw every night in her dreams. The same eyes that she wished she could see again, looking at her lovingly. The same eyes her son had. Knight still looked good, his body had filled out a lot since she'd last seen him. Sheka put on a little weight, but not nearly what he would expect for a girl who'd had four kids. She wore her hair in a curly sew-in, bob length and her eyebrows were perfectly beat on her face.

"How old is he, Sheka? He's 9, right?" Knight easily remembered because he was born around the same time his nephew Hermes was.

"How did you..."

"Do you have any idea how much that shit hurt? For months, you had me running around thinking I was going to be a father. So you cheated *and* got pregnant?" The pain in his face was undeniable. Even after so many years had passed.

"I'm sorry."

"Go get your kids some school clothes," he said and jumped in the car.

For them both, seeing each other put them in a bad place. They both were embarrassed and hurt about the way things had turned out. Even though the talk with the guys ventured away from memory lane, his heart ached from the moment he realized that was her. He'd hoped that she had done more with her life. He didn't get a chance to speak to her, to know if she was just there for extra money or in a transition period. But piecing together what he saw of her Facebook posts from Jo Jo's phone, it didn't look like her employment there was temporary or that she was on to better things.

```
Knight: WYD
Londyn: OTW home
Knight: Me too
Londyn: Drive safe baby.
Londyn: I mean, Knight.
Knight: Did you just call me baby, then
correct yourself?

Londyn: 
Knight: Why did you do that?
Londyn: Drive safely
```

```
Knight: Why did you do that?
Londyn: You ate mine
Londyn: *aren't
Knight: Whose am I?
```
Oh shit! Londyn thought.
```
Londyn: You tell me...
```

There was only one place he wanted to be. Only one. When the highway branched off, he could go to the left which would take him to Londyn's house or to the right which would take him home. He went left.

He got to her house and rang the doorbell. Inside, Londyn was spooked. *Who* was ringing her bell at that time of night? She wasn't expecting anyone, so that meant it could only be Micah or Knight. She tiptoed to the peephole and saw Knight's silhouette towering over the peephole. Micah was a few inches shorter and had dreads, so she could easily tell the difference. Just for good measure, she flipped the porch light on. He flinched away from the light, revealing beautiful, white teeth. The same teeth that Kenzie complimented him on the night they met.

"You said you were going home," Londyn opened the door wrapped in a towel.

He grabbed her face and kissed her, closing the door behind him. He picked her up and carried her to the room.

"I just needed a hug."

"Awww. What happened?"

"I saw my ex. Rubbed me the wrong way," he made himself comfortable and told her the whole story from the day he first met Sheka in Mr. Rehmeyer's fifth grade class 'til that night. They spent the night talking until hints of the sun danced through the blinds.

Jill Scott
"He Loves Me"

You love me especially different every time,
You keep me on my feet happily excited,
By your cologne, your hands, your smile,
your intelligence,
You woo me, you court me, you tease me,
you please me...

Chapter 15

"Maaaaaaa!" Ace yelled from the driveway. Londyn started laughing inside of her house. She was sure that her parents had only just put the car in park before he jumped out. The boys had been gone with them the whole summer. They hadn't seen Londyn since they left. When they were younger, she wouldn't let long expanses of time go without seeing them. The older they got, the less they seemed to be phased by her summertime vacay visits. With this summer being particularly rough, she thought it was best for her to just keep to herself. She didn't want them to see her breaking down that way.

"Wassup homies?" Londyn beamed opening up the garage to make it easier to bring the luggage in the house. They always came back with more than what they left with. The boys ran up to her and hugged her long and hard. Londyn even got choked up a bit. That was the longest period of time she'd been away from them. "Are y'all hungry?"

"YES!" All four of them said in unison.

"Great! Leave the luggage, it can wait. I have some smothered chicken and rice on the stove."

"Now that's what I'm talking about!" Londyn's father, Nat, excitedly said.

"Where did you learn to cook that?" Londyn's mother, Deshawn laughed.

"C'mon, mom," Londyn playfully rolled her eyes. "You can find a recipe for anything on Pinterest."

"What's Pinterest?"

"Mom!" Londyn screamed laughing. She understood that her mother grew up in a time when computers were the size of entire rooms. Technology was moving along so fast that Deshawn would still send Londyn pictures to post to her Facebook. Deshawn acted helpless to do it herself.

"Ooooh, Ma! These shoes are dope!" Deuce had already run to his room rummaging around. Londyn put their shoes on both of their beds for them to easily see.

"What?!" Ace questioned, then ran up the stairs to his bed. "Thanks Ma!" Ace yelled.

"Now, y'all c'mon down here to get something to eat," Nat shouted. The boys did as they were told.

"Here," Deshawn shoved the ringing phone in her daughter's hand, "Knight is calling. That's a mighty fine picture, too." Londyn blushed a bit and answered the phone. Her side of the conversation was brief and short. She let him know that her parents and boys had just gotten in off the road and she would call later.

Knight rolled out of bed to check on Hermes. Being that Pops and Knight helped take care of him, he had his own room at their house. Occasionally, he went to the oldest brother, Titus' house, but Titus already had three boys to juggle. Adding one more could be easy or another level of crazy, it all depended on what was going on.

"You up buddy?" Knight asked him.

"Yup," he said with his hands wrapped around a game controller clicking away.

"What are we gonna do today? We have to get you away from this game!" Knight said hopping on the bed.

"I have to get this playing in before school starts," Hermes' eyes never left the flat screen TV that hung on his cobalt blue walls.

"Oh yeah! School is about to start," Knight said. "Oooh, no more games for you!"

"C'mon Unc! Don't do me like that!"

"Oooh yeah. Games about to be collecting dust!" Knight rubbed his hands teasing his nephew. "Let's do something to get outta this house. Wanna shoot some hoops?"

"Nah."

"Wanna go to Six Flags?"

"Only if you get me some of that ice cream ball stuff."

"Bet," Knight said. Hermes hopped up and turned the game off. Knight went into his room to get ready.

He started to think that Hermes would get along well with Ace and Deuce. They were around the same age and with the distraction of the games, rollercoasters, and activity of the park, they wouldn't really be focused on getting to know each other, it would be all about having a good time. Ace and Deuce already had a built-in play buddy, so Hermes would be fitting in, but from the way Londyn described them, they would have welcomed him in.

Knight: WYD

"Now, Knight is texting you," Deshawn said shoving the phone at her daughter again. "Who is this Knight? And what is he saving you from?" she let out a naughty laugh.

"Mom?!"

Londyn: Just hanging out with the parents

Knight: Taking Hermes to Six Flags, wanna come?

Londyn: I'm straight

Knight: The boys?

Londyn: Aww thanks. They're good, I appreciate you.

She let him down easy. He knew Londyn wasn't going to have it before he even asked though. He mentioned meeting the boys when they came back from summer vacation and she laughed him off. He didn't press, plus they had a daddy, he should be doing that type of stuff with them.

Knight checked with his brother, Ares, to make sure Hermes was straight for the school year coming up. Being men, they weren't natural nurturers, but between all of them and his grandmother, Hermes was well taken care of.

Knight and Hermes got a late start at the amusement park, but they got their money's worth. Well, they got Knight's money's worth. They went on twisty, windy, rollercoasters, and were spun upside down and dropped out of the sky with no warning. Hearts racing then at a complete standstill. They even did a couple rounds of go-kart racing.

Even though Knight was the youngest of the brothers, he was very mature for his age. Londyn joked that he acted older than she did. Now, with the increased responsibility he had, there was more weighing on his shoulders. He had the firehouse and his legacy name riding on his success or failure. He was definitely feeling more pressure to get it right. But in those moments, it felt good just to let loose and have fun.

After Six Flags, they barely had any energy left, but they made it to the mall to grab him a pair of shoes. Everything had already been taken care of according to Ares. The bond between Hermes and Knight was stronger than it was even between Hermes and his own father. Hermes' mother passed away during child birth, so even though she didn't desert him, to a child, it all felt the same. She wasn't there. Not knowing her or hearing anyone talk about her was like a double death. People didn't want him to feel sad but at the same time, half of him was missing. Knowing just a little about her could have filled part of the empty void and maybe even revealed something about himself. Not knowing anything just added to the number of bleak walls that surrounded him whenever he tried to wrap his mind around what she was like, what types of things she liked to do, and what they had in common.

For reasons unknown to Knight, his mother had just up and walked out one day. Much like the unfunny jokes that float around the black community about fathers going out for milk and not returning; that's pretty much what happened. People laugh about it to hide the pain, but there was no hiding Knight's pain. He was being raised by someone who was not his mother. In Hermes' case, at least Regina was a blood relative. She wasn't kin to Knight, but treated him like he was her own.

Regina cheered from the stands of every football game, every basketball game, and even the three or four track meets he was in. She was there volunteering at the school in his classes and on field trips. She had her hands full with her three, but by the time Lil' Fran left, the oldest two boys were practically out of the house. It was actually therapeutic for Knight being that he had a mother figure and it was therapeutic for Ms. Regina in preparing for her empty nesting. It also was her way of showing Pops that she was the better woman.

Her heart was full of love, so was her home. Pops had long since realized that he'd made a mistake leaving her. He recognized he had been a fool to break up his family. But what was done was done.

Knight was able to relate to Hermes and even at nine, Hermes appreciated having someone who knew what it felt like to grow up without a mother.

Knight drove to the next shift at his job and called Londyn as usual. She answered every call, but her conversation was shorter than he was used to and there was more time between text responses. It was what he'd feared, that with the boys coming back, she was distracted. He instantly felt bad for feeling like her sons were a distraction. Really, he had been the distraction and now, the main event had returned. He was determined to stay in contact with her as normal. Here again, he also had the challenge of hoping that she and Micah didn't fall back into husband and wife mode. That would destroy him even though he felt like he didn't deserve her. He was treating her better than Micah ever could.

Londyn had been honest with Knight from the beginning. Or at least that's the way it seemed. She didn't have to tell him anything about Micah and how fresh the situation was or that she would give him another chance if he decided that he wanted to come back home. Knight was definitely beginning to become possessive about her. In his mind. And heart.

The first day of school for all of the boys came and went. Knight saw that with them being away at school, she could still devote time to him during the day, although now with it being fall, she was gearing up for her artist, Libra, to come back onto the scene. She was busy on the phone and email during the day, as well as doing research to connect with people and find events. The goal was to go into the New Year with a bang.

```
Knight: I need you
Londyn: Yeah?
Knight: Yes
Londyn: Do something about it
Knight: Come see me
Knight: How'd the exchange go with your
husband?
Knight: How was he acting?
Londyn: I really wish you'd stop calling
him that. We'll talk about it in person.
Knight: I'll throw something on the
grill
Londyn: I'll bring wine
Knight: Come around back
Londyn: Ooh, you want it from the back

Londyn: Wait...I read that too fast!
Knight: Get cha mind out the gutter, LOL
```

Just as she was instructed, when she arrived at Knight's house, she went straight to the back yard.

"Good evening, Sgt. Knight," Londyn said winding the stone squares that mapped out a trail from the driveway to the deck.

"Well hello," he said half-smiling. She couldn't tell if he was forcing the smile or trying not to. He didn't seem that excited to see her, but when he hugged her, it felt genuine.

"How was your day?"

"It was cool. Nothing particularly exciting happened today. But I am glad to see you," he said looking at her with the straightest face ever.

"How? Your face is super straight." She was a little annoyed, but then when she thought about it, she'd never really seen him excited about anything. What she noticed were the increased frequency of calls, the longevity of the calls, and the tighter hugs. She noticed a difference in his stroke, how powerful and emotional it felt. So she knew he cared, but she still felt like there was something that just didn't sit right. It was *too* good.

"It's Friday! Hey!" she piped up.

"What do you care? You don't even have a real job!" They both laughed. He took the two bottles of wine from her.

"The hate is so real. I bought red and white so you could have a choice."

"It's cool. I'm more of a beer and cognac man myself. You can kill these. Let me go get you some ice."

"I got it, you make sure you don't burn this meat. Just point me in the right direction."

"Girl, you better know I'm a grill master! A chef du jour! A beast with this meat!"

"You're a beast with the meat alright," she said giving him a quick tap on the butt. He told her where to get the ice bucket and she filled it with ice before bringing it back out. He lit candles to keep the mosquitoes from biting. "I'm waiting to hear about your exchange."

"Oh that? It was nothing," she brushed him off.

"So, you don't want to talk about it is what that means?"

"Nothing to talk about. He picked up the boys from the bus stop, brought them to the house and stayed in the car while they got their bags for the weekend."

"He didn't speak?"

"He waved."

"That's not too bad."

"I told you it was nothing. I just keep asking myself how did we get to this point? Like how did we get to a point where we don't even talk? We don't even look at each other? But when I do see him I feel like I say 'hi' to him twice before I even get half of a response. I still think about him. Like I feel the need to run things by him. I feel like at any point, he's going to walk through that door. I can't imagine making big decisions without him."

"I understand that. Why don't you tell him how you feel?"

"For what? That man has clearly moved on. He's not thinking about me. I can't make him happy. I'm not bitter or angry, but I am confused by it all. At this point, this is my reality. There's nothing I can do about it."

"Maybe you can change his mind," Knight said feeling her out.

"Here," she said handing him another beer and tossing the empty bottle in the trash. She saw that he'd taken the last swig out of the bottle he had. Knight made note of her thoughtfulness.

"Thank you," he kissed her on the forehead. Of course, he would have refreshed his own drink, but it sure was nice having her think a step ahead. That was one of the things he adored about Londyn, she seemed to genuinely care. She always asked about his days and how he slept. Before, it didn't bother him that he didn't particularly have anybody who seemed to care enough to ask. Now if he didn't get it, he missed her. Londyn was definitely different than the others.

Knight had skewered some lime and cilantro shrimp to throw on the grill for her and a steak for himself. He also grilled corn on the cob. They ate and talked, he reached onto her plate to snatch a few shrimp like always. They talked about work at the firehouse and the irritating call he'd had the shift before.

"Lemme tell you about Mr. Evans. He's an old, surly man. He calls 9-1-1 at least once a month complaining about trouble breathing," Knight shook his head.

"Why is he calling y'all instead of going to the doctor to get it checked out?"

"That's the thing. He has! Ya boy has emphysema and he still smokes!"

"What? That's insane!"

"I know. And it pisses us off so bad?"

"Yeah, because he's not trying to help himself."

"Not only that, but because if another call comes through, something more important like a car accident or fire, we can't ditch him for that call; one where we can actually save lives instead of babysitting his crazy ass. Sitting there coughing and smoking while hooked up to an oxygen machine!" After a few glasses of wine, and Knight downing a few beers, the sun had set on them.

"When do I get to meet Ace and Deuce?"

"Are you sure you're ready for that? I mean, you are a young man with no kids. What do you want to meet my kids for?"

"Why not? I'm gonna be their step-daddy."

"Chill out. I'm sure one of these young girls will give you kids one of these days."

"I want an old girl to give me kids."

"Maybe an old girl will," she smiled. He was crazy.

"It might be you," he grabbed her cheek.

"Nah, I'm good on having any more kids."

"You don't want any more?"

"Nope. My boys are good enough for me. You can meet them down the road, when I know that you aren't going anywhere. Not that I'm saying we have to be in a committed relationship, because I'm sure I'm not the only girl you're involved with, but I need to know that you're going to be around. The last thing I want is for them to get attached to you and you peace out on us."

"You don't think I'll be around?"

"I don't know what you'll be. You have the perfect schedule to juggle another person, especially if she has a job like a nurse or a teacher with a steady schedule. You could move us both around for months before any slipups."

"Wow! Glad to know what you think."

"It's true. I'm not tripping, I'm just saying I don't think we're at a place for those types of introductions yet." They both sat in their own thoughts. Neither of them really wanted to continue down that path of conversation. In general, their relationship was so light-hearted. They both knew she was right. There was no way for her to know if he was going to be around for any real period of time or if he was dealing with anybody else. Knight knew he'd gained her trust to a certain extent, but she was telling him that she was still skeptical. And showing him – by not introducing him to her boys. Londyn was treading lightly. Having sex with him was a big deal to her. That wasn't lost on him.

Coincidentally, they were both thinking about how they got to his back yard that evening. When they met, they left lasting impressions on each other. It was almost magical. And how crazy that they would both be fresh out of relationships, even though the waters around Londyn seemed to still be muddy. They were just what the other needed.

"This backyard is perfect. It's so peaceful out here," Londyn said changing the subject. She was enjoying her company and didn't want to call it a night yet.

"It is. I spend a lot of time out here. It helps me gather my thoughts."

"What thoughts? What's going on Knight?"

Londyn's question was met with a deep exhale. Knight looked over at her earnestly. He gently grabbed her hand and motioned for her to sit on his lap. She obliged. Face to face, they sat looking into each other's eyes. They each had a whole world on their shoulders. Neither of them could tell the future to know that a sure-fire storm was brewing ahead. Things were about to be shaken up for them both. But in that moment, it was Apollo Knight and Londyn Charles. Just the two of them. She cupped his head and ears in her hands and looked at him patiently waiting on him to tell her what thoughts he'd been gathering.

"Why are you looking at me like that?" she asked. "Just say it, whatever it is. I'm a big girl, I can handle it." She could sense there was something he needed to say. Some-thing that she probably didn't want to hear.

"I love you," he said. She laughed.

"No you don't."

"I love you, Londyn." She laughed again.

"You've been drinking."

He pulled her closer to him and put his lips to hers but didn't kiss her. He didn't say anything. He closed his eyes and breathed her in. He slowly moved his head from side to side, rubbing their lips together. This was a much different Knight than the one who barely acknowledged her leaving in the beginning.

"I love you," he said definitively. This time, she didn't object, but she didn't say it back. Instead, she parted her lips to let her tongue explore him. They kissed passionately, then he reclined back slightly and pulled her to rest on him. She stretched her legs out beside his to get comfortable. For a while, they laid there being lulled by the sound of the insects in chorus.

Once they cleaned up the deck, they made their way to Knight's room. They showered and turned on the TV, but it was really for the lighting. They entertained each other telling stories of their lives growing up and what they wanted for their futures.

T.I.
"Private Show"

Girl take it off for me,
You know just what I want,
It's always hard to leave, this private show
Let me see it, see it, let me see it take it off.

Chapter 16

"So how are things going with this Knight of yours in uniform?" Kenzie sang into the phone.

"Shut up!" Londyn laughed. "It's crazy. I know we both said we weren't here for anything serious, but we talk *all* the time. I see him on a regular basis. And at this point, I don't go 24 hours without seeing or hearing from him."

"Ok, so it sounds like you guys are moving in a different direction."

"He makes me feel so good."

"Orgasms will do that to a person, ya know?"

"No, I mean really. Like the warm and fuzzies in real life. He is such a gentleman," Londyn began.

"I remember. That's what got you the first night."

"Yeah and he makes me feel so confident, so sexy. I really feel like I can trust him."

"Girl, he's trying to keep you around because that snatch is good to him," Kenzie blurted in the phone. Londyn laughed too.

"As fine as he is, girls are throwing drawers at him. We were on the phone the other day. He walked into a store with his uniform on and a girl said, 'Come put out my fire.' "

"He told you that?"

"No! He had on his headseat and I heard her!"

"Wow!"

"Well, you know...the sex is good. Beyond that, we have good conversations, he's such a good guy. Kind of a loner, which I don't understand because he's freaking awesome! He just...oh!"

"Sounds like my friend is falling for him," Kenzie observed. Londyn toyed with the idea of telling her what happened over the weekend. She still was in awe herself. Knight had told her that he didn't want to fall in love, now he was telling her that he loved her. He was taking a step in the wrong direction. Not that he would be taking it alone if things kept going the way they were.

"I told you about him taking me shopping for the boys' shoes, then he tried to take them to Six Flags..."

"Oh no!"

"Oh, Kenzie! Of course I wouldn't let him do that."

"I was going to say it's way too early for all of that."

"Right!"

"Right!"

"He has me stepping outside of my comfort zone."

"Londynnnnnnn...what does that mean?"

"I sent him some nudes," she said really fast.

"NUDES!" Kenzie roared with laughter.

"Shut up, Kenzie, dang!" Londyn said through chuckles. "You're so loud your neighbors will hear you. Is Josh home?"

"No, chile! He's at work. This lil' boy got you sending him nudes? I didn't think you were into all that. You talk so much trash about me and my toys...and dressing up....and role playing...Now look at you coming over to the dark side. Did he ask or did you just send them?"

"He asked. I was sooooo nervous. After I sent the first one, he asked for another and another. It was so fun."

"I told you!"

"That's what I'm saying about him making me feel comfortable. He acted like he really enjoyed them."

"He did! See, different people bring different things out of you. Your crazy ass husband is the only person who talks trash about the way you look. You are beautiful and you have a nice body."

"Of course you'd say that, you're my friend."

"If it would make you feel better to lose a few pounds, then do it or shut up about it. But don't beat yourself up. Hell, aren't you actually *losing* weight?" Kenzie pointed out the obvious. When people commented that she was losing weight, she usually just said thanks and kept it moving. She didn't tell them she had no desire to eat because she was heartbroken and overwhelmed by the thought of raising two boys on her own. Something she never imagined she'd have to do once she and Micah were married.

"The wrong way."

"But you're still losing it! Girl, anyway! Was your face in the pic, Londyn?"

"NOOOO! Girl, no! I don't trust him *that* much. I'll send them to you when we hang up."

"Send them now. I'm about to run up to the shop real quick."

"You don't work on Mondays."

"You do when one of the Real Housewives calls you for an emergency appointment."

"I know that's right. And don't you do it for free!"

"I'm not one of these spring chickens trying to get on, honey. I been poppin'! Send the damn pics!"

The friends ended the call. Londyn went into the text thread she had with Knight and found the pictures. She selected them all, then unselected the money shot pic, *I'm sure she doesn't want to see all this! The boobs are enough*, she thought. Londyn hit the forward arrow at the bottom of the screen and began typing Kenzie's name. When Kenzie's name popped up, Londyn tapped it, then the send arrow.

"Why is the bubble green?" Londyn asked herself out loud. Kenzie had an iPhone, too, so Londyn was perplexed...that is until she saw that her forward had gone to a group chat. Her heart instantly stopped. "What the hell just happened? Oh

SHIT!" In 0.2 seconds, her heart went from a normal heartbeat to pumping out of her chest. *Who is in this group chat? Oh my gosh!!*

Londyn clicked the cluster of circle avi's at the top of the chat hesitantly, but necessarily. She shunned at the thought of who else could be receiving a plethora of full frontal pics of her in her birthday suit. The green line was still moving across the top of the message which meant the pictures were still going through. Her phone began buzzing out of control as texts started coming through that the first pic was received before the line even stopped.

```
T: Whew, Londyn!
TW: Yaaaaaaas!!!
CW: Who needs morning coffee?? Shots of
Londyn to wake us up in the morning!
        Incoming call...Decline
N: What is going on?
N: Am I seeing what I think I'm seeing?
Londyn: OMG! OMG! OMG! I'M SORRY! I'M
SORRY! OMG!
```

She clicked for the list to unravel. *Ten people.*

```
        Incoming call...Decline
        Incoming call...Decline
```

TEN PEOPLE! Every time she tried to see who they were, another call came through and interrupted the screen.

```
N: OMG!!
CW: Yes girl! SHOTS!
AL: Look at all that azzzzzzz!
AL: 😩😩
TW: LMAO
        Incoming call...Decline
CW: LMAOOOOOOO
N: ROTFL!
T: That body looking right, girl!
```

SG: 👀

SG: 👀

PMM: I still got ones in my purse from Magic last night!!

PMM: Looking like a MILF!

PMM: Two kids where???

T: 💰

      Incoming call...Decline

J: I am a married woman! A woman of the Lord! Please stop sending this kind of stuff to my phone.

CW: Who is that? Why you trippin? It was obviously an accident.

J: OH NO!! 🙈

CW: SEND MORE LONDYN!

CW: I got some ones two!!! Let's make it rain!

CW: *too

PMM: 💰💰💰

SG: I need to wake up to this eeeeveryday!

T: 😡😡😡😡😡😡😡😡😡

      Incoming call...Decline

NS: PUHAHAHA!

SG: 🍆 ☕

AL: I wanna see sommore! L ...WYA???

She quickly scanned down the list and breathed a half sigh of relief. They were all home girls who she could explain the situation to. Then when she clicked on the '+1' at the bottom of the list, 'Mom Dukes' appeared.

      Incoming call...Decline
      Incoming call...Decline

Incoming call…Decline

"OH SHIT!! MY MOM IS IN THIS CHAT!" Londyn felt her life flash before her eyes! She left the chat to call her mother, who was a junior high school teacher. As she went to call her, the phone kept vibrating with every text. She knew the girls were having a ball in there without her. Well…she was there in spirit…and in flesh. Right now, there was a real emergency. She had to figure out a way to get Deshawn to delete the text thread without opening it.

Buzz. Buzz. Buzz. More texts were buzzing through. She called Deshawn's phone…ring…*buzz…buzz*…ring…

b*uzz*…ring…*buzz…buzz…buzz*… "Hello, you have reached…" Click. *Buzz.* Londyn could barely think straight with the text thread constantly going off. Her heart was pounding, she was sweating and her hands were shaking. *Buzz.*

Incoming call…Decline

Deshawn was a devout Christian who practiced what she preached. Growing up, Deshawn had her children in the church every time the doors opened. *How am I going to explain this? Buzz…buzz…buzz…buzz…*

Then Londyn remembered that Deshawn's cell phone was set up to allow images of messages in the locked screen. So any text or picture message that she received automatically showed even when the phone was locked. *Buzz…buzz…* Londyn was mortified! She wanted nothing more than to crawl into a hole in the ground. But first, she had to find her mother who was not answering her cell. She called the work phone.

"Thank you for calling Beachside Junior High. If you know you're party's extension, enter it now," the automated female voice said. Londyn dialed the extension code then waited. *Buzz…buzz…*

"Mrs. Steele's office," a chipper teeny bopper voice answered.

"I need to speak to Mrs. Steele."

`Incoming call...Decline`

"She's teaching, may I take a message?"

"No. I need to speak to her."

"She's teaching, may..."

"Tell her it's her daughter and it's an emergency!" Londyn yelled at the my-life-is-so-perfect sounding teen who sounded like she had braces, freckles, and long blonde hair. The receiver dropped, then the next voice was her mother's. *Buzz...buzz...*

`Incoming call...Decline`

"Hey baby. What's wrong?"

"Mom, where is your phone? I called you."

"It's right here. I'm fine. Why do you sound like that?"

"Open your phone. I need you to do something for me."

"Oh! I mean, I have it with me at work. It's over there by my table with the kids."

`Incoming call...Decline`

"GET IT! Get it, I need you to do something."

"What's going on Londyn? What is this all about?" Deshawn was growing concerned.

"I sent you something by accident. I need you to delete it without opening it."

"LONDYN!"

"I know! I know! I'm sorry, Maaaaaa!" Londyn whined. Deshawn yelled out to one of her students to bring her phone into the office part of the classroom.

"What did you send?"

"Ok, go into your texts, but DON'T OPEN THE ONE AT THE TOP!"

`Incoming call...Decline`

"Somebody is texting me now," Deshawn was easily distracted. *Buzz...buzz...*

"No! Ma...that is from what I sent. I sent the pics to a group."

"My goodness!"

"Now, the message at the very top? Slide it to the left. It should turn red and say delete." As Londyn spoke to her mother, not only was she hearing and feeling her own phone buzz in her ear with every text, but she could hear her mother's phone buzzing on the desk! Her nerves were all over the place.

"It just opened the text. Oh goodness, there are a lot of people in here." *Buzz...buzz...*

"Left! Left! Slide it to the Left!"

"I just see times when I do that." Londyn took a deep breath, closed her eyes to calm down. On a scale from one to 10, she was at 20 trying to calm down to 15.

"Go out of that message, but stay in the text message screen where you can see the list of messages."

"I'm getting another text." *Buzz...buzz...*

"Ma! Please! Slide the text at the top to the left."

"Ohhh, it says delete. Ok, I did it."

"I'll call you later."

Londyn was completely exasperated. The ordeal was more than she thought it was going to be. Her senses were totally overloaded. She put her phone down on the table and it buzzed loudly again. Still jittery, she yanked it up and read the most recent messages.

PMM: Bust it wide open!

SG: Show us what you werkin' with!

Londyn burst into a fit of laughter, ran and dove across her bed. She was still shaking. She wanted to call Knight to tell him what happened, but she didn't know what was going on if he was on a call or at the station, so she texted instead.

Londyn: THE MOST EMBARASSING MOMENT OF MY LIFE!!!!

```
Londyn:  🙈🙈🙈🙈🙈🙈🙈
Londyn:  OHHHH EMMMM GEEEEE!!!!!
Londyn:  I AM MORTIFIED!!!!
```

It took about an hour, but finally Knight called. "What happened sweetheart?" She could hear him trying to conceal his laughter. Yelling at full blast, Londyn told him blow for blow what happened. She was sure not to leave out the sound effects of random buzzes from text messages and incoming calls. Knight was roaring! He was laughing so hard, he could barely catch his breath. That was the most emotion Londyn had seen from him since day one.

"I'm glad you're having a laugh at my expense," Londyn joked.

"Hey y'all! Listen to this!" Knight shouted to the rest of the firehouse.

"NOOOO!!!! Don't tell them!"

"This girl sent me some nudes, then accidentally sent them to a group chat." Londyn could hear one or two sorted laughs. "And her MOM was in the chat!" Everybody burst out laughing. They were slapping tables and cracking all the way up. It sounded like there were about 20 or 30 guys there, although she knew there wasn't.

"Say Knight," Josten said. He was obviously sitting right next to Knight because his voice was loud and clear. "Let me see them nudes, bwoy!"

"Nah bruh! Gone! You can't look at *my* ass!" Knight pushed him. Josten laughed another hearty laugh.

"What?" Londyn was confused. The pics she'd sent were of her, not him.

"*My* ass. You are *mine*." *Oh shit!* Londyn thought. "You think imma show 'em pics of my girl? Nah! I really needed that laugh though. We were just on a call where a little boy lost his leg."

"Oh no, bae!"

"Whaaaat? I'm bae now?" He asked. Londyn beamed on the other end of the phone.

"Sorry…lemme try that again. Oh no…Sgt. Knight!"

"Quit tryin' me. You had it right the first time."

"Bed time!" Londyn shouted.

"AHHH!" Deuce yelled.

"Five more minutes, Ma, PUH-LEEZE!" Ace begged. What child actually wanted to go to bed?

"Nope! It's nine! Time to go!"

"The light doesn't work in my room, Ma!" Deuce said. Londyn went into the mud room and looked for lightbulbs, that was where Micah kept them. She grabbed one and trotted upstairs to his room lugging a chair from the dining room table.

"What are you doing with that?" Ace said confused.

"You know she's a shorty! She can't reach the light," Deuce laughed. Londyn and Ace joined him in laughter.

"Let me get it, Ma! Do you even know what you're doing?" Ace asked.

"Boy! I been changing lights since I was your age!"

"OOOOOH diss!" Deuce cracked.

"I've never seen you change a lightbulb before," Ace noted. Londyn twisted out the old, dead bulb and replaced it with the new one.

"Flip the switch," she instructed. Ace hit the switch and the light came on.

"BOO-YA!" Londyn exploded sticking her tongue out and dancing on the chair. "Now, you can take this chair back downstairs. On second thought, I'll do it." Ace left the room.

"Thank you so much, Ma."

"Of course, Deuce. You don't have to thank me for changing the light bulb," she responded grateful that he was thankful. She kissed him and journeyed downstairs with the chair.

Londyn couldn't remember the last time she'd changed a lightbulb, or put the trash in the big can outside, or had to use a hammer. She didn't even know what a Phillips' screwdriver was. Micah was the ultimate handyman. She could empty a box of random pieces of wood, screws, washer/fastener thing-a-muh-jigs, and show him a picture of what the finished product would look like. An hour later, he'd have her bookshelf, or bed, or TV stand. He was amazing with his hands.

She definitely missed that. Apparently so did the boys. This was one of the things that Londyn had never even considered was a part of the transition from married to separated. The next day she bought a set of pink tools from the Home Depot. Just one more thing to re-establish the independence that she didn't want, but was thrust into.

Lloyd
"TRU"

This is me so please accept me for who I am,
And please accept me for what I do,
I'm just doing everything that I can,
Cause all I wanna be is TRU,
So please accept me for who I am,
And please accept me for what I do,
Cause there's no me without you,
And all I wanna be is TRU.

Chapter 17

Jo Jo, Knight's friend from high school invited a group of guys out to celebrate his birthday. It was the usual crew, Knight, Jo Jo, Derek, plus Abe and Shaheer. Knight made sure that Hermes was squared away before agreeing to go. It was his night to watch Hermes, but he was able to convince Titus' wife to have a sleepover with her sons. He told her he'd pay for pizza and Capri Suns, so she was game. He made sure to check-in with Londyn as well.

```
Knight: WYD??
Londyn: Chillin WBU?
Knight: Meeting up with some of the
guys.
Londyn: Really? Yeah right!
Londyn: I don't believe you, you need
more people 🙄
Knight: It's for a birthday
Londyn: What are you wearing?
```

Knight sent her a video of him in his driveway. He had music in his truck blasting and he was singing in his tone deaf voice to the phone. It was R&B singer Lloyd's song, "Tru."

This is me so please accept me for who I am,
And please accept me for what I do,
I'm just doing everything that I can,
Cause all I wanna be is TRU,
So please accept me for who I am,
And please accept me for what I do,
Cause there's no me without you,
And all I wanna be is TRU.

Londyn:

Londyn: Be good! Don't be out there giving MY stuff away.

Knight:

Micah had the boys, so Londyn was free. Still, she had no plans. She certainly didn't feel like dressing up to do any type of girls' night. As Atlanta culture would have it, there was really nowhere she could go on a weekend night and not dress up. So she just flipped through channels until her artist, Libra called her.

"Hey Londyn!"

"Libra! How are you hun?"

"Doing well. We're getting adjusted to being home."

"Oh gosh! I still haven't been over there. I'm so sorry!" The truth was, Londyn knew what it was like to be a new mom, having people fuss over you day and night in the beginning. She wanted to go when Libra had settled into being a mom, when Londyn could get more one-on-one time. Not to mention that school had started and so she was busy with football practices and games for the boys.

"You know you're more than welcome to come over. Anytime."

"What are you doing now?"

"Looking at the door waiting on you to come through."

"Ok, let me throw on something real quick. I'm not coming cute though," Londyn laughed.

"Chile please! You should see me!"

"See you soon!" Londyn hung up instantly excited...then somewhat melancholy. She did want to see the new baby, but didn't feel like making the drive to Libra's Buckhead condo. *Really, Londyn, what else are you going to do tonight?* It was drive to Buckhead or spend the weekend on the couch which she'd become accustomed to doing. She threw on a tank top and some shorts and jumped in the car.

```
Knight: I miss you already
Londyn: LIES!
Knight: FR FR
Londyn: Enjoy your friends!
Knight: I don't think we'll make it to
the next spot. The bday boy is drunk already.
Londyn: LMAO
```

"The problem with these women," Abe said, "is social media!"

"There's nothing wrong with social media!" Jo Jo slurred. "I love looking at ass and titties!"

"I get it, but they feel like that's all they have to offer. Some of them."

"Ass, titties, and hair!" Jo Jo said and they laughed.

"And waist trainers. Don't forget waist trainers," Knight said.

"I'm glad my queen ain't into all that fake stuff. Natural is beautiful," Shaheer added.

"You mean your baby mama," Derek threw in.

"Call her what you want. She gave me a beautiful daughter and she's raising her the right way. Just because things didn't work out between us doesn't mean that I don't still love and respect her. I'll slice somebody's throat if they do her wrong. She's still my family."

"I get what you're saying about the social media thing," Derek said. "Women say they want a good man...they want a relationship, #relationshipgoals, yet posting pics of everything they got all hanging out. What good man wants to see his woman out here looking like that?"

"Yep, they project the opposite of what they want," Shaheer nodded.

"They seem so materialistic. They post pics of long nails next to their Benz car emblem and LV bags and Chanel flip flops," Derek said.

"Steady making those folks rich, but wanna ask me for a discount when it comes to supporting my black owned business," Shaheer piped up. "Do you ask Louis Vuitton for a discount? Chanel doesn't have coupons!"

"Preach!" Derek said.

"Y'all just mad because these bad hoes don't want y'all," Jo Jo said.

"Shut your shallow ass up! When they see me pull up in that 9-11, they're all over me! It helps that a brother is pretty decent looking. But I don't want that. All body, no brains and no ambition?"

"And bad credit," Knight spoke up.

"Talk to me Baby!" Derek gave him some dap.

"We have to do better as a people. There's nothing wrong with looking the way you want to look, but have some respect for yourself," Abe chimed in.

"I'm talking to a community of people now trying to do something with their lives. I'm talking starting businesses, growing businesses, showing their kids how to be entrepreneurs, creating generational wealth," Shaheer stated.

"It's really a shame that we are so far behind, but I'm changing my train of thought now. I'm looking to do some investing. Small business is much more risky, but I'd like to talk to some of your community to see what change I can help make," Derek looked at Shaheer.

"No doubt," Shaheer responded.

"Look man...I'm trying to celebrate here. Y'all being all self-righteous and woke over there. Let's order a round of shots! Waitress! Waitress!!!!" Jo Jo started yelling over the music in the sports bar. "What's her name? Jennifer? McKenzie? Becky? Round of shots for me and my friends here!"

After three quick rounds of shots, the boys were feeling real good. They started reminiscing about glory days again. Jo Jo and Derek were sure not to bring up Sheka because of how poorly Knight reacted the last time. Nobody was trying to sour the mood. When it was all said and done, they raked up a $400 tab on drinks. Knight sent Londyn a picture of the bill, to which she just laughed at. They had to practically carry Jo Jo to the car. Then Knight FaceTimed Londyn from the parking lot.

"Hey you," she answered.

"Y'all say hi to the beautiful Londyn! Londyn, look at this fool," Knight said and turned the phone to his homeboys. They all started waving and saying hi, except Jo Jo. He was asleep, half of his body was in the car, the other half was out.

"Whoa! Looks like somebody had a good time."

"Yeah. Like I told you, we're calling it a night early. Where are you?"

"Visiting Libra and her baby," Londyn smiled.

"The singer Libra?" Shaheer jumped in the frame.

"Yes sir."

"She *is* pretty, Baby," Shaheer said matter-of-factly about Londyn. She was instantly embarrassed that she wasn't put together. The last thing she expected was to be on FaceTime with her young beau and his friends.

"Everybody looks better when you're drunk," she laughed it off.

"I don't drink," he said staring in the phone at her. "I know beauty when I see it."

"Ok, that's enough. That's enough. Let me see the baby," Knight asked. Londyn looked over at Libra who nodded yes. She turned the phone to show them the baby in her lap.

"Aww man," Shaheer said. "That's a good looking baby."

"Makes me want one," Knight said.

"Be here sooner than you think. Your life will never be the same," Shaheer said. "Nice meeting you Londyn. Congratulations Queen Libra. I love your work!" Shaheer bowed his head and moved out of the frame.

"Alright sweetheart, lemme try to get this boy in the car so I can drive him home."

"Later," Londyn said.

Knight and his crew hung out another 20 minutes or so while Jo Jo threw up. They were too busy laughing and taking videos and pics to really care. In addition, Derek, Abe, and Knight were drinking water to sober up. They helped to get Jo Jo in the car finally and said their goodbyes.

Libra turned her attention to Londyn who was sweetly looking at the precious baby girl in her arms. Londyn could hardly remember the twins being that small. It seemed so long ago, but at the same time, it seemed like yesterday. The new baby smell was intoxicating.

"That looks good on you," Libra said.

"It looks better on you."

"Don't you want to have another one? Maybe try for a girl?"

"Nah. Me and Micah entertained the possibility. I think that time has passed for me." Londyn was too embarrassed to say that her husband didn't want her to have any more kids because he didn't want her to gain more weight. None of the guys who tried to holla at her each day seemed to have a problem with her few extra pounds. "Plus, my boys are 11! I can see the finish line. Why would I start over now?" She laughed trying to make light of her own mental anguish.

"Very, very true. What if your new man wants kids?"

"It does make me wonder though, being out on the market, as they say. What if I get with somebody who doesn't have any kids?"

"Or wants another one."

"If he wants another one, he's on his own. But if he doesn't have one, that is something to consider. I would have to really, reeeeeeeeally be in love, like for real, to birth a baby out of this body." The ladies laughed.

"Well, don't knock it, that's all I'm saying. You'll find someone who you love and adore who loves and adores you. You'll get to a point where you wonder why you ever considered not having another baby."

"I guess. He's gonna have to *brang* it!" They laughed again. "This whole single life shit is scary. I don't want it at all."

"I can imagine."

"Like why is this *my* reality? Why was *my* family broken apart? It's just crazy to me. And the rules are so different now with technology and instahoes. Chile, I don't know what's going on!"

"Are you really seeing anybody? Your husband is," of course Libra had to throw that in. The few people who knew, threw it in every time the subject of her dating came up. Him introducing the boys to another woman really looked like he left Londyn for her. Insult to injury. It was also her friends' ways of showing her, not telling her, that it was ok to move forward. They thought it would help her move out of the pain.

"Knight is my friend, but I think we're both just passing the time."

"He's been calling and texting since you got here," Londyn bashfully looked down and snuggled the baby. She was really hiding her face to conceal the super-sized grin that exploded on it. "He FaceTimed you with his friends," Libra stared at Londyn with the straight face.

"Ugh! Hush!" Londyn laughed. "Let's talk about this new single and getting you back in the studio."

Knight: You still at Libra's?

Londyn: OTW home...you?

Knight: Taking my homeboy home. He's pissy drunk.

Londyn: You ain't gotta lie Craig. Just tell me you're going to spend the night with one of your other girls.

Knight: Where are you?

Londyn: Coming through downtown.

Knight: I'm ahead of you passing Grady curve. Pull over at University turn left. I'll be at Wendy's.

Londyn: What if I say no.

Knight: I know you wanna see this face.

Londyn: I look a mess.

Knight: You always look a mess, LOL! I'll be waiting.

Knight was sitting in the car looking at every car that passed until he saw Londyn's truck pull in. He immediately stood out of the car so she could see him. He walked over to her truck and opened the door. He leaned in and put his forehead on hers, gave her three quick pecks on the lips. She could taste the alcohol on his lips, it didn't bother her one bit. Being on his lips, any taste was sweet.

"Wassup?" he asked.

"You tell me, you're the one who wanted me to pull over here. I was headed home."

"You smell like a baby."

"I know," she acknowledged and he kissed her again.

"So where are you going?"

"I told you...home. Where are you going? Boys' night ended early, so who are you going to see?"

"Look," Knight pointed to Jo Jo passed out in the front seat. His mouth was wide open. "We rode together from his house."

"Oh my gosh!" Londyn cracked up putting her hands over her mouth. Knight pulled her hands down and pecked her again. This time, she leaned back away from him towards the passenger side seat. He leaned right over her. She grabbed his beard and rubbed it.

"I knew you wanted to see my face. Believe me now?"

"I guess. Dropping him off doesn't mean you aren't going somewhere else after."

Knight kissed her again then pulled himself out of the car. He closed the car door and ran back to Jo Jo's car and pulled out. She followed him on the highway until their paths separated. Knight took Jo Jo home and helped him into the house, then got in his own car to make the rest of the trek home. He called Londyn, "Talk me home."

A few days later, he went to have sushi at their restaurant. He called Londyn to talk to her while he ate lunch because he was used to going there with her. She joked about being mad he was eating there without her, especially when she heard some thirsty girl yell out, "Hey baby, can you put my fire out with your hose?" When he told her that was the reason he called, she turned her whole attitude around. They talked on FaceTime while he was eating then went on about their days.

Knight appreciated that even though her schedule seemed to be picking up juggling the boys and their friends, along with trying to arrange Libra's reentry into the entertainment world, she still made time for him. He knew if he asked her to meet him, she would have. Even if it meant rearranging what she had to do.

She openly asked for his opinion in how to handle a situation with one of the twins. Kingston, Deuce, had stolen money from her. In his defense, she told Knight that Deuce didn't really see it as stealing, but that he needed to. She didn't really know how to handle the situation.

"What did his daddy say? I know you told him," Knight inquired.

"I did. He gave me the tenth degree about it over the phone. Then when he called Deuce he just said, 'Your mother told me you stole from her. Do you know why that's wrong?' Deuce said yes, then Micah added, 'Don't let it happen again.'"

"That's it?"

"Yep."

"That's not enough. You need to make him return all of the stuff he bought with the money. Make *him* carry it in the store. Make *him* give it to the people to return. And when they give the money back, make them give it to him and have *him* put the money in your hands."

"That seems a little drastic. He's already opened some of the toys."

"Where did you say you got them from? Wal-Mart? They'll take anything back. Call me after you do it." Londyn laughed at his request. It was so direct, as they all were, but this sounded so differently.

"Look at you Sgt. Knight, trying to sound like somebody's daddy."

"I told you, you gon' have me with step-kids before I have my own. They ain't gon' like it when I move in. For real Londyn. Call me as soon as you hit the parking lot. I want to know that you did it exactly the way I said. You're being too soft on him. No matter what happens, what his daddy does or doesn't do, you are responsible for Deuce. You have to make sure you instill in him what needs to be there."

Knight, of course, was speaking from personal experience. Even though Regina was an integral part of his life,

Pops made sure he taught him everything that he needed to know. At the end of the day, the burden and privilege of raising him to a respectable, productive member of society fell on Pops. Knight also wanted to point out that even birth parents walk away, so at any time, Micah could chuck them the deuces and be out. Those were not his blood children, and even if they were, that wouldn't guarantee that he'd be active in their lives. Saying all that would have been taking it a little too far, so he just left it where he did.

"I'll take him on the way to football practice."

"Ok and you also need to have a talk with Ace. Let him know that he can't be doing that kinda shit either. You ain't raising no thieves."

A few hours later, Knight was in the bay of the firehouse doing an inspection of the truck. He was making sure to check the supplies that had been restocked on the truck replacing what was used in the calls that day. Londyn called, as she said she would to give a follow-up to the day's events.

"Did you make him do it?" Knight answered the FaceTime. Even though the boys weren't his responsibility, he still felt a tinge in his heart for them. His responsibility was to their mother. He knew that they weren't exclusive, but he loved her and she was important to him. He knew it meant a lot to her to have someone in her corner. She had been honest with him when she told him that she wasn't really venting about the separation or the drama, just dealing with it. He wanted to show her that he was there for her.

"Well, hello to you too, sergeant."

"You didn't do it, did you? I knew you were going to punk out!" he said. He was somewhat emotionally involved, as much as his half-heart would let him be.

"I did! Nanny, nanny!" On her end, Londyn stuck out her tongue and wagged her head from side to side. "I did exactly what you told me to do. Deuce was mad. When I gave him the bag with the stuff and told him he had to return it, he asked, 'Is all this necessary?' "

"Yes! It is!" Knight laughed. "Keep going."

"The cashier tried to give the money to me and I told her to give it to him. She said something about him being a big spender and having money. Then Ace jumped in with, 'No, he stole it from Mama!' so she tried to give it to me. I told her to give it to him to give to me. She told me I was being harsh. I said, 'Do you have any kids? I didn't think so. If he was in here stealing from your store, you would be asking where is his mother and how did she raise him. I have to train him now so he doesn't end up in the system.' Then I told her I didn't appreciate her undermining me in front of my boys."

"Slow clap, sweetheart. I'm proud of you."

"Deuce was in tears. I felt so bad."

"You'd feel worse putting up bail money."

"That's true."

"Give me a kiss," he demanded. She blew a kiss at the camera.

Knight ended the call with a little more positive reinforcement. Londyn felt better about getting across the seriousness of her son stealing from her. She toyed with the idea of pulling him out of practice and the game that week, but then that was teaching a whole different set of values. Values that went against him being there for his team and sticking to his word to follow through on commitments.

At the game on Saturday, she showed up in her yellow and black shirt with both of her boys' names on the back. Ace carried her pop-up chair and Deuce pulled the drink cooler. Once they got her setup, they ran over to speak to Micah who was sitting on the other side of the field, then on to warm-up with their team. Londyn cheered them on as usual and they won. The score was 14-0.

Londyn noticed a few Fulton County Police cars parked near the opening of the fence. She'd noticed them before, and thought about having them talk to the boys about the ramifications of stealing. As she approached them, one seemed to take notice of her. She could tell he was ripped despite the young officer wearing a bulletproof vest. He had crazy arm muscles and towered over her at about 6'3". He was definitely a tall drink of water. He turned to her.

"Londyn?" She stopped walking, surprised that he knew her name. Ace and Deuce looked a little scared. "Hi, I'm Officer Hill. I wanted to know if I could have a word with Ace and Deuce."

"Ummm...sure," she responded still perplexed. Officer Hill turned his gaze to the boys.

"Which one of you is Deuce?" Kingston raised his hand. "Deuce, I heard about you stealing money from your mother. Is this true?"

"Yes sir," Deuce answered looking down at his shoes.

"Look at me. Stealing is a crime. Did you know that?"

"Yes sir."

"So, if you know stealing is a crime, why did you do it?"

"I don't know."

"When you go before a judge, and they ask why you committed a crime, they don't want to hear, 'I don't know.' In the state of Georgia, stealing gets you up to a whole year in jail and you will have to pay up to a $1000 fine. The amount you stole is called a misdemeanor. Now, for a misdemeanor, you could also get your picture in the newspaper for all of your friends and teachers to see and have to do community service, like picking up trash on the side of the road. Is that what you want?"

"No sir!!!" Londyn and the cluster of officers laughed.

"Alright good. Now, Ace, you have to keep your brother straight. I'm giving your mother my card. It has my cell phone number on it. Londyn, if you have a problem with either one of your boys, call me and I'll come right over."

Officer Hill handed her a card, she thanked him then looked at both of her sons in the eye. "Tell Officer Hill thank you," she said.

"Thank you Officer Hill," the boys said in unison and they took off to the car.

Londyn: Do you know Officer Hill?

Knight: Who is that?

Londyn: He just walked up to me and the boys talking about Deuce stealing. You're the only person I told.

Knight: Really? I feel special.

Londyn: Don't 😒

Knight: Yeah, I know him. I sent him out there to talk to the boys. He's a really big dude, so I knew he would scare the boys a little.

Londyn: It worked! They got in the car talking about how big he was. They said he looked as big as The Rock.

Knight: LOL!

Londyn: Thank you so much for helping me. I really appreciate this.

Knight: I got you!

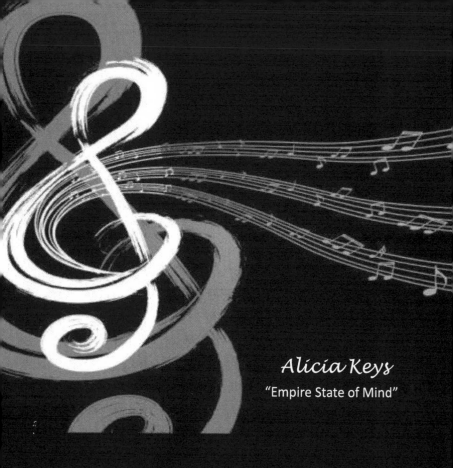

Alicia Keys
"Empire State of Mind"

New York, concrete jungle where dreams are
made of,
There's nothing you can't do,
Now you're in New York,
These streets will make you feel brand new,
Big lights will inspire you,
Hear it for New York, New York, New York.

Chapter 18

One way to get steady money coming in for Libra and Londyn was through endorsements. Londyn also figured that it would be a good way to get Libra's face back into the public. The endorsement company would freshen up her image using their marketing team to reflect the current make-up, hair, and clothing trends, even going a step ahead into the next season making her look more edgy. It was a win-win. Then Libra could use the refreshed image to go forward. She would be seen in the company's new campaign, as well as push her new single.

In Londyn's mind, it was a well thought out plan. Utilizing the resources of the endorsement company's make-up and hair team, half of the image work would be done. Since seeing Libra the week before, Londyn had lined up a few studio sessions to check out Libra's chops. Her vocals still sounded good, but they had some work to do on the new songs. Libra had been working hard working on her song lyrics. Together with her producer, they would pump out a hit. It couldn't be anything less.

Londyn kept the ball rolling by doing research into various companies that would benefit from having a new, fresh face for their campaign. The match had to be symbiotic, working to the advantage for both Libra and the brand. Clothing companies, cosmetic brands, perfume lines...Londyn spent days combing through old campaigns and researching the progression over the last few years. How often did they line up new spokeswomen? How much were the spokeswomen paid? How long were the endorsement contracts? What did they require?

Finally, Londyn had narrowed it down to a clothing company called, Anastacia. They had recently acquired one of those reality design show rejects to freshen up their offerings.

The design reject was truly a star in the making and came in second on the show. America was devastated that she didn't win, but Anastacia was thrilled and snatched her up. Although she brought a gamut of fans with her, they still wanted to pair the new line with a new face.

As quickly as Londyn thought she was knocking on their door, it turns out another manager had the same idea for her client. Talks seemed to be going well for Londyn and Libra with Anastacia, then all of a sudden, they came to a standstill. Londyn felt like she was losing her edge on the deal.

She was also at a point where she could see the end of her money. Micah was helping, but the amount he gave her in child support was unsteady. One month he gave her one amount, the next month, less than what he gave the month before. The dates he gave it were not steady either. She didn't want to ask him for anything. He knew how much it took to run the house and he knew what Ace and Deuce needed. It was up to him to stick to his word and give her what he promised to give her when he abruptly moved out.

Londyn received a call from a contact at Anastacia saying it looked like they were moving in a different direction, but Libra was not completely out of the running yet. The call was a Hail Mary because the contact did not have the final say, but was on the board considering which act to go with. The lady called so there wouldn't be a paper trail, but she was an older black lady who was pulling hard for Libra to represent the brand. She wanted to see some Black Girl Magic around the place. She told Londyn to get her ass to N.Y.C. with a new angle to blow the other talent out of the water.

Londyn called Knight. She wasn't going to burden him, she just knew that his voice could calm her down.

"Lon...dyn," he answered.

"Hey you. What's up?"

"Why do you sound like that?"

"No reason."

"You're lying. What's wrong?" he asked, then Londyn's face appeared on her phone. He was FaceTiming her. She answered. Just seeing his face made her exhale deeply. "What's wrong sweetheart?"

"Nothing!"

"Londyn, I'm looking at you. Your face isn't saying nothing. Tell big daddy what's going on," he smiled a gorgeous, megawatt smile. Londyn melted.

"Hey beard gang," she said trying to change the subject, looking at him lying in the bed shirtless. Tattoos dancing across his brown skin, his beard manicured to perfection. Knight was gorgeous. She still felt like this was all a dream.

"Don't you want a comfortable place to sit?" he said bringing the phone in closer so she could see him lick his lips L. L. Cool J. style as he rubbed his gorgeous beard in all of its splendor.

"Oooh, Sgt. Knight!" she said doing a shimmy in the camera, easily excited by the mental visual he'd just given her.

"Ok, I didn't call to talk about how awesome my beard is," he laughed. "What's going on?"

"Maaaaan! I'm trying to work this deal with Anastacia for Libra," she began, her face instantly filled with worry. "I think I'm going to lose it."

"Unh uh. What do you always tell me? Think positively! You can't approach it that way, Londyn."

"But they're looking at Destiny Reyes. She brings the Hispanic demographic. She's beautiful and popular and..."

"So is Libra. Who are you presenting? Destiny or Libra? Anastacia doesn't have a strong black demographic, so she's bringing our community with her. Not to mention she's a new mom. She's been gaining followers posting pics of her little baby, bringing new moms into her circle."

"How do you know?" Londyn was genuinely puzzled.

"I started following her after we started kicking it. I wanted to see what you do."

"Awww, Sgt. Knight."

"I had to check up on my baby!" Megawatt. Melt.

"I just got a call from an insider who said I need to get up there."

"Alright, so plan of action. Revise your campaign. You know who your competition is. Since Destiny is in the front-running, her camp isn't thinking about changing their pitch at all. You coming up with a whole 'nother campaign shows versatility and that Libra really is right for the job. Make them feel like they need her."

Damn. I wasn't expecting all of this. "Ok. Wow."

"I can't see you like this. I don't like you looking stressed. You'll be fine. The sooner the better. You want to stop them before making their final decision. Once it's made, and announced, they won't retract."

"Ok Knight! I see ya!" Megawatt. Melt.

"When are you thinking about going?"

"I hadn't thought about it. I literally just got off the phone with her. I was calling you to calm me down. I wasn't expecting a game plan," she laughed.

"If you win, *we* win," he said. Knight never imagined he'd be saying something like this on the night they met.

"Guess I need to book a ticket."

"And a hotel. Book it for Thursday. I can take you to the airport."

"That only gives me two days..."

"Get off this damn phone and get to work."

"Yes sir."

"Say, 'yes big daddy.' " Londyn just looked at him laughing and shaking her head.

Knight knew how critical this was for her. Of course, it wouldn't be the last opportunity to get an endorsement for Libra, but the timing was perfect. He wanted to motivate her. She'd been nothing but good to him. It made him feel good to give her a push in the right direction.

As he said, he arrived to take her to the airport. She was packed, for the most part. Her suitcase was open on the bed and she was running back and forth doing nothing really. He watched her frantic movements, the worry was all over her face. He tried to make small talk with her, but he could see that her mind was clearly in a different space.

He grabbed her breezing past him and put her face tenderly in his hands. He planted a kiss on her, gently she kissed him back, but her body didn't relax like it normally did when he kissed her.

He could feel then that she was at a place where she was starting to need him. He didn't want to let her down, but time was running out. Things were going to come to a head pretty soon and a decision had to be made. He had led Londyn get to this place, where she needed him to be part of her life. She didn't get here on her own. In fact, she'd tried not to get to this place where she cared about him so deeply. He coaxed her out of the shell of hurt and skepticism by calling her every day throughout the day...dating her...having sex with her...opening her up. He was in it too deep now. He couldn't bring himself to pull away from her. Not yet.

"Breathe sweetheart." She relaxed and popped her neck. He could feel her heart beating quickly, probably because of her shallow breaths. He laid down on her bed and pulled her down to him. He could feel her shaking. It reminded him of the first few times they had sex. Londyn really was nervous. He wrapped his arms around her, bringing her into his chest. He kissed her forehead over and over. They rested in that position for about ten minutes, until he could feel her calming down. "What do you need me to do?"

"Nothing."

"Are you finished with your bag?"

"Yes."

"Ok, I'll close it. Are you taking your laptop in the bag or in your suitcase?"

"The bag."

"Get yourself together."

"Ok."

Knight owed it to her to help her calm down. He wasn't going to be in New York with her. He wished that he could at least make the flight with her. Londyn was a complete basket case. He saw that her face was disheveled and she looked somewhat spaced out.

He closed her suitcase, and put the power cord to her cell phone along with her cell phone in her purse. He put her laptop and power cord in the lap top case. While she finished getting dressed, he gathered the trash bags she left by the door and put them in the big can outside, then loaded his pick-up.

"Londyn, you're all ready. I got ya loaded up in the truck. Let's go," his southern drawl was more evident because he spoke slowly.

"Ok," her eyes darted around the room. "I need my purse and my phone."

"They're in the car. Grab a jacket and socks, it's gonna be cold on the plane."

"Yes, yes," she mumbled.

"What else do you need?"

"Oh, ummm, the printouts on the desk in my office."

"I put those in the laptop case."

"Where is it?"

"In the truck." Knight couldn't believe how she had not seen any of his movements. He'd been in the house with her for 30 minutes and she'd been in the clouds, stressed out. Even in her few rants about Micah, he'd never seen her like this.

"Ok."

"Make sure you have your ID and let's get out of here."

Londyn checked her wallet and when she showed Knight that she had her ID, he backed out of the driveway. She asked him to pull into a gas station so she could grab some gum. He told her to get some juice to calm her stomach down as well.

Wearing comfy leggings and a thin pullover, she easily got the attention of the men she passed to walk into the convenience store. Knight saw the look of the guy holding the door open for her, then how his head turned to get a good look at her butt as she passed. He ran in the store. When it was her chance in the line, Knight put a juice on the counter. She jumped looking up at him; she hadn't even seen him walk into the store. She laughed a little.

"Oh, you wanted a juice too?" she asked.

"No. I knew you weren't going to do what I told you to do," he responded, she smirked. "Get in the truck, I got it."

Knight paid for the gum and juice. When they got in the truck, he pulled out a flask and handed it to her. She took a swig. He touched the flask to her mouth again. She took another swig, then he shook and popped open the juice and gave it to her.

"This is what it's like ridin' with a young nigga," he said.

He rolled down all the windows and blasted the music. She could feel the beat rumbling under her seat. They hit 75 headed to the airport. Londyn curled up in the seat and leaned onto the console between them. Then without warning, Knight felt her hand grabbing his crotch. She grabbed as much of him as she could, letting her hand comfortably rest there. He could feel her look up at him, he couldn't help but smile. He opened his legs to give room for his swelling. If that's what she needed to comfort her, he wasn't gonna stop her.

At the airport, he unloaded her.

"Why do you have diapers in your trunk?" Londyn asked confused.

"People have babies, they get gifts."

"Who do you know that's having a baby?"

"Do you want me to save these for you? For when you have my baby?"

"No," Londyn shook her head as he took her luggage out of the trunk.

"You got this sweetheart. You have to walk in there believing that you can do it. The only way you walk out of that presentation is with a yes. You got that?" He held her chin and looked in her eyes.

"Yes Sgt. Knight," she finally had a smile on her face.

"Big daddy loves you," he said in all seriousness. He was determined to get her to call him that. He kissed her on the back of the hand. She turned to walk into the terminal and he turned to get in his car.

"Knight!" she called out. He turned around. "I love you, too." They stared at each other for a few seconds, but it felt like an eternity. It was like their souls were communicating in the midst of Hartsfield-Jackson's busy airport drop off. There weren't any taxis, no skycaps, no police whistles, or passengers bustling to and from the row of sliding doors. There was just Knight and Londyn.

When Londyn touched down, she had a selfie from Knight waiting for her. *Aww, he's so cute*. After she got checked in, she texted Micah to have the boys call her before they got settled for bed. Their usual routine was to see their mother's face at the bus stop in the afternoons. Since she was out of town, they had to arrange for a sitter to pick them up from school and keep them until Micah got off work.

Ace and Deuce called her to give the run down on their respective days. Londyn felt like all was right in the world. Even though she was super nervous, she wanted to snuggle in for a good night's sleep to be fresh for her meeting at Anastacia's corporate office. She wanted to be ready for any objection they had. They needed Libra. Period. It was her job to get her client the gig. Londyn and Libra had little mouths to feed.

Knight: WYD?

Londyn: Wishing I could put my head in your lap.

Londyn, who was lying in bed, hopped up to take a picture of herself in the reflection of the hotel bathroom. She artfully took a few pictures from the back to show him the contour of her back and the roundness of her ass. *Click. Click. Click.* Pick the best one. *Send.* The lighting was amazing. The bright feature was perfect for applying make-up, the dimmer was great for sexy shots. Knight FaceTimed Londyn.

"I thought you said you didn't want any more kids," Knight said as soon as Londyn answered.

"I don't," she snickered falling onto the soft, hotel bed.

"Why are you sending me shots like that, girl? You gon' make me put a baby in you!"

"Shut up!" Londyn roared. "You know what? I forgot to take out the trash at my house. I always take it out before I go out of town."

"I took it out."

"You did? When?"

"When you were running around looking crazy," he laughed.

"Oh Knight! Thank you so much! You are so good to me." The smile on her face brought a smile to his. Megawatt. Melt.

"So...Ms. Londyn...are you going to let me see what's on the other side of that pic you sent?"

"You already know what it looks like."

"Refresh my memory...let me see what you're wearing."

"Nothing...I don't have on anything."

"I bet that looks nice on you. Lemme see."

Londyn coyly bit her lip and stared at his gorgeous face in the frame. He could tell she was thinking about his request. With the light from the bathroom sending a soft cascade into the rest of the room, she pulled the phone away from her face, extending her arm so he could see more of her body. His eyes widened as she used the other hand to rub on her breast. Soon, her face was no longer in view, but his was closer than it was before. She kept taking the phone down...down...down until the money shot was in the frame. She propped it up using a pillow giving him a view of her from the neck down.

Knight subconsciously licked his lips wishing he could put them on the set of lips he was looking at. She put her hand between her legs and massaged herself. Her breathing increased as she was as nervous to be doing something like this as she was excited that he was so in it. She could hear him moaning and encouraging her by saying, "Mmm hmm," without his eyes leaving the screen. "Cum for me," he whispered watching her pleasure herself. His sexy voice was all she needed to accompany the increasingly fast movements her hands were making. Knight heard her loud pants and saw her body writhing on the bed. He was all too familiar with what that meant.

She gathered the phone and brought it up to her face. They looked at each other, not saying a word.

"Sweet dreams, Sgt. Knight."

"I love you."

"I love you, too.

Kelis
"Caught Out There"

I hate you so much right now
   I hate you so much right now
      I hate you so much right now
Ahhhhh...

Chapter 19

Londyn woke up in her cozy hotel bed ready to take on the world. Surprisingly, she slept like a baby. She thought that was possibly due to ending her night on a high note. Knight had this way of making her feel completely comfortable. She was becoming more comfortable in her own skin and more confident in herself. He made her feel like she could take on the world. It was the same feeling that she felt with Kaden.

With Kaden, she lived each day like she was untouchable. He made her feel like that from day one. She had his full attention. There were other girls gunning for him, but he quickly made it known that she was the only one who he had a heart for. His eyes wandered, but not that heart. His intentions were good and he tried to do right by her.

Knight had that same charisma. Kaden was more outgoing and seemed to be more emotionally available. Up to this point, Londyn didn't really care about how emotionally available Knight was or was not. Surely, his level of emotional availability was tied to the hole his mother left in his heart. Londyn was convinced he held on to some deep seeded hate and feelings of abandonment that he didn't want to relive at the hands of any woman. Londyn wasn't in it to fall in love. She really wasn't in it for him to get her rocks off. She appreciated that he had good conversation and he was a gentleman. She was perfectly fine with the modern day pen pal system they had going; talking on the phone all day, every day. He's the one who took things to the next level. Sure, he was sexy and all that, but she wasn't really ready to jump into bed with him. Especially with her insecurities. The first time was really good, but she was sure that was just because it was the first time. Hell, Micah hadn't touched her in months! Somehow, she didn't think Knight would get better. Boy, did he surprise her.

Now, here they were several months later exchanging I love you's. She still had unresolved feelings for her husband although he'd seemed to be moving right along just fine without her. When she saw Micah's contact pop up in her phone when receiving a text or call, she still got butterflies. Nervousness, excitement, or anguish, she didn't know, but there was still a physical reaction.

It was all one-sided, though, so she didn't feel bad for carrying on with Knight. At all. At least she hadn't introduced him to her sons. She wouldn't even let him in the house when they were there. She and Knight were able to have a relationship that was separate from that aspect of her life. Even if he kept making hints about meeting them and moving in. It's like their relationship existed in a bubble, in a totally separate plane.

Londyn slid out of the amazing hotel bed. It was a painful process. The uber soft, down comforter was holding her hostage completely and she didn't mind it one bit. She missed her boys, but appreciated not waking up super early to wrestle them out of their beds and fight them to get ready for school. Micah was dealing with that this morning, something he wasn't used to.

When her phone started ringing, she was sure it was Libra. And it was.

"Good morning, sugar plum!" Libra sang into the phone.

"Well somebody's bright eyed and bushy tailed."

"Yes! I didn't get any sleep last night. I'm so nervous."

"I am too, but surprisingly, I slept well."

"I think my baby felt my energy, she didn't sleep either."

"Get off my phone! Girl, don't be sending all of that nervous energy over here! I don't waaaaaaaant iiiiiiiiiit!"

"Ok, ok, ok! I just wanted to wish you luck today. You are the best! I have faith in you! Brang home dat bacon gul!"

Londyn laughed and hung up the phone. Then the FaceTime rang immediately after. *What kinda crazy song and dance is this girl about to do on my phone?* "Hello?"

"Who are you having sex with Londyn?!" Micah boomed across the phone. Londyn looked at the phone, completely caught off guard. Thinking Libra was calling back, Londyn hadn't even bothered to look to see who was FaceTiming her, she just answered the phone.

"Is something wrong with the boys?" she asked. They had been the only topic of discussion since they had the text fight about Micah introducing Jennifer. And he was FaceTiming her relatively early in the morning.

"WHO ARE YOU HAVING SEX WITH LONDYN?!" He yelled louder.

"That's none of your business."

"It is if you're sleeping with him in our bed."

"You moved out, remember? It's *my* bed. And we aren't doing much sleeping."

"How many niggas are you passing your shit out to? I found a lot of rubbers!"

"Found?"

"The boys were playing and knocked over the trash. A bunch of condom wrappers fell out." *I emptied all of the trash cans.*

"Why were you in my house?"

"WHO ARE YOU HAVING SEX WITH LONDYN?!" *Oooh, he big mad.* Londyn's stomach was instantly nervous, the type of nervous she thought she was going to be waking up to with this huge presentation looming. The type of nervous she was yesterday when Knight picked her up.

"WHY WERE YOU IN MY HOUSE?!"

"It's OUR house!!"

"No it's not! Remember you moved out so you could be with Jennifer?"

"I didn't move out to be...THIS ISN'T ABOUT ME!"

"The hell it's not! You moved out on your own. I didn't ask you or make you leave. Now you're going through my damn trash and questioning me about some condom wrappers. Seems like a real stalker move to me."

"So you're calling me a stalker?"

"I didn't say you were a stalker, I said it was a stalker move."

"WHO IS HE?!"

"You don't know him."

"Oh, so it's not Jay or Terrell? The other guys you were sleeping with?"

"You know I didn't have sex with them. It was all talking! It was all emotional. I was getting the conversation and attention I wasn't getting from you. It was wrong and I apologized. Whatever. You're gonna bring this up for the rest of our lives I guess. I'm not doing this shit with you."

Londyn ended the call. She looked at herself in the palatial mirror with the amazing make-up lighting that just the night before was perfect for the sexy pictures she sent Sgt. Knight. Now, her whole disposition looked frantic. Her eyes were wild, her breathing was fast and her heart was beating out of control. She heard the buzzing from her phone vibrating as the ringer rang out. Micah was FaceTiming again.

She'd never just flat out ignored him. Londyn made it her business to have the relationship between them be as cordial as possible. He was helping her raise her sons, who he'd adopted as his own and treated as his own. Whenever he called or texted, she answered. She was still halfway waiting on him to come back and say that he was sorry and wanted to come home.

Instead, their communication was only about little league football games, pick-ups and drop-offs…all through text.

```
Micah
Missed FaceTime
```

She was retracing her steps back through the house as best she could with her foggy memory. It hadn't even been 24 hours, but since her nervousness had her all over the place she had a hard time remembering.

How did he get in the house? Micah had installed an external garage door opener that only needed a code to open the garage door. Since things between them were so cordial, well he barely even acknowledged her existence, she didn't see the need to change the code. Especially since he moved out on his own. Like why would he break back into a place where he didn't want to be? Which now seemed to be exactly what he'd done. So he'd gone in the house and went through the trash cans.

```
Micah
Missed FaceTime
```

She threw the phone on the bed so she wouldn't be discombobulated by the sound of it vibrating on the granite countertops of the bathroom.

But I emptied all the trash cans. Londyn thought back through her steps. There was only one can in the house that she hadn't emptied; it was in the corner of her room. She didn't empty it because she didn't use it. Apparently Knight had used it to dispose of a condom wrapper or two or three.

Why does he even care? She was anxious to get back home now. She didn't care about him having access to the house before, but now it was a different story. Who knew what he was going to do. Spray paint the walls. Destroy her TVs. Bleach her clothes. Set the whole thing on fire. Who knew?

This was not at all what she needed with the meeting she was about to walk into. She needed to be on her toes, with a clear head, not worried about whether or not her house was going to be still standing when she landed back in Atlanta the next day. She entertained the possibility of getting this deal wrapped up that day, maybe she could get an early flight back that night.

She proceeded to get dressed. To get her mojo back, she needed some music. When she grabbed her phone to open Pandora, she saw:

```
Micah
Missed call (3)

Micah
Missed FaceTime call (7)

Micah
iMessage (2)
```

She didn't think enough time had passed for him to have called her that many times. Londyn opened the texts. Micah had sent a screenshot of Knight's private Instagram profile. *Wow!* She started laughing. So many questions, not enough answers. She opened Pandora to her Beyoncé channel. That was exactly what she needed to get her head in the right space.

She got her whole life, singing and dancing for all of 30 seconds before Micah's calls interrupted the song again, and again, and again, so she just began speaking positive affirmations.

"I am strong. I am powerful. I am a goddess. Money comes easily and frequently in many different forms. I am a bad ass manager. I will close this deal today. I am a people magnet, they gravitate toward me. People love me and want to help me succeed. I have exactly what it takes to close this deal today."

Londyn looked at her phone before opening it to call her Uber.

```
Micah
Missed call (5)

Micah
Missed FaceTime call (4)

Micah
iMessage (7)
```

She couldn't even entertain him right now. The meeting she was about to have could change her life, and Libra's too. This was what they needed after being in the shadows for so long. Londyn didn't really want the spotlight, but she did want to be a successful manager and get a few other clients on her roster. Money was money, she had bills to pay.

Being a mother, she didn't want to turn her ringer off in case it was one of the boys calling her from the school. But they knew she was out of town and probably wouldn't call her. They'd call Micah first. She also couldn't afford to be in the meeting with her phone buzzing like that. It would throw her off her game and have the reps at Anastacia thinking she had too much going on to really be focused on the business at hand.

Walking out of the hotel, there was a chill as fall to New Yorkers felt like winter to a southerner. She bundled herself up as she walked through the automatic doors into the world that was still spinning no matter what she had going on. She braved the slightly hostile stares from random strangers she'd never seen before and would never see again. The doorman was the only person who seemed to be pleasant and Londyn knew that was only because he wanted a tip. There was such a sea of cabs, she didn't even need to get an Uber. That was the difference in culture between Atlanta and NYC. But not being accustomed to life in The Big Apple, the thought of catching a cab hadn't even occurred to her.

As she rode in the backseat, her eyes darted from high rise to high rise, block after block. There was scaffolding everywhere and people speed walking in front of cars while drivers barely hesitated to avoid hitting them. Then there were couriers on bikes malibuing in and out of walking and driving traffic. They weaved on the bicycles like they were taking leisurely rides on isolated country roads. The convergence of it all had Londyn on the brink of a heart attack.

```
Micah
Missed call (10)

Micah
Missed FaceTime call (2)

Micah
iMessage (7)

Knight
iMessage
```

Londyn opened her phone. She needed to tell him what was going on, but now was not the time. Still, she wanted to see what he had to say.

```
Knight: GM beautiful! U ready?
Londyn: As ready as I'm gonna be.
Knight: You got this sweetheart!
Knight: 
Londyn: 
```

Londyn appreciated him being her calm in the midst of the storm. Dealing with her emotions and the boys' emotions through this separation was enough. Now, it seemed that Micah actually cared...one way or another. She couldn't understand where all of his emotion was coming from. What did he expect was going to happen when he left? Did he think she was just going to shrivel up and die, never to be touched by a man again?

Londyn arrived at Anastacia and killed it. She rethought the entire campaign and gave the marketing team a fresh spin that they had not even considered. They were visibly impressed. When she saw facial expressions with raised eyebrows, she knew she had them. It was like she turned a lightbulb on in everybody's head all at once. She kept going with the pitch anyway. This was her last chance. Londyn had to give it all she had. She was prepared for the cookie cutter response of, "We'll discuss it and get back to you." To which she would let them know she was in town for another day and through the weekend if that's what was needed to seal the deal. Instead, they told her to wait in the hallway. To her, that was already a win.

She tried her best to conceal her giddiness. It was so hard, especially since she'd impressed herself, so she knew they were blown away. If Anastacia didn't take her deal for Libra, it was already perfectly packaged for another company. And with the adrenaline she was feeling from this presentation, she wouldn't stop until she got Libra a winning deal.

She was confident that Anastacia would bite. And they did! Libra was set to be the newest face of Anastacia! They would have their legal team draw up the paperwork to cover the details. The contract was to begin in 30 days! Londyn thanked them profusely and made a note in her calendar to send her insider a gift basket thanking her for the intel. Londyn couldn't wait to call Libra who she knew was chomping at the bit waiting to hear from her.

She dug her phone out of her purse:

```
Micah
Missed call (8)
```

```
Micah
Missed FaceTime call (7)

Micah
iMessage (1)
```

This man was determined to blow her up all day! She called Libra and gave her the good news. The deal was in the high six-figures for Libra, which meant low six-figures for Londyn. Talk about a win! Libra was over the moon. She screamed and cried, waking up her baby. She thanked Londyn over and over, along with professing how good God was. It was such a good feeling to be winning. Londyn stressed how much work they had to do to get Libra's album finished and the first single polished. It was grind time. Thirty days for a new mommy would fly by in no time!

Londyn made it back to her hotel and stripped herself. She wasn't the type to walk around or sleep naked, but Knight had her feeling so sexy that she'd begun to feel herself. She could look at herself in the mirror and not be ashamed or dislike what she saw. Micah called again.

"So you've been ignoring me all day."

"I had business to tend to." She gave him an explanation she was not obligated to give, but felt obligated. In some ways, she still felt like they were walking through life as husband and wife.

"I bet if your boyfriend called, you'd talk to him."

"He's not my boyfriend."

"Well, you sure are giving it up like he is."

"Damn, can I get a hi-five for using protection?" Londyn starting laughing.

"You think this shit is funny! It's not funny! Does he know you're married?"

"Does Jennifer know you're married?"

"SHE IS MY FRIEND!" Micah yelled into the phone. There was so much animosity coming from him. Londyn thought it was both cute and scary.

"He is my friend."

"Bullshit Londyn!"

"Micah, listen. What I do in my house is my business. What you do in your apartment is your business. I don't ask what you do, where you go, or who you do it with. That's for you. I only ask that when you take my boys on family outings that you don't do it with multiple women. It looks really bad. I don't troll through your trash looking for answers. That's crazy. It if doesn't concern the boys, don't ask me about my life."

Londyn hung up the phone, then powered it off. She knew he was going to be calling repeatedly and it would annoy him. Then she thought that Knight might try to call, so she turned it back on and put Micah on 'Do Not Disturb.' She needed to talk to Knight before Micah got stupid and reached out to him.

"They gave you that contract, didn't they?" Knight asked as soon as he answered the phone.

"You know it!"

"That's my baby," Knight said with a little excitement in his voice. She could tell he was smiling. "Let me call you back."

"Wait...wait...wait. Listen," she took a deep breath, "Micah knows who you are. He's called, texted, and FaceTimed me like 50 times since this morning. I don't know how he figured out who you were, but he has your IG profile. I'm letting you know in case he reaches out to you." Knight never liked or commented on Londyn's posts. The single, solitary time he did, her heart nearly exploded when she saw the two happy face emojis with heart eyes. She knew she must've been super cute that day.

"What? He has my...Londyn, I don't have time for this shit," Knight said and the call was disconnected. She expected his reaction not to be exactly pleasant, but not that extreme. Her heart crashed into her feet. Less than 24 hours before they were exchanging I Love You's now nothing. The rejection that she'd feared had finally happened.

Knight had a fight on his hands. Otto was standing in his office, face red. He was talking to Knight when Londyn called and was instantly irritated that Knight even took the call.

"Continue," Knight said bored and irritated at this grievance. It was always something with Otto. He managed to find a problem with everything. He acted like it was his duty to find fault in the way Knight ran his truck. Knight knew that as a whistleblower, Otto had no problem jumping over his head, which had happened a few times and Lieutenant Knowlen had no problem sending him back through the chain of command. Otto couldn't think that he could circumvent Knight to get his way. He didn't have to respect the man, he had to respect the rank.

"You gave Josten the time *I* requested."

"I gave Josten the time *he* requested."

"I put in for the 15th through the 21st. Those are my days!" Otto raised his voice. The other guys looked back towards Knight's office because they heard the yelling.

"So did Josten."

"I put in for it first. I know I did. I was talking about it before he did."

"Let me show you something," Knight opened his drawer. He was already prepared for this fight. He'd received Josten's request a week prior to Otto's and once he realized that he'd already given the time off to Josten, he knew this was going to happen. For that reason, he kept both written requests in his top drawer and counted down the days until the new schedule came out.

"I don't want to see anything! You boys always do this!"

"Boys?" Knight stood up out of his somewhat cushy desk chair. "Exactly what do you mean by that?"

"Well," Otto knew he meant 'boys' in the inferior racial connotation, but he couldn't get away with that. "You boys...boys from the truck...gang up on me. I don't know why you favor Josten over me. Maybe because y'all are so much younger than me! Y'all are homeboys and shit! Fraternizing after hours. Now you're showing favoritism."

"I won't be too many more of your boys," Knight was calm, but firm and still standing. "Here are the requests. I knew you were going to do this. I had 'em right here waiting."

"Don't gimme that shit!" Otto said knocking the requests out of Knight's hands. "You had him resubmit after I did."

"So what do you want to do now? You wanna go to Knowlen? Go ahead," Knight brushed him off, grabbed the papers and put them in the locked drawer of his desk. He walked into the common area where the other guys were. It would have been so easy to have Otto transferred with Pops being Chief of the entire department. There were 65 other firehouses Otto could've called home. Knight wasn't going to take the easy way out.

"You know he won't be happy until you give him his little vacation," Sterling said.

"Even if I switched Josten's vacation to different days, Otto will still find something to be mad about." Knight shook his head. "He's gettin' on my damn nerves."

"I already bought my plane ticket boss. Me and the lil' lady are going to Puerto Rico!"

"It doesn't matter. I don't care what you do. You put in for it first!"

"All Otto wants to do is sit at home and beat off all day!" Sterling said and they all laughed. Then Lieutenant Knowlen appeared around the corner. Before he could even open his mouth, Knight raised his hand and began walking toward his office. Lieutenant Knowlen started laughing.

"Lieutenant," Otto started.

"Pump the brakes Otto," Lieutenant Knowlen responded. "Knight, Otto thinks you're showing favoritism. Who put in their time off request first?"

"Josten. He put his request in eight days before Otto. I tried to show him the papers and he slapped them out of my hand saying I told Josten to resubmit with an earlier date."

"Did you?"

"No Lieutenant."

"Otto," Lieutenant Knowlen said, "it's hard to help you when you have a problem with everything Knight does. You gotta man up. And I heard Josten say he bought a plane ticket, so he has concrete plans. Even if we did move things around, which we won't, that would be an inconvenience to him. Next time, put your request in as soon as you *think* you want to have it off. I'm not going to keep being the peacekeeper between you two. It's getting old."

"Tell him not to favor those boys...uh, everybody over me!" Otto shouted

"Boys? Now, I'm not the one to raise your voice to. Check that attitude before you walk into my office."

"Yes Lieutenant."

"Now, you boys go play nice," Lieutenant Knowlen laughed. "Wait...Knight, you stay." Knight took a deep breath as both men waited on Otto to close the door. "You could've told Otto the time was already requested when he put his request in."

"Wouldn't matter Lieutenant, He'd find something else to complain about."

"Always does," Lieutenant Knowlen chuckled.

Knight walked past the common area straight to the bay. The bay housed two fire trucks and an ambulance. On the other side was a gym. They had free weights, a treadmill, an elliptical, a boxing bag and two bench presses.

He grabbed the boxing gloves and jabbed the bag a few times. Otto was like an annoying fly that you couldn't kill and wouldn't go away. He just buzzed and swirled, buzzed and swirled. The alternative to him being annoying was kissing ass, which he did every chance he got. So predictable, so annoying. Knight knew it really was nothing personal, because he'd watched Otto do this song and dance with two others. The difference with the other sergeants was, they had been transferred in. With Knight rising within the house, it presented a real problem to Otto.

Of the brothers, only Knight and Titus had advanced to sergeant. Castor was too busy chasing ass and covering his married tracks; Ares was focused on being a single father to Hermes. Pops was proud of them all. They were keeping the Knight name legendary in the firefighting community.

Knight continued to work off some steam, when he felt his phone vibrate. He saw Castor's name appear on the screen and rolled his eyes.

Castor: What's up for Sunday?
Knight: Chillin' wassup?
Castor: Everybody's off!

Castor: 🍔 🌭 🍖 🥬 🍳

Knight: Hell yeah!

Castor: 🍺

Knight: What about mom?

Castor: You know she'll be there!

Knight: I'll clean the grill. Tell her I want some mac n cheese.

Castor: You tell her!

The chances that all five of them were off only happened once every three or four months. Castor was usually the one who kept the band of brothers on track for their family gatherings. He had a big heart, like his mother Regina. Even though two of her boys were married, being surrounded by her sons, ex-husband, bonus son, and grandsons, she was always treated like a queen.

That exchange lifted Knight's mood. Now, he needed to deal with Londyn. She said Micah had found out who he was. He'd rushed her off the phone to deal with Otto and his shenanigans. Now, he needed to find out what was really going on.

"Hi," Londyn answered sounding somber. She was sprawled across her soft hotel bed. Her balloon was totally popped when Knight said he didn't have time for her drama. She couldn't imagine what insult he was going to add to the injury.

"Tell me again what's happening."

"Micah found condom wrappers in my trash and called me asking about you. Somehow, he figured out who you were."

"I took your trash out myself! Wait...why is he going through your trash?"

"I don't know."

"Didn't *he* leave you?"

"Yes," he could tell her feelings were hurt all the way around. She sounded so sad.

"Apparently, I missed a can when I was rounding up all of the bags." Londyn had emptied all of the trash into bigger bags and tied the bags up by the door. Knight actually put them in the trash. She knew Micah was lying about the boys playing over there because of the way that trash can was positioned, it was literally impossible for them to one, have knocked it down and two, they wouldn't have just been playing in her room.

"So what does he want with me? He scared now because you got another man in your face? The one who his sons are going to be calling Daddy?" Knight laughed. Londyn perked up in the bed.

"You aren't leaving me?"

"For his stalking ass? NO!" He laughed again.

"When I called you earlier, you said you didn't have time to deal with this."

"I had some shit going on at work. I'm not going anywhere."

"I know this is a lot for you to deal with. I'm sorry about all of this. If you want to leave, I totally understand. The last thing I want is to bring you drama."

"Londyn. I'm not going anywhere. I love you," he said. Londyn beamed.

Sam Cooke
"A Change Gon' Come"

It's been a long,
A long time coming,
But I know,
A change gon' come, oh yes it will.

Chapter 20

Londyn couldn't wait to get home. She hadn't received any calls from the security company, but that didn't mean her home was safe. Micah had the alarm code as well. She had been kicking herself in the ass since Micah FaceTimed her to ask who she'd been seeing. Kenzie told her to change everything. Londyn didn't see a reason to. This was a total invasion of privacy though. Her relationship with Micah, not as a couple, but as two people relate to each other, was going left at the speed of light.

Knight was calling hogs after a 24-hour shift, but he told her to plan to come see him once he woke up. After that new-age phone sex episode, he needed to see her in person.

As the Uber bent the corner to her house, Londyn became increasingly nervous. Surely she was over-reacting and her house was still standing. He wouldn't burn the house down. Or would he?

The house was intact. In fact, Micah even turned the alarm system back on, which surprised Londyn. Everything looked normal, until she got to her room. In the center of the bed was a family picture of her, Micah, and the boys, next to the box of Magnums and lube that she'd hidden in her toiletry closet so the boys wouldn't see it, which meant he actually had to look for it.

"I forgot I even had lube. Sure don't need to use this anymore," she laughed out loud. She'd gotten to the point where Knight practically made her wet on command. Londyn peeled off her clothes, poured a glass of wine, and took a load off. Once the call from Knight came through, she hopped in the shower and raced to his house. They'd both been through a range of emotions in the 48 hours since they'd seen each other. She was excited and anxious to be in his arms. As she drove along daydreaming about how he was going to lay her body down, she was jolted by the loud, grinding sound of metal. The semi-truck in the lane next to her swerved and bumped into her truck. She flashed her lights and right turning signal to say that she was pulling over.

She cautiously jumped out and so did he. They met between the vehicles. He expressed that he was sorry for hitting her. Londyn showed him on her truck where the touch occurred. There were definitely scrapes on her truck, the metal was dented, it was beyond cosmetic.

Londyn called the police, and called, and called. The number was busy. She called Knight to tell him what had happened and he freaked out. "Are you ok?" he asked with urgency in his voice. She told him she was fine and was trying to get through to 9-1-1. She half-heartedly laughed about 9-1-1 ringing busy. She was more concerned about the traffic speeding past. With her vivid imagination, she could see a car swerving, hitting her truck, then squeezing her body between her truck and a cement pillar. She decided to wait inside.

When the cop arrived, he was black, just like the truck driver. She thought, *Good. Let's get this over with. He's already admitted to it. Let's get this report and move on.*

"What happened?" the officer asked the truck driver first.

"I was drivin' long, an heard a *skurrrrr*, looked up and saw we had done touched," the truck driver said.

"Oh naw! You admitted to me that you swerved in my lane," Londyn corrected.

"Naw suh, I told her we touched. We touched!"

"Ain't no touched! You came into my lane," Londyn wanted to be clear without being an angry black woman. Her words were forceful without the added neck rolling and upset-hand-on-the-hip stance.

"Where you going looking like that anyway, ma'am?" The officer asked.

"Cut off shorts and a shirt?" Londyn frowned up her face.

"Got cha legs all showing. Let me see your license and registration." Londyn and the truck driver were prepared for that already. They handed it over. "Does your husband know you are out here dressed like that?" The officer asked seeing two last names on Londyn's license.

"I'm not out here dressed like anything. My ass isn't hanging out, my boobs are covered. It's not like he cares anyway. We're separated."

"Whatchu mean? He lef' alladat?" The truck driver chimed in, Londyn rolled her eyes.

"Good for you!" the officer said.

"Good for me, how?"

"You're free now. You can do whatever you want!" he said smiling.

"I don't see anything good about breaking up a black family. It's hard enough to raise our black boys to be upstanding black family men. This is just perpetuating the cycle. Nothing to celebrate," Londyn said with a straight face.

"Wow! Most women are excited about it."

"No they aren't. They aren't left with a choice, so they just feel like they have to make the best of it. I'm not happy about my marriage falling apart. I don't see anything good about. At all."

The truck driver and officer looked at each other. The three of them continued trying to figure out who was at fault. The officer wrote them both tickets and told them to duke it out in court. Londyn was pissed!

She hopped back in the truck and turned around to go home. She let Knight know she wasn't going to make it.

Londyn: Going to the crib

```
Knight: Why???
Londyn: Too upset
Knight: I need you
Knight: Bad
Knight: I'm frustrated
Londyn: Come work it out on me! I'm
frustrated too!
Knight: I don't know if you can handle
me like this
```

She drove home and hopped in the shower, feeling dirty from standing on the side of the highway with cars speeding past zooming hot exhaust on her. Her doorbell rang shortly after she toweled off.

"This was supposed to celebrate your contract, but I think it's more to calm you down now," he said holding a bottle of Moscato. She opened the door wide and stepped into his arms. He looked down at her putting his hand around her face and pressing his lips to hers. She was visibly shaken.

"Mmmm," she said sucking on his bottom lip while he tried to pull away. He got the hint and kissed her some more.

"Have you talked to your husband?"

"Would you stop calling him that?!"

"But that's what he is," Knight said laughing. He could see that she wasn't. Her face was straighter than straight.

"Yeah, he apologized for blowing up at me."

"Why does he care what you do? He's so confused."

"He wasn't confused when he packed his shit."

"What do you want Londyn? What do you want with us?" Londyn looked at him. She hoped to avoid this kind of conversation. She wasn't ready to make any decisions or put a title or boundaries on anything. He never said it, but she was sure Knight was involved with someone else on some level. Even though they saw each other regularly and spoke daily, he wasn't sleeping in her bed every night. And even if he was, he could easily find time to be with another chick. She saw and heard the way women responded to him. He couldn't fend them all off.

"I want you to be a part of my life. I love having you around. You encourage me, you motivate me, you make me feel sexy and desired. I don't want to give you up. I really, really like you…this…us."

Knight nodded his head and took a deep breath. He turned to her. Now was as good a time as any…

"What?" she asked. "Why are you looking at me like that?" He clearly wanted to tell her something. He looked down, then away.

"Let me tell you about this fool at work," he punked out. They talked about his beef with Otto and his family cookout the next day. Just talking about Otto got Knight riled up. She could see where the frustration was coming from.

He walked into her room, then called out for her.

"Come here big head! What's this?" She found Knight butt naked, spread eagle on his back. She approached the bottom of the bed and crawled up until he could feel her breath on the head of his penis. He looked at her and caressed her face. Using a flickering tongue movement, she licked up his shaft, then took the head in her mouth and let it fall out again. She repeated this movement until she could feel him squirming for more. She released a torrent of real black girl magic on him like he'd never experienced before. She loved feeling his erection in her mouth. It helped that every other time she tried, he wouldn't let her really do it. She had to show him what he was missing out on.

When he got to a point where he couldn't take it anymore, he leaned forward and picked her up, bringing her to sit down on him.

"We need protection," he said.

"I want to feel you."

"You sure you're ready for this?"

"Yes." She sat on him, slowly, cautiously. Londyn found a rhythm pleasurable to her hips and her man's needs. Knight pulled her face down and deeply kissed her, thrusting himself into her until she felt her body shake all over. He flipped her on her back and spread her legs apart, pushing down on her thighs. He was pounding her roughly, but it felt so good. This was clearly stemming from the frustration he said he had.

"You can't leave me," she moaned.

"I don't want to," he said slowing down his stroke.

"You can't, big daddy. I need this." Knight looked in her eyes and smiled. That was the fuel to his fire. She'd finally said it.

"Oh, I'm big daddy, now?"

"Yeah...it's all yours big daddy."

"This my shit?"

"Yeah....yeah...yeah!" He went harder and deeper.

"You mean it?"

"Yeah!" Londyn began clawing at his chest and squeezing his arms. Harder and deeper. He kept moving while her legs quivered uncontrollably.

"Mmmm, big daddy knows what to do to you," he turned her over and flattened her to her stomach. Londyn started shaking her own head. She knew it was about to be a wrap for them both. Watching himself go in and out took him over the edge. But not before she felt his whole, entire back in those strokes. The power of his big, strong body tense up and release let her know he enjoyed her body as his playground.

Knight collapsed next to her on the bed. He looked over at her and grabbed her face. "You my baby?" he asked, voice sounding innocent, like he hadn't just pile-drived her.

She shook her head 'yes.'

The next day was all about the Knight boys, and their women. Jasmine and Kori were in the kitchen while the brothers watched the youngest generation of Knight boys play around in the yard. Regina was back and forth between the kitchen and the deck. The fall weather was perfect. It was sunny out, but they weren't baking on the deck. There were hints of crispness in the air.

The grill was packed with hamburgers, ribs, and hotdogs. Pops manned it like the proud Pop he was, until Titus grabbed the tongs from him.

"Sit down old man!" Titus joked.

"Where do you see an old man? Boy, don't make me pull this here shirt off and show you were you got it from!" The brothers laughed. Both Pops and Titus stood at an impressive 6'4". Age aside, Pops was still in better shape than most of the men half his age. He still had a six-pack. Because he passed down those excellent genes to his brood, his boys maintained their definition with minimal workouts.

"Hercules! Hercules!" Regina teased.

"Ugh! Ma! Uggggh!"

"Both of y'all sit down, before I make examples out of you!" Ares belted standing up. He looked like a superhero and had a voice like Isaac Hayes. He was 6'6" and a half, plus a good 20 pounds bigger. Broad shoulders and a chiseled face. All muscle. And he always emphasized the half, as if it mattered at that height. Tall is tall. But having served a stint in the NBA, the half did matter to him. People always did a double take when he walked past. He looked like he tossed around cement blocks growing up instead of playing with G.I. Joes. Hermes was definitely taking after the Knight gene for looks and a firm, muscular physique.

"I bought y'all some fruit for those fine bodies! All of my boys look *good*!" Regina said placing a tray of pineapples, strawberries, and blueberries on the table. Jasmine and Kori brought out potato salad and baked beans, Castor sat out the bread and condiments.

"Before these Dirty Birds kick off and win this game against the Panthers, I want to propose a toast!" Everybody grabbed their respective beers, wine glasses, sodas, and Capri Suns. "I am so proud of you boys. I feel so blessed to have you in my life. And to think, all of my boys have made something of their lives. I could not have been more blessed to have a better bunch of sons, grandsons, daughters-in-law, and woman in my life."

"I'm not your woman," Regina cut her eyes.

"You'll always be my woman. You welcomed Baby with open arms and helped me raise him." Knight put his arm around Regina and kissed her forehead. "I love you all and I want you to know that nothing means more in this whole wide world than each of you...my family. Here's to many more family gatherings and will one of you fools give me a granddaughter *please*."

"Please!" Regina added.

"We haven't had a girl born in this family in four generations!"

"Jasmine?" Castor looked at his wife and winked.

"No hell! You better look at one of ya brothers! This shop is closed for business."

"Don't look at me," as everybody did being that Kori was the only other female of birthing age in the family. Kori shook her head and everybody laughed.

"Cheers!" Castor said. They all clanked drinks, hugged and kissed each other just in time for kick off.

The next morning, Londyn was awakened by the alarm on her phone. She barely opened one eye to find the phone. She hit the snooze icon and closed her eyes again. *What the hell?* She asked herself thinking she saw a locked screen full of messages. She squinted her eyes and held up her phone. Her locked screen was covered. Calls and texts.

"Maaaaaan, what is it now?" Obviously something had happened overnight, she almost didn't want to know what. From what she could see, none of those trying to reach her had anything in common really. Texts and a call from Kenzie, the same from Libra, then there was Andre, a friend of a friend who she only saw at events, but he rarely contacted her, then the group chat with Nika, Johna, April, and Ashley.

Londyn opened her text screen and saw the little blue circle next to few more texts from people aside from the ones she'd already seen indicating which threads were unread. She opened the top thread with the girls.

Nika: This is hitting home now. Did y'all see the news?

Johna: 😟😟😟

Johna: Why do they keep killing our men?!?!?!?!?!

April: OMG! AGAIN??

Nika: Yes! Right here in ATL!!

Nika: SMH

Ashley: This is getting out of control.

Nika: Exactly! Some people caught it on video and posted it on Facebook. I reposted it on my page. One of the vids showed everything!

Johna: NIKAAAAAAAA! That's horrible! Why would you do that?

Nika: People need to know what's going
on!

April: I just saw the video. That's
horrible.

As Londyn was reading the thread, feeling incensed that another incident had caused yet another black man to lose his life at the hands of the police, Kenzie called through.

"Londyn!" Kenzie didn't even wait for Londyn to greet her. "Oh my gosh! Have you talked to Knight?"

"Huh?"

"HAVE YOU TALKED TO KNIGHT?! Did you hear about what happened?" Londyn's heart stopped beating. At that moment, Deuce came running in the room and jumped on her bed. He lunged at her and she pushed him off. Instant reflex.

"What's wrong, Ma?" he asked.

"Kenzie. What are you talking about?"

"Turn on the news. A black firefighter was shot and killed by the police last night. His last name is Knight, they..."

Londyn hung up the phone and immediately called Knight. Straight to voicemail. Call. Straight to voicemail. Call. Voicemail. Call. Voicemail. Call. Voicemail. Call. Voicemail. Call. Voicemail. Call. Voicemail. She wasn't breathing, and her heart wasn't beating.

She called Kenzie back. By this time, Ace had jumped in the bed and was wrestling with his younger brother.

"His phone is going straight to voicemail! Stop it boys! Stop!" Londyn yelled with tears streaming from her eyes. "Turn on the news!"

"Listen. I don't know if it's Knight. They don't have a first name. They only said a firefighter named Knight."

"What the...?" She whispered trying to keep her composure from crumbling. Her twin sons didn't know what was going on, but their mother was upset. They hadn't seen her cry much since they came back from the summer. There was the time when Ace had his breakdown about Micah not being there. That was a hard conversation, but she'd managed to keep her tears to a minimum. Otherwise, when she got emotional she'd run to 'take showers' in the middle of the day when she needed to release them.

They wrapped their arms around her.

"How can they release a last name? What kind of shit is that? Don't they know how panicked that makes people?"

"I know, I know," Kenzie started tearing up hearing her friend choke back sobs. This was not what Londyn needed right now, not after all that she'd been through in the last six months. "It was a traffic stop at a gas station and it was caught by a couple recording with their cell phones. You can hear him yell my name is Knight, I'm a firefighter."

"And they shot him?"

"Yeah, more cops showed up, more people stopped around the station, it became a thing real fast. He was trying to get up to get his credentials and one of the cops shot him."

"No! No! NO!" Londyn wailed. Getting a description wouldn't help, Knight and his brothers looked so much alike physically. She hadn't met them, but she'd seen pictures on his Instagram. "Let me check his page," she said. She knew that people always went to the recently departed to post #rip and #rih comments saying how much they would be missed. There were a few praying hand emojis and people asking dumbass questions like, 'Are you ok?' and 'What happened?' They were just as clueless as she was.

"Let's be positive. Since people know his last name, there is a lot of pressure on authorities to release his full name. It will certainly happen soon this morning."

"I can't do this, Kenzie. I can't."

"It won't be Knight. *Your* Knight."

"It's one of his brothers! They all have kids! He's the only one without kids."

"Get your boys to school and I'll be at your house by the time you get back from taking them to school."

Londyn had all but forgotten it was a school day. Ace and Deuce were surely going to miss the bus now. They were glued to the TV watching the breaking news about the altercation that occurred while they were counting sheep. They hadn't started throwing smut on the deceased's name yet, because they hadn't released his name. Either way, they always try to make the boys in blue look like their actions are justified.

Meanwhile, Londyn's Instagram feed was jumping with snippets of the video and still shots. She got off. She hated that people shared stuff like that. Had they no respect for the dead? And their families? His body wasn't even cold yet. She also didn't have the heart to look because she wasn't ready to face the 1-in-4 chance that it was *her* Knight. Call. Voicemail. Call. Voicemail.

"Ok boys, let's go brush," her voice cracked and she started crying again.

"Did you know this guy, Ma?" Ace asked her. He was the more sensitive of the two.

"It may be my friend or one of his brothers. He and all three of his brothers are firefighters." As Londyn thought about it, a few of his cousins were firefighters as well. Pops and his brother were also firefighters. It couldn't have been one of the old men though. Still, that decreased *her* Knight's chances of being the victim to like 1-in-6 or 1-in-8. Somewhere in there.

"Let us stay home with you, Ma. To make sure you're alright," Deuce said. Londyn looked at him and wanted to laugh, but couldn't find it in her.

"If it was Ace asking, I'd say yes, because he's like that. But you, Sir Deuce? You're just trying to get out of going to school today! Go brush!"

Londyn turned the TV to a 24-hour music station and went to brush her own teeth. Her eyes were red and watery. It was a familiar reflection. Sadness. Desperation. Hopelessness. Feeling like nothing was going to dissipate the grey cloud hovering over her head. Sadness. Her eyes were so sad.

"Lord, please, *please*, let Apollo be alright. In the name of Jesus, I ask that you have covered him so that he is alright. Lord please, please give me a sign," she broke down crying. She stood at her vanity head bent down. Ace came up behind her, the same height as she was and wrapped his arms around her.

He knew his mother. She'd been through a lot with his dad passing away and his other dad leaving. He'd caught her crying a few times through it all. He seemed to be so in tune with her. Deuce wasn't as observant, but Ace noticed when Londyn just disappeared from the living room or the office. He knew what was going on when they couldn't seem to find her right there in the house. Ace would slip away from his brother and take Londyn a bottle of water and Excedrin or simply take her Kleenex. Once he hugged her and they cried together. Their heart beat the same rhythm. In some ways, he was more in tune with her than he was with his identical twin. Londyn felt like Ace had his father, Kaden's spirit. It was really Kaden who was looking out for her through Ace.

She turned around to hug him and cried harder. He held her, there was nothing to say. The ringing phone made Londyn turn around instantly. It was Libra.

"Londyn, sweetie," Libra spoke.

"I don't know," Londyn admitted, her voice shaky.

"What? Oh no! You haven't heard from him?"

"No."

"Londyn," Libra started crying as well. "It's not him. I already asked God. It's not him."

"Libra."

"I'm serious, Londyn."

"I'll call you later."

"I'm sitting on top of my phone. I mean it."

"Kenzie is coming over."

"Good. I know it's hard. You said their whole family was in firefighting, so he's still going to be affected. But he's fine."

Londyn ended the call. Call. Voicemail. Call. Voicemail. She encouraged Ace to get ready so they wouldn't miss the first bell.

The three of them ran out to the truck and Londyn dropped them off at school, then made her way back home. Her stomach was in knots. It was all over the place. When she turned onto her street, Kenzie was standing in the driveway. She walked over to Londyn, hugging her and handed her a bag of ginger ale and saltines.

"I know how your stomach gets when you're nervous. I bought a croissant from Burger King."

"You know I can't eat right now."

"Yeah. So I have fruit too." Kenzie thought of everything! She was such a good friend. The ladies walked into the house. Kenzie wanted to ask if Knight had called or texted, but she knew he hadn't. Londyn's first call would have been to Kenzie if he had. Only she and Libra knew his name or what was going on between them. Call. Voicemail. Call. Voicemail.

Now, Londyn felt like she could watch the news. She didn't have to be mommy or be strong. That's why Kenzie was there. The news confirmed what Kenzie had already told her, but they were holding the victim's name until his family had been notified.

"That's crap! The family already knows!" Londyn yelled at the TV. That's why Knight's phone was turned off. Either it was him or one of his relatives, but if he was waiting for information, why would his phone be off? "I can't take this! This waiting game! It's too much!"

Knight stood looking at the body of his second oldest brother, Ares. He was 37. As strong as Knight knew his Pops was, identifying the body of one of his sons would have taken him under.

Knight walked down the long hallway to where his family was. They already knew it was Ares, because the rest of them were there. Regina was the only female in the room with the exception of a single female firefighter. Castor and Titus were sitting next to Pops. Titus was closest to Ares in age, they were only one year apart. He was destroyed. Literally inconsolable. Ares was his best friend. The Knight boys hadn't ever had to deal with a loss this close to home. Both of their parents were still alive, so were Pops parents. Regina's father had passed away over 20 years ago, but her mom lived with her six months of the year and her sister the rest of the year.

When Knight hit the door Pops looked at him eyes bloodshot red, watery, and pained.

"Baby...Baby, tell me...Baby, say it wasn't my boy," Pops sobbed. Knight just collapsed in the chair and put his head down. Two of their cousins were there, along with a few members from each of their fire houses. The men who were there were obviously close to the Knight family, considering themselves family, so there wasn't a dry eye in the room.

As fathers, Titus and Castor were hurting on a different level. Yes, Ares was their brother, but they had sons and couldn't imagine the agony Pops was in. Knight hadn't seen his father cry since his mother left. That was 19 years ago.

"We were all just together," Pops cried. "What the hell happened? We were just having beer and watching football. We were...we..."

Somehow, a reporter got through the developing circus outside into the hospital. He found the mourners with blatant disrespect.

"Does the Knight family have a comment? I'm with the Atlanta Paper and we know that this is a developing story."

"I don't think this is a good time," Williams from Knight's house said.

"Hey, it's my duty to report the news. The public has the last name and people are anxious to know what's going on," he spoke hurriedly. Williams started pushing the reporter back toward the entrance of the hallway. "We have a right to the news!"

"We have a right to some damn privacy!" Castor jumped up. A few of the firefighters grabbed him. "Lemme go! I'll give him somethin' to report!" More men got between Castor and the reporter. They backed him out of the space.

"Are you ready for them to release his name?" Knight asked Pops who just looked back at him.

"Make sure Jasmine doesn't have the TV on. I don't want Hermes to see any of this."

"Chief, it's all over the internet. There were two people who recorded it when it happened. They immediately posted their videos to social media. People are already planning a march," one of the fellow firefighters said.

Pops knew that it was an officer who shot him, but the other details he got came from other firefighters, not from the police department. The boys in blue were not talking. The boys in red were trying to get intel, but everything was still developing and since it was between two entities that were supposed to work side-by-side, it was touchy. Pops looked outside. They were three stories up, but the window overlooked the ER bay. The bay and the whole street was full of people already chanting and being enraged. Along with a slew of news vans and reporters standing next to the sliding doors.

"Somebody has to pay for killing my brother!" Titus yelled at the wall. He was usually more calm, like Knight. "I can't even say his name in the same sentence as..." he stopped abruptly.

"Me either," Pops said, used to being in the face of the public, used to making tough decisions, used to being in control of his emotions.

Knight stood up and started walking toward the entrance. He tapped Williams and Josten on his way out and they followed him.

"Turn on the TV," Pops whispered. About five minutes later, they saw Knight appear outside of the sliding doors in the ER bay.

"On behalf of my family," Knight started and the crowd began to hush. Londyn, who had been on the edge of the couch since she got home, burst into tears of relief. "On behalf of my family, the Knight family, a family full of proud firefighters, sergeants, and the Chief of Atlanta-Fulton Police Department...we are deeply saddened. Words don't really express how we feel right now. My brother, Ares," Knight choked and paused, "was killed last night at the hands of a police officer. There is an ongoing investigation, I'm told. But my brothers, father, and I will not rest until we know the truth and someone pays for this."

The crowd erupted! Knight couldn't keep the tears from falling, but his expression was stoic.

"Before they try to decimate his character, let me tell you who he really is…was," he paused. "My brother was a single father to a 9-year-old boy, and volunteered as coach for the community league basketball team. He was an ex-NBA player and a member of the Atlanta-Fulton Fire Department for the last 12 years. He was a treasured member of our family and will be missed. Please give our family some privacy as we sort through this. Ares Knight is more than a hashtag." Knight turned around and walked back in the sliding doors followed by Williams and Josten.

Pops greeted his youngest son with hug and they both sobbed. They held each other unable to wrap their minds around the enormity of what was going on. It didn't take long for the authorities to get a picture for Ares floating around, as well as a full name for Knight.

"Wow! More than a hashtag! Sgt. Apollo Knight, the fourth, a representative for the slain firefighter spoke on behalf of his family," Raina, a reporter on the site began. Londyn, still feeling relieved, was then saddened because she knew Knight was hurting. It was nowhere near the sadness she felt when she thought it was her man who'd lost his life. "Sgt. Knight said that his brother leaves behind a 9-year-old son, who we are sure is upset by all of this. Firefighter Ares Knight served with Atlanta-Fulton Fire Department and we're told has an astounding 11 family members in fire departments around the metro-Atlanta area, including his father, highly decorated Chief Apollo Knight, the third and his three brothers, of course Sgt. Apollo Knight the fourth being one of them. His grandfather, retired Chief Titan Knight, is also highly decorated and revered in the community. This is indeed a tragedy, Bill?"

"My goodness, talk about firefighting in their genes. Thank you Raina. Just to help you our viewers understand the gravity of this situation, the victim's father is Apollo Knight, the third. He is the Chief of firefighters for the entire Atlanta-Fulton Fire Department. He is in control of 66 firehouses in metro-Atlanta." Bill took the camera's view inside at the news desk that appeared in the lower bottom corner of the screen. The on-site crew maintained a wide view of the crowd outside the hospital. "This is indeed a tragedy, and we will follow this closely. You can see in the camera angle that the hospital is flying their flag at half-staff. An investigation is pending. In the midst of other officer involved shootings, Atlanta does not welcome the possible unrest that could result from this. We are sure that the police department will take their time to fully understand what happened before releasing any details."

Londyn looked at Kenzie. "It's not him," she smiled and hung her head in relief. Call. Voicemail. Call. Voicemail. She did feel better knowing that *her* Knight was ok. In the face of what was going on, she could see that he was hurting, but there wasn't an overwhelming show of emotion that she would have imagined seeing with his brother being shot down in the street 12 hours before.

Now, knowing that Knight was alive, she could wait to hear from him. She knew the brothers were going to have to deal with this the best way possible, while taking care of their parents. All she could think about was if she had gone to the cookout the day before, she would have met Ares. It wouldn't have been so bad being there. Her boys could have played with Knight's nephews thinking they were meeting new friends.

She didn't go. She didn't meet him. Now he was dead. She would never meet him.

Marvin Gaye
"What's Going On"

Picket lines and picket signs,
Don't punish me with brutality,
Talk to me, so you can see,
Oh, what's going on,
What's going on,
Ya, what's going on,
Ah, what's going on.

Chapter 21

The next few days swirled around Knight. Taking that initial step to be the family's spokesperson made him just that, permanently. The men put up a good front, although Titus was never really able to contain his emotion.

Being firefighters, they stared death in the face on a regular basis. It was a part of the job. Not only were they saving people from death defying incidents, but they were trying to keep themselves and their fellow firefighters alive and in one piece. There were also a fair amount of days where they stared into the eyes of body-less heads, where victims had been decapitated. Firefighting encompassed much more medical injury than the average person thought. And in doing it day in and day out for years, they each had to deal with their fair share of death.

This was their brother though. Not a brother in arms, but a brother in real life. Someone who they had grown up with, fought with, who'd helped raise them, who played with them, schooled them on the court and about life.

Knight had a half court on the far side of the house. He went outside to play. It was dark, and he was alone with his thoughts, emotions, and the insects chirping mating calls to each other. Dribble. Shoot. Dribble. Shoot. Dribble. Run. Layup.

"So, I'm an orphan now?" Hermes said appearing from the shadows. He nearly gave Knight a heart attack.

"You scared the sh…crap outta me boy." His voice was always calm in every situation.

"Sorry Baby."

"What are you doing up?"

"I'm an orphan, now. Right?" Hermes beckoned for Knight to pass the ball.

"I mean. Maybe in the general definition of the word." Dribble. Shoot. "When people think of orphans, they think of a person who has no family. You have a family."

"I don't have any parents. Both of my parents are dead," Hermes looked at his uncle. Dribble. Shoot. Knight knew Hermes was going to have a tough heart-to-heart with somebody and that somebody was more than likely going to be him. He wasn't ready for it. He was still processing Ares' death himself. Not to mention all of the hoopla extending from Atlanta all around the country. Another black man killed by a white cop. The country was enraged. It was on every TV station, radio station, and blog. What really set the incident apart from others is that he was a firefighter. Nobody could argue a criminal record of any kind! The only dirt they could find were speeding tickets.

"You have me...Pops...Uncle Castor...and Titus. Then you have Mom, Jasmine, and Kori. We are not going to let you fall." Dribble. Dribble. Pass. "Have you ever heard that saying, it takes a village to raise a kid?"

"No."

"Well that means it takes more than just parents. Look at Kori and Titus. They have three kids, but I keep the boys sometimes, so does Mom, and Jasmine and Castor. We all chip in and their parents are still alive."

"Why can't my village still have my parents in it?" Hermes collapsed onto the cement. "It just hurts so bad." Knight took a deep breath and his own tears released when he exhaled. He sat down, putting his arm around Hermes and hugged him tightly. As he brought Hermes' head into his chest, he felt his nephew break down.

Under the moonlight, they sat on the cement mourning together. Pops stood in his bedroom window. He'd been standing there since he heard the first bounce of the rubber dribble on the cement. The house was full of broken men who didn't know how they were going to get through it all.

The next morning, Londyn called Knight to check on him. He told her he was doing ok, but that was his answer for everything. Everything was always, 'Ok.' She offered to come sit with him, he told her he wasn't up for company.

In the days after the shooting, there was a lot to do. The funeral service and wake had to be planned and paid for. Ares' life insurance had to be settled. They had to think about what to do with his home and belongings. Somebody had to be named Hermes' guardian. On top of all that, the story had picked up a life of its own.

A march was scheduled heading to the location of the wake. The city of Atlanta was behind the Knight family. So were countless other cities where marches and vigils were being planned. Because Ares was a firefighter, the black community was gaining support from the brothers in red. #aresknight had his own hashtag that was being tweeted and posted next to #blacklivesmatter.

Ares' firehouse started a college fund for Hermes, the donations were pouring in. By the end of the week, Hermes could've forked out Harvard's $65k annual tuition for all four years if he wanted to. Knight had been asked to speak at the march on the day of the wake. At first he declined, but he felt strongly about what had happened. Not to mention, the single time he'd been on Instagram, his feed was filled with people speaking out against the cops who shot Ares, and cops in general. People had a whole lot to say. The video of him being shot had gone viral. There was nowhere in the United States to find an untainted jury. In some strange way, getting justice for Ares would have been getting justice for all of the other black men and women who had been killed by the police in recent years.

The fact that Ares was a single father only compounded his influence. So many strong opinions were surfacing about deadbeat fathers, fathers who run away from their responsibilities and want nothing to do with their children. Then here was a man, an anomaly as a single father in the black community, doing the right thing and he was snuffed out early. It was too much for Knight to deal with. He got off of social media, but felt like he owed it to his community to speak.

Londyn: Just checking on you

Knight: I'm ok, thx

Londyn: Do you need anything?

Knight: nah

Londyn: You know I'm here if you need me

Londyn: You don't even have to call, just come over

Knight: What about the boys?

Londyn: I got that handled. Just know you have a place to get away where nobody can find you. My couch is great for vegging out.

Knight: So over it

Knight: Overwhelmed

Knight: It's a lot

Londyn: I know, but you're gonna get through this.

Londyn: You're strong! Hermes is depending on you!

Knight: Him and everybody else. It's scary, there's a lot going on.

Londyn: It'll be that way for a while. The Lord is with you, He will strengthen you. Isaiah 41:10

The wake was to be held that Friday. Local celebrities, the NAACP, Black Men of Atlanta, all of the fraternities and sororities sent high ranking officials to stand behind Knight. He was nervous to speak because he didn't know if he could stand in front of those tens of thousands of people to give a speech without breaking down. Not to mention that it was going to be aired across the country. He wasn't in shock like the first time he spoke. The pain of his loss was settling in.

The family had done a good job of keeping Hermes out of the spotlight, until somebody took pictures of Ares and Hermes from Ares' private social media and released it. It was a picture of Hermes standing next to a fish almost as long as he was from a fishing trip he went on with his dad and Pops. There was also a recent picture of all the Knight boys in their uniforms. The comments were all thirsty talking about how fine the brothers and Pops were. The family was irate that someone would do that, but their lawyer convinced them that it was good to show them all working for their community and showing Ares as a good father. It wasn't as much of a violation as it was somebody who loved Ares and wanted to get positive images floating around. The decision to have Hermes on the podium at the march with Knight would be a last minute decision.

Josten, Williams, Sterling, and even Otto gave their word and showed up at the family house to escort Knight to the march's podium. When Otto walked through Knight's door, he teared up. He certainly didn't expect to see Otto anywhere near a march.

The wake was scheduled to begin at 6 p.m., so the march was scheduled to begin at 3. Two private SUVs had been arranged to transport Knight, Hermes, Pops, the brothers and Knight's co-workers.

When they arrived, the crowd was thick. It was a challenge navigating the vehicles past the throngs of supporters holding signs, chanting, some using blow horns, all in the peaceful name of justice. People were even wearing shirts with Ares' picture and hashtag on them. Hermes began to get visibly uneasy. Knight grabbed his hand saying, "This is all part of your village." Hermes nodded.

Walking up to the podium, Knight saw local and national news vans and a slew of reporters in the front. He took a deep breath and spoke about his brother, and other black men who had fallen, while demanding justice on their behalf. It was moving. At points, the crowd was cheering, other times, tears were falling. Hermes cried and Knight put his arm around his nephew and kept speaking. As the crowd of over 15,000 parted so Knight and the family could get through to begin the one mile walk to the church, he was already trending.

#whoissgtknight, #firefighterbae, and #knighttime were floating around social media. He was being seen as everything from a sex symbol to a family man to a motivational speaker. There were two pictures that were predominantly floating around. One was Knight comforting his nephew while speaking powerfully behind the mic and another was of him looking over the crowd. From the angle, you could barely see the other people on the podium, but it looked like the sun was shining rays right over his head. His strong features and pristinely groomed beard making him look like a Greek god, much like those his family was named after. Even in a button down, his chiseled physique shined through.

The family led the way in the cool fall temperatures to the church feeling the love and support for their fallen loved one.

The next day, at the funeral, even more people showed up. It was more to make a stand, than to pay respects to a man none of them knew personally. Various fire departments lined the streets with their trucks end to end while standing in front of them, saluting the casket as it rode past in the hearse.

Londyn arranged for Libra to sing at the funeral. This could have been seen as a strategic move, but there were a number of celebs reaching out to support the family. Knight asked Londyn if Libra wouldn't mind and of course, she was eager to do it. It was a very moving service, the eulogy given by Regina's pastor. He'd known Ares his whole life.

A moving photo was captured of Hermes at the gravesite in a black, pin-striped suit paired with a tie that all the Knight men wore boasting a dope flame pattern. He was holding his father's black helmet. Tears streaming down his cheeks beneath the shades he wore. That picture, along with the picture of Knight comforting him on the stage became the 'faces' of the movement.

Londyn and Libra stopped by the house after the funeral. They decided to do the repass at the house instead of at the church to better control the crowd. There was just too much going on. The ladies showed up with cases of soda and water, some random guys helped them carry into the house. Libra was stopped for autographs and pictures, while Londyn was lost in the sea of people showing up to support. She wore a form-fitting black knit dress with leopard booties. Knight saw her turning heads all through the house. Guys were trying to figure out who she was with, nobody knew who she was. She was definitely put together, ya girl was flawless.

"You are bad, girl," a pregnant lady complimented her. Knight was close enough to see them talking, but too far to hear the conversation.

"Oh thank you," Londyn acknowledged sweetly.

"I mean it. Hair...make-up...and those shoes are everything!"

"They probably weren't the best choice. I've been doing so much walking today," they laughed. "Is this your first?" Londyn pointed to her belly.

"Yes ma'am."

"Awww, congratulations. May I?" Londyn asked not wanting to just rub on the stranger's belly. She wasn't that attractive, but she was glowing.

"Sure." Right at that moment, the baby started to move. Both ladies had happily surprised faces. "He likes you! Wow! He's moving a lot!" the expectant mom said looking down at her stomach moving and shifting. Knight saw the ladies laughing and just stood there watching.

"It's a boy? I have twin boys. I love boy babies," Londyn laughed.

"Yeah, we're going to name him after his father..."

"Londyn!" Libra called out, waving Londyn over to her.

"Well, congratulations again," Londyn said before trotting off.

Londyn barely got two minutes with Knight. She expected that. She couldn't find him to tell him she was leaving, but him seeing her there was good enough. He knew she was there, didn't show up empty handed, and came through with Libra at the funeral.

Walking to the private car, Libra and Londyn held hands. The day had been too emotional. There wasn't much to say, they were thankful to have each other.

"It's more fun if there's a man between you two," Knight came out of nowhere breaking up their hand holding by grabbing each of their hands.

"Sgt. Knight!" Londyn shrieked, Libra busted out laughing.

"Thank you so much!" he said hugging Libra.

"Thank you for letting me show my support. I know there were a ton of A-listers reaching out to you."

"You *are* A-list! How could I not have you?" he asked sincerely. Libra was one degree of separation away and he actually knew Londyn and knew she was trying to elevate Libra back into the spotlight. When other celebrities reached out to the family, Knight felt Libra should have the opportunity first.

"My prayers are with you, my brother," she said bowing and retreated to the car.

"Londyn. It's crazy in there," he started looking back at the house.

"I know, I know. That's why I didn't even try to get your attention really. You are #firefighterbae now, the spokesman of the Knight household. You are going to be in high demand."

"What?"

"Oh...you don't know? Maaaaaaan these girls out here are going crazy over you! #whoissgtknight is trending, but #knighttime is the best. Bruh, you have a whole fan club out here!"

"C'mon man!"

Londyn opened her Instagram and began typing 'whoissg' and it popped right up, 11,804 posts. "See," she shoved the phone in his hands. Then she deleted that and typed 'firefighterbae'. There were 14,001 posts.

"Wow!"

"Yeah, you are about to have hoes!" Londyn laughed, he did too. "Let me know when you are ready for representation. You'll be getting calls to appear on radio shows, talk shows, maybe even CNN and Fox News. Trending like this? You are going to be a household name."

"Whatever. I don't care about any of that," he responded bringing her in for a meaningful hug. "I saw you in there making friends."

"Mostly just floating around."

"I saw you laughing and smiling, rubbing on a belly," he paused and looked up at her, "like you want one."

"A belly? Nah, boss! The pregnant girl was telling me how good I looked and that she was having a boy who would be named after his dad. Libra called me before I could really talk to her any more. Who is she?"

"Who was she?"

"A friend of the family."

He kissed her on the forehead then opened the door and helped her into the truck. "Thanks again, ladies. I really appreciate the support yesterday and today." He stared at Londyn for a minute. "You're beautiful," he bit his bottom lip before leaning in to kiss her on hers.

After the emotion of the last two days, Knight wanted nothing more than to rest his head on a pillow in complete silence. With Ares in the ground, it was now time for the family to put the pieces of their lives back together.

In poor taste, the police department decided to make their announcement about pressing charges against Officer Blevins on the evening of the funeral. Thinking crowds would be exhausted, like the family, from the march to the wake on Friday and the funeral Saturday, they held a press conference before Ares' casket was covered with dirt.

One of Knight's friends, Derek, was on Facebook and saw a lot of posts about a news conference. He ran to the TV and turned up the volume. The house was still filled with family, friends, and supporters reconnecting and spending time together. A quiet fell over the house as they gathered around the 70" HD Smart TV to hear the news.

Pops kind of collapsed in his chair, anxious. Castor saw his dad holding his breath, so he went and stood behind the recliner with his hand on Pops' shoulder. Titus went to the deck and turned on the TV out there. His wife sat with him holding his hand. Knight sat next to Regina with his arm around her. The Knight family was paired up with the exception of Castor's wife, Jasmine. She took Hermes and all the boys down stairs to the basement. She wanted them as far away pending the outcome of the news. She'd be able to tell by the sentiments of cheers or cries whether or not it was good.

"We have chosen not to press charges against Officer Blevins."

Regina screamed and Knight pulled her in, a single tear sliding down his cheek. Pops hung his head and Titus took off running around to the front of the house, weaving around cars lining the long driveway, down the street. He needed to blow off some steam and be alone. Castor leaned forward and hugged Pops.

The resurgence of sadness and anger in the Knight family house was unreal. The extended family and friends were somewhat quiet at first, not knowing if their opinions would stir up more emotion between Ares' parents and brothers.

"This is complete bullshit. Bullshit! Bullshit! How can an officer shooting and killing a man in cold blood on a reflex walk away? A reflex my ass! He shouldn't have a badge! My son was complying. He upheld the law and served his community. He was a father. He was a father," Pops starting crying. Tears around the room were starting to flow. All of the brothers' phones were ringing and vibrating. It was going to be a long night.

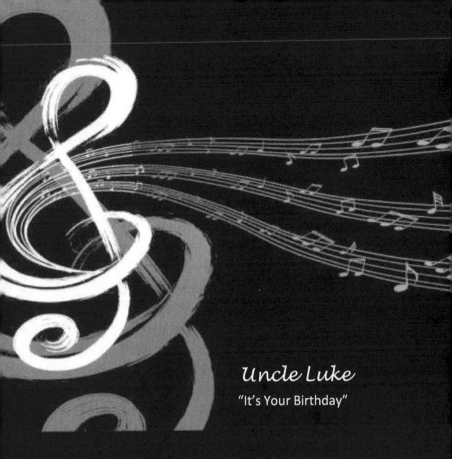

Uncle Luke
"It's Your Birthday"

Get busy, get, get, get busy,
Get, get busy, ah, it's your birth day,
It's your birthday, get busy,
It's your birthday, get busy,
It's your birthday!

Chapter 22

With all that was going on, Knight pushed his upcoming birthday under the rug. He didn't feel it was fair that he got to celebrate another year being on the earth when Ares wouldn't be able to celebrate anymore. He didn't breathe a word of it to anybody. He was more focused on helping Pops handle Ares' affairs and getting Hermes to a new normal.

Not surprisingly, he became Hermes' legal guardian. It was bittersweet, but Hermes wouldn't have had it any other way. Truth be told, neither would Knight. There was a lot to be done...packing up the house, selling, donating, or separating the belongings.

```
Londyn: Where is #firefighterbae
Knight: At your service
Londyn: You sure about that??
Knight: Fa sho
Londyn: how is your day going?
Knight: Ok
Knight: We're going through his stuff
Knight: This is so hard
Knight: FR,FR
Londyn: 🪦
```

Londyn was keeping her distance, but maintained checking in with him as he did with her. He was still calling her, but just not spending his days on the phone with her. He was completely overwhelmed. She totally understood.

```
Londyn: Hey sexy boy
Knight: Hi
Londyn: Mmmm...what's wrong?
Knight: I just got a lot going
Londyn: I know
```

Knight: I feel like I'm being a bad person right now

Londyn: How? You've stepped up for your fam, you're raising Hermes, you're helping get Ares' stuff handled, you're working hard every day under pressure in your new position. You have a lot going on, but you're doing great bae. Not to mention all of this social media crap pushing you in a spotlight you don't want.

Knight: My life is horrible right now

Knight: This sucks

Knight: 🌑

Londyn: Sgt Knight, I promise things will turn around. You have just had your foundation rocked. Trust me, I know what that's like.

Knight: You think?

Londyn: I haven't been in your exact situation, but yeah. You wake up one day and shit is just…different.

Knight: It's more than just

Knight: NVM

Londyn: You got this bae! No matter what it is!

Londyn: Try to find something good and positive about each day. Focus on that.

Londyn: I mean it, you got me in your corner 💋💋💋

She also knew his birthday was coming up. She recalled in a conversation about how close his birthday was to Kaden's. Their birthday was on the same date, just one month apart. Knowing he would say 'no' to any type of celebration, she decided to surprise him.

She walked into the firehouse and immediately the boys gave her their attention.

"How may we help *you*?" Josten jumped up.

"Good afternoon! Are you boys hungry?"

"I am if you're on the menu," Josten said. Williams and Sterling shook their heads. Knight was inside lying in his bunker so he couldn't see her walk up. The guys had been giving him space to be alone.

"Well...I am on the menu," she smiled flirting back. Williams and Sterling were surprised and leaned in to hear what she had to say next. "Just not for you," the older men snickered.

"That's too bad. You look like you taste good."

"I taste better than I look," she eyed him. The common area was silent for a minute while everybody waited to see how Josten was going to respond. Then Londyn burst into a fit of laughter and slapped his meaty shoulder, "Boy, go get that food out of my trunk." Williams jumped up to help him, teasing him the whole way.

"So you just bought...food for us?" Sterling asked.

"No, not exactly," she started. Williams and Josten were on their way back into the bay. "Today is Knight's birthday, so I wanted to do something special for him." They all looked puzzled.

"Who are you?" Williams asked with a scrunched up face.

"Umm...a friend." Londyn was starting to think this was a bad idea.

"You *do* know..." Sterling started and Josten nudged him. He stopped in midsentence.

"I *do* know what?"

"Uh, you do know he's...uh...he's in his bunker. I'll go get him."

"No! Not yet. Let me set up the food first. Can I use this table?" she asked referencing the table where they sat playing cards. They began clearing the table for her. It was actually a six foot rectangular table, but they were using it to play cards and hang out around. Londyn noticed Josten giving Sterling a look that said, 'You're a dumbass.'

Londyn spread out a table cloth over it and opened up the trays of chopped chicken and ground beef. The guys all moved quickly to help, they were against a clock. Either Knight was going to walk out at any moment or a call would come in. They spread out a feast of fixings from Chipotle, all of the toppings and sauces available.

"Go get him now," Londyn beamed to Sterling. Sterling glanced back at Josten, Londyn saw that, too. She grabbed a raspberry filled, glazed donut and put sparklers in the center and lit them just in time for Knight to walk out into the bay.

"Ha...ppy birrrrrrthday tooooo youuuu!" Londyn began. Knight's mouth dropped. He was genuinely surprised. The crew joined in and the Lieutenant came outside as well. When the sparklers fizzled out, Knight was placing the plate with the donut on the table. He hugged Londyn and kissed her, backing her out of the firehouse.

"Why did you do this?"

"It's your birthday," she said. He hung his head. "Hey, Sgt. Knight," she grabbed his chin, "you are still here. You still have to celebrate you. Even if it's something small. You deserve it. You're one of the good guys. You're *my* good guy."

"Why are you so good to me?"

"Somebody needs to be. You need to know somebody is in your corner. Somebody has your back. Somebody cares about you."

"I don't deserve you...this."

"Yes you do."

He kissed her again. "Come fix a plate to go," he said.

"I'm ok. It doesn't seem like I'm really wanted here. Two of the guys kept looking at each other funny. I know it was about me being here."

"Who?" his voice sounded concerned, but his face showed nothing. Londyn described Williams and Josten.

"Why were they acting like that?"

"I don't know. You know how guys act crazy sometimes."

"I think it's more than that. Who wouldn't want a pretty, young thang bringing them food? They were acting real protective of you."

"With all that's happened, they are protective." Londyn nodded that she understood.

"You look so sexy in this little uniform," Londyn said quickly changing the subject referring to his navy blue cargo pants and navy blue cotton tee with the fire house emblem. "Oooh wee! I can't wait to get my hands on you again, hashtag fire fighter bae. Mmm, mmm, mmm."

"You miss me?" he asked with his hands caressing her neck.

"You know I do." He rained kisses over her face and neck. "I bought two dozen donuts instead of a cake. Let *them* eat the donuts and get fat. You keep this body tight for me," she laughed. She turned around and sashayed towards her car. He strided behind her with his long legs and slapped her butt. She giggled. Knight opened the door for her.

"Thank you, Londyn. I really appreciate you."

Londyn winked at him and cranked up the car. She was annoyed by his crew, but Knight's response made up for it. It made her feel good to do something special for him. It had been a while since she was able to do something nice for Micah.

Londyn felt like if she didn't do something for Knight's birthday, nothing would get done. She was sure his family had forgotten with all that was going on. The crew didn't seem to be moved one way or another, and frankly seemed to be a little annoyed at her presence. She didn't even want to pry to find out why they were acting that way. He had a lot going on and nobody to take care of him.

"Say Knight, who was that?" Williams asked between bites of his brown rice bowl that seemed to be more chicken than anything else.

"Londyn."

"Yeah, we got her name, but who is she?"

"My friend."

"So we jus' gon' act like…"

"Aye bruh," Knight brushed him off and walked back inside the firehouse. Williams and Sterling looked at each other and shook their heads. He didn't feel like explaining anything to those fools. Instead, his mind drifted to the beautiful lady who'd just left him. She'd taken time to remember his birthday and tried to make it special, even with all he had going on.

Xscape
"Understanding"

What I need from you is understanding,
How can we communicate,
If you don't hear what I say,
What I need from you is understanding,
So simple as 1-2-3.

Chapter 23

Londyn had her own hands full. Micah hadn't been the same since he found out about Knight. He began sending random texts in the middle of the night. The texts were the same, all blaming her for the failed marriage. He told her because she had two relationships outside of their marriage, that he could never trust her. She argued back that he never trusted her which is why he didn't believe her when she told him that she didn't cross the line and have sex with the guys. He didn't own up to ignoring her before they came into the picture and didn't make the effort to find out what was lacking in their marriage that would push her to find emotional solace somewhere else. He only tried to hurt her in response, which he more than succeeded in doing.

The texts were long and hurtful. Blame. Blame. Blame. Londyn never brought up his past indiscretions. Once she decided to stay with him, there was no point in bringing up the past. Micah didn't feel that way. He threatened to divorce her several times. She'd ask what could she change to keep them on track. It was all superficial things, but she did them anyway. Got her hair done more often, painted her nails, tried to dress better. He didn't applaud her efforts. He didn't compliment her. She didn't think he even noticed. There were times when the boys would say, "Ma, you look so pretty, doesn't she Dad?" And Micah wouldn't even respond, or he'd grunt and leave the room.

When he wasn't sending hate texts, he was calling in the middle of the night. Londyn would call him the next morning and he'd claim they were butt dials.

"How Sway? How?" Kenzie yelled laughing in the phone. "How did he butt dial you from an iPhone in the middle of the night. Doesn't the phone have a lock screen? Doesn't he have a code on it? That boy is foolish!" she roared.

Londyn couldn't help but laugh herself.

"He just wanted to see if you were going to answer. Don't! Because you don't owe him anything. He decided to leave, so let him stay gone to find what he was looking for."

It was deeper than that for Londyn. Despite her falling for Knight, she still wanted her family. Micah, Kingston, and Kingsley...they were her family. Her parents had managed to keep their marriage together for almost 40 years. She thought she'd be joining them one day. She and Micah hadn't even hit ten years and they were falling apart. She questioned whether she'd done everything she could have to save it. Whether there was more that she could do. Whether she should go ask him to come back.

But why? All he'd done was point his fingers. Nothing he'd done seemed like he wanted to be back other than his blow up while she was in New York. Really it seemed more like he didn't want her to move on the way he had. *You can't make somebody love you. Micah just doesn't love me*, Londyn settled.

She was getting ready for a rare girls' night. Not that groups of chicks she knew weren't always getting together for something, she had just been keeping to herself so much lately. Steam from the shower was still bellowing out of the bathroom when a text from Micah came through. As usual, Londyn was listening to Pandora.

Micah: Have fun tonight.

Have fun? Yeah right. He just wants to pick a fight with me so he can ruin my night.

Micah: No answer?

Londyn: Thx

Micah: I can't even get a thank You? You can't spell out the words? How hard would it be to type thank you? How much time did you save?

Londyn: Thank you

Micah: Was that so hard?

Micah: I hope one day I can make you smile the way he does.

Londyn: What?

Micah: You seem so happy when you're with him.

How the hell did he see me with Knight? When was Knight last over here? That was just yesterday?

Londyn: So either you have cameras in my house or you're creeping around outside.

Micah: You run your mouth too much. Your friends aren't your real friends.

Micah: I see your boyfriend made you take down our painting.

Londyn: No, you did that when you filed for divorce.

Micah: Oh the papers you still haven't signed.

Londyn: So you mad I took down the painting or mad because I haven't signed the papers ending the marriage that the painting celebrated??

Londyn: Make up your mind!

Londyn: NVM

Londyn: You'll get your divorce, don't worry! I don't want you to be married any more than you want to be!

Micah: How many people know about him?

Londyn: When did you see him make me smile?

Micah: I saw you on the phone with him at the boys' football game.

Londyn: You assume I was on the phone with him.

```
     Micah: I haven't seen you smile like
that in a long time. I used to make you
smile. Don't you feel bad for breaking up our
family?
     Micah: You did this Londyn!
     Londyn: I'm not doing this with u. GN
     Micah: How are you so happy? Posting
pics smiling, like you didn't break us up.
     Londyn: Who said I was happy?
     Micah: You're dancing and singing in the
mirror.
```

Biiiiiitch! Londyn paused. There was no way she was going to have this conversation with him. He was crazy. Stalking. She was ready to get the hell out of the house. She quickly got herself together and got out of the house. Micah kept texting, but Londyn was frantic and a bit scared. She really didn't think he would hurt her, but this whole new Micah was a side that she'd never seen before.

She didn't know what to think about the person he was showing her that he'd become. Maybe this dark Micah was there all along and was just now showing it. She was distracted the whole time she was out. The ladies were laughing and talking all around her. Londyn laughed, painfully, and engaged in a bit of conversation until she was done faking like she was in a good place in her life. *This is why I stay at home. Pretending I wanna be here is exhausting.*

Micah's antics spilled over from Londyn's cell phone to social media. He knew better than to post comments to FaceBook because both of their parents and whole families would have seen them. He thought he was being slick by posting comments under her pictures on Instagram, then removing them. That way, they would appear in her notifications and not for everybody to see. Instagram. *Insta*gram. People saw things in real time. It never failed that every time Micah put a nasty or 'in poor humor' comment, Londyn's friends and followers would screen shot it and text or DM it to her. They would ask, 'Who is this? Why is he saying this?' or 'Isn't this your husband?' or 'Block this rude ass!'

Knowing he was paying attention to her every move, Londyn decided to have a little fun with it. She FaceTimed Kenzie.

"I found this pic on my explorer page of an ultrasound of twins. It had this long ass post about being surprised to be pregnant with twins, then at the end it was a joke!"

"Yes Londynnnnnn! I saw that. I was crying!"

"Girl! So since Detective Micah's stalking ass sees everything I post within seconds, I'm going to post it on my page."

"Ooooh, I dare you!" Kenzie spoke into the phone. Although they were on FaceTime, neither of them was looking at the other. They were looking at themselves in the little square on their respective phones. Kenzie was checking herself out from different angles and Londyn was just looking at her skin up close.

"How long do you think it will take him to text me about it?"

"Seconds!" Kenzie yelled. "But you gotta put some crazy hashtags. Folks love to read hashtags."

"Oh my gosh!" Londyn released a hearty laugh. "#babyfever, #momof2, #maybethree!"

"Girl!" Kenzie hollered. "Lemme go grab some popcorn for this!"

"You are so dumb!"

"No, *you* are! Do it while I'm on the phone. This is going to be hysterical!" Kenzie amped her friend up. Londyn went into her Instagram app, reposted the pic and uber long caption with the hashtags. They were both giggling like little school girls.

"He is going to have a fit!" Londyn giggled, but Kenzie knew she was nervous.

"And you shouldn't care. Did he think about your feelings when he moved out without telling you?"

"Ugh! Shut up! Dang! Done!" Londyn's face appeared back on the screen.

"Alright, it's 2:02...let's see how long this takes."

"I feel so devilish!"

"Girl, this is nothing. If you really wanna bring some pain, I got cha! How is Sgt. Knight?"

"He's fine. He was over here this morning."

"Yaaaaaas! Come through Sgt. Knight!"

Micah: Baby fever? You pregnant from this nigga?

"KENZIE!"

Micah: Or do you even know whose baby you are having?

"He just texted twice!!"

"NOOOOOO!"

"Girl!"

"OH MY GAWWWWWWWWWD!" They roared.

"What did he say?" Londyn read her the texts.

"Chile, its 2:05!"

"My goodness. That's ridiculous!"

Londyn: Jesus

Londyn chose to ignore his petty comments to her posts. His reactions were childish and there was no point to them. It frustrated her to no end that he would behave that way. She had done nothing but give him his space since he'd moved out.

Thanksgiving was the first big fight they had. Micah had taken the boys with his family for the holiday. They were out of school for the week and their little league football season was over, so Londyn didn't mind. She was not looking forward to being without her children for the holiday. It would be her first holiday without them since they were born.

Suddenly, she didn't mind the stress that came with helping her mother slave over the stove for two days leading up to Thanksgiving. Running back and forth to the store because they ran out of butter, or there wasn't enough sweet potatoes. Fussing over whose house was holding Thanksgiving dinner. Fighting over Hawaiian rolls.

It was times like these that brought her back down to earth. Times that were supposed to be all about family and she was without hers. Of course, she would have loved to be around her own parents and siblings, but she felt like it would make things worse. At some point her marriage would have become the topic of discussion. Her nieces and nephew would have asked about the boys and why wasn't Uncle Micah there and why wasn't she with them in Texas. Eventually, she would get overwhelmed and frustrated and shut them all out and retreat to her childhood bedroom wishing she'd never left her house in Atlanta anyway.

She gave her mother the abbreviated version of that thought process and lied saying she would go hang with the friends who'd invited her to have Thanksgiving with them. That was what she'd told everybody, "Aww, thanks so much! I already have plans, but I'll try to scoot by," she'd say with a heartfelt laugh. Then hang up and cringe. She didn't have the heart to be around other families all happy and loving and fighting and drifting to sleep in their tryptophan comas and watching football and playing cards and just plain ol' enjoying themselves.

It was too much.

Flipping through all of the cable movie channels that never seemed to have any good movies on, her phone vibrated with an email. She was hoping to quiet her thoughts by watching movies that had nothing to do about anything but would keep her mind focused on something other than the fact that her husband and sons were several states away and she was at home sulking on the couch.

She checked her email, anticipating to get the mastered version of Libra's single that was supposed to hit the airwaves the first week of December. The hint of excitement she felt was quickly doused when she saw that it was just an alert from Bank of America. She put the phone back down, then thought, *Did I just see what I think I...* She opened up an email that was a low balance alert.

"How?" She asked herself out loud. Working with limited funds, she was very good at managing money. She knew what was coming in and what was going out. She had two different accounts and this account was solely for bills. It was the account that Micah put money into for her to pay household bills from. She thought about when she'd last paid bills and there had been no activity in that account for at least a week. The longer he was out of the house, the less he contributed.

Londyn recalled which bills had been paid and that they had been paid around the 15th. Even with the water and insurance companies taking their time to draft the money from the account, it still only took about three days.

She logged into her Bank of America account and saw there was $2.13. She clicked on the account summary and saw the last transaction was a transfer to Micah Charles. Her eyes stretched wide. Her stomach tensed up. She could feel the sweat beading on her forehead instantly. *THIS FOOL TOOK ALL OF THE MONEY OUT OF MY ACCOUNT!* She called him instantly.

"Hey Ma!" Ace answered the phone. She knew how Micah operated. He knew that she would see the money was gone and would call him.

"Hey baby! How are you?"

"Cold!"

"I'm sure. Are y'all having fun though?"

"Yes ma'am."

"Ma!" Deuce's voice came through the speaker.

"Look at you, big head number two."

"Big head??" He asked, Ace started laughing. "Whatchu laughing at boy? Yo' head jus' as big as mine!" They both laughed, so did Londyn for about 1.3 seconds.

"Where is your dad?"

Ace passed the phone to Micah.

"What?"

"Micah, why did you take money out of the house account?"

"It's my money."

"It's not your money. It's the child support that you give me to take care of the boys."

"It's not child support! You still haven't signed the papers! I'm not going to give you money to take care of some nigga!"

"What are you talking about?"

"You got Knight laid up in the house, let that nigga pay some bills!"

"Whoa," tears exploded from Londyn's eyes. "I don't know where all of this is coming from."

"Oh, I finally get a reaction from you," Micah could tell that she was crying by the quiver in her voice. "I moved out, I introduced them to my friend, I filed for divorce, and I got nothing from you. I take money away and now your ass is on my phone crying."

"Oh my gosh, Micah! You are horrible. I have reacted. I spent my whole summer squirreled up in the house on this damn couch because I couldn't bear to go out. I cried myself to sleep and woke up crying, trying to figure out what was I doing that was so bad that my husband would just leave! I lost weight, wasn't eating, would go days without changing my clothes! You were too busy doing family shit with Jennifer like taking the boys to the beach, and making posting about finally being happy and dropping dead weight to notice that I wasn't around!"

"How long have you been fucking Knight?"

"He has nothing to do with our issues. He came into the picture after you moved out. Let's get that clear! And after you had that heffa around my boys six days after you moved out! Why did you take the money out?"

"It's mine!"

"It's not! That money is earmarked for bills. So what if I had just paid bills that had not been processed yet? What would you expect me to do?"

"Let them bitches bounce!" he roared laughing.

Londyn hung up the phone. She was hysterical. *Why is he being so mean? I'm going out of my way not to be an angry black woman! Not to act like a crazy, psycho baby mama, ex-wife, whatever! He's making it hard for me not to hate him! Now I understand why Andre 3000 wrote that song Caroline.*

That exchange began a torrent of angry, hate texts until she'd had enough and stopped responding. He called it ignoring, but this was something that had patterned over the last few weeks. He would randomly text her to start a fight, she'd respond calmly, then when he knew she was by her phone, he'd just light into her text after rapid fire text. Then, when she told him she was done arguing and to have a nice day, he'd say she was ignoring the rest of the ugly messages he sent. It was a sickening cycle. It was unhealthy and Londyn was tired of him.

By the time she hung up with Micah, her face was wet with tears and her head was pounding. They were only halfway through the Thanksgiving break.

What she wanted more than anything was to vent to Knight. He was keeping himself busy working extra shifts. He'd been hard to reach. She knew him losing his brother was going to cause a reaction. Honestly, she anticipated that he would cling to her, not push away. Being a full-time guardian for the first time, and to a 9-year-old who was also healing from the tragedy ushered in its own challenges. Juggling making sure he was cared for, he got to and from school, arranging aftercare, homework, chores, feeding and clothing another human being can be a shock when you've never done it before. He was instrumental in Hermes' life before, but not nearly to this extent.

On top of that, he was gaining more traction on social media. The thirst trap had not slowed down. Women were blowing up his DMs and posts with crazy comments. He was getting marriage proposals and all! His lawyer, who also acted as a PR for the family recommended that Knight keep his page open letting the world to see that they were just a normal family, strong and close. It would open up opportunities for him to speak on his deceased brother's behalf to help heal the wound created between the police and the black community.

Knight was uncomfortable with it at first. In his mind it would also keep pressure on the authorities to bust a move on the cop. Officer Blevins was a rookie officer who said his shooting Ares was a reflex reaction. The public was not buying it, nor was the Knight family. It was a mess. The culture of the relationship between officers and firefighters in metro-Atlanta had become particularly tense. It had become harder for them to be on scenes together. It was a constant dick measuring contest. There had even been a few fights between police and firefighter crews when tensions boiled over. The video of Ares being shot had gone viral to the point that it was impossible to pull it down. It was a clear case of Officer Blevins being in the wrong. The public was just waiting to see if the boys in blue were going to own up to it in any way.

Knight needed Londyn as much as she needed him. It had been over a week since they'd seen each other. He reached out to her.

```
Knight: I love you.

Londyn: 🫧
Knight: Londyn, I love you for real.
Londyn: I love you too bae
Knight: No, I really fucking love you.
Londyn: I wouldn't say it if I didn't
mean it.
Knight: I'm not saying that, I'm just
letting you know how I feel.
Knight: I need you.
Londyn: I'm right here
```

Londyn looked at the phone. She reread the latest string of messages. It came off as being weird to her. *What did he do?* She thought. This just came out of nowhere. She hadn't talked to him in days, then this.

When he knocked on the door, she was excited to see him. She opened the door to let him in. She stood there wearing a black masquerade mask with beautiful swirling black and silver glitter designs. It covered half of her face. She wore it with a tight, black satin chemise with straps that crisscrossed over her back and butt. His eyes widened with surprise. Knight made her feel so comfortable with her body. She knew he'd appreciate her dressing up for him. And he did. Especially with the chill from the late November air turning her nipples hard enough to poke through the thin fabric. He looked at her, playfully bit her nipple and moaned, "Mmm hmm."

"You told me to try it...try dressing up for you," she said boldly. Inside, she was so nervous she wanted to just run away.

He instantly grabbed her face and started kissing her passionately. She laughed and kissed him back. There was such a hunger in him, she'd never seen him like that before. He needed her, she could feel the intensity behind his kiss. He backed her up into her room and laid her on the bed.

He laid down on top of her and kicked his shoes off, then removed his shirt. Londyn cradled his head and returned the fire he was giving her. He slowly removed the mask.

"I just want to see how beautiful you are," he looked at her for a moment. He began hungrily sucking her breasts. Back and forth between them, he held them in each hand making sure to give them both attention.

He reached his hand between her legs and moaned again. It felt like a lake. She was ready. He stood up and dropped his pants in one movement. He dove on the bed, sliding right in. They both moaned as he pushed the first stroke as deep as he could go. He pulled her leg up, bent down to kiss her, cradled her head, and stroked all at the same time. She came in about ten slow, long strokes.

Then he grabbed her around her back and rolled over so she was on top. They moved slowly, in perfect synchronicity. Londyn massaged her own breasts, until he put his hand around her neck and squeezed.

"Oh Knight!"

"I miss you, sweetheart. You miss me?"

"You know I do."

"Show big daddy how much you miss him," he said barely above a whisper. The light from the living room creeped around the corner offering the perfect dim lighting for him to see her bronze skin shining.

Londyn swiveled around reverse cowgirl, still sitting on him and leaned forward. She easily found a good rhythm bouncing up and down, while he spanked her butt.

"Mmm!" she moaned, "mmm, mmm, yeah!" He sat up behind her wrapping his hands around her waist, twisting her face to him so he could passionately kiss her more. He reached up the nape of her neck and grabbed a handful of hair, gently tugging.

"Yeah big daddy! Yeah!"

"Say it again."

"Yeah big daddy!"

"Say it again," he tugged at her.

"Big..." she climaxed again. As she felt a powerful surge run through her body, she felt him squeeze her harder. He winced as he grinded in slow, purposeful strokes. She could feel that he'd reached his peak too. He scattered kisses all over her back. She smiled, grabbing his hands. He laid her down next to him and continued to passionately kiss her. It was so out of the norm, but what woman complains about being kissed like that?

They laid in the bed embracing each other. He had made love to her. The sex was always good, but he took it to a whole different level. His movements were so passionate. His kisses were endless. He'd told her he loved her and he'd just shown her.

They made their way to the couch. Londyn sat in the middle and Knight sat half lounging on the left side. They watched TV and talked about what was happening on the show. Staring straight ahead, she tilted her head to the left. He sat up and shifted his body so his head was leaning to the right, towards her head. Then he slid his head over until their heads touched. He intertwined his fingers in hers, drawing figure eights on her hands. He turned his head and kissed her on the forehead.

Londyn could feel him staring at her, but she didn't want to look in his eyes. He brought her hand to his mouth and kissed it. Then he kissed her cheek. Still, some time later as he prepared to leave, he felt somewhat dis-connected.

"You ok, Knight?"

"I'm ok."

"You sure? You seem...off. Different. Like your energy is completely off."

"I'm ok. Juggling a lot."

"Something is different. I know you have a lot going on, but it's not that. Your energy, man..." she paused before going forward. "Are you married?"

"No," he laughed.

"Engaged?"

"No."

"Do you have a girlfriend now?"

"No.

"Do you have any kids?"

"Taking care of Hermes full time is a lot harder than I thought it would be. You know, I didn't know how much went into taking care of a child. Not fully. Then I picked up a few extra shifts and this whole PR shit." Knight held his head low, "I certainly wasn't expecting all of this. The first day I spoke to the public, I was trying to take some of the burden off my dad. Now, everybody is looking to me. It's like I'm the movement."

"Remember when I showed you the hashtags? I knew this was going to happen. Use it for positive change. You can be a liaison between the community and the law. Because you already work in community service, you have a unique perspective. It's different than people who are parents or advocates for change just because they see that change needs to be made. You live in the face of the public every day. You see things from the law's side, but also from the laypersons' perspective. And you have been promoted to sergeant. That says a lot about your higher ups having faith in you."

"USA Morning is flying me to NYC for a segment."

"That's huge, bae! Do you want me to come?

"A last minute ticket two days before Thanksgiving will cost a fortune."

"You're right, I'll watch.

"Man," he said scratching his head. They stared at each other standing in Londyn's living room. She reached out and playfully bit his nipple, it was mouth height for her. He cradled her head into his chest, then kissed her forehead.

"I know it's a lot. I'm here for you Kniiiiiiight! Don't forget it."

"I know. I love you."

"Love you too, Sgt. Knight." He kissed her on the forehead again and was gone.

Puff Daddy
"I'll Be Missing You"

Every step I take,
Every move I make,
Every single day,
Every time I pray,
I'll be missing you.

Thinking of the day,
When you went away,
What a life to take,
What a bond to break,
I'll be missing you.

Chapter 24

Thanksgiving for them both was sad. Londyn decided not to even peel herself off of the couch and while Knight was surrounded by loved ones, he was openly sad. The whole Knight clan was lackluster. They'd tried their best to put on a usual Thanksgiving, but the spirit was just not there. Not even in the kids. The family was planning to sue, but their lawyer advised them to wait. The weight of the injustice Ares was dealt hung heavy in the air. Knight wished that he'd picked up a shift for Thanksgiving Day.

Once the day was over, and the house was back in livable condition. The disposable plates and cups were trashed, the leftovers divided up between the households, and all of the counters wiped down. The third generation of Knight Boys were in charge of trash clean-up and the brothers folded down the tables and chairs. The ladies washed, dried, and put away dishes. Everybody left and the house was quiet once again. Pops and Regina sat on the couch watching TV after all of the clean-up was done. They were exhausted. Pops put his arm around her and she relaxed in his embrace. Although it wasn't totally uncommon to see them like that, Knight still raised his eyebrows at the two of them. No matter who was in Pops' life – or bed – Regina always came first.

Knight trotted up the stairs to his room and saw the light from his room shining in the hallway.

"Dang, this light must've been on all day!" he said to himself. He hadn't been up there in hours. He passed Hermes' room and saw it was empty, but there were pictures of him and Ares laid out on his bed. Knight stood there looking at the collection. There were pictures of his parents together, a few of his mother while she was beautiful, glowing, and pregnant. There was a picture of Hermes being pushed on the bicycle for the first time. Knight laughed at that one because he vividly remembered that day. Titus' middle son was learning too, so all of the brothers were out helping. They promised Hermes and his cousin that they'd take them to get ice cream if they learned how to ride their bikes. It took a few tries and Hermes still had the scar on his knee from a nasty fall while learning, but the toothless, cheesy grin he had all day, even after the ice cream reward was worth the day's frustrations.

There was a picture from his kindergarten graduation, with his father, uncles, and grandparents all there supporting him. Knight's favorite was from Halloween the year before when Ares and Hermes dressed up like Incredible Hulks to go trick-or-treating. In the picture, they had green face paint and the whole nine, standing with angry faces and flexing their muscles. Knight shook his head, he needed to get out of there before his emotions got the best of him.

As he pushed the door to get in his own room, he found Hermes laid out on the floor…eyes closed, unconscious with a pill bottle just inches away from his hand.

"Mes! Mes! Get up man! POPS! POPS!" Knight shouted. He scooped Hermes up and carried him to the shower and doused him with water. "What did you do, Mes? POPS!"

Pops rushed up the stairs. His nerves had pretty much been on edge since Ares was killed. True to their firefighter roots, both men knew how to maintain relatively calm composures when assessing a scene. He moved quickly past the pill bottle to find Knight with Hermes in the shower.

"Is he breathing?"

"No…his pulse is weak and thready."

"Take him out, begin CPR," Pops ordered as he dialed 9-1-1. "This is Chief Knight. I have a nine-year-old, who's OD'd on…" Pops went back into Knight's bedroom to find the bottle on the floor, "...aspirin. Not breathing...weak, thready pulse. We need EMS right away!"

By that time, Regina had made her way up the stairs to see what the commotion was. Tears had already formed in her eyes, "I'll go pull the truck out of the garage," she said and rushed downstairs to get her purse and Pop's keys.

EMS arrived quickly, and put Hermes, who was still receiving CPR by Knight, on the gurney. The paramedics began taking care of him, started an IV and got him in the ambulance. Knight hopped in too. Pops followed closely with Regina in the passenger side. They didn't even think to call the brothers, they were all too concerned with finding out what was going on with Hermes.

Knight looked down at him, holding his hands, crying silently. Looking at his nephew in the back of the ambulance, he couldn't imagine how much pain he was in to do something like this. Hermes was sad, of course, but he seemed to be doing well. With them all healing, they were not paying as close attention to him as they should have been.

Because of his age, the police and children's services were going to have to be notified. In any other case, there probably would have been a thorough investigation as to what type of care was being given in the home; whether it was unfit or not. With tensions as high as they were between the forces, Knight and Pops knew this was going to be a problem. Since it happened in Pop's home, chief-to-chief, he knew the police chief would be over the investigation.

One thing...after...another.

Knight looked at his nephew in the bed hooked up to tubes and monitors. He beat himself up for taking Hermes to the march, then to the wake. Those were events he should have missed. In a way, Hermes being there made his loss more monumental. Knight felt like he should have paid better attention to him, talked to him more, been...there.

The next day when Hermes opened his eyes, Knight was sitting in one chair, Pops was laying on the bootleg hospital couch, really which was just a thin, uncomfortable cushion to sit on with the wall acting as the back.

"Unc," he said in a weak voice. Knight jumped up and stood beside the bed.

"Mes! You scared us, man! Let me go get a nurse. Don't move," Knight poked his head out of the room. Pops stood up too.

"Say man," he rubbed Hermes' head full of long, curly hair, "you had us so worried." Knight held the door open for the nurse, who purposely brushed against him when she walked in. She'd asked Knight if she could have a picture before he left. As pretty as she was, he was annoyed by her. His nephew was hanging on to life by a thread and she was talking about taking pictures to post.

"How are you doing, Hermes?"

"I'm ok," he said. Pops poured him a cup of room temperature water and handed it to him with a straw. The nurse did her check-up and when she was satisfied said she'd get the doctor. When she left them room, the men talked to him.

"What happened, man?" Pops asked. There was no denying the concern splashed on his face. "Why did you take all those pills?"

"I'm just sad," Hermes looked down at the stark white blanket that covered him, but wasn't keeping him warm. "I'm hurting. Like, it hurts. It hurts so bad. I miss my dad," the tears started falling down him cheeks.

"Do you understand what you did?" Pops asked. Knight stood on the other side of the bed looking at Hermes.

"I just wanted the pain to go away. Pops, when your head hurts, you take aspirin. I just wanted the pain to go away. My head hurts, my stomach hurts, my heart...my heart hurts," Hermes described and Pops starting crying along with him. He wrapped his arms around his grandson. They cried together.

Knight: FYI...Been at the hospital since yesterday. Mes OD'd.

Londyn: WTF? OMG! OMG! OMG!

Londyn: What's going on? How is he?

Knight: He's ok, they're going to keep him another night. This shit is crazy. He said he was hurting and wanted the pain to go away. I HAVE to spend more time with him. I don't think Pops is going to let Mes outta his sight for a while.

Londyn: Bae, I'm SO sorry! I'll be praying for y'all. You want me to bring you something treat?

Londyn: *to eat?

Knight: Nah, Mom is bringing food up here. Thx.

Londyn: 🌸

Knight: Need one in real life!

Sunday, Micah brought the kids back from Thanksgiving vacation. Londyn was excited to see her boys, but she could give two shits about her ex and his antics, especially after the stunt he pulled taking all of the money out of the house account. She knew that he was going to do or say something. Only God knew what it was going to be. She would try to keep it classy as usual, Micah didn't seem to care as much.

As soon as she heard his car pull into the driveway, she opened the door, eager to see her sons.

"Maaaaaaaa!" Deuce jumped out of the car first. He was always first.

"Deuuuuuuuuce!" she copied. He practically lunged into her arms. "I missed you so much!"

"Yeah, I missed you too!"

"Did you have fun?"

"Yes!"

"HEY MA!" Ace made his way up the sidewalk to the door where Londyn's face was beaming. They hugged each other warmly.

"Y'all go help your dad with your luggage," she directed the boys back to the driveway. They returned to the front door with their suitcases, which by then Micah was making his way to the door with the extra bags. "Hi," she said to him.

"Whatever," he grunted without lifting his eyes to look at her. He leaned into the house to drop the bags just beyond the threshold.

"Ace! Deuce! See y'all later!" he shouted in a jovial tone. Deuce came downstairs, hugged Micah then flew past Ace who was coming down to do the same.

"Bye!" Londyn said nicely.

"Fuck you!" Micah threw out.

"Whoa! That was harsh!" Ace was standing just beyond the wide opened door. Londyn pushed Ace inside and closed the door slightly.

"Did you change the password to the house account?"

"I did. After you took all of the bill money out, I had to change it."

"You're such a bitch!" he yelled.

"What did I do? I changed the password to the bank account that is in *my* name? You shouldn't be taking money out, only putting money in. My action was a *re*-action to your action."

"You changed all of the security questions, too!"

"I did!"

"I don't have time for this!" he yelled. "Dumbass!"

Londyn shook her head as she opened the door. Ace was still standing there. She was sure her eldest son had heard everything.

"You know what, Londyn? Fuck you! Fuck your whole life, stupid bitch!"

"Dad!" Ace said staring at Micah in disbelief. Londyn pushed Ace in the house, closed and locked the door. "Why would he?"

Londyn shook her head. She embraced her son and kissed his forehead.

"I'm so sorry, Ma. I don't know why Dad is being so mean."

"Don't apologize," Londyn responded trying to choke back the tears. She couldn't believe her husband had just called her out of her name and in front of her son. That was the first time he'd ever called her out of her name since they met. Of course, Ace was going to tell Deuce. As a mother, she knew how much they were going to need a man in their lives. To help raise them right, to show them the ropes, to help them navigate as black men in America. With the tragedy of Knight's brother looming over her head, the wounds of hate crimes were fresh in her head and on her heart.

What Micah had done was absolutely uncalled for. There was no reason why he should have called her out like that. She didn't understand why he was even upset.

"He hurt my feelings though."

"Mom and Dad are having a hard time getting along. It's not your fault. It has nothing to do with you or Kingston. We love you both."

"But you don't love each other." Ace snatched himself away from her and stormed up the stairs. She went into her walk-in closet, fell on the floor and cried.

"Lord," she whispered, "I need you. I need you to work this out. I'm not perfect, nor have I ever claimed to be. I can't do this alone. This situation is getting harder and harder. Your word says that your burden is light. Bring rest to my soul. Give me the strength to make it through. This is all on you. I give this all to you. The sadness, confusion, loneliness...I'm tired of hurting, tired of being in constant pain. It's your battle to fight for me."

The separation was supposed to be easier as time went on, not harder. Micah seemed to be more upset. Londyn had given him the freedom he wanted. She didn't want it, but she also didn't want to end up on a t-shirt because she was begging him to stay or acting out. Too many people had stayed in relationships they weren't happy in or tried to force relationships to the point where one killed the other. She had two sons to think about. So when Micah said he was out, she didn't try to hold him back. Her mom always said, "If you love something, set it free. If it comes back it's yours, if it doesn't, he never was."

She wiped the tears and they kept flowing. Her heart was sad. It was hurting for her. It was hurting for her boys. It was hurting for the way Micah was treating her; he was obviously hurting about something to lash out at her like that. It was hurting for Knight. It was hurting for Hermes. So much pain was swirling around her. Just when things seemed to be moving in the right direction, with the boys healing, her healing and finding the peace to move forward, *BOOM*! One thing after another.

She had already spent so much time over the holiday crying. Getting her sons back should've been a bright spot in her day. The last thing she wanted to do was waste more tears on a man who didn't want her, didn't love her, and didn't seem to care that she was even alive other than finding ways to make her life harder.

Londyn decided to take the boys to Sky Zone. She would play with the boys at the trampoline park. She stood up and instantly felt dizzy, then a wave of nausea led to her rushing to the toilet. She threw up and looked at the vomit in the bowl. "What the hell?" she asked out loud. She thought back over what she'd eaten that day. Londyn knew the milk was questionable when she ate cereal that morning, but it was only a few days past the expiration date. It must have been labeled incorrectly.

"Ace! Deuce!" she called out and threw up again. "Man!" she said, again, out loud to herself.

"Yes ma'am?" Deuce answered first.

"Tell your brother to get ready, we're going to Sky Zone."

"YES! SKY ZONE! SKY ZOOOOOONE!" Deuce said running off.

Londyn flushed the toilet and walked to the sink to brush her teeth. She was not a throw up-er. She only threw up when she was pregnant or hung over and she hadn't had anything to drink in days. When she had, it was only a glass or two of wine. She and Knight had been doing so good using protection until only recently. Still, his pull out game was strong.

She changed her clothes into some comfortably decent athleisure wear. Once the boys were changed, they piled in the truck and spent half of the day at Sky Zone.

Tye Tribbett
"What Can I Do"

So here's my heart,
Here's my mind,
I give You my soul, Lord,
Need You to take control,
'Cause I've tried it,
Tried it on my own but,
What I found is I can't make it,
On my own.

Chapter 25

Londyn got her boys off to school bundled up in jackets. The high was 49°. She woke up feeling frisky. She instantly felt bad for Knight being in and out of the elements. Being a Florida girl, anything below 70 called for a jacket. Anything below 50, the world was coming to an end. So, according to her weather app, the world was officially coming to an end.

The whole time they were getting ready she was sending the boys rushing back and forth to their rooms for the right jackets to give good coverage, skullies for their heads and having them give last looks in the mirror before heading out to teach them to look for anything they forgot to do or put on, her mind was on how she could warm herself up. And Knight.

After dropping them off, she sashayed in the house, pulled on some sexy, black fishnet stockings with six inch, black stiletto pumps. She was excited to take the picture, but she needed to pose. She propped her phone up, then posed on a chair so the picture would be taken from the back. That was her most comfortable angle and probably his most favorite view. She set the timer on the phone, then ran to get in position for the clicks. Not wanting to mess up the perfect frame she had, she walked over to the phone, then ran to get in position. After doing that a handful of times, she had a good seven or eight pics to choose from.

"Look at that waist girl!" She gave herself kudos. "I could probably do better if I actually used my gym membership," she said. The depression diet Micah put her on was showing the positives. She had lost a noticeable amount of weight. It was only about 15 pounds give or take, but on her short 5'4" frame, it made a difference. *Maybe if I lost the weight before he left, he would still be here*, she thought. That would've been the 15 pounds she needed to lose for him to get her pregnant. The smile on her face quickly faded, then she shook off the thought and went through her pics. She didn't want to put clothes on in case she didn't have any winners.

Bingo! One of the pictures was flawless! The stilettos made her legs look long and the fishnets oozed sex appeal. Facing the back of the chair, her butt was hanging off just enough to make her look thick. Her legs were spread wide open and she was leaned forward on the back of the chair. It was a beautiful pic even if she had to say so herself. Londyn added a filter to highlight her in the center of the frame.

She pressed send and ran to cover up while she waited on his response. Standing in her closet, she found a warm, jogging suit to lounge in. She did have work to do looking at the photoshoot Libra did over the weekend. As Londyn smiled and danced feeling good, a wave of nausea sent her running to the bathroom.

"What is happening here?!" she screamed. *My period is coming...what's today? Lemme look. It's supposed to be herrrrrrrre, ummmm, around the 18th. Today is the 28th, sooo....wait...IT'S THE 28TH?* She *sat on her bed trying to remember if she had the 18th correct. When did it come last month?* She wasn't the type to mark her cycle, because it was always consistent. When it first started, her mother bought her a calendar and told her to always keep up with the first day of each period. After a year, the first day only deviated by a day or two, never more than that, so she stopped tracking.

Her phone vibrated shaking her out of her thought process.

Knight: Damn girl! Big daddy likes that!

She smiled, nervously. She had thrown up every morning for the last three mornings. Now that she realized her cycle was late, it was going to bother her if she didn't...know.

She ran to the corner store, bought a pack of pregnancy tests and ran home. Anxiously, she waited.

Two lines. She checked the box, "Two lines will appear if you are pregnant," she read out loud. She took the other test. Two lines. Londyn went to the kitchen, downed a glass of water, ran back to the store, bought a different brand of test and ran back home.

Plus sign. She checked the box, "This test is the only pregnancy test with a Color Change Tip that turns pink when urine is being absorbed, blah, blah, blah. Plus means pregnant." Londyn rapidly shook the test. "A plus sign."

She didn't even bother taking the other one. She hopped back in the truck, got another test and took it once she arrived home.

Pregnant. She exhaled deeply. Ran into the kitchen, drank a glass of water, then drove up to the corner store again.

"Baby, I'm not going to sell you this test," the cashier said. She was an older lady, maybe around Londyn's mother's age. Her skin still looked really good, though her glasses were thick. "You're pregnant. This will be your fourth test. You are pregnant, hun."

"I can't be."

"You are. I can see all over you that your spirit does not sit well with this news. It'll all work out."

"What does that mean?" Londyn's eyes brimmed with tears. "Why do people keep saying, It'll all work out? What does that mean?" she started to cry.

"Listen, life throws rocks at us that we can't dodge. We have our lives planned out and God laughs. Didn't you just fall on your knees and give this whole mess to Him?"

"Huh?"

"You were crying, you were overwhelmed and you gave this all to Him. You were laying on the floor crying," the cashier said. She could see that Londyn was weirded out. "He heard you. You gave it to him. You can't have faith and worry. The two just can't exist in the same house. You're trying to figure things out and you can't. Right now, the water is cloudy and it's going to get worse before it gets better. Keep praying for peace and trust *Him*."

"Everything is just so fu...messed up."

The cashier laughed. She caught Londyn's slipup and how she respectfully corrected herself. "I know. Do you think everybody else is supposed to go through obstacles and you're exempt? No ma'am! The obstacles are what make you stronger. You're going through this because you are going to help somebody else get through theirs."

"Who's going to help me?" Londyn sobbed. She dropped down on the counter crying. She didn't know anybody else close to her who was going through a divorce. Or who had been through a divorce with children. All of the divorcees she knew were her parents' age.

"This is just the beginning. There is a storm brewing around you and you don't even know it," the lady spoke with conviction. As she spoke, she looked around Londyn off in the horizon.

"What do you mean?" Londyn asked confused.

"Baby, just pray," she shook her head in disbelief. "Just pray for strength and wisdom to know what to do. Be still."

"What do you see? Tell me! What do you see?" Londyn begged wiping her tears.

"Be still."

Londyn went from being sad to afraid. She stopped by that store at least once a week. She had never seen that cashier before. Londyn believed in angels walking on earth and receiving signs from God. She was far from a saint, but tried to live a good life. Seeing that lady on that day was no coincidence.

Londyn buying a barrage of pregnancy tests that day was no coincidence. *Where had she come from? And how did she know I cried on my floor? I didn't tell anybody about that! What did she see? Why wouldn't she tell me what else she saw?* There were more questions than answers. Londyn would do what the lady instructed. She'd be still.

Knight would be excited. He always talked about wanting to start a family. Of course, he wanted to be married first, but knowing Londyn was carrying his child would be good news to him she was sure. Micah was going to go absolutely ballistic. She wouldn't worry about all of that quite yet. She spent the day trying to calm herself down. She wasn't ready to tell anybody.

Low-key stressed out, the next day, Londyn busied herself securing Libra a New Year's concert performance. She had the new album and partnership with Anastasia to use as leverage to make her more appealing to potential venues and promoters. It was late in the game for a gig of this magnitude, but clubs and cities were getting desperate to find talent to bring in for their New Year celebrations.

Libra's single release was just days away, making the chance of a New Year's gig more promising. Keeping the end goal of elevating her status in mind, Londyn was scouring for something big, like Vegas, Atlantic City or Miami. Places people traveled to celebrate the holiday.

As she sat with her laptop on the couch trying to work to distract herself from the recent news that she was with child, breaking news hit the national news morning show that she was watching.

"Welcome back to Every Morning America, in the 9:00 hour. If you are just joining us, we are excited to announce that Stacey Mack is pregnant!" one of the female anchors said. *Great! The whole world is pregnant!*

"Yes, she and husband, drummer, Truth, are expecting their first child!" another too-bubbly-first-thing-in-the-morning anchor said.

"Sadly," the first anchor began with an overly dramatic frowny face, "her manager has let us know that she will not be able to perform at our New Year's concert!"

"Oh NO!" the second anchor cried. "My friends were begging me to come up to New Year's just so they could see her perform. Well, Stacey Mack, we love you! We are happy for you, but we will miss you!"

"Maybe we can FaceTime her singing from her living room and project it on a big screen," the first anchor gushed. There was a collective laugh in the studio.

Londyn had a genius idea. Surely, they would be trying to replace Stacey Mack with another performer of color, preferably a female. She began working hard to get in touch with the producers of Every Morning America. Other A-listers, the Beyonces and RiRis of the world would already be booked this late in the game. This would be perfect, but she had to jump on it immediately. Since Stacey Mack had only just released news of her pregnancy the day before on Instagram, the show's producers were caught off guard as well and hadn't trimmed their list of performers down to a workable, realistic short list. Londyn had time.

She put together a proposal and summoned the same confidence she had when presenting to Anastacia. Only this time, it would be her secret. She didn't want the added pressure of trying to come through on something so monumental. Tens of millions of people watched the Every Morning America's New Year's Show each year. They had a huge countdown in Times Square. It was thee largest countdown in the country.

"Good morning, sweetheart," Knight said when Londyn answered on the first ring.

"Sgt. Knight."

"Whatchu doing?"

"Working."

"Yeah right, you don't have a job," he laughed.

"Some how, these bills are getting paid."

"Mmm hmm. You been going to amateur night at Magic and not telling me?" Knight joked about her going to the most popular strip club in Atlanta.

"Ha...ha...ha..."

"What's wrong?"

"Nothing."

"You miss big daddy?"

Londyn burst out laughing. She missed him. But she also didn't know how she was going to look him in the eye and not blurt out that she was carrying his child. "Not really."

"Well too bad. I miss you. I'll be over there in a minute."

"You must really miss me coming over here from work. Are you hungry?"

"Starving."

"I'll fix you breakfast."

Knight arrived and smelled breakfast as soon as she opened the door. He hugged her like he meant it, although he didn't smile. Smiling was a rare occurrence since Ares passed. Knight made a bee line for the bathroom; she had already laid out a fresh washcloth and towel for him. While he showered, Londyn fixed his plate. Eggs, grits, sausage, and fruit. That was about the extent of Londyn's breakfast skills. She'd get fancy every now and then, but the boys didn't require much beyond that. They preferred cereal or waffles.

"Londyn!" he called from the bedroom. She smiled and bit her bottom lip.

"Yes!"

"Come here, sweetheart." She walked into the room and found him sprawled across the bed. She began to crawl between his legs. "Unh uh, take that off," he said speaking about her clothes. She wore an oversized 'Silently correcting your grammar' tank top and leggings. She stood back up and put Raheem Devaughn on her phone. He crooned, "Guess who loves you moooooore..."

Londyn looked in Knight's eyes, he leaned his head to the side. Just like that, everything she worried about was forgotten. She stared in his eyes removing her tank top slowly. Then she let it fall back down. She turned around, shimmied the tank top up above her butt, pushed her leggings down. Left side, right side. Left side, right side. Until they made their way to the ground. She stood with her legs spread apart and lifted her arms so the tank rose off her butt completely.

"Mmm," Knight said, his mouth watering to taste her. Images of her from the pic she'd sent the day before flashed in his head. "Come a long way from you not even wanting to see me in person to this," he chuckled. So did she. She pulled the shirt off and climbed on top of him. Knight still made her nervous. It had been six months and he still gave her butterflies.

He yanked the tank top away from her, but sensing he was about to do that, she gripped tighter.

"No," she said.

"Man, get rid of this," he reached up to take her bra off.

"It's so pretty. I want to leave it on," Knight stared at her.

"I want to see you. Your sexy ass, not this ugly ass bra."

"It's not ugly!" Londyn whined. She loved the hot pink lace bra, sad to see him unhook it. She pouted out her lips. Knight picked up the tank top, and tied Londyn's hands behind her back with it.

"Mmm hmm," he laughed when he felt her juices begin to drip down with her sitting on his lap. She was turned on instantly. He was as hard as could be.

After they made love, he warmed his breakfast in the microwave, ate, then fell asleep in her bed. She woke him up just in time for him to leave before the boys came. She wondered how the news of the pregnancy was going to affect her boys and Hermes. She didn't want Hermes to feel sad and left out with Knight having to divide his attention more than it already was. Hopefully, they would all come to find excitement about it.

Donny Hathaway
"This Christmas"

Hang all the mistletoe
I'm gonna get to know you better,
This Christmas,
And as we trim the tree
How much fun it's gonna be together,
This Christmas,
Fireside blazing bright,
We're caroling through the night,
And this Christmas will be,
A very special Christmas for me

Chapter 26

Knight's firehouse did an annual toy drive for kids who were less fortunate. Williams and Knight went back and forth about who was going to be Santa. Williams had been Santa for the last seven years. He and Knight both had enviable beards, but Williams' was more salt than pepper and he didn't need the potbelly cushion. Knight's stomach was ripped, Williams' was just as hard, but it was nice and round. Knight patted his subordinate's belly and told him to get ready.

The event turned out to be a spectacle. Knight posted a picture with him and Williams dressed in his Santa suit with a caption saying he was one of Santa's helpers, urging the community to come out to the drive donating unwrapped toys.

"Bring the thirst buckets out, Knight!" Josten joked.

"Boy stop."

"I'm serious. You know the Sgt. Knight Fan Club is gonna come out and support their man."

"Y'all make this out to be much more than it is," Knight brushed Josten's comments off.

"Naw Sgt. Knight, ain't no need to be bashful," Sterling said. "If I was younger, I'd be getting in on some of that leftover tail."

"You can't handle it all Knight!"

"Says the man who sex game ain't made his wife crazy in 19 years!" Josten said. "You could get all the tail you want, and when I hit 'em, they'd still feel like they ain't been touched!" Josten roared.

Two of the local news stations came out to interview Knight and talk about the toy drive. He tried his best to steer the interviews to the men of his firehouse and the needy children who were now going to be getting a Christmas thankful to the men and women in the south Atlanta community. He knew they'd ask about Hermes, which they did, along with how his family was dealing with this first holiday season without Ares. They inquired about if the family had plans to file complaints with the city, try to get Officer Blevins fired or put a civil suit against him.

Knight did a great job keeping his cool and redirecting the interviews to the topic at hand. When the interviews were over, he went inside the firehouse and sat at his desk. He closed and locked his door, shedding a few tears. Castor, Titus, nor Pops were being harassed at their firehouses about how the family felt, what the family was going to do, how the family was getting through their first Thanksgiving and Christmas without Ares. Only Knight was. It was hard enough dealing with what he had on his plate and now trying to heal from the tragedy.

When he gathered himself, he walked back outside and saw a clique of Santa's Helpers walking up. They were all dressed in red Santa dresses with white fur trim. Some wore Santa hats, some wore red and white ear muffs. Some wore knee-high black boots, while others opted for red and green knee-high stockings with black pumps. The ring leader wore sexy, velvet, black knee-high leg warmers.

"We are here to offer our assistance as Santa's helpers to Sgt. Knight," the ring leader began. She slightly looked over her shoulder at the women who walked up in a 'v' shape behind her. The camera crews turned their cameras on them, while the newspaper journalist quickly snapped a few pics. The honorable women who were there to drop off toys, laughed or scoffed at the desperateness and the men laughed waiting to see how this would all played out.

"Here is Fireman Williams, he's Santa," Knight said pulling Williams over to the ladies.

"Ladies," she pointed and they all walked over to Williams. The photo op was perfect for them all. They were giggling and handing the other firefighters and community people their phones so they could take pictures to post on their own social media. They were not going to leave until they took pictures with Knight. He knew that.

Knight stared at the ring leader and she stared at him. She was gorgeous. Her hair was styled perfectly, falling in big curls over her shoulders, her make-up was on point. It accented the natural beauty she already had. Her eyes were hazel and her skin tone was burnt caramel. Lips...Ruby Woo. He watched her approach him.

"Thirst...bucket," Josten whispered. Their eyes glued to the ride of her hips as she slowly walked to where they stood.

"I'm here to assist you," she said. "What can I help you with, Sgt. Knight?"

"Nothing."

"Is there really nothing you need?" she asked openly eyeing him up and down.

"Not at the moment."

"Sheeeit," Josten whispered.

"I think he could use some help," Knight said, his eyes not leaving hers.

"I'm not here for him. I'm...here...for...you...My girls and I are not walking away until we've taken a picture with you and until you have my number in your phone."

"The picture thing is easy, my love life is complicated."

"That's fine. I'll help relieve some of the stress around those...complications."

"Is that right?"

She winked at him extending her hand, "Milan."

"Knight." He turned around and she followed him into the firehouse. There was so much commotion around the other ladies, the only person who noticed what was happening was Josten. Knight took her to his office. "This is my office."

"This is where the magic happens?"

"It can."

"Good, I'm already ready," Milan squatted down and unzipped Knight's pants. She proceeded to give him head until she felt he was ready, then unrolled a condom on him and turned around. Knight arched her back so her breasts were smushed on the desk and he starting pounding from the back. Five minutes later, they were walking back outside to where everyone else was.

As he waved them away, he felt so empty inside. It was a good quickie, fast and exciting at the thought of being caught; but it meant nothing. She was sexy, but beyond that, she was easily forgettable.

He felt horrible about it. His life was going downhill fast. As bad as things were going, he needed something he could hold on to. He craved more. He didn't even know why he'd done it. There was no reason for it.

```
Knight: WYD??
Londyn: About to go pick out a tree.
Knight: Where?
Londyn: Fayetteville
Knight: Can it wait?
Londyn: You coming over? 👀👀
Knight: I wanna go with you.
Londyn: Huh? Really?
Londyn: Ok. Tmrw?
Knight: Fa sho
```

Knight arrived at Londyn's house and she was dressed in muted shiny, skinny jeans, Timbs and a cute grey sweater with oversized, pink sequin lips on it. He leaned in to kiss her as soon as she opened the door, she grabbed her purse and they headed down to the Christmas Tree farm.

She was reluctant to decorate at all. She decided that not decorating would make Micah's absence more noticeable.

Londyn was really trying to begin a new tradition with this being her first Christmas without Micah, so she wanted a fresh tree and was going to have it decorated by the time the boys got home from their weekend with their dad. Knight was interested to hear talk about how big the holidays were for her family and how this was her first real tree in years. His story was not nearly as exciting, being from a family full of men, but the ladies did what they could to make it festive.

They walked around the petting zoo and saw a huge bounce pillow. Knight grabbed her hand and they took off running.

"Are you crazy?" Londyn asked.

"About you!" he said sliding out of his shoes to go bounce. Londyn followed suit and they played around like little kids. Once their blood was pumping, keeping the cold at bay, Knight bought tickets for them to ride around the property on the hay. The wind created by the hayride made the 40° feel more like 30. As the air whipped around them, Knight wrapped his arms around Londyn, snuggling her close to him. He planted kisses in the nape of her neck, she gushed with love.

He knew her situation was complicated, but he was really into her. His situation was complicated as well, but he was the one who made it that way. He had to come clean with her. The day was going so smoothly, he couldn't dare ruin it for her, especially knowing the motive behind picking out a real tree to begin with.

Knight could see the love in her eyes. When she looked at him, she saw a man who cared for her, who released her from a degrading, sad prison of self-doubt and insecurity. Her impression of him was going to come crashing down. And soon. He couldn't hold out much longer. It was eating him alive. The longer he waited, the harder it became. She brought him so much joy and support as well. He didn't want to let her down, and he wasn't prepared to lose her.

The air flowed through her ponytail as they talked and laughed. He bought hot apple cider to warm them up for the hunt. Londyn paid for her tree and was instructed to go to the blue section to pick her tree. He grabbed a hand saw and wheelbarrow before they embarked on the hunt. They walked up and down the aisles, making jokes about the trees and the people. Just like when they were shopping for the boys' school shoes, throughout the day, Knight hugged her and patted her butt.

Londyn saw her tree and took off running. It was perfect. It was hers.

"I don't know why you're running, they all look the same," he teased in his calm voice.

"They don't. He has his own personality." She stuck her tongue out at Knight, "keep talking trash, I'll be calling this tree big daddy."

"Doubt that. He can't do what I can do," Knight winked. He cut it down, but not before letting Londyn have a spin at using the old-school hand saw. Once they had it in the wheelbarrow, it was put on a machine to shake it free of bugs and loose spindles. Knight was tickled by Londyn's amazement. She'd never done this part of the process. Her father and brother did the tree hunting, she was on the decorating committee with her mom and sister.

The tree was netted and put on the back of Knight's pick-up. He drove Londyn home, helped her get the tree in and set up. The intoxicating smell of evergreen quickly filled her house.

"Ace and Deuce will be home soon. So does that mean I can't get any?" Knight asked looking at his watch.

"You did this because you wanted some ass?" Londyn asked trying not to look disappointed.

"Not. At. All. I did it because I love you." He kissed her. "I miss being around you." He kissed her. "With everything that's going on, we haven't really spent time together."

"Mmm hmm," she rolled her eyes, then started laughing. "It's not my weekend with the boys."

"Awww shoot nah!" Knight started gyrating to a beat only he could hear in his head and still couldn't keep up with. "Let's decorate this tree. You order us some pizza, I'll put some wine in the freezer."

"It's already cold. Look in the fridge!"

"That's what I'm talkin' 'bout!" Knight rubbed his hands together and got comfortable. He took his shoes and jacket off, washed his hands, and emerged around the corner with two glasses of Cabernet Sauvignon. "Cheers to...mmm..."

"Happiness, honesty, and being our true selves," Londyn filled in. She could see that her beau was at a loss for words.

"Yeah, all that!" They toasted glasses and took sips. She knew he was still acting somewhat strange. He wasn't as available to her as he had been. The time they did spend together seemed more heartfelt. The sex was deeper and more meaningful.

Londyn had already pulled out her bag of assorted red, black, and white ornaments, along with a few signature Falcons' pieces. This year's theme was the falcons to get the boys more excited about the holiday. The pizza arrived, they ate and decorated, drank and decorated. Londyn had door covers and random celebratory pieces for the coffee and dining tables. Knight was glad to help, but it was more than he bargained for. Seeing her excitement made it all worth it for him.

After they were finished, they took showers, and fell asleep on the couch watching movies. They woke up the next morning in bed. This man is even gorgeous when he sleeps, Londyn thought. As if he could feel her looking at him, Knight's eyes opened. He smiled.

"It's so good waking up to you," he said tugging her arm across the bed in his direction. Londyn giggled and let him pull her to him. The size difference between them made it easy.

"You hungry?"

"No. I want some booty though," he said quickly. There was no sound between them for a few moments.

"It's yours," she conjured up the boldness to say.

"Hmmph," he said rolling her on her stomach. He kissed down her neck, down her back, down the crack of her butt. He reached between her legs and the party had already started.

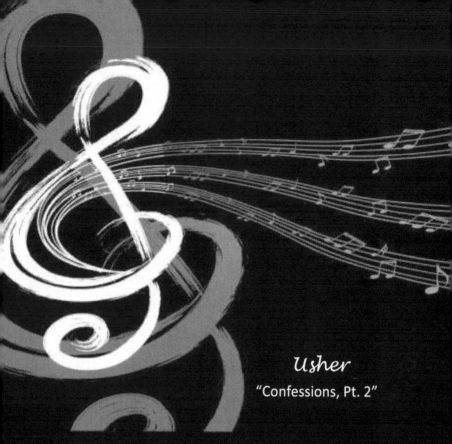

Usher

"Confessions, Pt. 2"

These are my confessions,
Just when I thought I said all I could say,
My chick on the side said she got one on the way,
These are my confessions,
Man I'm thrown and I don't know what to do,
I guess I gotta give part 2 of my confessions,
If I'm gonna tell it then I gotta tell it all,
Damn near cried when I got that phone call,
I'm so throwed and I don't know what to do.

Chapter 27

Knight had fallen completely off the map. All of a sudden, Londyn's calls and texts were going unanswered. He didn't know any other way to separate himself from Londyn than to go cold turkey. He had to let go of her. It pained him. His heart ached with every beat just thinking about her. She consumed his thoughts every minute of every day. When she called or texted, it meant she was obviously thinking about him too.

For two weeks, she didn't hear a peep out of him. She came to the realization that he was done. Either, he didn't want to buy her a gift or it was late into cuffing season and she wasn't the one he chose. Londyn found herself let down by a man...again. She knew at some point he'd come back. They went from hardcore sex to love-making. It was evident he cared, she could feel the difference. She made it up in her head not to even respond when he attempted to reach her again. He'd ghosted her before and came back twice already. Three times was just going to be too much.

His conscience had gotten the best of him. He could no longer live the lie he was living. But he felt bad for ghosting on her. She'd been nothing but good to him, he owed her an explanation.

```
Knight
Missed Call

Knight: WYD?
Knight: Londyn

Knight
Missed Call (2)
Knight: Please answer me
```

```
    Knight: I know you're looking at your
phone
    Knight: I know you're mad at me
    Knight: We need to talk
    Knight: Londyn please

    Knight
    Missed Call
```

He knew she was sitting, probably with her phone in her hand, ignoring his calls and texts. The first call and text were about an hour apart. Not used to her taking more than five minutes to respond, he called and texted closer together.

Londyn was mad; she had every right to be. She had been understanding with his work schedule when he picked up extra shifts, she kept her distance when Ares passed while he got used to being a full-time caregiver to Hermes, which seemed to push Knight further away. Through it all she'd given him his space while still letting him know she was there for him.

```
    Knight
    Attachment: 1 Image
```

Londyn held the phone in her hand. She knew that whatever was inside this message, she did not want. Part of her wanted to delete the whole text thread and block his number. The other part wanted to know. She opened the message and saw a picture of a baby.

A baby.

A newborn baby.

Londyn started shaking, her whole heart exploded into her throat.

What...thee...entire...hell...

Knight's heart jumped when he saw Londyn calling him. She didn't even hear the phone ring on her end he answered so quickly.

"Hello."

"Who is this?"

"Hi Londyn."

"Who is this?"

"A baby."

"I can see that. From the looks of it this baby is between four and eight weeks."

"Isn't he cute?"

Londyn scoffed. She could feel the temperature of her blood boiling. "Who is this?"

"His name is Apollo." *BOOM!* The weight of Knight's words hit Londyn like two tons of bricks. The line between them went silent. Londyn's mind was completely blank, while Knight was trying to imagine what she was thinking as she processed what he'd just said. She wasn't even breathing.

"Apollo?"

"Apollo Knight the fifth." *BOOM!* Another blow. As if she needed any confirmation. What reason would he be sending her a picture of a newborn baby for? She knew it was Knight's baby the moment she opened the text.

"He's yours," she said rhetorically.

"Yes."

"Bring your ass over here. Right now," the calmness of her tone worried him.

"I'm at work."

"Bring you ass over here. Right now. This is not a phone conversation." Londyn disconnected the call.

Londyn's stomach was in knots. She didn't even know how to respond, what to say. Nothing. Her whole world was spinning around her. She didn't want to jump to any conclusions, maybe he'd just found out himself. Whatever he had to say, it had better be good.

Knight approached Londyn's door and she opened it before he could even knock. She searched his eyes, they were sad. Then again, he'd had the whole ride over to her house to play like he was upset about having to have this conversation. She'd seen him genuinely sad; this seemed genuine.

"How old is he?"

"Six weeks."

"When did you find out?"

"This was the ex I told you about." Londyn did the math in her head really quickly. Unless he was born early, which he didn't appear to be a preemie, he was conceived before they met.

"When did you find out?"

"She told me a while ago. Then she told me it wasn't mine. Then she said it was, but she didn't want anything from me. She changed her number, blocked me, blocked me on social media. She said they would be fine, she wasn't going to let me see him, nothing. I had no way of contacting her. She clearly didn't want me around."

"She didn't move."

"No, she didn't. She did everything but." Awkward silence.

"Your son has your name."

"At the end, she called me crying saying that she was wrong to try to keep him from me and she wanted me to be a part of his life."

"Why didn't you tell me?"

"I didn't know how."

"BULLSHIT!" Londyn had been perfectly calm up to that point. "You say, 'Londyn, I just found out I have a baby on the way! My ex is acting crazy!' You don't just keep going like nothing is happening! It's not like we weren't talking every damn day! Spending time together on a regular basis! I have been honest about my issues with Micah every step of the way! I don't tell you blow-for-blow all of the drama that we have going on, but where things concern you, I let you know!"

"You do."

"Didn't I just ask you if you had a baby? That was a few weeks ago. He was already born! That was the perfect time to tell me! Your spirit was way off, and I knew it was more than the promotion and Ares and Hermes. I knew there was something you were keeping from me. It was all over you!"

"I'm sorry."

"Sorry? Were you there when he was born?"

"Yes."

"So..." Londyn squeezed her eyes and rubbed them in frustration. "You've known about this baby for at least three...four months. You still saying shit to me like calling my sons your stepsons and saying, 'I'll have stepkids before I even have my own kids,' knowing good and well this girl was pregnant."

"Londyn, I'm sorry."

"I just don't get why you didn't tell me! You don't think I'm worth the truth? You didn't think *my* truth was worth *your* truth?"

"I didn't think we would still be dealing with each other this long. I thought you and Micah would've been got back together," Knight said to which Londyn shot daggers from her eyes. "I didn't think it would matter."

"Annnnnnd after you realized that I wasn't going right back to Micah, then what?"

"You're my baby, Londyn."

"No, *this* is your baby!" She opened a picture of Apollo V again. "You are such a liar!" Londyn yelled and Kinght turned his face away from her. Awkward silence. They were stretched out on the couch by then. He was laying down and she was sitting up, facing him. He buried his face in the couch cushion.

Knight knew he had messed up. He'd known it for a long time. He wanted to tell her, but he genuinely thought she was going to go back to her husband leaving him to be a distant memory and their time together an occasional, enjoyable reminiscence. He didn't think he would matter.

"You just spent the night over here! We went Christmas tree shopping! All hugged up on me knowing you were keeping this from me! Why would you do this to me?"

"I didn't want to lose you." Awkward silence. "I tried to tell you, it just never seemed like the right time. I couldn't ever get the words out. I need you. I didn't...don't want to lose you."

Knight looked at Londyn hoping that she saw the sincerity in his eyes. She couldn't tell if it was sincerity or BS. She was angry...hurt...angry...confused...hurt...angry.

"How old is she?" Londyn needed to know, feeling like all of the confidence boosting compliments he gave her were just to keep her from knowing that he really didn't have a thing for older ladies and she was only a childhood fetish for him.

"You know I like 'em old," he joked. Londyn had the straight face. "Thirty-two." She twisted her mouth to the side to keep from smiling. *So I guess he was telling the truth about liking us old chicks.*

"What is going on with you and her?"

"Nothing."

"Are you going to try to work it out? Get back together?"

"I don't want to miss my son growing up, but we aren't really like that."

"What does that mean?"

"I spend as much time with him as I can, but we aren't together. I don't know if we should try again or not." Knight pulled Londyn over to him and embraced her. She was so angry, but she couldn't resist him.

"If you want to be back with her, I can't do anything but respect it. You choosing to have a family would hurt me, but I'd totally understand. It hurts me more that you felt like you couldn't tell me. Why would I leave you when he was conceived before we even met? And it's not like we've put titles on anything."

"I love you, Londyn. I mean it." Awkward silence. "I just don't know what to do. Pops raised me. I can't imagine not being around."

"You can still be around, if y'all aren't together. The question is...do you want to be with her?"

"Not really...but she has my only child."

"You, sir, need to figure out what you're going to do. Like I said, if you decide that you want to try to work things out with her, I get it. Could you please be honest with me?" Londyn sat up off of him.

"Yes."

"I need that. There is no reason to lie," Londyn said.

"I'm so sorry, sweetheart." He grabbed her hand and kissed it.

"I guess now is the best time to tell you that my period is late," Londyn stirred the pot. Awkward silence. Knight slowly shifted his eyes around to meet hers.

"You need to take a test?"

"No."

"How late?"

"A week," she lied.

"So you do need to take a test."

"I'm sure it's stress," she spoke confidently, but couldn't look him in his eyes. He put his hands over his face.

"No, man! You need to take a test, Londyn! You can't be pregnant!"

"Chill out. I'm not worried, so you shouldn't be." Suddenly, she wasn't so mad about him not telling her about his newborn son. Seeing his reaction, she wasn't ready to share the news that she had a gut full of Knight too. It was time to change the subject again.

"Show me another picture of my Cinco."

"Cinco?"

"Duh, he's the fifth. Don't you call him Cinco?"

"No, we've been calling him Apollo since nobody calls me or Pops by our first name."

"Well, I'm going to call him Cinco."

"Really?" Knight looked at her confused. Londyn held out her hand and beckoned him to hand her his phone. He opened up another picture, then held his breath, cautiously...nervously watching her while she looked at it. He saw her fold her lips in. Knight knew she was trying to hold back the tears. She stared at the innocent baby taking the world's slowest inhale and releasing the world's slowest exhale. That was the only way she could keep the tears from falling.

"You're ok with this?"

"With Cinco's lil' sexy self, yes. With you lying? No. I'm not ready to give you up, though." Londyn looked in his eyes. He could see that he really hurt her. Knight picked her up and sat her on top of him, then pulled her face down to meet his. She swerved.

"I'm sorry Londyn, I really am. I should have told you. I need you sweetheart. I need you in my life." He pecked her face and neck. Then as he felt her slowly open up to him, he kissed her passionately.

"Let me get back to work," he said between pecks, his lips still lingering on hers, tasting the elixir of anger and love swirled together.

The conversation was indeed hard, but not nearly as hard as he anticipated. He thought she was going to completely flip out and get angry black woman mad. He expected throwing dishes and shoes. It was nothing like that. She was much calmer. She was angry and yelled, but was much calmer than he thought she'd be. That was one of the advantages of dating an older woman. Less time and tolerance for drama.

Londyn watched Knight's truck pull out of the driveway and called Kenzie as soon as he was gone.

"I have a whole stepson, sis."

"Whaaaaaaat???"

"This fool texted me a picture of a baby, talkin' 'bout, isn't he cute?"

"Knight?"

"WHO ELSE!"

"Oh my gosh!"

"I know!"

"Well, at least now, he has a child so if things get serious between y'all, you won't have to have a baby like you feared."

"I was kind of entertaining it, though. I mean, I wouldn't mind having another one."

"That's not the story you were singing before this boy started knocking all ya walls down," Kenzie burst out laughing.

"Good peen will make ya change ya mind!"

"So what's the deal with him and the mom?"

"She's the ex from before me. I told him if he wants to work things out with her, I'd be messed up about it, but I'd understand. At the end of the day, all we want is for someone to choose us. Someone to say they are down for us and want to try this thing called life with us. If he chooses her to try to be a family with, how can I be mad? Hell, I've been sulking, and crying, and depressed, and losing weight over Micah. He didn't choose me. That's all I wanted, was for him not to give up on me. On us."

"It's different though. You and Micah are married. He's not married to this girl. And the way you two have been carrying on, I'm sure there wasn't much between them anyway."

"He said he wasn't sure if he wanted to work it out with her."

"Be careful. Babies change everything," Kenzie spoke as a warning. "Why didn't he tell you sooner?"

"He said he didn't want to lose me."

"I feel that. I wouldn't ruin my good thang either. He probably thought you and your crazy ass husband were gonna get back together."

"That's what he said."

"Yeah...there was no reason to tell you until he felt he was at a point of no return with you. He couldn't hide it anymore and he wasn't prepared to let you go. Shoot, I'm not mad at the youngin'."

"Really?"

"Nope. He could have told you. Should have, especially with all that I love you and carrying on. But I totally get why he didn't."

Londyn's mindset was pretty much like WTF for the rest of the day. Knight didn't say exactly how long he'd known about Cinco, but he knew long enough to have told her before he was born. The more she thought about it, the more upset she became. Confronting him earlier that day, she reacted more in shock. She didn't have time to really think it through. She thought back on all of the times Knight referenced them moving forward, wanting to date her, being an item, them moving in together. The whole time, he knew there was a baby on the way with 23 of his chromosomes and he didn't mention a word.

Waking up the next day, Christmas Eve, Londyn had to gather her boys up to catch their flight home. She stared at the ceiling thinking, *This is a helluva way to begin the holiday. Did that really happen?* She snatched her phone off of the comforter next to her, opened the text thread she shared with Knight and saw it. The picture of Cinco. She tapped it to make it bigger and stared at it until her phone automatically closed. She pressed her thumbprint to the phone to open it and stared at it until her phone automatically closed. She did it over and over until tears brimmed in her eyes.

What if Knight decided to work things out with her? Whoever she was. He never even said her name. What if he wants to try to work on being a family? Where does that leave me? Broken-hearted again? Lonely as hell? The tears ran onto her pillow. She wrapped the long, king sized pillow around to cover her face and she let the sobs free. In dealing with Micah, she'd become a pro at stifling the sounds of her sorrow. In fact, it was the opposite. Fear of losing her is what made him hold on to the secret for so long. That and being immature. Clearly, his age had a lot to do with how this all played out.

In reality, there was still the chance that Knight could choose her. He hadn't ruled her out. She felt that if he wanted his family, their conversation would have gone totally different. He also wouldn't have carried on with her the way that he had been. He'd had plenty of time to go back and forth over this in his mind before telling her. Knight and Londyn had been all over the city, out in the open, during the day, sometimes even at night. He wouldn't have risked being seen with Londyn if he was focusing on having a happy home. Or he would have just cut her off.

Still the thought of Cinco being newly in the picture planted a deeply-rooted sense of worry in Londyn. She could lose Knight. She could lose her happy place.

She felt heavy again. Nauseous. Not because of the baby, or the fact that she, too, had a secret that she had yet to disclose, but because if he didn't choose her, she wouldn't know how to handle it. Two heartbreaks in the same year.

The plane was not going to wait on them. Londyn washed the tears from her face, brushed her teeth and looked at her reflection in the mirror. Her eyes were red, but she could still get away with it. She woke up the boys, hustled the three of them out of the house, drove to the airport and caught the plane. She wore a pair of light brown aviators to keep random strangers from looking into her soul and seeing that her life was falling apart. The only time she took them off was going through security.

Nat and Deshawn were waiting outside of the airport for them. Deshawn may as well have been wearing bells and whistles as loud as she was when Deuce made a bee line for her. As soon as she spotted her grandson, she started screaming like she was being surprised that they were coming. She certainly caused a stir with the West Palm Beach airport being as small as it was.

Ace wasn't far behind his brother, the two immediately shedding the jackets they wore. All three of them were thankful that the temperature was 30° warmer. Londyn brought up the rear. She didn't have nearly the amount of energy that her sons had, nor was she as happy to be up and out of the house. She would have much rather preferred to spend her holiday sulking on the couch.

"Honey," Nat grabbed Londyn, pulling her close. "What's wrong?"

"Nothing Daddy," she spoke unconvincingly in a bland tone. The boys had already hopped in the truck with Deshawn also sitting in the back to enjoy talking to them about their trip.

"You and Micah seeing each other again?"

"What? No," she scrunched up her face. "Why did you ask that?"

"You're pregnant," her father said and Londyn yanked back from his grasp. He could see her eyes, wide as she looked at him through her sunglasses. "You're glowing," he added, smiling with his lips, worried with his eyes.

Londyn turned away and got in the front seat of the truck. She buckled up and leaned her head on the seat facing toward the window. Deshawn looked at her daughter's reflection in the passenger side mirror, then at her husband, who gave her the 'I don't know' Kanye shrug. Deshawn was anticipating that this was going to be a difficult holiday as it was their first holiday without being a family. It was all over Londyn's face.

When they arrived at the house, Londyn ran up to her room and closed the door. She blew right past the beautiful, live tree her mother put up with neutrals and peaches. Deshawn decorated it with seashells, sand dollars, and starfish. Londyn didn't acknowledge any of the decorations that made her parents' home feel festive. Her hand barely touched the garland rounding the rail as she flew up the stairs.

"Let me go check on my baby," Deshawn said.

"Give her some time Deshawn. Give her some time," Nat said patting his wife on the shoulder. Deshawn was clearly worried and could tell her husband knew something she didn't.

"What ya know good?"

"Give my baby some time," he said again more sternly.

"She's been like that all day," Deuce volunteered taking his shoes off. "She hasn't said much all day and her voice sounds sad."

"I think she's sad about Christmas," Ace added. They had seen her through the last year or so of emotion, they knew when to leave her alone.

"Me too babies," Deshawn said looking upstairs to her daughter's room door.

The whole day passed and Londyn did not come out of her room. Deshawn realized that it had been several hours since they'd heard a peep from her. She went up to check on her and found her balled up under the covers.

"Londyn, what is going on? You've been up here all day," Deshawn set a tray down with Nilla wafers, Nutella, and milk on the end table next to the bed.

"Ma, please," Londyn growled.

"Can I at least see your face?" Deshawn gently tugged at the down comforter.

"Ma!"

"Is it a crime to want to see my baby?"

"Here's a baby for you to look at," Londyn said. As she emerged from the darkness of the comforter, her hair looking a tousled mess, Deshawn saw how red and swollen her eyes were. Her whole face was flushed. Londyn put her thumbprint on the phone and it opened up to a newborn baby picture. Deshawn side-eyed her daughter.

"It's Knight's son. Not Micah's."

"Your *friend*?"

"Yep."

"Wait...this is a new baby."

"I know," Londyn said and she covered her head again, wailing. Through sniffles, she summed up the conversation between herself and Knight. She didn't have the heart to tell her mother she was pregnant too. That was a conversation for another day. She didn't even want to bring a baby into this situation, but felt crushed at the mere thought of going to a clinic.

"He's calling," Deshawn said placing the phone back in her daughter's hand. Londyn looked at the picture that showed up with his contact. Seeing him looking fine and svelte in his uniform, stirred her at the pit of her soul. She really did love him.

She silenced the ringer. "Mom, I'm going back home."

"You just got here."

"I can't do this. I don't want the boys to see me like this. I told them I had a migraine, but I don't think they believe me."

"They think you're sad that Micah isn't here."

"That works just fine. Let them think that. I need to get myself together. Plus with Libra's performance on Every Morning America, I can tell them I got called back early."

"Whatever you need, just let me know."

"I'll leave midday tomorrow, after prayer meeting and presents."

"And my sweet potato muffins," Deshawn boasted. She knew her daughter so looked forward to those. "He's calling again, baby. Talk to him," Deshawn excused herself.

Londyn answered the phone, listening to the air move around on the speaker.

"Hello?" Knight asked.

"Hi," she responded dryly.

"What's wrong?"

"What's wrong?" her voice was barely audible. "The man I've been seeing told me he has a six-week-old son. He's been lying to me from day one.

"Damn Londyn." Knight knew that she was going to get to this point. He also knew that she had every right to be angry.

"Damn Apollo."

"I can count the number of times you called me Apollo." He tried to FaceTime her, she declined. "I want to see you."

"Not like this."

"You're beautiful to me no matter what."

"Lies."

"I'm sorry. I really am. It was so messed up what I did. I should have told you sooner. I just didn't know how. I didn't want to fall for you. I didn't think I would. But once I did, I didn't want to lose you."

"Bye."

Londyn disconnected the call. Tears were forming again and she didn't want him to hear her like that. She didn't want him to know he mattered that much.

```
Knight: Did your period come on?
Londyn: No
Knight: You need to take a test
Londyn: Do you love her?
Knight: I mean, she's the mother of my
child
Londyn: Do you love her????
Knight: I love her for bringing my son
into this world. I'm not in love with her.
```

Just like she told Deshawn, Londyn made it through presents and lunch on Christmas. The boys didn't mind her leaving, although they told her they would miss her and would check on her every day. Since she'd dated Kaden, this was her first Christmas without a man. She'd never felt so alone.

```
Knight: Merry Christmas 🎅🎄
```

Knight saw the bubble with the dots going. He was nervous about her response. She hadn't said anything to him since the last text. He meant what he'd said. He was not in love with the mother of his child. The bubble disappeared, then reappeared, then disappeared. Londyn typed, 'Merry Christmas! You're going to be a father of two!' *Delete. Delete. Delete.* Then, 'Tell my bonus son Cinco I said Merry Christmas.' *Delete. Delete. Delete.* Then 'I'm pregnant.' When it was all said and done, she didn't respond at all.

Londyn was becoming more distraught by the day. The fetus in her belly was growing, its father didn't know it existed because its mother didn't know how to handle the situation. Londyn wasn't even sure she wanted to deal with Knight anymore because of his deception. She reflected on the distance that had grown between them over the last month thinking it had more to do with his brother passing and him getting Hermes when really, he'd had a child.

To make matters worse, she had no clue who this girl was. He never said her name, Londyn and Knight didn't have any friends in common. He had so many followers now, she could only scroll through the women who he followed. Half of them had private pages, so that was useless. It bothered her that he never said Cinco's mom's name. Saying her name would have personified her, but it also meant that there was more to hide.

She kept replaying the day when Knight kept texting her he loved her, then came over and made love to her so intently. It was unlike any other time. That was probably when she got pregnant. They had graduated from having sex to making love. That was also probably when reality hit him that he couldn't keep going on with her like his son hadn't entered the world. He knew he had to tell her and wasn't sure how she was going to take it. That's when he knew he genuinely loved Londyn and couldn't just cut her off or pull himself away.

Londyn and Libra flew to New York and braved the frozen tundra. It was freezing for the southern gals, but they handled it well. It was worth it. Only the day before, Anastacia had announced Libra as the new face of the brand. Libra was on fire! Her single was doing well. Londyn had done a great job of getting her client back on the map. All that day as they ran around doing appearances, interviews, and keeping up with all of the outlets who wanted to speak to Libra, Knight kept texting and calling Londyn.

Knight: Londyn, please say something.

Knight: Did your period come on? Please
go take a test. I can't have another child
right now.

Knight: Londyn, I need you

Knight: Don't shut me out

Knight: ●●●

Londyn left him to keep up with her the same way the
rest of America was...social media. She wondered if the only
reason he was still reaching out to her was to find out if she was
pregnant or not.

The thought of going from zero children to three within
one year was enough to stroke anybody out. Beyond that,
Knight was going through withdrawals. This is what he was
afraid of, the reason he didn't want to tell her in the first place.
He was afraid she'd turn her back on him. He needed to hear her
voice, read a text, anything.

It was impossible for her to push him out of her mind.
He'd broken down her walls, given her something she was not
even looking for, he made her love him. Now she was carrying
his child.

All day, she'd managed to plaster a faux smile on her
face when inside she felt like dying. It was so hard to constantly
be 'on'. But Londyn wasn't about to bring that type of energy to
Libra. There was too much riding on the last 24 hours of the
year being perfect.

As the clock ticked down, Londyn tried to think about
what she had to be thankful for. The year had brought far more
grief and heartache than any one year should. She still had her
health, her boys were healthy, she was clothed, fed, and she was
arguably in her right frame of mind. The ladies held each other's
hands screaming the countdown, releasing positive vibes in the
air.

It had been nine days since she'd found out about Cinco. Whether or not Knight decided to choose her, Londyn prayed to walk into the New Year with gratitude and direction.

Libra had been invited to a million and one after parties throughout the concrete jungle once her name was released as performing on Every Morning America's coveted stage. They hit two or three of them, taking pictures, stuntin' for the Gram to show some of the legends they were partying with. This further solidified Libra's return, gaining her over 100,000 more followers that night alone!

By the time they made it into the hotel room, the sun was chasing the dark skies away. They were exhausted and hungry. Libra ordered room service to be delivered to the suite while the ladies took their showers. They recapped the wonderful last 24 over mimosas, pancakes with fresh berries and cream, and sausage. Londyn closed all of the drapery in all of the rooms of the suite so that not a peep of the New Year would shine on them until they were ready. They had a whole day of sleep to catch up on.

"Londyn! Wake up!" Libra jumped up and down on Londyn's bed.

"Didn't I tell your ass not to wake me up? Oooh...and I'm cramping. Bad." Londyn remembered cramping badly with the twins. *Lord, please don't let this be twins again*, she thought.

"C'mon girl! Let's go spend some of this moolah we just made!" Libra beamed. Londyn opened one eye to squint at the clock. It was past three in the afternoon. "LONDYN! THERE'S BLOOD IN YOUR BED!"

Londyn jumped up and Libra yanked the covers. The sheets between Londyn's legs were soaked with blood. Her mouth flew open. She just stared at it. Libra, too. Libra knew it was much too much blood to be a period.

"What's...what's...we need to call you an ambulance!"

"I'm pregnant."

"Pregnant? From Knight?"

"Yes," Londyn said and a tear fell.

"We'll call him from the hospital!" Libra jumped off the bed and dialed the hotel operator requesting an ambulance.

"Libra, we can just take a taxi. They drive just as fast," Londyn said weakly.

"A taxi driver can't stop this bleeding." Libra led the way. What was supposed to be a fun-filled first day of the New Year was spent in the ER. It was confirmed that she was having a miscarriage. Being a new mom, Libra's heart went out to Londyn.

As she lay in the bed, Londyn was quiet. Enveloped in a bottomless abyss of thoughts, she was used to getting lost in the darkness of the deep. She was so unsure of how she even felt about the pregnancy. Not really the pregnancy itself, but the situation around it was so murky. This must've been the brewing storm that the cashier warned her about. If she'd signed the divorce papers when Micah first sent them, she didn't think she'd have felt so conflicted about being pregnant. Maybe this was God warning her to be more careful with Knight. Surely, it was the news of Cinco that made her so emotional that her body couldn't hold it together. She had been absolutely distraught over the course of the last week. She'd barely eaten, had probably only slept a collective four or five hours during that time.

Libra was with her every step of the way, even once they flew back to Atlanta. It took a day of two for the clotting to subside. Libra was there to offer her support.

"What a way to start a New Year," Londyn said.

Childish Gambino
"Redbone"

But stay woke,
Niggas creepin',
They gon' find you,
Gon' catch you sleepin',
Ooh, now stay woke,
Niggas creepin',
Now don't you close your eyes.

Chapter 28

For the next month, Knight got the hint that Londyn didn't want to talk to him. His calls and texts became more sparing until he stopped all together. Three weeks of that time was dead silent between them.

It's not that Londyn didn't want to talk to him. She didn't know what to say. She was healing from not one, but two heartbreaks. There was so much swirling around in that head of hers, and his as well. They were both trying to figure out how to move forward with their lives whether they should put forth the effort to be in each other's lives or not.

The January winter in Atlanta made the time pass by even slower. There was not a lot going on. People were broke from overspending during the Thanksgiving and Christmas holidays, so socially, the scene was quiet. Plus, who was trying to go outside in temps that felt like a bone chilling 10°? Chattering teeth are not sexy.

Londyn's heart was cold, her bed was cold, her mind was cold. She really started to miss Knight. She would look at her phone and wonder if he was thinking about her at that moment. She willed him to call her, text her, DM her, anything. She just didn't want to make the first move. Since they'd met, they had only gone beyond the span of a week without communicating once. Four weeks had turned her angry, confused heart to a longing heart.

Knight was miserable. He couldn't believe that she had completely shut him out. He apologized over and over. She just stopped responding. He didn't know what else she wanted from him. Perhaps, she didn't want anything, not even to be bothered. He had a lot on his plate with his newborn son, who everybody was now calling Cinco thanks to Londyn, and then there was Hermes. The holidays had slowed down the marches and benefits as people focused more on their own families than holding signs and chanting bundled up in jackets marching up and down wintry streets.

Knight decided there was nothing to lose. He wanted to see her, talk to her, touch her. He needed to be wrapped up in Londyn. He was unsure how she would receive him, but since his calls and texts went unanswered, his approach needed to be different if he hoped to be successful.

He turned into her driveway, turned off the ignition and just sat there. With no heat running, it was going to be cold inside the truck soon. Rejection was something that he did not do well. He was Sergeant Apollo Knight, IV, there was nothing to reject about him. People loved him, women threw themselves at him, he was a hard worker and a great firefighter.

He walked to the door and rang the doorbell. On the other side of the door, Londyn was cozy on the couch with a blanket watching Netflix, eating pizza. She figured it was her mailman and just opened the door.

Knight was standing at her door. He looked tired and worn. He did have a newborn after all. But she could see past that, she saw that he was hurting too. She opened the door and he stepped in. He sat on one couch, she sat on the other. They just looked across the room at each other, not knowing where to begin, if there were any words at all that could encompass what their hearts felt.

He outstretched his arms toward her. She picked up her plate and motioned to give it to him. He shook his head 'no'. He beckoned her again. Slightly reluctantly, she walked to where he was and tried to sit next to him. He grabbed her hips and sat her on top of him. He ran his hands down the length of her arms and interlocked their fingers together. Brown skin on brown skin. He buried his face in her chest...inhale... exhale... inhale...exhale. He released her fingers, hugging her tightly around her waist.

He turned his head to the side and just laid it there...inhale...exhale...inhale...exhale. He moved slowly, deliberately.

Londyn tilted his face up towards hers and she tenderly stroked the back of his head. He leaned back on the couch, looked in her eyes, put her hand over his mouth and kissed her fingers, up her arm, across her chest, down the other arm, ending with the other hand over his mouth. He stared into her eyes. His eyes watered, and he buried his face in her chest...inhale...exhale...inhale...exhale.

Londyn grabbed his face and looked in his eyes. The man before her was broken...tired...overwhelmed. He'd lied to her. She was hurt, he was hurt. Yet, there was nothing to say. She ran her hands down his beard as they searched each other's souls. Their eyes told the story, that their mouths could not. She bent down, pressing her lips to his. Her eyes watered as well, as they pecked slowly, painfully, then hungrily began searching each other's mouths with their tongues. There was so much passion between them, it was undeniable.

Knight slid to the edge of the couch, and picked her up. Keeping her hands enveloping his face, she continued kissing him while he carried her into the room. He laid her down, then peeled off her shirt, bra and cozy thermal pajama bottoms. She sat up and ripped his shirt right off of him. He got on his knees and went straight for her other set of lips. He licked and sucked and licked and sucked. Londyn heard sniffles and opened her eyes. He had tears running down his face.

Londyn grabbed his face, pulling it up to hers. She wiped his tears, kissed his cheeks and kissed his lips. She navigated him inside of her, where they both wanted him to be. That boy put his whole back into that stroke. Like his life depended on it. She felt every centimeter of how big and long he was. With all the passion in the world, Knight did not hold back as he showed

Londyn how much he'd missed her. She squeezed her legs around his waist as he slid his hands under her butt to pull her cheeks apart.

"You're so deep, bae," was the only thing she could say. He loved the way her body felt. This was what he'd craved; healing his throbbing with her wetness and warmth. The way she held him...caressed his face...sucked his lips. She excited him the way no other woman ever had. It was deeper than just sex. The person who Londyn was made him feel such a deep connection that all he wanted was to be inside of her. To be with her. To touch her. To kiss her. To be around her.

He held her feet, one in each hand and spread them wide as he looked down at her. He was driving her wild. It seemed like an eternity since he'd seen these faces. In person. He dreamt about them every night, saw them when he closed his eyes during the day. Londyn was a real-life daydream.

"You make me feel so good," she moaned and threw it back, making each stroke more intense.

"Oooh, Londyn!" He yelled, pulsing in breathtaking pleasure.

The air was filled with the stench of their love. They laid there just looking at each other. They'd both imagined being in each other's arms. Now, here they were. She wiped the sweat from his brow, he littered her body with infinite pecks. From head to toe and back up. Literally. They held each other until they fell asleep.

The next morning, they freshened up and played catch up. Knight showed Londyn pictures of Cinco and Hermes, and spoke of how exhausting it was to be a new dad. Londyn laughed and shared stories about having the twins and how different life was for her becoming a first time mom.

He had a taste for waffles. That was beyond the scope of Londyn's kitchen. She ordered IHOP take out. He offered his truck since he had an automatic start so the truck could heat up while she threw on a cute jogging suit to dash out to the restaurant in. Plus, his debit card was in his wallet in the truck. She walked in the restaurant which was slammed! Her order was ready to go, for which she was thankful. She paid and shuffled to the car. An order of waffles, an order of pancakes with strawberry syrup on the side, and two Denver Omelets. She also ordered two juices to go.

Rushing to get the food home so Knight could enjoy it while it was piping hot, she turned a corner a little too quickly. One of the drinks tipped over, so she whipped into a parking lot to clean it up. Men are crazy about keeping their vehicles clean. She didn't want to clean up the juice in her driveway and have to hear his mouth.

Londyn reached into the glove box for napkins and as she found them, an insurance card fell out. *Maya Brown? Who the hell is Maya Brown?* Londyn read her name on top of Knight's name. Londyn instantly felt a tinge in the pit of her stomach. She clicked a picture and sent it to Kenzie.

Londyn: Find out who this is
Kenzie: On it boo

Londyn exhaled deeply and shook it off. There was no need in getting upset before she had any information, and there was no need in asking Knight when Kenzie was the damn FBI. Working at the salon, she'd learned all kinds of ways people got caught cheating and snooping. The girl was a whiz at finding dirt on people.

As hard as it was, Londyn played it cool. Of course her mind instantly ran at 3,000 miles per hour. He didn't have any sisters or females she knew of who would be close enough to have him on their insurance. Calmly, she walked into the house with the food. She set up TV trays, they ate and talked like nothing had changed. Knight hung out for most of the day, then left, but not before planting infinite kisses on her face and neck throughout the time he was there.

```
    Kenzie: I don't like this situation-ship
friend
    Londyn: 🌑
    Londyn: I'm scared
    Kenzie: Bout to call you in a sec
```

"Listen girl," Kenzie started about to spill the tea, "what did he tell you about his relationship with this damn girl?" Londyn felt sick. She closed her eyes. Whatever Kenzie found couldn't be good with her starting off the convo like that.

"That he didn't want to be with Cinco's mom. He was staying there on occasion to help out."

"Friend," Kenzie paused dramatically, "they live together."

Londyn was silent, she didn't say anything. Her hands were shaking the same way they were when she opened the picture of Cinco on December 23rd. *This is not happening.*

"Londyn, go to her Facebook. Her name is Maya Hotness Brown."

"Hotness?"

"Girl, more like hot mess. Have you seen her?"

"No, I just found the insurance card in his truck," Londyn said putting Kenzie on speaker and opening the Facebook app. She searched Maya Hot and her private page came up. "That's him," Londyn's voice cracked looking at the background picture of Knight holding Cinco in the hospital. "That's her! That's the damn girl from the funeral! The repass! The pregnant girl!"

"Huh?"

"At the repass at his house, a pregnant girl was telling me how bad I was...am...was...ugh!"

"Wow! You were literally standing there talking to her?"

"YES! Rubbed her belly and felt Cinco kick!" Londyn slid onto the floor. It was amazing how their lives had touched and they didn't even know they had *their* man in common. They were one degree of separation away from each other, but were really closer than that. They were both in Knight's heart, in his mind, and in his bed. "I asked him who she was, he never answered...but he mentioned that he saw us talking."

"They bought a house together."

"What? How? When?"

"October."

"October!" Londyn fought back the tears. She couldn't believe what she was hearing.

"It gets worse, friend. Are you sitting down?"

"Maaaaaaaan!"

"Scroll down," Kenzie instructed. Even though Maya's page was private, certain updates were still visible.

"What the fuck?" Londyn whispered. "That's the first time he told me he loved me. I remember that day because it was Daddy's birthday. He proposed to her that same day?!" She felt like she was going to be sick.

"Well, that's when she changed her status," Kenzie acknowledged. Londyn sat on the floor with her back up against her bed. She was flabbergasted.

"So he's telling me that they had broken up, he didn't know about the baby, she didn't want anything to do with him, he doesn't know if he wants to be with her, AND THEY ARE ENGAGED AND LIVE TOGETHER?!"

"Sis!"

"Kenzie, I can't believe this. I'm like completely in shock. I knew there was more to it. He never said her name to me. Never. Not once. I knew he was hiding something. Girl! And the way he just made love to me in here was crazy. He put his peen in my soul!" Kenzie laughed. "And he's over here with a whole fiancée and a whole baby."

"She's a teacher. I found out where she works, her cell phone, house phone, address, and two emails. I even got her resume sis!"

"How did you...never mind," Londyn shook her head. She wanted to laugh, but laughter eluded her.

"I saw their house, well condo in Midtown. It's cute or whatever. Listen, if you wanna get this fool, you know I got peoples!" Kenzie yelled in the phone.

"Lemme think through this."

"He's not who he says he is."

Knight's façade had come crashing down. His mask had fallen off. Londyn had the missing pieces to the puzzle, that 'thing' she couldn't put her finger on. It made so much sense now. His distance, his frustration. Him looking at her like there was something he needed to say. The way the guys looked at her, then each other at the firehouse. He *was* stressed. Knight and Maya were looking for a home to buy, expecting their first child, and Londyn had no clue about it. Not to mention what happened to his brother in the midst of it all. Instead, he was still trying to save face with her.

The phone was shaking in her hands. Londyn was crushed. Absolutely crushed. She didn't know how to deal with the news she'd heard. She couldn't cry, she was too angry. She did feel an air of vindication. Her gut was dead on. She knew something was off. Now she had to decide how to handle it.

Should she confront him or go straight to Ms. Maya Brown?

Londyn stared at the private Facebook page. She had so many questions. Far more questions than answers. The girl in the profile picture looked nothing like Londyn. She was light-skinned, brown eyes with a straight bob. Even in the small profile picture, Londyn could tell it was a weave. It was bone straight, nothing like Londyn's naturally long hair.

Londyn flashed back to seeing her at Knight's house. She replayed the entire interaction in her head. She was sure that Maya Brown would remember her. There was only one thing keeping Londyn from beginning to get the answers she needed.

She clicked 'Add Friend' on Maya Brown's profile.

BOOK CLUB QUESTIONS:

1. What do you think made Londyn really fall for Sgt. Knight?
2. Describe how Sgt. Knight's character evolved through the story.
3. Do you think Londyn and Micah tried everything they could to salvage their marriage?
4. Do you think Londyn's separation affected the way she received Sgt. Knight?
5. How do you think the separation affected the boys who've already lost their birth father?
6. Why do you think Micah kept lashing out at Londyn?
7. Do you think Sgt. Knight really cared for Londyn, or was he just stringing her along?
8. Were there any signs that Londyn missed where Sgt. Knight was showing her that he was living a double life?
9. What do you think of racial tension in America?
10. What should Londyn have done when she found out about Cinco?
11. Why do you think Sgt. Knight kept Maya a secret?
12. Do you think Londyn should have a woman-to-woman conversation with Maya or confront Sgt. Knight?
13. Do you know anyone who has experienced a similar situation?

@writewithcarla

#WhoIsSgtKnight

Show me where you are taking Mask Off! Tag me in

pictures of you enjoying this great read!

Made in the USA
Columbia, SC
15 December 2018